Guardians

Book 4 of the One True Child Series

Guardians is a work of fantasy fiction. Names, characters, places, and incidents are the product of the author's imagination or are used fictitiously. Any resemblance to actual events, locales, or persons, living or dead, is coincidental.

Liminal Books is an imprint of Between the Lines Publishing. The Liminal Books name and logo are trademarks of Between the Lines Publishing.

Copyright © 2018 by L.C. Conn

Cover design by Cherie Fox

Between the Lines Publishing and its imprints supports the right to free expression and the value of copyright. The scanning, uploading, and distribution of this book without permission is a theft of the author's intellectual property. If you would like permission to use material from the book (other than for review purposes), please contact info@btwnthelines.com.

Between the Lines Publishing
9 North River Road, Ste 248
Auburn ME 04210
btwnthelines.com

First Published: 2018
Original ISBN (Paperback) 978-1-7321723-2-6
Original ISBN (eBook) 978-1-7321723-4-0

Second edition:

ISBN: (Paperback) 978-1-950502-84-4
ISBN: (Ebook) 978-1-950502-86-8
ISBN: (Hardcover) 978-1-950502-85-1

The publisher is not responsible for websites (or their content) that are not owned by the publisher.

Guardians

Book 4 of the One True Child Series

L.C. Conn

Also available from L.C. Conn

Realm of Dragons: Fight for the Crown

The One True Child Series

Sentinels (Book 1)
Domination (Book 2)
Awakenings (Book 3)

Praise for *Sentinels*:

"An excellent beginning to a fantasy epic. From page one, you'll be swept up into this battle of good and evil with all of creation at stake."
– Jo Neiderhoff, San Francisco Book Review

Praise for *Domination:*

"Once more, Conn weaves her spell, and we are immersed in Carling's spectacular world. Adventure, magic, and romance leave us hungry for more!"
— Tamara Benson, San Francisco Book Review

"Fantasy is alive and well and exerting its power to enchant and beguile in this novel of foretold destiny." **– Diane Donovan, US Review of Books**

Praise for *Awakenings*:

"Once more, Conn gives the modern young female reader a heroine to look up to. Her prose is accessible, and her storytelling skills shine brightly, leaving us waiting for more in books to come." — Manhattan Book Review

Early praise for *Guardians*:

"Friendship, family, and fate all play a part once more in book four of Conn's engrossing One True Child series. The best thing about this book? The fact that it isn't the last!" — **Manhattan Book Review**

To Jody, Aunty Trish, Julie, Barbara, Ann, and Sharon.
Thank you, ladies, for all your support, encouragement, and
friendship

Chapter One

Claire Brown sat on the floor of her bedroom amidst piles of clothing, toiletries, shoes, books, and bags. She stared around her at the posters and bookshelves that lined the walls and wondered again at what she was doing. Was she really going to give up all her creature comforts to live rough on a hillside in the middle of Scotland for three months? Yes, she was, and she was very much looking forward to it.

Having gained her bachelor's degrees in arts and science, Claire was now in the final stages of her honours in archaeology, and this dig in Scotland was going to be the trip of a lifetime. Her professor and mentor, Maggie Hallaran, had picked Claire to join her on this new excavation. She had been on other smaller expeditions around the country and a couple in Australia, but never had she been so far away from her family and the security they gave her.

Pulling a pile of clothes towards her, she started to sort them and remembered the other reason this was an important trip. In some ways Claire was running away, but for a very good reason. It was a painful one and one that still cut deeply at her heart—the raw and explosive breakup of her five-year relationship with Adam Ryder. He had been her childhood best friend, her confidant, and finally her boyfriend. Up until six months ago, that is, when she had caught him cheating on her with a very beautiful redhead.

She flicked her blond hair from her face with some irritation at her thoughts and shoved the clothing into the bag with a bit more force than she should have. The anger stemmed from the fact that he would not let up trying to get back together with her—calling, messaging, and never giving her a wink of sleep with his constant attempts to contact her. Claire was getting very tired of it all and wished he would just accept it and find someone else.

"I would pack some warmer clothing if I were you," a soft but deep voice said from the doorway, making Claire jump. Geoff was leaning on the door frame, watching his great-niece as she was miles away in her thoughts. His kind brown eyes twinkled down at her along with his cheeky smile.

"Uncle Geoff, you scared me," she told him as she laid out the shirt she had been holding. "I didn't hear you come in."

"That's because you were somewhere else and not employing your Talents. What's on your mind?" he asked, tiptoeing around the mess on the floor to sit on her bed.

"Stuff, I suppose. Just thinking about my life and everyone since I moved back to the apartment." Claire dropped her head and looked at her hands.

"I miss her, too," Geoff told her quietly, misinterpreting her contemplation of her breakup with that of the loss of her Aunt Lilith. He placed one of his big hands on her shoulder gently, trying to give her comfort. "But I know what Lil would say to you right now. She would tell you to stop being silly and just get on with your life."

"I know, it's just…I'm going to be so far away from you all and I'm scared—" Claire's voice trailed away, not wanting to say the words.

"You're scared of losing more of us. But it happens to everyone at some stage, Claire, and we can't stop it. Your field of work should remind you of that. But look at us. We are all healthy and happy. There's nothing to worry about."

"I'm just being stupid, I guess," she told him somewhat embarrassed by her feelings.

"No, not stupid—just caring." He paused for a moment, then broke the sombre mood. "Now, how is the packing going?"

"I have no idea what to take. Have you got any idea what a Scottish summer is like?" she asked as she looked around the room at the mess she had made. There were jeans and shorts, shirts and hats, shoes, socks, and underwear all scattered around in badly combined piles.

"Maybe. When we had built up the business a bit, Katy and I took a flying visit to the British Isles. I wish now that it had been longer. Katy had heard about some historical site in the highlands from a small B&B we were staying at, and we drove up to see it. I swear we had four seasons in one day! By the time we hiked up to it, we were soaking wet and shivering, and then the drive back was glorious sunshine. I've got the photos somewhere." Geoff smiled at the memory.

"So that means…what? Make sure I take good wet weather gear?"

"Plus, plenty of jumpers and warm socks."

"I am never going to get packed at this rate." Claire gave out a great sigh as she looked at the mess before glancing down at her watch. "I only have twenty hours left!"

"Hang in there, Kid." He leaned on her shoulder as he stood up and used his long legs to get back across the room. "What you don't have, you can always buy when you get there. Anyway, I wouldn't leave it too long, otherwise Grace and Lynnie will do it for you, then God knows what you'll end up scrabbling around in the dirt in. Everyone will be here soon." He left the room and headed out to the lounge.

She watched him leave and then went back to packing. Grabbing the rucksack she had been using for field trips, Claire started to throw clothing and other items in, then pulled open one of her drawers and started to stuff a couple of jumpers and other warm things in after. She pulled the drawstring closed and clipped the cover shut, then pushed it to the end of her bed.

This party was not her idea. She had hoped just to leave the city with Maggie and start their journey without any fuss. But her grandmothers, Lynnette, and Grace, had insisted that everyone travel to the city to give her a good send-off. She loved them dearly, but they did fuss, and she marveled at the strength her grandfather Malcolm had. Her maternal grandfather, Bob, had been gone for three years now, and with the recent loss of her Great-Aunt Lilith, it hurt a bit more. She had only just met them all six years ago.

"Claire, come and help, please. You've changed everything around, and I can't find a damned thing anymore," Geoff yelled from somewhere in the apartment.

The apartment was where Claire had lived from the age of ten after her parents were killed. Geoff Brown was her guardian and great-uncle, and she had come to love him as a father. When she started university, he had let her live in the apartment rent-free while she was in the city. And when she turned twenty-one, he had made the deed over to her and handed her a portfolio of shares he had invested on her behalf. Claire was now in the very enviable position of being young and financially stable.

"Where are your serving platters?" he called again. "Claire! Are you even listening to me?"

"Coming, Uncle Geoff." She untangled her legs and went out to help. The décor she had changed as soon as she possibly could. Out went the old green leather bachelor couches and in came a more practical and comfortable suite. The colours on the walls no longer resembled those of an English gentleman's club but were now bright and softly coloured with tasteful artwork.

The doorbell rang, and she went to answer it. In flowed a troop of people, young and old and some in the middle. All were family, and she greeted each with love and kisses. Her grandmothers immediately took over the arrangement of food, and her aunts and uncles made themselves at home. Her younger cousins headed directly for the spare room to set up whatever game console they had brought with them. Lastly through the door was her grandfather Malcolm, who enveloped her in an almighty bear hug.

"Your parents would have been so proud of you, Claire. We all are," he whispered to her, and Claire detected a slight catch to his voice. Not one to show much emotion, Malcolm had always been strong—he had to be, with Grace as his wife.

Geoff came and shook his hand as he handed his older brother a bottle of beer. Claire left them to talk and went to the kitchen, but she was soon banished. That was the way it had always been around her grandmothers. They liked to be in charge and busy, and Claire liked to indulge them.

In the lounge, her aunts and uncles were catching up. David Fuller—her mother's surviving twin—and his wife Beth had made the long journey from the village with their two boys, Jasper and Hunter. But Ben Brown—her father's younger brother—and his wife Charlie and their twins, Oliver and Owen, lived in the city. They were not like aunts and uncles to Claire, but more like much older siblings.

"We are thinking we might make the move at the end of the last term, just in time for Christmas," Ben was telling David.

"What's this?" Claire asked as she sat in between them.

"Charlie and I are moving to the village," Ben replied.

"The elders have asked me to head up the little hospital. So, we're jumping at the chance to get out of the city and have a bit of quality family time in the village," Charlie told her with a big smile.

"That is really great. I'm so happy for you. Let me know when and I'll help with the move," Claire offered.

"You probably won't be here," David exclaimed with a cheeky grin. "No, you'll be off on some adventurous archaeological dig, finding some important artefact that will change the world. Like that chick in that movie—you know the one, the curvy one with big lips."

"No, not even. It's all dirt, dust, mud, and grime in a dig." She dug her elbow into his ribs.

"Dinner! Come and get it while it's hot. Claire, will you go tell the boys?" Lynnette asked her. "They won't have heard me over the noise of that thing."

"Sure." Claire walked to the spare room and ducked her head in. "You lot, dinner—and you better not have messed around with Uncle Geoff's things, or he'll kill you." She dropped her voice menacingly.

"Get real, Claire! As if," Hunter told her as he filed out with Owen and Oliver. Jasper came last, now much taller than her and filling out to be the same build as his father.

"Claire, wait," Jasper said, grabbing her arm before she could leave. In his hand was his phone. "Adam wanted to know if he could come over. What do I tell him?"

"Tell your half-brother that using you as a messenger is not cool. And that if he turns up tonight, I will not be happy."

"I'm sorry it didn't work out for you guys. I really did think you would get married."

"What, so you could claim that not only are we cousins, but brother- and sister-in-law? I don't think so. Now get before they come looking," she said with a half grin.

What she had told him would have been true, but all completely aboveboard. Adam was her Aunt Beth's child. She had given birth to him before she married David, so technically they were not related.

With dinner over and done with, and the dishes having been cleaned by the boys, they were now gathered in the living room waiting for Geoff to speak. This always seemed to take a while, as his old, ingrained habits as a lawyer were hard to break. He stood and waited for them to be quiet.

"Right," Geoff began, taking charge of the room. "I'll only keep this short, because I know Claire hates being the centre of attention." There was a small bit of laughter at this, as everyone knew that Geoff did not really keep speeches short. "Tonight, we are here to farewell Claire as she embarks on a great adventure. She leaves her family, whom she has only just got to know, to go in search of people who have long since disappeared. If you would all raise your glasses, I would like you to toast our Claire."

The shortness of his speech took Claire by surprise, and she went and hugged him. And then she thanked everyone for coming and told them that they shouldn't have. She was still blushing when the doorbell sounded through the apartment. Claire was there before anyone could answer it, but when she opened the door, she wished someone else had.

"Claire, please. I just want to talk." Adam—tall and just as good-looking as ever—stood there pleading with her, his hand holding open the door she was about to shut in his face.

"Adam, no. I have told you so many times already, and I know Jasper sent you a message not to come." She looked back into the lounge. "I'll be back in a minute," she called to her family, then turned back to join Adam on the steps outside.

"I'm sorry I came. I know you have the family over, but I wanted to talk to you before you left. I wanted to let you know I still love you."

"Well, you had a funny way of showing it. How many others were there, Adam?" Claire asked, her eyes narrowing.

"I've already told you that she was the only one, I swear. I was so drunk that night, I didn't know what I was doing," Adam told her. Even though he had tried to put some conviction into his words, they still didn't ring true to Claire.

"Oh, it looked like you knew exactly what you were doing. Now I want you to leave and not talk to me for a very, very long time. And stop the other thing too—I can't sleep properly." She eyed a man over Adam's shoulder as he walked past them, watching them argue. He had a cap pulled down over his face and a dark leather jacket with the collar turned up.

"I'll try. Sometimes it's just automatic."

"Try harder, Adam." Claire turned and walked back into the building, leaving him standing on the steps.

"I'm sorry, Claire. I did tell him not to come tonight, and I thought he had agreed not to." Beth was there waiting for her.

"It's not your fault, Beth, if he can't get the message. I'm sorry that you're stuck in the middle of it."

"It's been a bit difficult, but I'm sure he will calm down soon. You going away will help to put some distance between you, I hope."

"We can but hope, Beth," Claire told her aunt and then went back to join her family.

The looks they sent her way did not go unnoticed by Claire, and she wished that they would just forget that Adam had ever been in her life. But it would have been impossible with him having been her first boyfriend. Her Aunt Lilith had warned her that first loves were the hardest, and she had been right. It was at times like these that she missed her most.

After moving to the village, Claire had spent a lot of time with Lilith, especially after school, poring over the archives of The Community and helping to sort them. That is where her love of history and discovery came from, and it was her aunt who had suggested she go to university and study history—from there, she discovered archaeology.

The evening started to wind down and the goodbyes and good lucks were said. There were lots of hugs and tears from Grace, and once they were all gone, there was peace and silence once more in the apartment. Geoff started to clean up the coffee mugs, rinsing them and putting them upside down on the draining board, while Claire took the rubbish out.

Heading out the front door and down the steps, then turning to a little alcove at the side of the building, she dumped the bag of rubbish in the bin that was hidden there. As she walked back to the door Claire wasn't paying attention to her surroundings, her mind still on the matter of Adam. Her thoughts were interrupted when a man bumped into her.

"Sorry," he said as he put his hands out to steady her.

"It's fine." Automatically, Claire put up her defences and stepped back from him.

The man nodded to her once and then kept on walking, moving down the road at a brisk pace. Claire watched him go as she climbed the steps to her front door. He had a cap and a dark leather jacket on, that shone a little in the above streetlight, and she was sure she had seen him before. Shutting the door and locking it behind her, she relaxed and felt calmer.

"Cup of tea?" Geoff asked her as she entered the lounge.

"No, I don't think I could drink another drop," she said, collapsing into the couch and putting her head back. "I love them all, but they are hard work sometimes. I didn't realise how much they talked over the top of each other."

"Yes, they do that, but then so do you, Kid." Geoff chuckled. No matter how old she got, Claire thought he would always call her Kid, and she didn't mind it one bit. "Penny for them?" he asked.

"Nothing, really…just how much I am going to miss them all. To tell you the truth, I'm a little bit scared of what is to come."

"You've been overseas before—this shouldn't be any different."

"There is a bit of difference between jumping the ditch to Australia and going halfway across the world to Scotland, Uncle Geoff. There'll be no backup support," she told him, slumping further into the couch.

"You'll have Maggie with you."

"You mean I will be babysitting Maggie the whole way to make sure we don't miss our connecting flights. I love that woman, but she has no sense of time or where she is." Claire laughed quietly.

"Don't be mean. I think Maggie is lovely," he told her off.

"Do I detect a little bit of romance in the air?" Claire asked with a cheeky smile.

"Just because I compliment a woman does not mean I like her, Claire," he told her, looking at her down his long nose.

"I wish you would. You need someone."

"I had my one love and I lost her. I don't have enough time left to train another to the way I like things," he joked. "Besides, I'm still looking out for you."

Claire got up and placed a kiss on his forehead. "Thank you for looking out for me, but you can stop now. In case you hadn't noticed, I'm all grown up." She placed a hand on his shoulder, and he patted it.

"Never. You will always be the Kid. Now get to bed. You have a big day tomorrow."

"Yes, Uncle Geoff. Good night," she said and walked to her bedroom.

"Night. Sleep well." Geoff sat there for a few more minutes reflecting on how he had come to be the guardian of this special girl.

Chapter Two

Claire threaded her car through the traffic in the city as she headed for the university to pick up Maggie, who had insisted that she still had things that needed to be sorted out before they left. She parked and left Geoff in the car while she went to find her professor. When Claire returned, she was struggling to carry Maggie's large bag while the older woman followed along behind, searching through her oversized handbag.

With Maggie now safely in the back seat and her bag in the boot, they drove to the airport. Claire had made sure to tell her mentor an earlier time than was needed, just to make sure they did not run late. At the airport, Maggie stopped Claire just as they entered the terminal.

"Here, you better hold on to these. I'll just lose them," she said in her American drawl. Maggie handed Claire a bundle, which included their airline tickets and her passport. "Thank you, Geoff, for the lift, and I'll say goodbye now. I'll let you two have a moment." She wandered off and Claire kept her eye on her as she held out the keys to her car.

"I'm not going to hang around. It's just going to cost more in parking," Geoff told her as he took the keys dangling from Claire's fingers and gave her hug and a kiss.

"Good idea." Claire agreed with his practicality, also knowing he hated saying goodbye at the airport. "Look after the car. No hooning around in it, got it?"

"As if, the way I drive these days! Well, look after yourself, and call me when you get there." He nodded briefly, and then he was gone, walking out the glass doors with his long, loping stride.

Claire turned to find Maggie waiting just a short distance away.

"All done?" she asked when Claire joined her.

"Yep. Shall we check in?" Claire led the way through the maze of barriers to join the end of the queue of other travellers.

Once checked in and free of their baggage, the two women walked through the terminal, looking through the shops and duty free. Maggie would stop, inspect various items and compare prices, but ultimately not buying anything and complaining how expensive everything was. The only purchase she did make was a pack of mints, which she added to the other three packs already in her handbag, and a couple of magazines for their crosswords. For her part, Claire only needed her music and the book she had been looking forward to reading.

The unlikely pair made their way through customs and found their departure gate. As Claire sat nervously waiting to board, she looked out the window at the plane sitting on the tarmac just outside and again wondered how it could fly. She knew the theory, but her own experience with the Talent had clouded her judgement.

Maggie nudged her out of her daydreaming and pointed to the line that was now forming of those about to board. She stood and looked around her to make sure they hadn't left anything behind. Claire handed Maggie her boarding pass with her passport, and they joined the line.

Inside, the quarters were tight in economy, and Maggie was having a hard time putting her large handbag into the overhead locker. Just as Claire was about to get up and help, a tall man with dark hair and darker eyes lifted it out of her hands and placed it in for her. He gave them a wide smile, complete with dimples.

"I hope you and your daughter have a lovely flight," he said and moved past them before Maggie could even thank or correct him.

"Well, I must say, he is a very good-looking young man. What did you think, Claire?" she asked as she sat down beside her.

"Very nice, but a bit young for you, don't you think?"

"Oh, enough. I was talking about you. You're footloose and fancy free now." Maggie gave her a side glance and a slight hint of a smile as she fumbled about fastening her seatbelt.

"I'm fine the way I am at the moment, thanks, Maggie. I don't need you setting me up with complete strangers."

"It's a long flight." She swiveled in her seat and looked down the aisle where the man had disappeared, and then turned back to Claire. "He's only a couple of seats down."

"Will you stop it, otherwise I am going to have to start calling you Grace. You're as bad as my grandmother. She wouldn't stop going on about it last night. Poor Beth had to put up with it."

"I've met your family, remember, Claire, and I don't believe half the things you say about them," Maggie said laughing. "Now I suppose you're going to plug in your headphones and drown me out with your music."

"Yes, I am. Do you have a pen for your crosswords?" Claire asked.

"I have my pen and my magazines. I think I'm set. I'll nudge you when the meal comes."

Claire waited until the safety announcement was over, then sat back, put her music on, and enjoyed the first song as the plane climbed into the air. The flight to their first stop over in Singapore was uneventful, and Maggie's hopes of Claire talking to her mystery helper came to nothing.

From Singapore, it would be another long flight to Heathrow Airport. There was a short delay while they waited for their next flight, and Maggie was disappointed that the man was nowhere to be seen. That was, until they boarded the new plane and he helped her again.

"This is becoming a habit, ladies." He smiled but only had eyes for Claire. She pretended not to hear and was playing with her phone.

"Thank you. It's so very nice of you." Maggie spoke for them both.

"Where in the States are you both from?" he asked Maggie.

"Well, I'm from New York originally, but Claire is from New Zealand. We're colleagues, not mother and daughter," she put him straight.

"Oh, I just automatically assumed. My mistake. Well, I hope you and Claire have a nice flight." He went to find his own seat further down the plane, and Maggie took hers.

"Here are your magazines and your pen, and no, I don't want to talk about him. Really, Maggie, did you have to?"

"It's just a bit of fun. What's wrong with talking to nice men? There aren't many of them around," Maggie replied seriously, but not enough to hide just a hint of sarcasm.

"It's embarrassing. How about you tell me about Gerry Drummond instead?" Claire asked, hoping to change the subject.

"Oh, Gerry and I go way back to when we were at Oxford together. Unfortunately, he was already engaged to his now wife. That's a sad story in itself. But he is a brilliant academic, sharp as a tack and so knowledgeable. He is also the brother-in-law of Robbie MacCallum—you know, the guy who presents that archaeology show. They go in for three days somewhere and see what they can find."

"You mean destroy any archaeology they find."

"Claire, you can be such a snob sometimes, you know that?" Maggie asked, flipping the magazine to the crossword she was in the middle of.

"I just don't like how they treat sites. There is no method in it," Claire argued back.

"They only have three days."

"There's no excuse for sloppy workmanship. Never mind that now. What is this Gerry like to work with?"

"Very much like you, madam. Thorough and careful. He likes to make sure everything is recorded and tagged. His son is going to be working with him this summer—I haven't actually met him. He has some unpronounceable Scottish name, but wisely uses his middle name, Matthew. He'll be picking us up from Glasgow Airport."

"How do you say so much while explaining so little?" Claire asked her with a teasing smile.

"It's a gift. Now hush and go back to your music." Maggie retorted, trying to suppress a smirk, not taking offence where none had been meant.

The two women had taken to each other immediately when they first met three years previously and had become fast friends. When this opportunity came up, Maggie told her that Claire had been her first and only choice for the trip. And Claire in turn was very flattered.

The sound of Maggie talking roused Claire from the sleep she had fallen into, her book resting on her chest and the silent earbuds were still pressed into her ears. It took her a moment to understand what her professor was saying.

"Oh, no. We're not visiting London. We are going on further to Scotland—near Perth, in fact. We've been invited by a friend to join him on an archaeological excavation near Loch Tay."

"That sounds very interesting. So, you're archaeologists?" a deep male voice asked.

"Yes, though I do more teaching these days than actual fieldwork. I'm getting a bit old for roughing it. Claire is one of my students—well, I'm her mentor, really. She is finishing her Honours degree, so this experience will be fantastic for her."

"How is she doing? As her mentor, you must know if she will pass."

"Oh most definitely she will. She's the brightest student I've ever had," Maggie said proudly.

Claire opened her eyes and looked to see who Maggie was talking to, thinking it was a steward, but found laughing brown eyes staring back at her.

"Good, you're awake. Claire, this is Tony—sorry, I didn't get your last name," she prompted him.

"Tony Benning," he introduced himself, holding out his hand for her to shake. Claire took it and just as quickly released it. "I'm sorry our talking disturbed you."

"It doesn't matter," she told him, sitting up straighter in the seat and tugging on her earbuds.

"I'll leave you alone, I see the drinks trolley coming and I don't want to be a nuisance. It was lovely chatting with you, Maggie. Claire." He stood and made his way back to his seat.

"You are incorrigible, Maggie," Claire hissed at her.

"What do you expect me to do when he starts talking to me? By the way, you were snoring," Maggie replied superiorly.

"No, I wasn't. I don't snore."

"You do. Loudly. Now shush. I want a drink."

The rest of the flight to Heathrow was quiet with only a little turbulence to mar it. As soon as they landed, Claire made sure she was the one to help Maggie retrieve her handbag, and then nearly pushed her off the plane so they didn't have to see that man again. She didn't know exactly what it was about him, but she felt uncomfortable knowing he was near. Claire left Maggie standing at the baggage carousel waiting for their bags while she went to get a trolley. Their journey had still not ended. Once through customs and border control, they had a two-hour wait for yet another connecting flight to Glasgow, where they were to be picked up.

When she returned, she saw Maggie yet again talking to Tony. Their height difference did seem a bit comical, but she fought the laugh down, telling herself it was just jet lag and lack of sleep that was affecting her.

"There you are. Tony has agreed to help lift our bags off for us. Isn't that nice of him?" Maggie told her.

"I'm not sure that's a good idea, Maggie. We still have to go through customs," she replied quickly.

"Claire, don't be so rude. I'm sure Tony is a very honest person."

"I just don't like seeing someone who needs a hand struggle. But if you would rather I didn't—" Tony said.

"No, sorry. That came out all wrong," Claire apologised. But she was grateful for the help, especially with Maggie's bag, which felt like it had a ton of bricks in it.

"Have a great trip, ladies. I hope the dig is a successful one." Tony pulled on a baseball cap and smiled at them, then walked away. As Claire watched him go, she felt that there was something familiar about him, but she couldn't put her finger on it.

Another queue, another wait, and another airline. Claire just hoped that the car that was picking them up was going to be comfortable, because she was sick of being squashed into small seats with no leg or elbow room. She felt sorry for guys like Tony, who were so much larger than she was.

Glasgow was yet again another airport. They were always the same, and Claire was starting to wish that someone would put some thought into helping the traveller navigate them. With bags once more on a wonky trolley, they searched for their ride.

"What does he look like?" Claire asked Maggie over the noisy crowd in the terminal.

"How should I know? I've never met him," she replied testily. "Look for a sign—Gerry said he would have Matt make one up."

Claire searched the terminal, but she could see no sign with their name on it. People were everywhere, and being only fractionally taller than Maggie, she couldn't see over their heads. Claire pushed the trolley over to a row of seats and stood up on one to get a better view. Waving further up the concourse was a piece of brown cardboard with one name on it: *Maggie.*

"I think I found our ride. Over there." She pointed as she got down and started to push again.

Maggie followed, her legs working hard to keep up with Claire's quick steps. She almost ran into the back of her when Claire came to a sudden stop. In front of them, holding the sign, stood a young woman about the same age as Claire, with bright red hair and soft blue eyes.

"Are you waiting for Maggie Halloran?" Claire asked her.

"I am, but you can't be her. You're too young. I was told that Maggie was old," she told Claire in a very English accent.

"I am!" Maggie came out from behind Claire. "And we were expecting Matthew Drummond."

"I'm Addy MacCallum, his cousin. He's in the car down the road waiting for my call. Follow me," Addy told them and led them outside to the drop-off and pickup area. Her phone was out, and the message sent. "He shouldn't be too long. The tight-arse hates paying for parking."

"He and my uncle would get along. He feels the same way," Claire laughed.

"You don't sound Scottish, Addy. Where are you from?" Maggie asked.

"I was brought up in London, but now I'm in Oxford, finishing my degree," she told them. "And before you ask, yes—my parents are Robbie and Fiona MacCallum."

"Well, I wasn't going to ask, but it is nice to know," Maggie said with raised eyebrows to Claire.

Claire was searching down the road, not really sure what she was looking for, when she spotted someone getting into a black car. It was the baseball cap that caught her attention, but she supposed that there were a lot of caps like that one in the world and she was just dreaming.

"Here he comes," Addy said, waving an arm frantically.

A very old Land Rover pulled up beside them. It was covered in just about as much rust as there was mud splattered over the faded and dull blue paintwork. A tall man with dark hair ran around the car and opened the rear door, then came to meet them.

"Hello, I'm Matt. Pleased to meet you. Dad's told me a lot about you." He addressed Maggie in a very broad Scottish accent and had remarkably bright blue twinkling eyes. They were the first thing that Claire noticed, and they took her by surprise. He then turned to Claire. "Nice to meet you, Claire." He held out his hand to her and she took it. It was a brief handshake, and she found she wanted it to linger a little more.

"Come on, Claire. Climb in," Addy told her, pushing her to the rear door.

Claire sat in the back behind the driver's seat and settled herself in. They were soon on their way, and she noticed that Maggie took no time at all in asking questions of Matt.

"What's your field, Matt?" Her voice was raised to speak over the noise of the loud diesel engine.

"Landscapes—lumps and bumps is me," he replied.

Claire could see his eyes in the rearview mirror and liked how they crinkled when he smiled. He caught her looking, and she looked quickly out the window.

"Uncle Gerry said you're Maggie's student," Addy said, hoping to start a conversation with Claire.

"Yeah, I'm doing my Honours at the moment. What about you—you said you were at Oxford?"

"I'm reading history. It seems to be a common theme in our family. Lots of archaeologists and historians and then there's my mother, who likes to play old, dead people."

"I like your mother's work," Claire told her.

"You would be the only one. I find it a load of rubbish. I hope you're not one of those people who loves my father's show as well, are you?"

"No, sorry; can't stand it. I hate how they trample all over the place and ignore all the good stuff."

"I think you and I are going to be very good friends." Addy smiled at her. "Have you got a boyfriend?"

"No, not at the moment. I just got out of a long relationship, and I'm not really looking for another just yet." She glanced back up at the mirror in time to see Matt's eyes moving back to the road.

This exchange was not lost on Addy, and she stored it away for future use to torment Matt with.

"I know what you mean. My 'supposed' boyfriend was 'supposed' to be joining me up here, but apparently, we haven't been working out well lately and he didn't think it was a good idea."

"His loss," Matt said from the front as he drove.

The drive to Loch Tay took well over an hour, and both Maggie and Claire fell asleep. Addy woke them up as they were entering a town. Little cottages sat on one side of the road and a wide river ran down on the other, which made it look to Claire like a postcard. They crossed over a bridge and Addy told them that it was River Dochart, which fed the Loch. The cottages and houses continued on the other side, and Claire was determined to come back and have a good look around as soon as she could.

Matt continued to drive, and soon the countryside opened up to them. The green hills and fields reminded Claire of around the village back home, and she smiled a little. It almost felt like home to her—all it needed was the New Zealand songbirds to make it real. She shook herself a little and couldn't believe she was homesick already.

"Just up after this corner if you look to your right, you should see your first glimpse of Loch Tay," Matt said in his best tour guide voice and smile.

True to his word, they did. It lay between them and the hills in the distance. The sunshine sparkled on the ripples which were whipped up by the wind. The dark waters reflected the blue of the sky above, and Claire fell in love with the place. Each vista brought her a new and even lovelier setting, and her hands itched to get her camera out and take some photos. But she didn't want Matt to stop the car. She wanted to see what was around the next bend.

On they went, passing farmhouses and barns, cottages, and guest houses. Stone walls and bridges, animals in pastures—it was all too much to take in and sped by so fast, but she was already hooked.

"That's the way to the site," Matt told Maggie as they passed a fork in the road. "But Dad thought you would like to spend a night in a hotel before joining us at camp. Instead, he booked you into the Ben Lawers Hotel. It's a little way up the road. There's a bit of history around it and he thought you would enjoy discovering it."

"This could be New Zealand, couldn't it, Claire?" Maggie looked back at her, echoing her own thoughts.

"Yes, it could," Claire responded. She dared not look in the mirror again but kept her gaze out the window—until she spotted Matt in the side mirror.

Ten minutes later, Matt pulled the old Rover into a car park with a view of the Loch. Claire opened the door and stretched. It seemed such a long time since she had been able to stand properly.

"You coming, Claire, or are you just going to stand there daydreaming all day?" Maggie urged.

"Coming." She bent down to pick up her bag.

"I've got that," Matt offered and picked it up before she could.

"Thanks." Claire followed him into the stone building that was to be their home for the night and she got her first real look at him.

Matt had dark, wavy hair, and gingery stubble on his face, which set off his incredibly blue eyes. He was taller than her—but that wasn't hard—and thin in a wiry, athletic sort of way.

"We'll leave you here, but I'll be back in the morning to pick you up. Have a good night," he told Maggie as he placed the bags by the front desk.

"You don't want to stay for a drink and rest before you go on?" Maggie asked.

Addy looked like she was ready to accept the invitation, but Matt spoke before his cousin could.

"No, I don't think so, but we thank you for the offer. Dad wants us back as soon as possible. There's still a lot to organise. We'll see you in the morning," he said with a quick glance at Claire. Matt then took Addy by the arm and walked her out before any more could be said.

"Such a nice boy." Maggie raised an eyebrow.

"No, Maggie," Claire warned.

With their room key obtained and bags stowed safely away, Claire and Maggie set out on the short walk to the nearby village ruins. As they explored them, Maggie read out the story of Lady of Lawers. A shiver ran down Claire's spine as she heard the story of the woman who could reportedly predict the future—and how some of her predictions had come true. Maggie passed it all off as just local myth and went on about how everyone's granny in the highlands has the second sight.

They spent the evening in the bar enjoying a good meal and a drink or two. Maggie was in fine form sampling the local tipple, which she discovered was brewed on the banks of the loch. But Claire cried off, saying she didn't have a head for alcohol. The landlord of the hotel regaled them with stories of the area, and when he learnt that they were to join the dig, he told them that the past should remain in the past.

Later that night Claire lay in bed, her thoughts on home and Uncle Geoff. Maggie snored loudly, startling her. Claire rolled over. Sleep was not coming so quickly for her that night. Her mind raced away with her as she tried to keep it calm and stop it flitting from one thought to another. Lying on her back, she put to use the meditation techniques she had learned when she first came into her Talents. They helped to relax her body, which had been unconsciously tense, and soothed her worries.

Slowly she drifted off. The dreams that followed were disturbed with images of Adam trying to call her, but she pushed him away repeatedly.

Morning broke too soon for Claire, and she had a hard job getting out of bed. Maggie had to call her several times before she even let her feet touch the ground. She dressed slowly and packed up her things. By the time she arrived downstairs, Matt and Addy were already waiting.

"Here," Maggie said as she handed her an apple, "since you missed breakfast."

"Thanks, Maggie. I didn't get much sleep last night," she told her.

"Well, come on, you wasted the last comfy night you're going to get for a while." Maggie thanked the lady behind the desk and led the way outside. Matt had already loaded the car with their bags and was waiting behind the wheel.

Before Addy could claim it, Claire climbed in and sat behind the front passenger seat. She had found the previous day to be a bit uncomfortable in more ways than one. Addy gave her a small secretive smile and climbed in beside her, sending her cousin a wink in the mirror. Matt threw a glance in Claire's direction and then concentrated on driving out of the car park and onto the main road.

They turned off at the intersection that Matt had indicated the day before and onto a one-lane road. In his running commentary of the landscape, Matt informed them that the road wound its way along the side of Beinn Ghlas, which sat beside and lower than Ben Lawers. On one side of the road the mountain sloped steeply upwards, and on the other a stream tumbling over rocks. Trees were sparse once they made the highest point, and they had to stop in the passing bays to let other cars pass. Driving down the other side, they passed small brooks that fed the larger stream.

Matt pulled up onto a gravel track and sat waiting. Behind him, Addy started to mutter, and she got out of the Rover to open the gate that stood in front of them. He drove through the opening in the fence and waited on the other side for Addy to shut the gate and get back in.

"He's such a pain," she whispered to Claire as she climbed back in.

"I heard that," he told her, giving her a grin as he drove up the bumpy track.

Maggie held on to the dashboard in front of her with one hand and her head with the other. Claire could tell that the effects of the previous night's drinks were a bit worse than she had let on, but she too was holding on, so she did not roll about too much.

They finally made it to the camp site, set in a stone-walled field next to a large forest of tall Scots pines. Tents were lined up in military precision, all the same make, colour, and size. A large building housing a cookhouse and shower block stood off to one side and dominated the hillside. At the actual excavation, the turf had already been taken off one part of the site, in a marked-out area, and people were on their hands and knees scraping away at the dirt.

Matt parked with the rest of the vehicles and helped Maggie and Claire get their bags out of the back. He and Addy showed them to their tents and waited while they stowed their luggage into the homes they would have for the next few months, and then took them to meet Gerry. To Claire, Gerry looked like the quintessential English professor but with a strong Scot's accent. He had a mass of messy greying hair, a thin scarf looped around his neck, and was slightly shabby looking. He greeted them warmly, with hugs for Maggie and a handshake for Claire.

"Come and see our project. It's already looking good," Gerry told them proudly and with enthusiasm, talking more to Maggie than Claire as he led the way to the site.

"I can already see things are a bit different than normal. What's with the building and glamping accommodation?" Maggie asked as they walked.

"That is down to our new benefactor. He insisted that we be well looked after, and if he wants to spend his own money to do it, then who am I to stop him? The food is fantastic. It beats beans and sausages on a camp stove any day," he told her.

Chapter Three

Claire was put to work straight away in the opened trench. Armed with a small trowel, she was given a pegged-off area to work in and got down to it. This was the reason she came, to get her hands dirty and work hard, and she was soon sweating in the warming sun.

"There you are! I was looking all over camp for you." A pair of booted feet stopped in front of Claire, and she glanced up to see Addy looking down at her.

"Why waste time when I can get stuck in? I didn't come here for a holiday," she told Addy as she sat back on her heels and rested dirt encrusted hands on her thighs.

"You're going to earn some brownie points for that, Claire." Addy laughed. "Tell me about yourself—where in Kiwiland do you come from?" She started clearing the dirt in the next pegged area.

"I come from a little village in the middle of the North Island," Claire told her as she bent back down to her own work.

"Ahh, small town girl. I can relate."

"I thought you said you grew up in London?" Claire asked, confused.

"I said I'm from London, but I didn't spend all my time there. My Granny lives here in Scotland. I spent most of my holidays up here, especially when Mum and Dad were too busy to spend time with me."

"I was going to ask what it was like, but that just spoke volumes to me, so I won't," Claire told her.

"I really like you, Claire. I can see us becoming very good friends," Addy told her. "So, tell me about your family."

"There's really not much to tell. I have grandparents, aunts, uncles, cousins. Most of them still live in the village, but some live in the city."

"That's not an answer! Come on, I want details. Any good-looking, single cousins or brothers?" Addy laughed.

"Yeah! I have four cousins, all guys and all single, and I think they are pretty good-looking. Remind me later to show you a pic." She laughed back at her.

"Can't wait. Now tell me more," Addy encouraged.

"Well, my parents both died in an accident when I was ten. I'm an only child and I lived with my Great Uncle Geoff, who is my dad's uncle. I lived with him from then until I left for uni. I have three grandparents still alive. I have two aunts and two uncles and my four cousins. That's it, really—not a big family."

"It's bigger than my family. Have you been on many excavations before?"

"A few. Not on this scale, though, or this age. Mostly first-settler stuff in New Zealand and a couple in Aus. I've been looking forward to this since Maggie told me about it. How about you?" Claire asked, not looking up from her work.

"Well, it is the family business, so I've been dragged to a few."

"But you're reading history, right?"

"Yep, I plan to be behind a desk. I'll leave the great outdoors to people like you and Matt." She laughed.

"You never thought to go into your mother's line of work?"

"Ha, you are funny! My mother doesn't want the competition. She only drags me out when she wants a good photo shoot. You know, the kind of thing magazines do, famous-mother-and-daughter shit. That's why I left London as soon as I could."

"Okay," Claire said slowly as she sat back. She wiped the sweat from her brow and caught a couple of guys at the other end of the trench watching them. "Um, I think you have a couple of fans, Addy."

Addy looked towards where the guys were working. "No, I don't think it's me they're looking at. Well, maybe some of them." They looked at each other and laughed.

Later, after one of the best dinners Claire had tasted in a long time, she joined Addy around the campfire. Addy passed her a beer and Claire handed it straight back, instead picking up a lemonade. She made herself comfortable beside her new friend and was introduced to some more of the crew she had not met yet.

"Anyone sitting here?" a voice asked behind them. Claire looked up and saw Matt standing behind the camp chair next to her.

"No, no one is, I don't think." The words tumbled out of her mouth and she quickly looked away, embarrassed and feeling like a complete idiot.

"We were just comparing the guys in camp—you know, making one decent-looking one from the lot," Addy said to her cousin as she leaned across Claire, offering him a beer with a mischievous look.

"And if it were two guys doing that, you girls would call it sexist," he rebutted, cracking open the beer she had just handed him.

"But it's fun. Claire was telling me that she would take Chris's arse, Taylor's muscles, Scott's height, and Cory's sense of humour."

"I did not! Those were your choices," Claire protested quietly, blushing furiously.

"What do you say to that, Matt?" Addy went on as if Claire had not spoken.

"I would say that you are teasing Claire too much on her first day," Matt told his cousin.

"No, Claire can take it. She was teasing me earlier about her cousins, so it's only fair." Addy finished her drink and picked up another.

"I wouldn't have much more of those either—you heard Dad yesterday. Just because it's being supplied doesn't mean you should overindulge. You don't want to be kicked off the dig in the first few days."

"Uncle Gerry wouldn't do that to me! He loves me." She smiled. "Speaking of which, I think you're wanted." Addy indicated behind him as she watched Gerry walking towards them.

"There you are. I want to go over a few maps with you tonight, so we know where we are in the morning," Gerry spoke to Matt.

"But we know where we are, Uncle Gerry. We're right here," Addy piped up, gesturing to the surrounding landscape.

"Yes, very good, Addy. No more for you tonight, please." Gerry gave his niece a stern look and then turned back to his son. "Now would be good, Matt."

Matt stood up and followed his father to the Site Director's tent and disappeared inside, but not before one last look at the place he had just left.

From across the fire, a voice called out to Addy. "Hey Addy, help us settle an argument. You're not Robbie MacCallum's daughter, are you?"

"Oh, God no! Why, you got a thing for him?" Addy arched her eyebrow at the guy who had spoken.

"Nah, I'm not into oldies," he told her right back with a cheeky grin.

The talk then turned to that programme, and it was soon the main topic of conversation. A few liked the show and rabidly defended it against those who were of the same opinion as Claire. It made for a great debate, and she was very much enjoying it, adding her voice to the argument, just as she had with Maggie many times.

Addy nudged Claire as the voices were being raised to new levels, handing her a beer. This time Claire took it and began drinking. *One couldn't hurt*, she thought to herself and was about to reenter the discussion when Addy stopped her.

"My cousin seems only to have eyes for you," she said quietly, so the rest wouldn't hear.

"What? Don't be daft." Claire automatically turned to where Matt was now sitting, alongside his father at the other fire. He was not looking, but talking to Maggie, who was next to him.

"In the car on the way from Glasgow he did. And I noticed you looking as well."

"Now you're talking rubbish. How many of those have you had?" She indicated the beer Addy was once more raising to her lips.

"Not enough. Stop changing the subject. You were—I saw you. You blush very prettily. I wish I could, but I just get all blotchy."

"You're being ridiculous," Claire told her in a quiet voice.

"Am I? There he goes again—look."

"Addy, this isn't funny," Claire said and reluctantly Claire turned her head again, but once more he was facing Maggie.

"Just keep looking, he'll do it in one more second—" she said slowly, encouraging her new friend. Matt did as she said he would do. He turned and looked directly at Claire and just as quickly looked away again when their eyes met. "See, I told you so. And there's the blush."

"Shut up," Claire said as she sank deeper into her seat.

"You two would make a lovely couple."

"No, we wouldn't, because I'm not looking for anything at the moment." She finished the beer in her hand. "Were you two close growing up?" Claire asked, desperately looking for something to stop Addy's teasing.

"We only saw each other in the holidays when my parents would pack me off to Granny's while they tripped around the world. Gran lives with Matt's mum, but he's a bit older than me, so we weren't really into the same things. Plus, who wants to hang out with their younger cousin?" Addy offered Claire another bottle, but she declined.

"But you seemed close on the drive here."

"We are now. He is kind of cool. He's a great sounding board when I actually get down to doing some work and when I want to vent about my parents. Poor thing. He hasn't had a decent girlfriend in ages." Her eyebrow rose suggestively.

"You can keep that idea to yourself. Why does everyone try to match-make me?"

"So, what is Claire's type? He wouldn't happen to be tall, dark-haired, blue-eyed, and dimpled, would he? For instance, sort of like Matt?" Addy laughed at Claire's blushing.

"I don't have to answer that! We don't know each other well enough, Addy. But I will say goodnight now." She laughed nervously a little as she rose from her chair and the world tilted a bit. Jet lag and alcohol just didn't mix well with Claire, and she steadied herself. "See you in the morning."

"Spoilsport!" Addy called after her.

As Claire went to pass the other fire, she deliberately did not look in Matt's direction but kept her head down and made a beeline for her tent. She thought she had gotten away, until Maggie called out to her.

"Claire, just a moment." Claire turned and saw Maggie beckoning her over. "I was just telling Matt that you had shown an interest in Landscape Archaeology and asked him if he could talk to you about it." A smile played on the older woman's face.

"That would be lovely, thank you." She made herself look at him and felt a jolt inside as his blue eyes pierced hers.

"Any time—just let me know," Matt told her quietly.

Claire felt awkward and flustered. It took her back to being a teenager again and she did not like the feeling.

"I'm just off to bed," she told them. "See you in the morning." Turning quickly, she fled straight to her tent.

The tent was made of a white canvas, and the inside was very spacious for one person. It reminded Claire of those in old black-and-white expedition movies. Inside was a stretcher, a small table, and a chair, both made out of the same wood and the same material as the tent. Hanging from the centre was a battery-powered light, and she fumbled with the switch to turn it on. Claire picked up her bag from the stretcher where she had left it and moved it to the chair, pulling out an old T-shirt and shorts as she did so.

The taste of the beer she had earlier was now souring in her mouth and was making her feel slightly queasy. *Or,* she wondered, *was that feeling from something else?* Holding tightly to her toilet bag, she ran on silent feet to the shower block and started to brush her teeth.

From one of the stalls came Addy, and her face lit up. "Good, you're not in bed yet." Seeing that Claire could not object, Addy looked around them to make sure no one else was within listening distance. "I need your help, and I think you are sensible enough to give me good advice," she started. "It's about dear old Daddy. He has heard of the dig, probably from Gran, and he wants to come up for it with his crew. I'm not supposed to say anything, because the details are still being worked out. But with all the talk tonight about how everyone feels, I think I should warn Uncle Gerry. What do you think?"

Claire swished the toothpaste from her mouth, then wiped it on her towel. She stood up and leaned against the sink.

"I think you should tell Gerry. If you don't and he finds out you knew, it could make things worse," she replied.

"See, I knew I could rely on you for being the sensible one. I'll tell him in the morning." Addy looked in the mirror and pushed back her auburn hair. "So what did happened in this old relationship that has turned you off men, especially my cousin?" Addy asked teasingly.

"I don't really want to talk about it right now," Claire said, picking up her things and walking out to the cool night air. She shivered slightly and sped up to reach her tent quickly.

"Come on, I'm in the mood for a good sob story." Addy stopped for a second as she realised that sounded harsh. "Sorry, I didn't mean that—it came out wrong." She raced to catch up with Claire and followed her into her tent.

Claire dumped her things on the chair alongside her bag and hung the towel around the back of it. When she turned around, Addy was sitting on her bed, her pale blue eyes turned up to her new friend.

"Come on, you've got to give me something! Just the smallest of details?"

"Has anyone told you that you're frustrating to be around?" Claire asked as she sat down.

"Many times. Repeatedly. You're changing the subject again."

"We were together five years. It was a long-distance relationship. He cheated. I dumped him, and now here I am."

"Wow, that sucks. The way you reacted before, I thought you were the one who was dumped."

"No," Claire said simply. "But sometimes it feels like I was. But I've never been dumped before, so I don't really know what that's like either."

"Never? You've never been dumped before?" Addy asked, a little shocked.

"No. Adam was my first boyfriend," Claire told her.

"That's even worse. What an arsehole!" A moment of silence passed between them, in which Claire could see the cogs of Addy's mind working. "That's all right. Matt will do nicely as your new, improved boyfriend. He would never cheat on you—he's too loyal."

"Stop right there. Why won't people stop fixing me up? Maggie tried it on the airplane with this old dude who was nice to her, and then just now she was trying to get Matt and me together on some pretext of me wanting to know more about landscapes. Now you too? No. No more. Now out, I want to get some sleep!" Claire exclaimed, only half-heartedly.

"All right, but I can't help what I see. What was the guy on the plane like? At least tell me he was good-looking." Addy stood at the tent flap.

"Yes, in a creepy, young uncle sort of way. But not my type."

"No, your type has stunning blue eyes," Addy said giggling, and quickly left before Claire could retaliate.

Alone at last, she zipped up the tent, pulled out her sleeping bag, and switched off the light. The dimness was a haven, and Claire lay on her bed and tried to relax. She felt extremely tired, but she went through her nightly routine as normal to set herself up for a peaceful night's sleep. She did not need to draw unwanted attention to herself. Soon she drifted off into a dreamless and peaceful state.

Claire was just unzipping her tent the next morning when Addy walked past her, a look of determination set on her face. Claire watched as her new friend walked straight up to Gerry, who was talking to one of the ladies from the finds tent. She saw Addy say something to Gerry, and his whole demeanor changed in an instant.

"You have got to be kidding me, Adaira! Did he send you here as his spy?" he shouted loudly enough for the whole camp to hear.

"That is not fair, Uncle Gerry, and you know it! Why do you think I'm telling you now? Because I didn't want you to be blindsided," she retorted.

From out of nowhere, Matt came running, and Claire could see he was trying to calm them down.

"Bloody Robbie is what's wrong!" Gerry yelled at him. By now, a crowd was watching the unfolding screaming match.

"Okay, let's go somewhere else and talk about this." Matt then said something that Claire could not hear, and they moved into one of the site office tents while everyone else went about their business.

"Do you have any idea what that was about?" Maggie asked her, coming up from behind.

"Yes, sort of. Apparently, Addy found out that her father and his crew are trying to come to the site for one of their programs."

"Oh dear. That's why Gerry was yelling. He cannot stand the man."

"Really?" Claire asked her.

"There was a bit of a rift in the family when Gerry split from his wife. As I understand it, Robbie and Gerry haven't talked much since."

"Wow. Glad I'm not mixed up in that!"

"You said it, sister. Now go on, get to work. We're not here for a holiday," Maggie said, nudging Claire along.

Grabbing a bite to eat first, Claire then headed off to the site and got her orders for the day. She was not in the main trench that day, as they had gotten down to the level where they had expected to find artefacts and now more experienced hands were working there. She was put to work further up at another lump in the ground that had the geophysicists interested.

Matt turned up shortly after, as Claire was attempting to make her first sketch of the stones on the ground and numbering them. He looked at her work over her shoulder.

"No, not like that. Where did you learn to draw, in nursery school?" He knelt beside her and took the pad from her hands. "Like this," he told her as he made a few strokes of the pencil.

Within minutes he had drawn a perfect representation of the rocks and their situation in the ground, talking all the time. His instructions seemed formal and straightforward, but Claire knew she still wouldn't be able to follow them, as she really had not been listening. Matt stopped drawing, as he realised he had completely taken over her job and handed back the pencil and pad.

"Sorry. I got a bit carried away." He stood and moved further up the hill.

"It's all right, but I don't know how I'm going to pass this off as my work," Claire said to his back. She looked back at her sketch pad, sighed, and carried on, trying to emulate Matt's artistry.

"I'm not interrupting, am I?" Addy joked as she joined them, but the question fell flat as both Claire and Matt answered *no* at the same time.

"Here, make yourself useful." Claire handed Addy a shovel and pointed to the area that was already marked off for digging. "Get started." She smiled when she saw Addy's grin drop from her face.

Claire snuck a peek at where Matt had gone and saw him now sitting on the still-damp grass, a sketch pad on his knees. His face was lined with concentration and his hand was moving over the page. She was not the only one watching him. Addy was curious to know what he was drawing so furiously. Carefully she laid the shovel down and made her way around behind him.

"I knew it!" Addy crowed softly so Claire could not hear.

"Shit, Addy, stop doing that. And you know nothing." He quickly hid the drawing he was doing, which just happened to be a portrait of Claire.

"You're in love," she said quietly.

"No, I'm not," he retorted quickly.

Claire looked up at the force of the words Matt had said, and he switched to Gaelic so she would not understand.

"Oh, you're no fun, Galen Drummond," Addy told him in English.

"And don't call me that!" he called to her retreating back, and she picked up the shovel again.

"What did you call him?" Claire asked.

"His real name, just like mine, is a traditional Gaelic name, but he hates it."

"What is it?"

"Galen—it means *tranquil* or *calm*. You wouldn't believe it now, though," she said with a sly smile.

"And what does yours mean?" Claire asked.

"Something really stupid. Adaira means *the oak tree by the ford*. What does Claire mean?"

"*Bright* or *clear*. What language was that he was using? I don't think I've heard it before."

"Gaelic. Granny taught us when we were younger. It infuriates Matt when I pretend not to understand him," she laughed. "Do you speak any other languages?"

"Not really—just enough to say *thanks* and *hello* in some. So why doesn't Matt like his first name?"

"It's the way it sounds. You can imagine what the boys at school would call him, so he switched to his middle name: good old solid Matthew. My dad is the same. He calls himself Robbie, not because that is his middle name; no, it's because of his total obsession with Robbie Burns. His real name is Talorgan, and before you ask, I think it was the name of a king or something like that."

The pair descended into silence for a while as they both got down to work uncovering the lump in the ground. They had made some progress when Claire remembered the confrontation earlier that morning.

"Was Gerry really upset with you?" Claire asked.

"The news, you mean? A bit, but when he calmed down, he apologised. I think I'll wait to ask if I can slope off when my dad arrives. I have a feeling that I might be pushing my luck with that one. I know, how about you come with me and visit my granny? She would love to meet you and she's never met a Kiwi before."

"Thanks for the offer, but we'll see."

"Hey, you're allowed a couple of days off every now and then. You're not a slave." Addy laughed. "Now get back to work."

"Look who's talking."

Chapter Four

A week had passed, and the days settled down into a nice, easy pattern for Claire. Early rising, quick breakfast, work, lunch, more work before dinner, drinks by the fire, and then bed. But she was soon feeling the effects and longed for some decent exercise. She woke extra early one morning after a night of dreams of trying to fend off Adam and headed out to run down one of the tracks in the forest of tall Scots pines beside the camp. The wind through the tall branches made a soothing whooshing sound, and the wood creaked as the branches and trunks bent under the force. The ground under the towering trees was covered in thick brambly undergrowth, and a slight mist caught at the trunks in the cool morning air.

Claire ran for an hour before even thinking of heading back. She stopped, stood in the middle of the track, and drank from her water bottle. The quiet descended on her as her breathing stilled, and she soaked in the serenity of the forest. It had a more ancient feeling than the forests of home, and she felt elated to be there. The crunch of branches being stepped on caught her attention, and when she peered through the trees, she saw a large deer with a great set of antlers, walking through the bushes and long grass. She watched him pass, trying not to be seen. This was the first time she had been close to such a large buck that was not surrounded by a fence, and she didn't want to frighten it away.

A sense she wasn't alone made her aware that there was someone nearby, and she turned to look. Matt was coming down the track with his camera, watching the same buck she had seen. She stood and waited for Matt to realise that she was there, but when he looked right through her, she realised what she had done and quickly stood behind a tree to transform. Once back to herself, she stepped out from behind the tree and almost bumped into him. In the process of trying to catch her before she fell, he dropped his sketch pad that had been tucked under his arm.

"Oh God, I'm so sorry." Claire apologised and stooped down to pick it up at the same time he did, with the result of them bumping their heads together.

Claire ended up on the ground and laughed at their clash, and all the while Matt was apologising profusely. She picked up the pad and looked at the drawing of the deer, impressed once more with his skill.

"That's really good," she told him, handing it back and getting up. "Can I see some more?"

"The rest are just boring site drawings, nothing that great," he told her self-consciously as he closed the pad.

"Have you done any others?"

"I have, but they're in my tent."

"I would love to see them. You're very talented. I wish I could draw like that," she told him, finally getting to her feet, and brushing herself down.

"Anyone can draw. They just have to practice. Are you going back now?" Matt asked.

"Yeah, I should get back." They walked together in silence for a while.

"If you're impressed by my drawings, you should see my mother's work. She's a local artist and has a good following—she's sold quite a bit."

"I would like that." Again silence, though more companionable than awkward. Claire was not really sure how to take this man.

Claire found him to be quiet and reserved with her, but she had seen him joking around with others—women as well as men. She wondered if he did not like her and was just being polite. Was Addy's teasing just her way of making a dig at Matt? It was all too complicated for her, and she really did not want to start thinking about anything like a relationship with anyone at the moment.

He broke into her thoughts with a question. "Do you often run? Only I haven't seen you out before."

"Normally I run every day, but I've been very lazy since I've been here. I woke early this morning and just had the need to clear my mind and get some of this good, clean air into my lungs. Do you run?"

"Me? Nah, hiking is more my thing or a good bit of canoeing on the Loch."

"You look rather fit." Claire blushed as she realised how that must sound. "I...I mean..."

"It's okay, I know what you mean," he replied, laughing slightly. "It must be good genes, but honestly, you don't want to see what's under this shirt." It was his turn to blush, and they both laughed nervously.

Matt held out his arm and stopped Claire in her tracks. Further up in the middle of the cleared path stood a red squirrel on its hind legs, its tail erect and bushy behind its small body, its little front paws up to its mouth nibbling on something. Claire was transfixed. She had never seen a squirrel before, and the cuteness of the little creature filled her with wonder. A sound off into the forest startled it, and it soon bounded away and then up a tree to safety.

"We don't have things like that back home," Claire said in wonder.

"What, no squirrels?"

"You've never been to New Zealand, then?"

"No—I would love to go. I love seeing it in movies. The scenery looks amazing. Some of it reminds me of Scotland," Matt told her.

"It is great, but we have no native mammals, except for a bat that likes to walk on the ground and seals. The only other mammals have all been introduced. Our forests are filled mainly with birds. I love the songbirds here, but they don't have a patch on our natives. I've got a sound bite on my phone." She pulled her phone out of her pocket and took the earphone jack out. Fumbling for a second, she found the file she wanted and pressed play. The glorious sounds of Tui and Bellbird, Wood Pigeon, and Saddlebacks, to the smaller sounds of Thrush, Blackbird, and Wax Eye called out into the stillness of the new morning. They listened in silence to the bird calls of a foreign land in the atmosphere of an ancient one. When it finished, Claire put the phone back in her pocket.

"Sounds beautiful," he said.

"My cousin Hunter is mad on nature, and he wanted to give me something from home to bring here so I wouldn't miss it," she said, slightly embarrassed.

"Have you got a big family?" They started to walk again.

"Not really. I'm an only child and I have four younger cousins, two from each side. I've got two uncles, two aunts, and a great-uncle who was my guardian, and I have two grandmothers and one grandfather."

"You lived with a great-uncle?"

"Yeah, my parents died in a car accident when I was ten. Uncle Geoff was named as my guardian, so I went to live with him. It took us a while to get used to each other, but we got there in the end. How about you?"

"You know Addy and my dad. There is also Gran, Mum, Uncle Robbie and his wife Aunt Fiona, and Dad has a sister who lives in Australia who has three kids. I know he writes to her occasionally, but I've never met them."

Claire wanted to tell him that it had only been six years since she had met her family, but she was reluctant to go into that particular story.

Matt looked at his watch. "If you want breakfast before you start working, you'd better get a move on." The mood changed with his words. Claire felt they had been on the verge of sharing something then, but it was gone in an instant. Since there was no *we* but only a *you*, she felt like she was being dismissed.

"You're not going straight back?" she asked him with slight disappointment.

"No, I'm going to stay here for a bit. There's a few bits and pieces I have to get down for Dad. I got distracted by the deer for a while, so I'd better get it done." It sounded like an excuse to Claire, but she didn't want to accuse him of lying to her.

"See you back at the site, then."

"Yep, will do." Matt gave her a small wave, then continued to watch her as she ran down the track, back towards camp.

People were up and moving about when she arrived back, and she didn't speak to anyone until after she had grabbed a quick wash and an apple to eat on her way up to the site. She was stopped by Maggie, asking her where she was going.

"Work—or are you getting as senile as my uncle?" Claire asked with a laugh.

"Smart ass. No, it's your day off, but if you're keen to keep on working, then be my guest," Maggie replied loftily with a wave of the hand.

"And no need to worry about what you're going to be doing, because I have that all covered," Addy said, coming up from behind her. "Hurry up and change, 'cause I am not taking you anywhere looking like that."

"What's wrong with how I look?"

"Don't get me started. Oh, and if you don't want to wait in the long que for the washing machines, then bring your dirty washing with you."

"Where are we going?" Claire asked.

"The comforts of home, lass." Addy inflected a very good Scots accent and put her arm around Claire's shoulders, steering her back to her tent. "We just need to find Matt and surgically remove the keys to his Land Rover from his pocket. Have you seen him?"

"I saw him in the forest on my run this morning."

"You run? Oh my God, I don't know if I can be friends with someone who actually exercises," Addy teased.

"You're in a good mood this morning."

"Yep, especially when it comes to time off from slave labour and visiting my granny and her homemade baking. You have not tasted anything until you taste her cakes. My mouth is watering just thinking about it. So go, get organised and meet me over by Matt's rust bucket." Addy pushed her in the direction of the tent and walked off.

Fifteen minutes later, Claire was lugging a bag of dirty clothes over to the Land Rover and saw Addy walking to the car with Matt hot on her heels.

"You forget, Matt, I learned how to drive in this old thing," she was telling him in response to something he had said.

"Yeah, I know. I'm still getting over teaching you. That's why I'm telling you to be careful."

"Are you going to give me the keys or not? Because Claire and I have a big bag of stinky washing each that needs to be cleaned and we both need some fussing over. You're not going to stand in the way of two girls getting some home-baked goodies, are you?" She stood with her hands on her hips, staring her cousin down.

Reluctantly, he handed over the keys. Addy gave a squeal of delight and hugged him.

"Say hi to Mum and Gran for me," he said.

The two girls jumped into the old Land Rover and Addy tried to start it up. It turned over and over, refusing to start, before Matt opened the door and told Addy to get out. Reluctantly, she relinquished the driver's seat to him and stood back, waiting. He started muttering something under his breath that Claire couldn't understand, and as he turned the key of the old vehicle, it started up the first go.

Just as he was about to exit the car, his father hailed him and made his way over to them. To Claire, he looked very tired and worn.

"Ah, Matt, when are you going to be back?" Gerry asked as he neared.

"Are you okay, Dad?"

"Just bad dreams—you know, the usual. Now, when are you back?" Gerry asked again.

"I'm not going anywhere. Addy's just borrowing the Rover to visit Gran. I was just starting it up for them," Matt replied as he hopped out of the driver's seat.

"Go with them. You could use the time off, and I know your gran would love to see you. And in that heap of shite, they'll probably break down along the way—it's a death trap." He looked critically at the old car as if it were about to suddenly disintegrate in front of his eyes.

"She is not a heap of shite, Dad. She just needs a bit of work," Matt protested, looking fondly at the Rover.

"You've been saying that since you got it. Have a good time and say hello to your mum for me." He walked away and left them to it.

With no more objections and only waiting for Matt to return with a bag, Claire climbed into the back of the car, leaving the front for Addy, who raised an eyebrow at the change.

Down the newly made track they went, with both Claire and Addy taking turns opening and closing the gates as they went. It was not really a very long drive to their destination, but Claire dozed off with the rhythm of the car. Totally unprepared for any type of dream she was left wide open and defenceless. Adam was once again the focus of these dreams, calling to her, asking her to listen to him. Claire yelled at him to go away and leave her alone and then her father was there, standing between them, looming large over Adam. The next thing Claire knew, she was being shaken awake by Addy. Claire sat up with a start. The car was pulled up on the side of the road and Addy was leaning in through the back. Concern was written over not only her friend's face, but also Matt's, who was leaning over the front seat of the Rover.

"What happened?" she asked them.

"You were screaming in your sleep. You were telling someone to leave you alone," Addy told her. "Are you okay?"

"I'm fine. Sorry, I must be overly tired." Claire didn't want to explain, and she felt extremely embarrassed. Addy slammed the front door of the Rover and climbed in beside Claire, pushing her behind the driver's seat.

Matt pulled the car back onto the road and they continued on in silence, with Claire still feeling highly embarrassed. A little way down the road, he turned up a gravel track and crossed through a shallow ford. A little further on, they passed a large and very old oak tree sitting solitarily by the gravel track, its large branches shading the earth around it.

"Look, Addy. It's your tree!" Matt declared as he looked back at her.

"Yes. You make that observation every time we pass it, and it's getting very old." There was a little bit of venom in her reply that confused Claire. She looked between the two cousins and Addy, seeing her confusion, clarified for her new friend. "I told you, Adaira means *oak tree by the ford*."

"Oh." Claire nodded. "How much further?"

"Not far—just over this rise and down into the next valley," Matt replied.

As they crested the hill, Claire saw laid out in front of them a valley with a small stream running down the middle, a flat expanse of land dotted with sheep and a few cattle, tapering up the valley to where the hill they were on, and the one opposite met. Nestled at the base of the two hills stood a two-story stone farm cottage with outbuildings and pens, all surrounded by a low stone wall. They headed down the other side and pulled up outside the white painted cottage.

As Claire got out of the car, the door opened, and a plump woman exited. She was wearing an apron that was covered in paint of all different colours, and she bustled out to greet them. She gathered Matt up in her arms and told him off for not coming sooner. Rounding on Addy, she hugged her and told her the same. Then she turned to Claire.

"You must be Claire. I'm Leana; welcome. Come in, come in! Don't stand out here. It's going to rain soon." Claire looked to the sky and saw that it was a clear blue—the only flaw in the day was a cold wind.

She led them inside, then turned and told Matt to go get the bags.

"Aunt Leana, the only bags we have are dirty washing," Addy told her.

"That's all right. Matty can bring them in and put them through the washer. Do you two need a good shower? I'm sure the ones on site aren't up to much."

Claire was the first in the shower, followed by Addy. By the time Matt made it in, there was no more hot water. From out in the living room both Addy and Claire could hear some swear words directed at them, and when he had used up his English repertoire, he started on Gaelic. It was getting so bad that Leana banged on the bathroom door.

"If you don't stop that right now, I will come in there and wash your mouth out with soap!" There was silence from within. As Leana entered the living room, she spoke to the two women. "He's lucky he didn't wake Mum. If she doesn't get her nap, she gets so cranky lately."

"How is Granny?"

"She's the same, Addy dear, just a bit shorter-tempered. Now, Claire, has Addy made you a cuppa yet? No? Addy where are your manners? Well, while I make a pot, can you go get Mum up? She will want to meet you, Claire." She pointed a paint-smudged finger at Claire and then walked back out.

Addy gave Claire a smile and a roll of the eyes but went and did as she was told. Claire stood and went to look out the window. As she looked out over the bare expanse of land towards the opposite hill, a great wall of rain washed over the cottage and worked its way across the fields. She stared out the window and a shiver went up her spine.

"Don't worry. If you wait five minutes, the weather will change again. I remember one summer when it snowed," Matt spoke behind her. She had not even sensed him coming into the room, and she jumped.

She turned just in time to see Addy walking in with a woman in her late years, still standing straight and walking unaided. This woman did not fit the image that she had built in her head of a bent-over little old Scottish lady. She walked straight up to Claire and shook her hand.

"Welcome, Claire. I am very pleased to meet you." She indicated for Claire to sit down and sat beside her on the couch. "Addy, can you go help Leana get the tea? She has probably drifted off in dream world again."

"Yes, Granny." As Addy left the room, a beeping sound could be heard. "That'll be the first load—back in a tick." Matt jumped up and left them alone.

"Claire, before they come back, trouble is coming, and you need to be ready. You have the Abilities…no, that is not how you put it, is it? Talents, that's the word. You need to use your Talents to their fullest. Listen to…"

"Here we are," Leana called out as she and Addy reentered the room, and Granny stopped talking. They bustled around the coffee table, pouring tea, and handing them round. Matt joined them soon after and was the only one to notice that Claire was a bit pale. He sat on the other side of her and quietly asked if she was okay. She nodded and just as she was about to say something, Granny told him to stop fussing and to pass Claire the biscuits.

"Matt mentioned you would like to see some of my work, Claire," Leana said after they had finished their tea and small talk.

"Yes, please. I would love to." Claire followed Leana with Addy in tow, and as they left the living room, she could hear Matt and his grandmother talking in Gaelic to each other. Somehow, she knew they were talking about her. She decided right then to try and learn the language. She didn't like people speaking in a different language around her, especially coming so shortly after the strange message from Granny. Her use of the word "Talents" haunted her, and it was not lost on her that she had at first called them "Abilities."

Leana's studio was small, light, and airy. A couple of easels stood with beautiful but unfinished works on them in different stages. One more stood in a corner, out of the way and covered with a paint-splattered cloth. Leana busied herself tidying up a bit, and Claire couldn't help but notice an empty bottle or two discarded in the rubbish bin under her crowded desk. Matt's mother then pulled out a couple of pieces that were finished and waiting to be framed. Claire could definitely see where Matt got his talent from.

Claire began to lift the cover of the painting in the corner and got a small peek at the face of a little girl. Leana was beside her and pulling the cover back into place.

"That one isn't ready to be seen yet," Leana told her quietly, just as Matt entered the room, and Leana looked at him wistfully. "You need to shave. You look so much more handsome clean-shaven."

"Mum, don't. I like it like this." He scratched at his stubbly beard, which glinted ginger in the light and contrasted with his dark hair.

"Now that the rain has passed, the rest of the day is going to be beautiful. You should take Claire up to the stones. I'm sure she will find them interesting," Leana told her son. Claire caught a hint of something passing between mother and son, but she couldn't really put a finger on it.

The rain had stopped, and the clouds, puffy and white, skimmed the tops of the surrounding hills, giving glimpses of the blue sky above. The ground was muddy and, in some places, boggy, and Claire was glad Matt had insisted she wear wellington boots for the trek up the hill. Sheep scattered out of their way, their thick, woolly coats dripping with water as they bleated at them.

Claire lagged behind Matt and Addy as they walked up the narrow trail, and she gave in to temptation and sent out feelers to see what human life there was out there in the wilds of Scotland. Apart from themselves and the two ladies in the cottage, Claire could not sense anyone else close by. The emptiness surrounding them was almost complete, and it calmed her. The message Gran had given had upset her, and she wondered who it was she was supposed to listen to.

When she shook off that thought and looked around, she found that they were halfway up the natural amphitheater that had a small stream of water bubbling down the middle. What she did not see was the small glances that Matt gave her.

Addy, finally getting sick of it, nudged him. The look he gave her was one of surprise. "Would you just make a move on her already?"

"What?" Then realising what she had said, he replied quickly. "No. I can't. What if she has someone already?"

"She doesn't. She broke up from her last boyfriend some time ago. But from what Claire has said, he wants to get back together. So, if you are going to make a move, this would be the perfect time."

"I can't, Addy. Gran has told me not to—yet."

"Gran has told you what?" It was Addy's turn to be confused, but not for long. "Oh—oh, I see, and your Mum hasn't..."

"No. At the moment I would believe Gran over Mum. Gran has told me she has been drinking again."

"Um, I don't mean to sound rude, but is it considered polite in Scotland to talk in Gaelic about someone when you are right in front of that person?" Claire had stopped and was looking up at the cousins.

"Sorry, Claire. It's these hills. We just sort of slip into it when we're here," Addy said as Matt looked away. Claire could see that he was embarrassed to have been caught out.

"Can I ask what it was that you were discussing about me?" She walked up and joined them.

"Nothing, really. I just wanted to know what Gran thought of you, being an outsider, so to speak," Addy told her quickly, but for Claire it did not ring true.

"On the way back to camp, can we stop off at a bookshop or information centre?" she asked the cousins.

"Sure, why?" Matt asked.

"Because I want to pick up a 'Teach yourself Gaelic' book. It's about time I learnt another language, and I think that one will do nicely." She strode off and left them looking up at her as she continued to climb the hill.

A craggy outcrop of rock stood in the centre of the flat grass area which covered the summit of the hill. It was large enough to hide the entrance to the standing stones just beyond it, and Claire climbed to the top to get a better view of the circle. For some reason she could not concentrate on the ancient looking upright stones. They seemed to force her eyes away from them and down into the valley and the cottage below.

Thin, wispy blue smoke was trailing out of the chimney and drifted on the wind to disappear, before it reached the other end of the valley. The clouds were still clinging to the sides of the hills, but they were less substantial than before. The sun was now shining down, and the air was warming up.

"The spring is down here, Claire. Come and have a look," Addy called to her.

Claire didn't know if she did what she did next because she wanted to show off or just because the mood came to her. But to loud gasps of the cousins below, Claire launched herself off the rock she was standing on and performed a forward somersault with a half twist. She spotted her landing and brought her body upright and prepared for the impact, but as her toes touched the wet ground, her left foot slid out from under her and her right ankle started to roll. Her ears took in the unmistakable crack of bone breaking just before her body hit the ground, and the shock knocked the wind out of her.

From somewhere to her left, she heard her name being called. She tried to gain control of herself as waves of pain emanating from her leg and foot came screaming up at her. Claire cried out. She sat up with great difficulty and grabbed at the boot on her right foot to pull it off, but other hands were soon there to stop her.

"Don't, you might do more damage." Matt held her leg in place, and the pressure did not help the pain at all. "Addy, hold on to her, and I'll try to take the boot off."

Addy held on to Claire's hand and was soon regretting it as it was squeezed tightly. Matt gently started to tug the rubber boot from the heel first. Claire closed her eyes and her face drained of all colour.

"Okay, I'm going to do it again. Ready?" Matt said softly, and Claire opened her eyes, looked directly into his, and nodded. For a second time he gently pulled on the boot until he could slip it off easily and placed her leg on top of his thigh.

"You are going to have to strap it. Hang on." Claire reached under her shirt and took her bra off and pulled it out. "Use this." She handed it to Matt, and he took the red undergarment gingerly.

"It's not going to bite you, Matt. Get on with it," Addy told him.

"Just put my heel into one of the cups and then wrap the straps around the ankle. It should stabilise it."

"Are you sure?"

"Yes. My aunt is a doctor, and she gave me a few first aid tips. Never thought I would need it, though." Her breathing was heavy as she fought to control the pain.

Matt followed her instructions, and soon the red bra was wrapped tightly around the ankle and foot, using the existing clips to fasten it. He sat back and looked at her. "I think I better go back and get the Rover. I don't want you to try and walk on it."

"I'll be fine," Claire said.

"Or I could carry her down—" Matt started while looking at Addy.

"No, Matt," Addy cut across him before he could finish. "Just go get the Rover and hurry up," she said firmly, holding Claire's shoulder down to stop her from trying to get up.

Matt placed Claire's leg onto the wet grass and stripped off the jumper he wore to use as a cushion for her ankle. "I'll be as quick as I can," he assured them and took off down the hill with Addy yelling after.

"Be careful, you idiot. We don't need you hurt as well!" The two girls watched him run towards the start of the path.

"Is he going to be able to get up here?" Claire asked, thinking of the steep track that had brought them there.

"There's a track that circles around, but it'll take him a bit longer than just trying to come straight up." Addy was still watching the retreating back of Matt when Claire reached down with her hand and grasped her ankle.

She sent out a searching thought through her hand and found the break area in the fibula. She quickly looked up to Addy and made sure she was not looking before sending out a signal to the bone to repair itself. Under her touch, she could feel it knitting together. She stopped when it felt like a normal bone should, then made sure the tendons were where they should be. The bruising and swelling she did not touch. She couldn't help the fact that Matt and Addy would expect there to be some visible damage to the ankle, even for just a sprain.

"What are you doing? Leave it alone," Addy told her, catching her in the act.

"I think it's only sprained," Claire tried to tell her.

"I heard a crack, Claire. I'm sure you've busted the bone. What were you doing, anyway?"

"Showing off, I suppose. But the ground is wet, and my left foot just slipped out from under me."

"You've done it before, then?"

"Have you heard of freerunning or parkour?" Claire asked.

"Yes, of course I have. They are all over the colleges in Oxford."

"Well, when you get to a computer next, search up *Kiwi Chick Freerunner* and see what comes up." She winced as she moved to a more comfortable position. There was no real pain, but she needed to keep up the pretense.

"That's you? I had a boyfriend who thought he was good at it, but he wasn't. He was obsessed with those videos," Addy told her.

"We had a few fans."

"We?"

"Well, I didn't do the camera work myself." She didn't feel like talking about Adam, and she looked around. "Is Matt coming back?"

"No. He's only just reached the cottage," Addy said with a glance down the hill. "Stop changing the subject."

"I'm not, Addy." Claire felt like Addy was interrogating her. "What is it that you want to know?"

"What do you mean?"

"Well, you're trying to ask me something, so what is it?" Claire asked.

"Sometimes I feel that you're not telling me everything. You tell me about your family, but you don't go into much detail. You tell me about Adam, but there is still something more. You're holding out on me."

"Okay, fair enough. I don't know why, but I wasn't told about my family until I was seventeen. I only know that my parents didn't have anything to do with them when I was born and my uncle kept it that way, because that's what they wanted. And Adam is still too raw to really talk about."

"So, what changed? How come you met them?"

"Addy, can we do this later, when I'm patched up and dry?"

"Sorry. Are you cold? Do you want my jumper?" Addy asked, already moving to take it off.

"No, just my butt is wet."

"How's the ankle feeling?"

"Throbbing. Can you see him?"

"Not yet. He has to circle all the way around," Addy told her then paused before adding. "You know he likes you, don't you?"

"Who, Matt?" Claire asked, trying to keep her voice calm.

"No, the Loch Ness Monster. Yes, Matt."

"But he hardly talks to me, and every time he does, he finds an excuse to stop talking. Like this morning," Claire added with a frown.

"This morning? When this morning?" Addy asked confused.

"I told you...when I was out for my run. I bumped into him in the forest, and we started to talk, but he shut me down and sent me back to camp." She reached down to her ankle.

"I've never met any of his girlfriends or even seen him around a girl he liked before, so I'm sorry, I can't tell you if this is normal behaviour for him." Addy walked a little to the other side of the hill and tried to look down. "I can see the Rover. Won't be long now."

"What makes you think he likes me, then?" Claire asked despite herself.

"The way he keeps looking at you. You haven't noticed?"

"Not really," Claire lied. Of course, she had seen him looking, she wasn't blind, but she was not going to tell Addy that.

It was shortly after that the Rover crested the hill and came to a stop close to Claire. Matt came running around the vehicle, knelt down beside her, and picked her up. Claire thought to herself that he was stronger than he looked. Addy opened the back door, and Matt helped her into the back seat of the Rover.

"I can manage. It's only a sprain." The look that passed between the cousins told her that they still thought it was broken.

"I think the quickest way back to the cottage will be straight down," Matt said as he got behind the wheel.

"That's too steep. Can't we just go back the way you came?" Addy asked.

"No, too bumpy, and part of the track has been washed out. I've done it before, Addy."

"Not with an injured person on board," Addy protested.

"Look, it's okay. I can brace myself." Claire put her voice to the discussion.

"Are you sure?" Addy asked, turning around to her. Claire nodded her response. "Fine. You're the one who's injured. Let's go, then, but carefully, Matthew. That is the word for today—carefully."

"Yeah, I know." Matt turned the wheel to point the car down the way they had climbed up. "Hang on. This could be a bit hairy."

The nose of the Land Rover pointed down, and he pressed the brakes as the rest followed. Carefully picking his way down, he managed to avoid most of the major rocks and boulders that jutted out of the grass on the hill. In the back, Claire held herself in place by bracing her hand up against the back of the driver's seat. She closed her eyes, not wanting to witness the gradient they were traversing. The one time that she did open them, it was to find Addy had her own tightly closed and Matt's piercing blue eyes set in concentration as he maneuvered the car down the slope. Claire concentrated on the depth of colour, finding them somehow comforting, and trusted that he would make it down with them all and the car in one piece.

As the car was about to level out at the bottom of the hill, there was another obstacle in their way—a boggy patch that had nearly caught Claire out on their walk up. Matt revved the engine and sped through the waterlogged area, with water and mud spraying out either side. They made it through and then scattered the sheep in all directions as Matt drove directly to the cottage.

The door opened even before they had entered the walled enclosure of the small farm, and Leana and Gran filed out to meet them as they pulled up. Claire scooted to the door and opened it.

"Will you please just wait?" Addy asked in a frustrated tone.

"It's only a sprain!" To prove her point, she stepped out of the car and stood on her left leg, gingerly placing her right down. "It only hurts if I put weight on it."

Matt was suddenly there, putting his arm around her waist to take the pressure off and guiding her inside.

"Put her in the living room, Matt," Gran instructed, taking charge. "I'll look at it in there. Addy, go to the bathroom and get the first aid kit. It's under the sink."

Matt lowered Claire slowly onto the couch, lifted her leg, and placed it on a cushion. He carefully and tenderly unwrapped her bra from around the ankle and handed it back to her with a shy smile, and she tucked it under her shirt.

"My butt!" Claire whispered to him.

The whisper was so quiet he had to lean in to hear her. "What?"

"My butt is wet. I don't want to leave mud and dirt on the couch."

"Don't worry. I'll sort it," he told her.

"Right, let's have a look at it," Gran said, coming up and moving Matt out of the way. "Matt, can you get a frozen bag of anything out of the freezer to ice it?"

"Aye, Gran." Matt went to do her bidding.

Gran started to peel Claire's sock back, and when Claire started to make the sounds she should make for a sprained ankle, Gran looked up and gave her a stern look.

"You don't have to pretend with me, young lady. I know what you are, and I know what you have done. What I don't know is who you are and where you have come from—or even how. You and I need to have a very long talk when everyone is out of the way." She gave Claire a very significant look and then turned back to the ankle. "Well, the bruising is starting to show. It is going to be black and blue by tomorrow. At least you didn't mess with that. You have a very clever head on your shoulders."

At the same time, Addy and Matt entered the living room, Addy with the first aid kit and Matt with a towel and a bag of frozen corn. He helped Claire put the towel under her and she gave him her thanks, and then he just stood there holding the bag of corn.

Granny bound the ankle and pushed a safety pin into the bandage to hold it in place, then she took the frozen corn from her grandson and placed it on the ankle.

"It's only sprained, just as Claire said," she pronounced.

"But we heard a crack," Addy told her.

"It was probably the tendons moving. But it is not broken. Now, I believe Claire would like to change her jeans and get into something a bit drier. Matt, help her upstairs. She and Addy are sharing the rose room." Then to Claire, she said, "All of your clean clothes are there. I couldn't tell which were yours and which were Addy's."

"Thank you, Mrs. MacCallum."

"Call me Gran. It will be easier," the old lady said with a smile.

Matt helped her up from the couch even though Claire told him that she could do it herself, and again he wrapped a strong arm around her to help her to the stairs. Claire felt very foolish and a fraud having to pretend that she was injured, and the look on Gran's face told her she deserved it.

The warmth of Matt's body as it pressed against hers was both comforting and uncomfortable at the same time. The thrill of his touch awoke something inside her, and she was very conscious of how different he was from Adam.

He helped her hop up the stairs and steered her to a door at the top of the first landing, opening it for her. The room deserved the name Gran had given it. The walls were covered with beautifully hand-painted roses in a multitude of colours. She stood in the doorway drinking in the garden that was the room. She only moved into it because Matt made the first step. She could almost smell the perfume they would have given off if they were real. The curtains were white with stripes of pale pink roses, and the bedcovers matched.

Her mouth hung open as she stared around her. The detail in the paintings on the wall were so incredible that they seemed to be real, only larger. Matt noticed her expression and gave a small smile.

"Mum painted them," he told her simply.

"They are the most amazing things I have ever seen." Her arm was still around Matt's shoulder, and she automatically brought up the other one and placed her hand on his chest to steady herself. "They are so beautiful. I saw her paintings downstairs, but those are nothing compared to these." She turned her head to face Matt and saw how close she was to him. She blushed as she stared into his eyes.

"Hey, Matt, did you do all the washing?" Addy's voice came from the landing and Claire broke away from Matt, her face going redder. Matt, in turn, blushed as well and headed for the door as Addy entered.

"Sorry, was I interrupting something?" Addy asked with a raised eyebrow and a smirk.

"No!" Claire and Matt both answered at the same time, and Addy laughed.

"All the washing was done, Addy. Claire, when you want to go down, just call," Matt said as he left the room.

"So, did I interrupt?" Addy asked Claire once they were alone.

"No, you didn't. We had only just entered the room and I was admiring the roses."

"Aunty Leana painted them. I always stay in this room when I'm here. It was Breena's room."

"Breena?" Claire asked as she sat on the bed and started to pull her legs out of her jeans.

Addy sat on the other bed and started sorting the pile of clothing. "She was Matt's younger sister," Addy said quietly, then realising what she was saying, jumped up and made sure the door was shut properly before going on. "Breena and I were the same age, and it was after her death that Uncle Gerry and Aunt Leana separated, and she started to drink. My cousin died in a biking accident, near the oak."

"I'm sorry, Addy. I had no idea."

"Of course, you didn't, how could you? Matt doesn't like talking about her and neither does anyone else. It's almost as if they think if they don't mention her, then she was never here, and the pain will go away." There was a catch in her voice, and she refused to look at Claire.

"Is that why you reacted to Matt's comment when we passed the tree?"

"These are yours," she said quietly, nodding while handing Claire a pile of clothes.

"Thanks." Claire put the clothes down and hobbled over to Addy, sat down beside her, and put an arm around her friend. "Were you close?"

"Yeah, I pretended to complain whenever Mum and Dad packed me off here in the holidays, but I loved it. We were like twins, well, that's what Gran used to say. Always getting into trouble together." She looked around the room. "Aunty Leana painted these when Breena was born. When she died, Gran stopped her before she could paint over them. I'm glad she didn't. I love staying in this room. It's almost like she's still here. When it happened, Gran told me that she had gone to join the fairies, just as her name suggested."

They remained silent for a while, looking at the beautiful flowers. Bob and Lilith came to Claire's mind as well as her own parents, and the pain of loss came quickly bubbling up from the place that Claire liked to suppress it. She fought to keep it down, telling herself this was not her pain, but theirs, and not for the first time in her life she cursed herself for prying.

"Did you just kiss my cousin?" The question was so far out of left field that it took Claire completely by surprise and she didn't respond at first. Addy turned to watch her, waiting for the answer, and she smiled slightly. "You did, didn't you?"

"No, we didn't. When he does, you'll be the first to know."

"But you are attracted to him?" Addy asked, still prying.

"This conversation is making me feel very uncomfortable."

"You haven't had many girlfriends, have you?" Addy's eyes squinted when she looked at Claire as if she were seeing her for the first time.

"I've had friends who are girls, but I've always felt more comfortable around guys. And if my uncle were here right now, he would call you the same thing he calls me when I ask too many questions. A ferret."

"Oh, I love ferrets! They're so cute. Their little faces and paws, so sweet." She put her hands up to her face and mimicked a ferret in motion. Claire laughed and was glad the sadness had gone from Addy's eyes.

Claire changed into a new pair of jeans with the help of an insistent Addy, hoping she was making all the right noises that were supposed to go along with an injured ankle. Just as she was straightening herself down, a knock came at their door.

"Are you decent?" Matt spoke through the gap.

"Yes, Galen, we are all changed and presentable for downstairs. You may enter," Addy called to him in a haughty voice.

"Gran said lunch is ready and to fetch you down." He walked into the room and opened the door wide.

"She is ready to descend." Addy stood and stepped aside dramatically for Matt to help Claire.

"Don't you ever stop?" he asked her.

"No. My mother would be horrified if I ever did." Addy swept out of the room before them and waited at the top of the stairs. As Claire went past, aided by Matt, Addy gave her a big smile and a wink.

Later that night they were all in the living room, except for Leana, who was in her work room. Stories of Matt and Addy's childhoods were being told, with much laughter. From the other side of the house came some tuneless singing. At first everyone seemed to ignore it, and Claire took her cues from them. But the later the evening got, the louder Leana became.

"I'll go put her to bed." Matt stood and headed for the door, his face a mask.

"Thank you, Matt. I'm finding it harder and harder these days," Gran told him softly.

"I'm sorry, Gran," he said at the door.

"Nothing for you to be sorry about, Matt. I just wish your father would come back and look after her."

"I'll try," Matt said as he left the room.

Claire could hear Leana protesting to her son that she didn't want to go to bed, that she wanted another drink. She could not hear what Matt said in return, but she heard them moving around the house. The stairs creaked and groaned as he helped her stumbling footfalls. There were more voices, both loud and soft.

"Addy, can you make sure Claire has enough blankets for tonight?" Gran said, turning to granddaughter.

"Yes, Gran." Addy was as subdued as she had been in the rose room as she left Gran and Claire alone.

"Matt will be a while settling his mother in. And I think it's about time we had that talk. I know you come from New Zealand, but where did your people come from?" Gran asked, her full attention on Claire now, and the girl found it a little unnerving.

"I don't know. My great-aunt and I were working on the history of our village, but there are no references to where we came from. We tried all the different genealogy sites to trace family trees, but it's almost as if they deliberately changed their names to leave the persecution behind them."

"Persecution?"

"The only thing we have ever been able to find out is that the group of twelve families were expelled from where they were in the 'old country', and they made their way to New Zealand with some of the first settlers. The village is made up of the descendants of those families. We have a library that holds all the writings of those who have investigated our history. We have a book listing the families and who is connected to whom."

"What about names...are there any Gaelic or Scottish-sounding names?"

"No. They are generally like my own surname, Brown or Fuller. In all our studies, we have just assumed that they changed their names to fit in. We can't even find the boats that may have brought them to New Zealand."

"Brown can be a Scottish name, you know. Are there any symbols associated with any of the families or Abilities?"

"Before I tell you anything else, why are you asking me these things? What is it you are not telling me?" Claire asked shrewdly.

"That is a fair question, Claire. I can understand that you have some reservations about telling a stranger something as important as your Talents. I have a feeling you have already guessed that I have a Talent and what it is."

"Isn't it well-known that the Scots have the Sight?" Claire smiled at the older woman.

"Aye, but do you know where that comes from itself? I can see you don't. Claire, it comes from the old people. The Romans called them Picts, but our people are much older than those of that name. Like your ancestors, ours are lost in the mists of time. Our lands have had many waves of invaders but none have never really conquered us. We instead assimilated into their cultures, all the while carefully preserving our own."

Gran left her seat and went to a bookshelf. Carefully, she chose a small book and then handed it to Claire. The younger woman took the book and opened it. Inside, strange symbols leapt at her from the pages, and she read the headings beside each one. Symbols of animals with the clan name and where they came from were in the first part of the book. The second had more familiar titles, but the symbols held no meaning for her.

"Which is your Talent, Claire?" Gran's voice broke through to her.

"I, umm—" This discovery stunned her, and she felt confused. "I'm Flying and Hide."

"Two majors?" When Claire nodded, Gran went on. "Neither of which I would have picked you as having. It has been our experience that someone with Abilities has one major and one minor. It is rare for anyone to have two majors. Do you have a minor?"

"I don't understand what you mean by minor Ability," Claire asked, closing the book, and placing her full attention on Gran.

"A minor Ability is something in the arts, like painting, which is Leana's."

"Oh, I see. I've never really explored any of those. I would have to think about it. Does that mean that Matt and Addy are Talented? Is that what you were discussing with him earlier today in Gaelic?"

"Aye, they are, but it is up to them to tell you in their own time. And no, he guessed I had told you something and he wanted to know what it was. But it is not my place to tell him a message when it does not involve him; and no, Claire, he does not know that you are like us. I am going to have to do some hard thinking as to which clan your people may have come from. I'm guessing, though, that you have more Abilities that you are hiding, such as Healing?"

"Yes, Healing is only a new one. Charlie, my aunt, is a Healer and she taught me how to do a few basic things," Claire said, returning her attention to the book and flicking through its pages.

"You have learned another's Ability? That is very interesting."

"Gran, what was the last part of the message? You told me to listen to something, but we were interrupted."

"I was about to say listen to your dreams. That was all that came through." Gran could see that the rest of the message had perplexed her and watched as she opened and closed the book in her hands. "You can take that book with you if you like, but please don't let it be seen by anyone."

"I promise. I'm used to dealing with secretive books. My Aunt Lilith and I used to pore over them together."

"She sounds like a fascinating woman. I would love to meet her one day."

"She passed last year. At her funeral, The Community's Elders asked me to fill her role as archivist, but it felt wrong at the time and Uncle Geoff doesn't want to push it on me just yet."

"I am sorry for your loss. I would say it was a wise decision, though. You are still young and need to be out in the world learning things. But I think you have had enough information for one night, and you still need to pretend to have a hurt ankle. I'll go see where Matt is."

It didn't take long. Gran had only crossed half of the room when the door opened and the man in question entered.

"Are you ready?" he asked Claire.

Claire looked at Matt in a new light, trying to see if there were any traces of what his Ability might be. She already guessed that his minor was art, just from his work at the site, but she doubted she would be able to tell what the major one was. This trip was turning out to be very enlightening, and it was slowly dawning on Claire that she may have solved the riddle of where the people in the village had come from.

"Claire?" he asked, closer to her this time and holding out a hand. She looked up and his startling blue eyes were waiting for her, like pools of crystal-clear water she could drown herself in. "Are you all right?"

"I'm fine…just a bit tired, I guess." She placed her hand into his and felt the warmth of it seep into her own. He pulled her to her feet and placed an arm carefully around her while she clung to his shoulder.

Claire did not see the small smile that had snuck onto Gran's face as they passed her and wished her goodnight. She had seen many things in her life and had imparted many a message. But now as it was starting to fade from her, this was, she thought, the best one yet. The coming of this girl into their sphere made her happy for more than one reason.

Chapter Five

The morning dawned, and it was not bright. Clouds had once more descended on the valley, and it was promising to be a misty grey one. Claire woke before Addy and dressed quickly and quietly, then headed down the stairs. As she reached the bottom step, she could hear someone moving about and she froze for a moment, not knowing what to do. The noises seemed to be coming from the kitchen and she set out again, this time remembering to hobble.

Warmth and cooking smells greeted her when she opened the door and bustling around the space inside was Gran. The wonderful aroma was coming from a variety of baked goods sitting on the bench tops, and Gran was just pulling more out of the oven when she greeted Claire and told her to sit down.

"You should have called. I would've come to get you," Matt's voice came from the other side of the kitchen. Claire had not seen him initially and waved him back to his seat before he could even stand properly.

"I'm fine. It's just a bit sore today. I'm a fast healer." She hobbled across the space and sat down opposite him.

"Can I get you a cup of tea, at least?" he asked, still standing.

"That would be lovely, thank you." She sat back and watched as Matt ducked and dived around his busy grandmother. It was like a dance, a very unconscious one at that.

Gran placed another tray loaded with biscuits into the oven and then joined them at the table.

"What are your plans for today, then?" Gran asked the pair of them.

"I need to get back to site, so I think we'll be leaving mid-morning when sleeping beauty wakes up."

"So soon? I was hoping for a proper visit."

"Not this time, Gran…sorry. Did you talk to Mum about my suggestion last month?" he asked her.

"Aye, and I got the response that I warned you about. Leana needs to come to the conclusion on her own."

Matt said something in Gaelic and Gran told him off. "That is rude, Matt. Say it in English so Claire can understand."

"I said, 'She never will.'" Matt looked down into the depths of the cup he held.

Claire found herself yet again in another awkward conversation that had nothing to do with her. Guessing that they were discussing Leana's alcohol problem, she didn't want to be part of it and wished they would speak Gaelic.

"Have you talked to your father about it?"

"Dad is just Dad. He won't come back unless she asks him to, and until she gets herself cleaned up, she isn't going to ask. What about her other problem?" Claire noticed the sideways glance directed at her from Matt and made out that she had not understood what he meant.

"Erratic, to say the least. And that then sends her on a downward spiral again. I thought yesterday she was doing all right, until—" Gran trailed off and Matt nodded. There was silence for a while, punctuated only by the clock ticking on the wall. Claire didn't know what to say, so she sat waiting and drinking her tea until her stomach growled loudly. Matt and Gran both looked at her, and Claire apologised.

"I think our guest needs feeding. Can you organise some breakfast for her please, Matt, while I clear up this mess?" Gran asked.

"Aye, Gran." Together the pair rose from the table. "How do you like your eggs?" Matt asked her.

"However, they come. I'm not a fussy eater."

"That's good, because he's not a fussy cook." Gran laughed as she began wiping down the bench.

"I do all right," Matt argued. "I just get distracted and forget sometimes, that's all."

"Just like your father."

Again, like a well-rehearsed performance, they worked together in the kitchen. Claire wondered what it must have been like for Matt growing up, his sister dead, mother an alcoholic, and his father gone. Growing up in this house with his gran must have been lonely for him, and she could now see why he was so close to Addy. She would have been like a bright ray of sunshine. That sunshine broke through the room as the messy red hair poked around the door.

"There you are. I woke up and you were gone." She entered the room fully, still in her pajamas. Grabbing a cup of coffee on the way through the kitchen, she wove in and out of the others and Claire could see the family resemblance. Sitting down next to Claire, she stretched like a cat.

"How did you get down the stairs? Did Matt help?" She blew on her drink before taking a sip.

"No. I hobbled down myself. I have had injuries before, you know." It was as she was saying it that she realised she hadn't had any such injury before. She had been knocked out a couple of times, but never any broken bones or sprains.

"Oh yeah, Matt, did you know we have a celebrity in our midst?" Addy called across to him.

"Addy, no," Claire whispered as she remembered their conversation from the top of the hill.

"She's a YouTube star. Kiwi Chick Freerunner. You know those videos Stephen kept showing you when you visited that time?"

"Stephen?" he asked quizzically.

"Yeah, that guy I thought at the time was so cool but turned out to be a total tosser," she responded.

"Adaira, watch your language," Gran told her as she was packing biscuits away into a container.

"Sorry, Gran. But you remember. He thought he could do parkour, but he ended up in hospital with a broken leg and ribs."

"Oh, him…yeah, he was a—" He looked at Gran, who shot him a warning look. "What you said, Addy. I don't remember the videos, though."

"When you've finished cooking our breakfast, go get your laptop and I'll show you."

"*Our* breakfast? Since when am I cooking for you as well?" Matt asked her but Claire could see he was far from serious.

"Since I am the best cousin you have, and you just love and adore me." She battered her eyes at him and gave him a beaming smile.

"Go get the laptop. It's in my room," he told his cousin with some resignation.

Addy jumped up, and as she passed him, she planted a kiss on his cheek. "You're the best." She was soon back and switching the device on. With a few simple keystrokes, she was in and searching.

"Addy, please don't," Claire begged her quietly.

"Shh, it'll be fine," Addy replied, still searching.

"It's been years. They probably don't even exist anymore."

"Look, here's one. Take a look at this, Matt." She turned it around so he could see the screen.

"Give us a minute," he called back to Addy.

The image had caught the attention of Gran, and she watched the footage of Claire leaping over the gap between two buildings with ease and gasped when she landed it.

"This is you, Claire?" Gran asked with surprise.

"For my sins, yes." She remembered the stunt. It had been the night before everything went wrong in the city.

A plate was put before her, heaped with bacon, eggs, and toast. Just to keep her hands occupied, she started to eat, but she had lost her appetite when Addy had brought up her freerunning. Matt sat down beside his cousin and started to watch the same footage, and then another and another. Until he came to one more.

"This one was only posted this month. I thought you said it had been years?" Addy asked.

"It has! The last one should have been the first one you saw. Let me see?" The bacon went dry in her mouth, and she washed it down with the remains of her tea.

Matt turned the screen to her, and she watched a younger version of herself jumping and tumbling, leaping, and contorting her body as she flowed over different obstacles. She looked at the info bar on when it was posted and who had posted it, and her heart sank. Adam. He must have found some old footage and decided to put it up.

"You okay, Claire?" Addy asked.

"I'm fine…just ghosts of the past coming back to haunt me." She turned the screen back to Matt, who was looking at her strangely. He closed the laptop and sat back in his chair; his food untouched.

"How did you get into doing something like that?" Gran asked.

"Mucking around with mates. I had always been good at running and jumping, and it sort of progressed from there." She concentrated on the plate in front of her and managed to eat all of it before sitting back, feeling embarrassed by their scrutiny.

"So how do you go from doing something like that to squatting all day at a dig site?" Matt asked her.

"You grow up, I suppose, and find a different interest. I haven't done any of that kind of stuff for a few years now — well, if you don't count yesterday's pitiful attempt." She gave a small laugh and noticed quickly that it wasn't shared with the rest of them. She picked up her mug and remembered that it was empty and put it back down.

"Do you want another?" Gran asked her.

"Not really." Claire was blushing and wishing that she was anywhere but here, sitting opposite Matt, who was watching her.

"I want to check that ankle of yours before you go, and now seems like a good time. Matt, can you find me another bandage in the bathroom, please?" Gran looked between the two of them and could see her grandson brooding on something.

Gran came around the table and pulled a chair out, then sat down and lifted Claire's leg onto her lap. With deft hands, she had soon unwrapped the ankle and exposed the skin to the air. The bruising was now a purplish colour with green and yellow tinges. Matt returned and handed a fresh bandage to his grandmother, then cleared the table wordlessly.

Later that day, they arrived back at the camp and Matt went straight to fetch the site medic. They met Claire at her tent just as she was entering, and he insisted that Claire let the medic have a look at her ankle. She agreed reluctantly and headed inside.

"It's not that bad. It looks worse than it is, but it's only bruising," she insisted as she took off her shoe and sock.

"I'll be the judge of that," Bernie told her gruffly. He was also the Health and Safety Officer, and his word was final.

He unwrapped her bandages with rough hands, and Claire was pleased he hadn't been there when she had first been injured. He turned it this way and that, and Claire winced and gasped at the appropriate times until he was satisfied.

"Well, you won't be doing any digging for a while with it in that state," he told her.

"Please, I have to! I can't just sit around and do nothing." She looked up at Matt. "Please, Matt, there's got to be something else I can do," Claire pleaded.

"I'll go see Dad. I'm sure we can find you something to do," Matt reassured her.

"No overdoing it, young lady. Did you get x-rays done?" Bernie asked her.

Claire panicked for a moment, but the choice of lie was taken out of her hands.

"Yes. It didn't show anything, though. We took her to our local near home," Matt told the medic.

"Good. Well, rest up. It shouldn't take long to heal." He then left the tent.

Matt stood there for a moment more looking at her. "I better see Dad and let him know." He came back to himself and left as well.

Claire lay back on her small bed and put an arm over her face. She did not like this one bit—lies were starting to filter through into her life once more. There were two things she hated above anything else: secrets and lies.

"There you are. Here, this is for you to munch on." Addy entered her tent and handed her a plastic container. "Gran told me to give them to you. It's some of her biscuits."

"Thanks." She took them from her friend and put them at the end of her bed.

"Matt asked me to tell you that Uncle Gerry has agreed to let you work in the finds tent for now. At the cleaning table. Sorry—it's the best he could do."

"It's fine. At least I can do something." Claire sat up and started to stand. Within seconds Addy was there to help her, but Claire waved her off with some frustration. "I can manage. Stupid medic. Why did Matt have to go get him? I could be back on site by now."

"Don't you blame him. You did this to yourself," Addy told her sharply and Claire could see how protective she was of her cousin.

"I'm just grumpy—ignore me."

"Yes, you are grumpy, but I refuse to ignore you. Do you want a hand or not? I can't promise I can hold you the way Matt does, but I can try." Addy couldn't contain the smile she was trying hard to hide.

"Oh, ha, ha, ha," Claire said sarcastically and slapped her playfully on the shoulder. "You can stop that too. It's not funny anymore."

"It still is to me, so when I stop laughing at it, then I'll stop teasing." Claire pushed Addy out of the tent and came limping behind.

It's not too bad working in the finds tent, Claire thought. She was out of the weather, sitting on her backside, and cleaning small bits of pottery with a toothbrush and cold water. The ladies she was working with were lovely. They had welcomed her easily into their group, and they gossiped like no one else she had met before. Nobody was off-limits, including Claire. Thankfully they had not connected her with Matt, but she had been connected with every other young man in the camp, which she denied most furiously and with some amusement at their teasing as they good-naturedly fished for information.

Claire knew they were fishing, hoping to get from her the past she had been hoping to leave behind, and she didn't mind their gentle jokes. But she did blush furiously whenever they started to talk about their sex lives, and they talked about it frequently. Having not really hung out with a group of women before, either her own age or older, apart from those in her family group, Claire had at first not known how to take it, but by the time she could leave the tent on her first day, she found she had learned a lot.

It was one of these bracing conversations a few days later that a tall man with a mop of curly blond hair walked into the middle of. His easy smile let them know he had heard what was being said, and his grey eyes twinkled with mischief.

"Good afternoon, ladies. Sorry to interrupt such a scintillating discussion, but I was wondering if you could tell me where I could find Gerry Drummond." His Irish accent lilted gracefully, and Claire could see it had an effect on more than one woman in the tent.

"Try the site director's tent a couple along, or up on site," one of the older ladies told him, looking him up and down.

"Thank you kindly. When I've finished with him, I'll come back and join the conversation. It sounded delightful." He smiled and winked at them, then walked out.

"Just what we need—another digger," the older lady said.

"But what a body! Did you see how tight his pants were?" another said, and they all laughed.

Claire kept working and enjoyed the talk around her. She picked up the next piece from the tray in front of her and dunked it into the bucket between her feet. Clods of dirt came away in her hands and she could feel grooves on the bare stone, still filled with earth. The toothbrush she had in her hand started its job, and soon she had a clean piece of dark stone. The grooves she had felt now came out in sharp relief. Turning it in her hands, she called for the finds supervisor and reluctantly handed the piece of stone over to her.

Sheryl turned it over and felt the surface of the stone, her finger gently tracing the outline of the design on it. She took it to the entrance of the tent for more light at the same moment Gerry was walking past with the Irish visitor.

"A moment, Gerry—have a look at this. I think it might be Bronze Age or maybe even earlier. It is very in keeping with other types of carvings that have been found in the area. It is either a boar or a wolf symbol, I think." She handed the stone to Gerry, and he took it carefully in his hands as if it might break at any moment.

"Yes, I think you might be right, but I would definitely say Iron." He looked closer at the carving. "It's a boar, I think—look at the snout. Well done." Claire watched him very carefully and could tell there was an undercurrent of excitement he was suppressing.

"What the hell are you doing here, you Irish bastard?" a shout came from outside the tent. The Irish man turned, and a great grin spread across his face.

"You little Scottish prick! Has your wallet loosened yet, or are you as tight as ever?" He left the tent and Claire could see from her seat Matt giving the newcomer a large man hug.

Gerry handed back the stone to Sheryl, telling her that he would like to look at it a bit more closely later. Then seeing the expressions on some of the faces in the tent, he explained that Matt and the other man were old university friends.

That evening Gerry called a meeting, and everyone gathered in the cookhouse. He stood before them, looking slightly harassed and annoyed. Addy shifted uncomfortably in her seat, and Claire could guess the reason for her unease.

"We all here? Okay, I'll try to make this short and not hold everyone up, but I have some news that is going to affect our little working group. I was informed this afternoon that we are soon to be graced by the presence of my brother-in-law, Robbie MacCallum, and his merry band of land rapists. Sorry, Nick, no offence intended."

"No need, Gerry. I quite understand." Claire recognised the Irish visitor from earlier as he responded.

"Apparently, they have had full permission from all authorities and our benefactor to come on site and film their little program. We are—I have been told—to give them every degree of civility and help while they are with us. Thankfully, they will only be with us for a short time, and there is nothing that can't be fixed after they leave—I hope. Now, I would like to introduce to you Mr Nicholas O'Brien—or Nick, as he likes to be known. Nick?"

The tall Irishman stood and looked comfortable in front of a large crowd. Claire could see he had some fans already amongst some of the female staff and maybe even some male.

"Okay, I am here to find out exactly what it is you have found so far. Work out where we can set up our own tents and caravans, what and who Robbie would possibly like to film," he said with a wink at one of the girls. "I will try not to get in your way, but I will be around and talking to people. That's it—I hope I get to meet as many of you as possible. Thank you."

"Don't believe a word that comes out of his lying Irish arse!" Matt called out from where he was sitting at the table in front of Claire and Addy. He laughed at the discomfort his words had caused his friend.

Nick sat back down, and Gerry stood up. He waited for the buzz in the room to settle and then started to speak once more.

"Yes, thank you for that input, Matt, and thank you, Nick. I just want to add that everyone is doing a fantastic job and the finds that are coming in are superb. I want you all to keep up the good work. That is all. You can now go and have fun." He picked up his papers and left the cookhouse before anyone else.

Claire and Addy stood up to move out, and she could see Matt approach his friend. "So how the hell did you end up working for my uncle?"

"Easy one to answer. You turned it down, so he got the best at last. No, really, I did hear that you turned the job down and so I applied. I did mention your name and Gerry's a couple of times, and I think that clinched it. Are there any nice girls around? I thought I saw a couple out there when I was talking. There's also a tasty blond I saw earlier."

"Keep it in your pants, Nick. Hey, I mean it. Leave them alone," Matt warned him.

"All right keep ya hair on." They stayed in the cookhouse while Claire followed Addy to the campfire.

The fire was crowded that night with the younger ones. Someone had decided it was a good idea to have a type of karaoke night as a form of entertainment. Everyone had to sing at least one song. It didn't matter if it was well-known or even a child's rhyme. Guitars and other musical instruments were pulled out of tents and tuned, waiting to try and accompany the singers.

Claire and Addy were sitting together and talking, not really listening to the instructions being given. Claire had taken the bandage off, as the bruising was starting to fade, and she was now walking on it normally. She was in the middle of telling Addy that she was hoping to be back on site and digging again when her name was called.

"Claire, come on—keep up. It's your turn." A tall guy with a shaggy blond beard was looking at her.

"I can't sing, and you guys really don't want to hear me, honestly. It sounds like two cats fighting."

"You are here and so you have to abide by the rules. Come on, anything will do," another called out and they were all looking at her.

"All right," she said in resignation and scoured her mind for a song to sing. From somewhere in the dark reaches of her memory a song she had learned in primary school came up, and she started to sing *Pokarekare Ana* softly. The words of the traditional Maori love song came easily to her memory. As Claire sang, she was surprised that the notes were not her normal out-of-tune caterwauling, and her voice grew in confidence. Unlike the other singers who had gone before, there was no attempt by the musicians to accompany her clear voice.

The haunting refrains floated out onto the wind, and soon the other campfire had quietened their voices to listen. The air was still, and not another sound could be heard. No scuffling feet, no coughing or even a murmur. There was not even the sound of the birds settling for the night. It was eerie how calm everything seemed to be until she finished, as if the world was holding its breath.

For a moment the last note hung in the air, and there was silence until someone started to clap. The applause was deafening, and people were calling out. Claire blushed and hid her face in her hands and when she looked back up, the group around the fire asked her what the words meant. When they finally quietened down, she recited the English version rather than sing it.

Oh restless are the waters
Of mighty Rotorua
That separate my true love
And keep her far from me.

But still I'll face
The raging tide,
Until I am near her
Once more at her side.

I wrote to her a letter
To tell her that I love her
To tell her that I need her
And think of her each day.

Though sunlight may be fading
Though summer may be through, love
As long as I have true love
I'm richer than a king.

Though winter fast approaches
I will not fear the cold dear
As long as I am with you love
I'll feel forever warm. *

"I thought you said you couldn't sing?" Addy asked her quietly.

"I didn't think I could. Was it good?" Claire replied.

"Was it good, she asks! How am I going to beat that? Claire, it was beautiful and sad-sounding and wonderful and…and… I can't describe the chills up my spine."

"Shut up! It wasn't that good." Claire blushed again.

"Well, you had a certain someone watching," Addy said, pointing to the other fire.

When Claire looked over, both Matt and Nick were still looking at her and both raised their bottles of beer in salute. She smiled slightly in reply and then hid behind Addy.

The next person was taking their time deciding what they were going to sing, and Addy passed Claire a bottle of beer. She started to refuse. Claire didn't like drinking, as she didn't want to lose control of her Talents and be discovered by anyone. But tonight, she made an exception and decided that one wouldn't hurt.

"Right, we have known each other for a while now, Claire, and I think it's time to spill."

"About what?" Claire asked, taking a sip of her beer.

"Your old boyfriend, that's what. Come on, I've been very good and not asked before now. You have to tell," she begged her friend.

"There's nothing more really to tell. He cheated, and I dumped him. End of story."

"That's not all, though, is it? Come on, Claire. I need a good bedtime story. I could hear it in your voice when you sang."

Claire took another gulp of the beer, trying to decide whether she should tell Addy the story. Then she took a deep breath. "We had been together since we were seventeen."

"Hang on, what's his name?" Addy interrupted her.

Claire rolled her eyes and resumed. "Adam. I thought I already told you that. Anyway, we had been together since we were seventeen. Happy?"

"I will be if you would just get on with it."

"Okay. We did the whole long-distance relationship thing while we were at uni, and about six months ago I found him in bed with another woman, so I stormed off and broke up with him."

"You're not giving me the details that I need, Claire. Didn't you ever talk about this kind of thing with your best friend back in New Zealand?"

"He *was* my best friend. Adam and I grew up together and were best friends from kindergarten. He was my cameraman for those videos you watched. He was my confidant, my mate, my everything. Until I caught him with that other woman—a redhead." By now, the music was swelling and thankfully for Claire, it hid her voice as it started to rise.

"Wow. I had no idea. So, he was your first boyfriend as well."

"Yep, lucky me! My childhood sweetheart turned out to be my cheating ex." She gulped down the rest of her bottle of beer and placed it on the ground beside her.

"Do you miss him?" Addy asked.

"No, but yes. Stupid, huh? Five years we had been together. I don't know if I actually miss him or just miss the thought of him being there."

"Do you still love him?" Addy asked, grabbing Claire's arm.

"Now I know how my uncle feels when I ask a lot of questions."

"That is not answering my question, Claire. Do you still love him?" Addy asked seriously.

"I don't know. When I saw him the night before I left, there were some of the old feelings, but I was still so angry with him. I didn't leave it very well." Addy grabbed her up in a big hug that nearly pulled Claire out of her chair. "What the hell are you doing? How much have you had to drink?" She extracted herself from the grasp and righted her chair.

"I've not had nearly enough." Addy laughed. "Sorry, I get a bit overenthusiastic when I've had a couple."

"Okay, Addy. I've told mine, now yours. You were supposed to be here with a guy, so what happened?" Claire asked her.

"Same old thing as I usually do. Get drunk and either say something stupid or do something stupid and drive off the good ones."

"Was he a good one?" The shoe was on the other foot now, and Claire could think of several questions she would like to ask.

"Oh yes, a very good one. The bad ones leave me crying and the good ones I say goodbye to, although this time he broke up with me. I just don't have any luck with guys." She paused while she went for another couple of bottles and handed one to Claire. "I think I'm due for a bad boy, though." She looked purposefully at Nick near the other fire.

"Well, Addy, if what I heard this afternoon is correct, he is up for anything," Claire told her.

"Really? Well, maybe I should go and get myself reacquainted with Mr Nick and show him I have grown up." Addy winked at Claire and smiled.

"Addy! You're not really going to, are you?" The beer was starting to go to her head, and she was beginning to enjoy herself.

"Addy, you're up!" came the call from the other side of the fire.

"Woo hooo! Yeah. Okay, what am I going to sing?" Addy stood up and looked around her. "Oh, I know. A classic and I am sorry if you don't like country." She started to hum a little as she got the tune in her head and then belted out the first words of the song.

"Crazy, I'm crazy for feeling so lonely…"

Each word and every line Addy sang felt like a stab in the heart and in the back to Claire. The first thought she had was that Addy had dragged her pain out of her only to throw it back in Claire's face. Her face was set in stone, and she gripped the neck of the bottle tightly as she threw back the rest of the beer while listening to her friend sing.

When Addy was finished, there was as much applause for her performance as for Claire's, but she was not as shy as her friend. She took pleasure in the adulation and bowed repeatedly to the ovation. When she sat, her face was beaming, and she looked to Claire for more. But she was not expecting the response she got.

"Well done, Addy. You have a beautiful voice." Claire's words were light and spoken with a smile, but her body language spoke a whole different story.

"Claire, what's wrong?"

"Nothing, Addy. I'm going to bed." She stood with such force that her chair tipped over as she stalked off between the two fires to her tent. Claire heard her name being called by more than just Addy, but she didn't slow her step.

The zip to her tent caught on something, and she had a hard job trying to get it open with trembling hands. Claire tried over and over to open it and finally gave up, sat on the ground in front, and started to cry. A footstep behind her warned of the approach of someone, and quickly she got up and headed to the shower block. If she couldn't hide in the safety of her tent, then a toilet stall would have to do.

Sending out her senses, she could tell someone was following her, but she didn't want to see anyone—especially Addy. Her anger was still building, and she wasn't ready to vent it. She shut herself in the cubicle and leaned against the door just as the footsteps entered the building.

"Claire, you okay, honey?" The voice belonged Maggie.

"Yeah, just needed the loo." She tried to make her voice sound as normal as possible, and it seemed to work.

"All right. Well, if you need to talk, you know where I am."

"Yep, no probs, Maggie," Claire responded, just wishing she could be left alone.

"Okay. I'll leave you now."

"Cheers." She heard Maggie leave and she sat on the toilet with tears streaming down her cheeks. It felt like she was seventeen again and had been tricked once more, just like Adam had done when he lured her into his father's building. The feelings she had tried so hard to keep in check all these months came pouring out, and she wept.

"Claire? Are you in there?" Addy's voice was at the door, and it startled her. She didn't hear her come in, but Claire was sure she had heard her crying. "Claire, I can hear you. Please, what is wrong?"

How could she confront Addy? Everything screamed inside her to yell and rant, but she didn't know how. She was not the type of person to rage—lose her temper, yes, but rage, no.

"I'm not leaving until you talk to me. I can stay all night if I have to." Claire heard Addy lean against the door. "I don't know what happened to make you angry at me, Claire, but I'll be damned if I'll be accused of something I didn't do."

"Go away, Addy. I don't feel like talking anymore."

"She speaks! What did I do?" Addy asked her.

For a brief second, Claire flirted with the thought of turning invisible, shrinking down, and flying out, but that would only create more questions—ones she was not willing to answer. But before she could come up with an answer, Addy's head poked over the stall door.

"What the hell, Addy?"

"Well, if you won't open up, then I'm coming in." Deftly she climbed over the door and dropped down in front of her.

"Don't you run and hide in here and not tell me what I have done. So come on, out with it."

"Why did you sing that song?" Claire stood up and faced Addy.

"The song? What—wait—what?" Addy stammered, clearly confused with the question.

"Why did you decide to sing that song?"

"Because I like it and that is the way I was feeling. Is this why you stormed off?"

"Yes. So, you didn't sing it to get at me?"

"Why would I do that? No, Claire! You have let your imagination run away with you."

Claire wiped her eyes on her sleeves and stood looking forlorn at Addy. "I think I overreacted."

"You think? God, you scared me. I thought I had done something really bad." She put her arms around Claire and hugged her.

"Do think I'm the kind of girl who gets upset and starts crying when she has a drink or two?" Claire asked into her shoulder.

"I'm sorry to say that you are that girl."

"See, this is why I don't drink." Claire laughed.

"Are you ready to come back and join everyone?"

"Yes, but I feel so stupid."

"You are stupid, but only you and I know why, so that makes it all right." Addy opened the door and as Claire moved into the brighter light, she stopped her. "Wash your face. You're like me. We can't cry gracefully."

Claire took one look in the mirror and grimaced, then splashed some water on her face to try to get rid of the redness around her eyes and her cheeks. Looking in the mirror again, she straightened her hair.

To get back to the fire circle, they first had to pass the other one. Arm in arm they walked, and as they passed it, Claire stole a glance at Matt. He was talking loudly with Nick, and it was obvious that they were both well on the way to having the mother of all hangovers the next morning.

Claire and Addy resumed their seats and were soon offered another beer, which they both refused and stuck with those of the non-alcoholic variety for the rest of the night. The feelings of despair were replaced again with joy and fun, and the embarrassment she had felt was fading. The noise of Matt and Nick soon outdid that of the karaoke night. Their singing was definitely off-tune, and the more they drank, the funnier they thought they were. Soon they were the only ones left at their fire, so they stumbled over to the dwindling crowd around Claire and Addy's, bringing their bottle of whiskey with them.

In short order it was only the girls sitting with them, their loudness having chased everyone else away. In their drunken state, their accents thickened to the point where Claire could no longer understand what either one of them were saying. But to them, it was hilarious. Claire stood up and started to clean up the area, picking up discarded bottles and cans and putting them into a bin for recycling. Then when she had finished, she bade them good night. As she was passing Matt, he stood up and stepped in front of her.

"Claire don't go. Stay a bit longer." He reached out and grabbed her arms.

"Matt, let me go, please," she asked calmly.

"No, no, don't go. I want to tell you that I like you, that I really like you—and I thought your singing was grand, just grand." He tried to stare into her eyes as he wobbled on his feet. He reached up and cupped her face in his hands and then leaned in, kissing her full on the lips. Claire could not only smell but could also taste the whisky he had been drinking, and it was very stomach-churning. He broke the kiss and held up a finger.

"Wait right there. I'll be right back." Matt stumbled off into the bushes nearby, and they heard him throwing up very loudly.

Nick was now standing talking to both Claire and Addy. To their ears it sounded like gibberish, but they got the point when he pointed in the direction of Matt and followed him to the same bushes.

"I'm outta here," Claire said, looking at Addy.

"I'm not staying to look after them." She stood and was on Claire's heels in a second.

Chapter Six

The next morning there was a distinct amount of noise around Matt and Nick's tents. Large metal trays just happened to be dropped from great heights, shovels clanged together, annoying ringtones sounded on phones, and anything else that made a loud noise seemed to be coming from that direction. Also—for some strange reason—everyone seemed to feel the need to yell at someone who happened to be on the other side of the camp site.

The torment carried on until they both had been forced from their tents. Hangovers definitely did not look good on either one. Their faces still carried the green tinge, and bags under their eyes did nothing for their boyish good looks. Addy took great delight in teasing them both very loudly in the cookhouse while they sat over their coffee. Claire was enjoying watching from a distance by the door while she waited for Addy to finish.

"So, do you remember anything from last night, cousin dearest?" Addy asked in a sickeningly sweet voice.

"I don't know what you're talking about. Can't you just leave me to die in peace?" Matt groaned with his head in his hands.

"Oh, my goodness, gracious me. You don't remember? Claire, he doesn't remember. Sorry!" Addy called out to her friend. Claire blushed but still watched with a smile.

"Addy, please, stop. Just tell me what I did so you can go away."

Addy squatted down beside her cousin, so she could see his reaction. "You don't remember kissing Claire?" she said softly so only he could hear.

Matt's head came up so swiftly that his vision blurred, but he had no problem focusing on Claire, who stood at the doorway. His face, already pale, went another shade whiter. He watched her leave, not giving a second glance back at him, and he knew his cousin was telling the truth.

"Oh my God. Why?" he asked in barely a whisper.

"Because you were drunk...and I think Nick had something to do with it as well. How about you talk to him, because I'm not sure that Claire is very impressed with drunken kisses before going off to throw up. If you want her, Matt, you are going to have to do some serious apologising." She patted him on the back hard as she stood. "I'll see you boys on site." Addy left them to their misery.

Outside, Claire was waiting for her and walked with her to Gerry's administration tent. Addy pushed her in and followed her soon after.

"Uncle Gerry, Claire has something to ask. Go on," she prompted Claire.

"I was wondering if I could go back to the site today. My ankle is better, and I have no problems walking on it at all." She had planned what she was going to say while waiting for Addy, but now her voice faltered, and she forgot her carefully rehearsed words.

"I can't see why not." He looked down at his notes for a moment. "Are you on the top trench, Addy?"

"Yep."

"Good, she can join you there. Hopefully we should get something out of there today, otherwise we are going to shut it down. Have you seen Matt this morning?"

Addy smiled. "He's in the cookhouse, Uncle Gerry, along with Nick if you want him. And I wouldn't be gentle with either of them if I were you."

"Oh, I intend not to. I am going to have very strong words for the pair of them. Now, off you go, ladies. I want some progress, please."

"Yes sir!" Addy saluted, and she grabbed Claire's arm as they walked out.

They collected their tools and walked up to the trench. Not much had been done to it since the last time Claire had been there. Most of the hands were still working on the other trench, especially now that a round house had been uncovered. Claire started where she had left off and got to work.

She had enjoyed the companionship of the finds tent, but this was definitely where she wanted to be. The sun was shining down, the dirt was coming away easily, and she had Addy there telling her a litany of adventures with various boyfriends. *It's a good day to be alive*, she thought as her trowel hit something more solid than the fertile earth she was scraping away at.

Carefully, she used her trowel to push the dirt out of the way so she could see what it was she had come across. She worked on that little patch of dirt for some time and brought to light two stones, both roughly the same size.

"Addy, what do you think of this?" she called to her friend.

"Two more stones on the side of a hill strewn with them," Addy said, looking down on them.

"Very good. Can you work that way and I'll keep doing this? I just have a feeling there are going to be more."

"How about we stop for lunch and come back after?" Addy asked. When she did not get a response from Claire, she carried on. "It will still be there after you've eaten."

"No, I think I'll work through. Can you bring back a sandwich or something?"

"What did your last slave die of?" Addy asked, laughing while walking away.

"Boredom—because she had nothing to do, so be grateful," Claire called after her and went back to work.

By the time Addy had walked back to camp, eaten, got a sandwich and bottle of water for Claire, then walked back to the trench, Claire had uncovered another four stones all in a row. She was sitting on the uphill side of the trench and looking down at them, trying to puzzle them out. A pad was lying beside her, and she had tried to make some drawings, but they were pitiful attempts.

"Have you seen Matt?" she called down to Addy as she made her way up to her.

"No, not since this morning when I dropped the bombshell on him. Why? Do you need another smooch?" she teased.

"Stop it, Addy, or we will have a falling out. No, I need his artistic skills. I can't get this right no matter how many times I try." She pointed to the piles of screwed-up papers that were moving slightly in the wind.

Addy handed her the sandwich and water, and then picked up the pad. "You really can't draw, can you? How on earth have you managed to get this far and not at least picked up a hint or two on how to draw?"

"I winged it, I suppose," she said with a mouthful of ham and salad sandwich.

"Claire, you could have washed your hands first," Addy said, scrunching up her nose at the sight of dirt on white bread.

"It's just dirt. It's not going to hurt me," Claire said, taking another large bite. "Here comes Nick. See if he knows where Matt is, will you?"

"I would rather not, if you don't mind." Addy said with the same look she had given Claire's dirt smeared sandwich.

"You were keen last night. I thought you wanted another bad boy?"

"I've changed my mind. I've decided to wait until I find someone half decent. And I find that Nick O'Brien is not that person."

"Afternoon, ladies. Enjoying the sunshine?" Nick asked as he neared with a smile.

"It is summer, after all," Addy said with a superior tone.

"I would like to apologise for last night. I think we may have had a touch too much to drink."

"Is that all you wanted to apologise for?" Addy asked before Claire could say anything. "There's nothing else you can think of that might have happened?"

"No, nothing I'm ashamed of, anyway." He eyed Claire. "Weren't you working in the finds tent yesterday?"

"Yes, but I've done my time and now I've been released back into general population—on probation, of course," Claire told him straight-faced, but she almost lost it when Addy had to turn away from Nick to hide her smile. "Is there something we can do for you, or are you just here to waste our time?" She picked up the water bottle and drank half of it in one go.

"No. Just checking on the archaeology and meeting everyone." Claire could feel him trying his hardest to be charming and nice. Having been around people who had that Talent before, she felt more creeped out by him than charmed.

"I was wondering if either one of you ladies had any objection to being on camera?"

"Claire might, and I definitely do. No cameras for this MacCallum," Addy told him and sat next to her friend.

"Oh, that's right. You're Matt's little cousin. Wow, you have grown up. You wouldn't like to go to the pub later, would you?" he asked.

"No, I wouldn't. And I should think you would have had enough last night."

"No, never enough. How about you, Blondie?" he asked, now turning his attention on Claire.

"What a charmer. You have just said my name and he couldn't remember it. I would say that his brains are well and truly pickled, wouldn't you, Red?" Claire asked her friend.

"You're right, Blondie; well and truly pickled," Addy agreed.

They sat there looking at him, waiting for him to either leave or say something else—hopefully something they could throw back at him.

"I'm sorry I forgot your name. Yes, I'm still a bit hungover, so I'm not as sharp as I should be. But the question still remains. How about the pub this afternoon?"

"No, thank you. I don't really drink. Plus, I have a date tonight," Claire said.

"Oh, well, doesn't hurt to try. Must be a lucky man to be going out with a girl like you. I'll see you round." He walked away back down the hill to the other trench.

"You have a date, and you didn't tell me?" Addy rounded on her as soon as Nick was out of earshot.

"Yeah, of course I do. With a long, hot shower and my ever-so-comfy cot bed. Heaven!" Claire sighed dramatically.

"You idiot, get back to work," Addy said and laughed at her.

Claire decided to knock off early and left Addy in the trench uncovering more stones. So far, they had now found ten, and it was starting to curve. There was still not enough there to get too excited about, but they hoped it would be enough to convince Gerry to keep the trench open. Addy had promised she would talk to her uncle about it later.

Down in her tent, Claire changed out of her dirty, sweaty work gear and into a T-shirt and running pants, then pulled on her trainers. She zipped up her tent and started to stretch, only to receive a few catcalls from some of the guys who were nearby. Claire was in a good mood, and she flipped them the bird with a smile, then took off at a run, back down the track through the forest she had taken before.

It was good to be running after squatting and kneeling all day. Her body was stretching out and becoming limber again. She could feel the knots in the muscles of her back and neck becoming untangled and free, and she breathed a bit easier. The forest was quiet and cool compared to the dig site. The wind wound its way through the trees, which stood straight and tall, and made the branches sway in a calming way.

On she ran and on some more until she decided she needed to get back. The light under the trees was dim with only a few small patches of late afternoon sunlight filtering through. Claire's music blared in her ears, and she was lost in her own world. The tune seemed to fit her mood and enhanced her experience of the forest as she ran. The run back to camp turned into a walk while she listened, not really paying attention to what was going on around her. Her eyes were on the depths of the forest and its undergrowth, as she hoped to see the buck again. But it was something entirely different she saw that day.

Hands grabbed her shoulders and stopped her in her tracks. Whirling around, she saw Nick's face smiling down at her. She pulled the earbuds out of her ears forcefully.

"What the hell are you doing?" Claire demanded, still in shock, pulling away from him.

"Well, you see, my darling, I was getting the feeling you didn't want to answer me the way you really wanted to earlier, in front of your friend," Nick told her

"No. I answered you correctly. I don't want to go to the pub with you and I don't want to be on camera, thank you very much."

"Oh now, you don't mean that, do you? I can tell when a woman wants me or not and you, Blondie, want me something fierce." He took a step towards her, but she stepped out of his way.

"Is that what you tell yourself? That girls are all up for it when you want? I have met my share of narcissistic men in my time, but you take the cake!"

"Now, don't be like that. I can make your dreams come true, darling. You are looking at the man who will be hosting the show next season. That's right, the old man is going to be out on his ear. He's past his use-by date and I will be taking the reins. It'll be a nice little earner and I'll be getting the say on who is on and who isn't." He looked pretty pleased with himself.

"And does Robbie know this? That he's been stabbed in the back like this?"

"No. That's the beauty. They are waiting to tell him at the end of this year, then it's bye-bye, Robbie, and hello, Nicholas. So why don't you come and give me a kiss?" He stepped closer to her again.

"I don't think so, Nick. I have a bit more self-respect than that," she told him, backing away but not fast enough.

He made a grab for her and held her wrist firmly in his grasp. Pulling her in towards him, he wound his arm around her shoulders and bent down. Claire acted and struck out with her knee, coming up hard and fast and connecting with Nick's tender man parts. He let her go immediately and crumpled up in extreme pain.

"You try it again and you will get something worse," she yelled at him, then turned and fled down the track with the sound of his stumbling footfalls chasing her. She ducked behind a large tree, and as quickly as she could, while fighting off the shock that was starting to set in, she cloaked herself in invisibility and flew to the nearest branch. She sat and watched as he came skidding to a halt where she had disappeared and searched for her.

"You bitch!" he called out to her. "If it's Matt you are wanting, you'll be waiting for a while. He's no good with women, except when he's blind drunk!"

To Claire, it sounded as if Nick felt Matt was competition and that he had to have her before his friend did. She wondered if he was going to be a danger or whether he was braver when he was by himself. Claire did not have a clue what to do next. Should she tell someone what had happened or leave it and wait to see what he would do, she wondered, still trembling from the encounter.

It felt like a dark cloud had just fallen over her trip. This was not how she had imagined it at all. She flew to the next tree and the next, keeping Nick in sight always. She followed and watched as he exited the forest and re-entered the camp, and she floated down to the ground.

Walking out of the trees, she went immediately to her tent and grabbed her wash things. As she stalked her way to the shower block, Addy intercepted her.

"Um, Claire, I have a question. It's not from me, but from someone I care a great deal about and who is really cut up about something he has just heard, and I really want the answer to be the right one so he can be happy again."

"Did you take a breath at any time with that?" Claire asked, still trying to get her own emotions under control.

"No. Now I'm serious. Before we go into that sweat box of a shower room and we can be overheard by every woman in the camp, I want to know."

"Know what, Addy?" Claire said angrily. She knew what was coming so got in before her friend could. "You want to know if what Nick said was true? That he and I got it on in the forest and that I was gagging for it?" Claire's voice was getting angrier.

Addy nodded. "I know it can't be true, but Matt—"

"Matt has nothing to worry about. Nothing happened except Nick attacking me. And if he is saying otherwise, tell Matt to ask *Nick the Dick* how his balls are feeling and if he needs some ice. Oh, and while you are at it, tell him I am not impressed with his choice of friends." Claire stormed off into the shower block and stayed there for a very long time, trying to get the feeling of Nick's hands off her.

Claire avoided everyone she could that night. After her long shower, she grabbed a quick bite from the cookhouse and then went straight to her tent. She could hear the noise from the campfires, the laughter and music, and felt like a stranger all over again. The book she was reading was at her side, untouched and unread as she drifted off to sleep before she set her defenses.

The dreams began as they always did: with darkness and white mist. This didn't frighten Claire as it once had, because she knew what it meant—that her parents were with her. The more she wanted to see and speak with them, the more a persistent banging she could hear, like someone thumping on a door. The thumping became louder and louder and finally having no more energy to resist, Claire gave in and let Adam in.

Adam was anxious, and he rushed into the dream with great force. So much so that it scared Claire, and the black smoke that was her father surrounded him, shielding her from Adam, while the white mist of her mother curled around Claire comfortingly.

"Claire, please. I just want to talk. There's something very important I have to tell you," Adam cried out from around the blackness.

"Adam, we're not together anymore. You can't just keep trying to get my attention. It's not going to work. You hurt me too much," she said, sounding almost defeated.

"I know, and I don't know how many times I have to say I am sorry, but I will keep on saying it until there is absolutely no hope. I still love you." He struggled against the blackness, trying to get closer to her. "Can't you call this off for a moment so we can talk privately?"

"I don't think so, Adam. Dad is only trying to protect me."

"All right. Fine." He put his hands up in surrender and stepped back from her. "But I need you to listen to me. This is really important. I found out a few weeks ago that Jack has been seeking people who could change our father back." He struggled again. "Please, Claire. I promise I won't try to touch you. We have to talk. I'm worried he might go after you."

Claire thought about it for a moment and asked her father to let him go.

"Are you sure?" John asked her.

"Yes, Dad, I am," she told him with a heavy sigh. John released Adam and went to stand beside his daughter, the white mist of her mother curling more tightly around her like a blanket.

"Thank you," Adam said to Claire. He had never really believed that these silent entities he only saw as black smoke and white mist were part of her parents that had been planted in her subconscious before they were murdered by Marcus, his own father.

"Just say what you came to say and then please leave me alone. I have enough to deal with in the real world," she said with a sigh and closed eyes.

"Are you all right? What's going on?" he asked, sitting down across from her.

"Adam, it's not your place to put things right in my life. You lost that right when you cheated on me."

"I know, but that is part of what I have to tell you. Jack set me up! He was trying to break us up, Claire. He paid her to come on to me."

"But you didn't need to act on it. You chose that. You thought you could get away with it and you didn't. I am sick of this conversation. I am tired of going round in circles. I just want to move on."

"He is trying to get back at everyone he thinks hurt him and his mother." He stepped forward, only to be blocked by her father again.

"Do you have any proof?" Claire asked him.

"I have come across a few things at work. He's been trying to ruin Ben by destroying his construction business. There are hidden paper trails that I've discovered, and I managed to stop it before it happened. But there are other things that are not adding up. Mysterious payments for different things. I am trying to build up a picture of what he's up to."

"Okay, you have a few bits and pieces that could be him doing something. Adam, you have told me what you wanted. Can I go and get some rest now?"

"You don't believe me?"

"I'm not saying I don't believe you, but only that I can't do anything from over here. And as for trying to change the suggestions we both put on your father, he won't find anyone to do that. I made sure that they were iron tight. Has there been any change in Marcus?" Claire asked, going over what the suggestion they had secured in Marcus' mind all those years ago.

"No, he's still the same. And I'm ready to make sure that it stays there. I don't understand why you won't let me do the same to Jack. It would solve all our problems and we can—"

"We can go our separate ways," Claire finished for him. "You know the reasons we don't want you to. Aunt Lil explained it to you. There is a difference between what we did to your father and what you want to do to Jack."

"I still don't see it."

"I know you don't," Claire said, the exhaustion creeping into her voice, and she rubbed her face with her hands. "Please don't try anything without investigating it properly first. Can you promise me that?"

"I promise."

"Is that all? Can you leave me alone now?"

"Yes, if that's what you want. But I'm going to be in England for business. Can I come up and see you?" he asked hopefully.

"I don't think that's a good idea, Adam. Didn't we say enough before I left?"

"All right. I won't."

"Goodbye, Adam," Claire said simply and started to push him away from the connection.

"See you, Claire." His words floated back to her.

The white mist swelled and enveloped Claire as the wrench of the disconnection overwhelmed her, and the feelings of the loss of the relationship renewed. The strong arms of her father were joined by her mother and both comforted her. There were no words between them, only the love she had missed out on for years. Slowly they began to fade, and she passed into a full and dreamless sleep.

Claire lay on her cot for a while before she realized that the sun was still a while away before it started to climb into the sky. But the sound of bird song was beginning to fill the air beyond the thin canvas of her tent. The camp was still quiet except for the odd snore, and she couldn't hear anyone moving around. After getting up and dressing slowly, she left her tent and filled her lungs with the new morning air. Claire was so pleased that she could use her Stealth Talent and not disturb those closest to her tent as she set off on silent feet. She was still not ready to talk to anyone in the camp, especially after the previous afternoon.

Taking a different trail through the forest, she ran on. Claire ran without thinking, trying to put as much distance as she could between her and the camp. She kept a wary eye out for anyone else and—keeping her senses on alert—was grateful when there were no return signals in her path, other than a few rabbits and squirrels.

Claire slowed and finally came to a stop. She stood in the middle of the track, which weaved its way through the tall trees on either side, with her hands on her hips. Her breathing calmed and her heart rate came back to normal. The morning air felt clear and crisp, and the birdsong was swelling in the treetops above her. The horrible memory of the afternoon before slipped away from her mind to be replaced by this perfect, calming, and cleansing morning.

Leaning against the trunk of a massive pine, she sunk down and sat with her back against the rough bark, closing her eyes. She let the world just be and felt it rise and fill her. This strange land she had come to was beginning to feel like home to her. It had an ancient voice that seemed to envelop her, building up in her mind and soul, capturing her and holding her close with its acceptance.

She opened her eyes, feeling so relaxed and calm, at peace with herself and the world around her. Across the trail, Claire noticed a doe with a fawn following closely behind it, walking through the brambles under the trees. Their awareness accepted Claire, and they were unfazed by her close presence. The animals crossed the track, near enough for Claire to reach out and touch them as they passed by. Claire felt an uprising of her spirit and a detachment from reality with the scene.

"How did you do that?" a whisper asked her, and she came crashing back to the present. Matt was looking at her, his eyes wide in amazement as he stood in the middle of the track.

"I just sat, and they were there," Claire told him. He came and sat with her, crossing his legs as he did, and he handed her his camera.

Claire took it and looked at the digital screen. She saw herself with a serene expression on her face, the animals with their heads bent and right beside her.

"Can I have a copy of that?" she asked as she gave it back to him.

"Sure, not a problem." He looked at the picture and then back at Claire. "I wanted to apologize for the other night. I was way out of line, and I embarrassed you." He tried to meet her eyes but was having a hard job.

Claire didn't know what made her do it, but she leaned forward, placed a hand on the back of his neck, and kissed him. The kiss lasted about as long as the one he had given her.

"There. Now we're even," she told him plainly.

"I... I..." he stammered as Claire stood up.

"Matt, it's fine. I didn't appreciate it at all the other night, and I was a bit angry. But it's fine now."

"You, umm... I..." he was still stammering as he stood to face her.

"Look, I really like you, Matt, and if you feel the same, then the ball is in your court." She gave him a quick peck on the cheek, turned, and ran back down the track. Using the same trick she had used on Nick, Claire ducked behind a large tree and disappeared.

She watched Matt standing there, clearly confused as to what had just happened as he looked around him. Then he did something that surprised Claire. He leapt into the air and flew off into the forest. She smiled.

When Claire got back to camp after wandering slowly through the trees, she saw a convoy of trucks and four-wheel-drive vehicles driving up the hill. Gerry came running out to greet a tall man with long, grey hair climbing out of the first vehicle. He wore round sunglasses perched on his nose and had a small goatee beard the same shade as his hair. She had seen him before and recognized him instantly as Robbie MacCallum, the host of Archaeology Adventures. He was also Addy's father and Matt's uncle. She looked around and found Addy coming out of the cookhouse.

"There's my girl!" Robbie's voice boomed out over the camp, and Addy looked up and gave a tight smile. Robbie crossed the ground between them and gathered her up in a bear hug, lifting her off the ground.

Nick was soon out and greeting him with a handshake while Addy walked over to Claire. "My dad. All happy to see me, until there is work." She looked at Claire and studied her a moment. "You seem different this morning. Did you do something with your hair?"

"No. I've just got back from a run."

"That's not it. Something has happened. I can sense it."

Just then, Matt came walking up to Robbie to greet him, and he looked their way and smiled. Claire returned the smile while Addy was watching. She grabbed Claire's arm excitedly. "Claire!"

"What?"

"Something has happened! Between you and Matt—tell me I'm wrong."

"I don't have to tell you anything, Addy."

"It has…so what happened? Tell me!" Addy spent the rest of the morning while they were at the dig site trying to get the secret out of Claire, but she wouldn't budge.

The mound where Claire had started to uncover the stones before she was whisked away and supposedly hurt herself was now a full-blown trench, and more shaped stones were emerging from the soil. A pattern was starting to form, and Claire and Addy stood at the edge of the trench looking down on the collection. With the help of some more of the other students, more than one wall had been uncovered. Maggie came to check on their work and after they had told her what they found, she sent the two younger women into the trench to help her see better what they were talking about. Maggie then became excited. She headed off to go search for Gerry and returned shortly with Robbie following closely behind. Addy groaned.

"What have you found, lass?" Robbie asked before Gerry could, looking eagerly at the trench.

"We are not sure at the moment, Dad, which is why we called Maggie over."

"Use your head and tell me what you see," he demanded.

Addy described the layout of the walls, how they converged and curved. She also put him straight and told him that Claire had discovered it first.

"And you, lass, what's your name?" Robbie's attention was now on Claire.

"This is Claire. She is Maggie's protégé I was telling you about," Gerry answered before Claire could.

"Ahh, so you're the one we have to thank for this dig."

"I beg your pardon?" His comment gave Claire a moment of confusion. She couldn't see how she could be responsible for the dig.

"Claire started this trench, aye," Gerry broke in before Robbie could answer, but Claire felt there was more to that comment. "Maggie, I think you might be right. It definitely looks like we may have not just the round house down there, but also a broch. If it is, then it's the first hill fort in this area. Well done, girls."

"This will make brilliant footage, Gerry. We can have the camera set up after lunch and start rolling."

"Well, let's not jump the gun, Robbie. We have to open the trench up further to be really sure."

"Aye, that's no trouble. We have the JCB for that. It'll be done in no time," Robbie said enthusiastically.

"We discussed this—there will be no mechanical digging on this site. We have some amazing artefacts from the top of this trench already. Claire was the one who cleaned the stone plaque and brought it to our attention."

"Oh, really? And did you understand what it meant?" Robbie directed the question to Claire.

"Gerry said that it was a Pict stone carving of a boar," Claire answered.

"Do you have no knowledge of your own, girly?"

"Our archaeology in New Zealand is a bit newer than that of Scotland, Mr MacCallum, but I know that it has been a struggle for academics to decipher the meaning behind the Pict carvings."

"Well said, girly." A call from behind interrupted Robbie, and he turned to find Nick walking towards him. "Ah, just in time, Nick. I want a camera here on this trench this afternoon while the girls are working."

"I'm afraid they won't be working here this afternoon, Robbie. Matt will be here recording the find so far." Gerry sounded frustrated and annoyed at Robbie.

"That's good. They can start enlarging the trench while he is doing his arty thing." Robbie dismissed him and walked away, with Nick discussing other parts of the hillside dig site they could possibly utilize.

After lunch, the clouds crept down the sides of the hill they were working on. A light, misty rain soon started to cool the air and wet the ground. Claire had rugged up in a jumper and a light jacket to keep most of the moisture away. She was looking forward to the afternoon's work enlarging the trench, but she was feeling that odd butterfly sensation when she thought about Matt being there as well. She smiled at the memory of earlier that morning, having caught him by surprise.

It kept her going while she was breaking up the tough turf to uncover the fresh dirt underneath and while she was scraping away the top layer as it turned to mud in the drizzling conditions. Addy was prattling on beside her, but Claire wasn't really listening, until the words "Nick is coming" shattered her thoughts.

Looking up, she could see Nick and a man with a camera making their way up to their position. Claire stood behind

Addy and slowly faded out. She was not in the mood to deal with the Irishman.

"Addy," Nick greeted her, puffing.

"Nick," Addy said back very stiffly.

"I thought Claire was working with you."

"She is. She's right there." Addy turned, but there was no Claire, and she looked around trying to find her.

Taking the opportunity, Claire used her Stealth with the Invisibility to make her getaway. She turned as she was about to hide behind some bushes and saw Addy's eyes moving with her.

"Oh, well, maybe she had to go to the loo. What do you want?"

"To do my job. Hey, have I done something to offend you?" he asked her casually.

"Oh, nothing much, really—just attacking my friend when you know my cousin is interested."

"Oh I see, you're jealous. Maybe we can hook up tonight?"

"I don't think so, Nick. I'm done with bad boys."

"You think I'm a bad boy." His eyebrow rose suggestively.

Claire was feeling guilty now that she had left her friend to deal with Nick, and releasing her energy, she walked back to the site.

"There she is. Shall we get on with it?"

"Do you really need to be here?" Addy asked him. "Can't the cameraman do it by himself?"

"I'm not staying. I was just showing him what we needed. I thought Matt was supposed to be here. It was all part of the shot."

"Why don't you go and fetch him, then, Nick. We're a bit busy doing real work," Addy told him pointedly and turned back to the new trench.

They could hear him muttering as he left, and Addy gave Claire a smile. There was a question building up in that smile and Claire could guess what it might be, but she hoped that her friend would wait to ask it until their company had left.

Ten minutes later, Matt arrived with a satchel slung across his chest, a large sketch pad, and a folding camp stool, which he set up near where the girls were working.

"Afternoon," he greeted them.

"Nice of you to make it. Have a nice lunch, then?" Addy asked him politely.

"Very nice, aye," he answered and pulled out a camera from his bag and shot a smile at them. He raised it to his eye and took a couple of photos of them.

"Lovely. You could've at least waited until we put our lippy on," Addy told him.

"I think you both look perfect as you are." He blushed slightly, and Claire turned before her face could give her away.

Matt turned the camera back to the trench and started to photograph it for the survey records. The cameraman that Robbie had sent was getting in his way, and he had to ask him to move every couple of minutes.

"Look, man, just go over there and film those two. You're in my way."

"Sorry, dude, just doing my job," the man apologised and then obligingly, he did as Matt asked and tried not to be annoying over by Claire and Addy.

Something in the trench caught Matt's eye, and he went in to have a closer look. He bent down and fired off another couple of shots, zooming in with each one.

"Claire, can you come and have a look at this for me?" he called to her, still looking intently at the ground.

She stood and stretched out her back and then moved over to him. He indicated with his finger what he wanted her to have a look at. Bending down beside him, their heads almost touching, Claire saw what it was that had caught his attention: a small, smooth stone that had some evidence of tool work on it. Carefully she started to scrape away the wet dirt from around it, digging down deeper, while Matt took more and more photos of the process.

"Addy, can you pass my tool kit?" she called out without raising an eye from the object.

"Sure." Addy came over to them with the small plastic case in hand and placed it beside Claire. "What do you need?"

"One of the small picks, please." A tool that looked very similar to those that a dentist would use was placed in her hand. Slowly and gently, she started to scrape away underneath the stone to loosen in from its place. When Claire had decided that it was free enough, very carefully she dislodged it until it fell into her hand.

The object was more oval than round, and the other side was encrusted with dirt. Claire took it over to her water bottle and wet it, smudging the dirt away from the surface, until a little design came into view. It was the same design from the plaque she had cleaned—a boar symbol and a small hole above it. She showed it to Addy and Matt and became aware of the cameraman standing over the top of them.

"Give us a look?" he asked, pointing the camera down at her hand. She washed the item some more with her water.

"I think it's an ornament of some kind, like it was meant to be worn around the neck." Claire held it up for them to see, and they agreed. Carefully she placed it into the finds tray, and a shiver went up her spine. She had seen the symbol before on the plaque, but also more recently in a book. It was only when she saw both Matt and Addy look at her that she realized which book.

The little ornamental stone also triggered something in the back of her mind. It seemed familiar to her, as is if she had touched it before. She shook herself free of the feeling of déjà vu and looked up, catching a similar look in Matt's blue eyes.

"Hey, um, cameraman, you done here?" Matt asked, not looking around.

"Why, you trying to get rid of me?" the scruffy man asked, his camera still filming them.

"Ah, yeah, I am," Matt replied, still gazing into Claire's eyes.

"Yeah, no probs. I got some good footage, so that should make them happy." He walked off with a wave and the three of them were alone.

Claire sat on the edge of the trench looking down at the stone, then looked up to find that the cousins were still watching her.

"What, do I have dirt on my face or something?" She wiped at her cheek, but there was nothing there.

"Claire, I'm going to ask a question and I hope you trust us enough to answer honestly," Addy said tentatively

"Okay," she replied slowly.

"Before, when Nick was coming up the hill..."

"Yes?" she interrupted.

"You were there one minute and gone the next."

"Yeah, I hid behind the bushes."

"That was only after he got here. I'm going to say something, and I want you to say yes or no." Addy paused, looking at her friend hard. "Special Abilities."

It was a simple phrase, and Claire knew exactly what Addy was asking. The time had come for her to either keep her secret or open up to these two people who had come to mean so much to her.

"We call them Talents," was her simple answer in return.

Matt and Addy stood for a moment staring at her and then looked at each other. Addy went to say something then closed her mouth, unsure of exactly what to ask next.

"Your gran is a lovely lady. She loaned me a very interesting book." When they still didn't say anything, Claire continued. "We, The Community, have been searching for decades for the answer of our ancestry. I think they are going to be very pleased with what I have discovered over here." Again, there was silence. "Are you just going to stand there all day and gawk at me?"

"So, you are one of The People?" Matt was the first to ask.

"I think so. I do have these Talents lurking around me." She laughed at the sudden weight that had been lifted from her. It felt good to talk about it with someone and not try to hide the secret.

"Talents? Well, it's obvious that you have Hide, the way you disappeared, but you may want to work on your breathing. I could hear you."

"My Uncle David told me that once." Claire smiled at the memory.

"What's your other ability?" Matt asked her.

"You mean others. I'm a Chameleon."

"A what?" Addy came and sat beside her. "That's a funny-looking lizard."

"It is a term we have for a person who can take on more than two Talents."

"Your ankle was broken, wasn't it?" Matt asked speculatively.

"Yes. I'm sorry I lied. I have Healing as well."

"But that is only two—you said more than two," he said, confused.

She looked into his bright blue eyes and came out with them all. "I have Flying, Hide, Light, Stealth, Mind Touch, Recall, Seek, and Healing."

"Wow," Matt said quietly while letting out a deep breath. He slowly sat down on her other side.

"I don't understand. Gran always said that people only have one major Ability and one minor one. But you seem to have all major," Addy said.

"Not quite. I don't have Strength, Longevity, Foresight, or Charm."

"Those are the ones you have to be born with," Matt said to no one in particular. "I'm with Addy on this. How?"

"I don't know. I didn't even know I had any Talent until I was seventeen. Hell, I didn't even know that The Community existed until then. I got into a bit of trouble in the city and my uncle had to get me out of there pretty quick. That's when he took me to the village. Along the way, he explained to me that my parents were killed because they had Talents that a man named Marcus wanted to use, but they didn't want to join him. He also explained that I had two Talents, Flight and Hide. I was sceptical, to say the least—one minute I'm a normal girl, and next he's telling me we come from a long line of people with these special abilities.

"Anyway, so now I'm introduced to all this family I didn't know I had, some of them totally dysfunctional all because of this Marcus guy. I am then told that it is up to me to defeat him and put everything right. Long story short, I did a lot of study and had a lot of ideas that nobody had thought of before. With the help of my aunt, I suddenly had Talents coming from everywhere. But I wasn't alone. With the help of Uncle David and Uncle Geoff, we tracked Marcus down to a cabin in the hills to deal with him and save Adam. Oh, I forgot to mention, Adam is Marcus's son."

"Adam? As in your ex, Adam?" Addy asked her.

"Yep—oh, it gets better, just wait. After Charlie had healed Adam, we go and totally mess with Marcus's mind with suggestions and make him the complete opposite of what he was. We also discovered that Adam is the illegitimate son of Marcus and Beth, who is married to my Uncle David. She had him before they were married. Marcus also has another illegitimate son called Jack, who was the one who taught me how to use Hide. Now apparently—according to Adam, who still is Dream Messaging me, no matter what I tell him—Jack is now getting his revenge on those who changed Marcus. And he has been looking for someone who can remove the suggestions we made. So basically, that is my whole story on how I found I had Talents."

"There weren't any others who could have taken on the task but you?" Matt asked her when she had finished.

"There probably were many who could have, but we were told by Mary, our Elder with Foresight, that it had to be me. But I think I thought it was up to me, because I was taking pieces from different Talents and combining them. I was a bit arrogant back then. I used to act before thinking, like the other night." She looked at Addy, who smiled back.

"Don't worry. We all grow up eventually, Claire," she said, bumping shoulders with her.

"Speak for yourself, Addy," Matt said.

"Um, I did ask her, but your Gran wouldn't tell me. But I think I have worked it out for myself. The way you tracked me, Addy, you have Stealth—and Matt, I saw you Fly this morning after we, um, had that talk."

"I knew something had happened. *'Claire and Matty sitting up a tree—'*" Addy began to sing.

"Cut it out, Addy," Claire told her, blushing, and looking around to see whether anyone else had heard.

"Watch out—olds alert," Matt said quietly, getting up.

"I heard you found something," Gerry called out to his son before Robbie could speak. The same cameraman who had left them was following with his camera already running.

The three of them stood up. Claire left them and went to the new part of the trench to continue working. Cameras made her nervous, and she didn't want anything to do with this program. She did watch as Matt picked up the stone and showed it to his father and uncle. The piece was turned and cleaned further by Gerry and inspected closely. His face lit up with the results and he passed it on to Robbie to look at. Matt was pointing at Claire and saying how he had seen it, but it was she who dug it out.

The cameraman had already started to film this new discovery when he put the camera down, complaining about the battery dying. He turned and fled down the hill, calling out that he would be back in a flash.

"Well done, Claire, but next time let us know before you start to excavate something." Gerry came to where she was using the trowel to dig down into the soft earth.

"I will, sorry. I got a bit excited, but Matt took some photos before I did," she explained.

He looked at her for moment longer. "Good. Make sure you do," he replied and left her to it, returning to the others.

"Do you think it could be?" Matt's voice carried to her.

"It's possible. This is the second image we have found from the same trench. If it is, then we are getting close."

"I'm still not convinced. These lands were scattered with our people, and it may not be what we're searching for," Robbie counted Gerry's statement.

"It's a broch. There have been two clan symbols found. But you are right, Robbie. Let's not get ahead of ourselves. We need more evidence," Gerry responded with a sigh. "Many an archaeologist has thought one thing only to be proved wrong by the evidence. Keep up the good work, kids."

The pair walked off a short distance, and Claire was puzzled as to what it may be that they were looking for. The book came to mind, and the strong drive she'd had to do research at seventeen renewed itself. This was becoming a dig within a dig.

Chapter Seven

Claire did not join the fireside antics again that night but went straight to her tent and took out the booklet that Gran MacCallum had given her. It was slightly thicker than her red book of Talents back home, and Claire opened it with anticipation. The typed pages were slightly worn, and she wondered if Matt had read this particular one, but then she shook her head free of those thoughts. There was time enough to think about him once she had finished reading.

The first section was dedicated to the family groups. A symbol of an animal accompanied each name, written, she presumed, in Gaelic. The names of the areas laid out on the small map were confusing, and she didn't have any references to go by in her tent. There was only one place in the camp that she could get internet connection, but she didn't want to go there and take the book with her. It also reminded her that she hadn't sent any emails to her family for nearly a month. It was soon to be July, and the realization that she had been there a month made her a bit homesick. She missed her uncle and—funnily enough—her younger cousins.

Claire read the brief description of the boar, which seemed to be the symbol that had caused the stir earlier that day. The only detail that she gleaned from it was that this was the last known surviving clan descended from Picts. Matt had called them "The People," in a similar way to her Community. Her excitement was growing, and she read on.

The next section was very familiar to Claire. The Abilities were exactly the same. There was one difference, however; there was no mention of a Chameleon. Her own Talent was missing from the list. Questions again started flooding her mind, just as they had when she first started on her journey six years before. The symbols were simple enough to understand, like the bent arrow for flight, but still others were a bit more complex, and she would have to ask Addy and Matt. As she came to the end, Claire sat up and placed the book back into the pocket of her backpack.

Matt. Now there was a complex question in itself. She did like him, but was she ready for a relationship so soon after breaking up with Adam? There was something about him that stirred her heart and made her feel alive again. *A feeling I did not have for a long time with Adam*, Claire admitted to herself. She reorganized her thoughts on their relationship and found that in the last year she had only been going through the motions. Yes, she had enjoyed his company and attention, but when she really analysed it, there was no depth of feeling. Had they been apart too long, and the relationship came to its natural conclusion?

There was too much noise outside in the campground to really let her concentrate better or even get some much-needed sleep. Adam's constant battering at her had not helped her get a restful night's sleep in a while, as she had to hold her defences up so tightly. She looked forward to the day when she could lay her head down and just relax.

Someone started to strum a guitar, and Claire groaned. *This could go all night*, she thought as she hooked her fingers into her sneakers and dragged them to her. She thought back to earlier that morning and spying on Matt as he flew through the forest. Claire had never seen anyone else flying and seeing his gracefulness in the air made her think on her own technique, cringing at the clumsiness of it. This gave her an idea on how to spend the rest of the evening.

After putting on her sneakers, Claire crept out of the camp and into the forest beside it. She waited until she was sure she was out of sight and lifted off the ground, up into the treetops. Weaving her way through the upper branches, she searched until she found one that suited her needs and drifted down onto it. Claire sat with her feet swinging in the expanse of air, looking up at the darkening night sky. The clouds had cleared and left a beautiful vista above her. The Milky Way glittered into existence as the last dull light of the sun left the world. It stretched out and was so much clearer here in the open spaces of Scotland than she had ever experienced it before. Under its starry trail she felt small and insignificant, but calm and comforted at the same time. The feeling of belonging to something so much larger than herself agreed with her. It was there in the treetops she found her peace she had wanted, and she drifted off to sleep leaning against the trunk of the pine.

The sunlight moved slowly down from the top of the tree as the morning dawned. When it finally touched the eyes of a sleeping Claire and awoke her to the new day, she remembered where she was. The first initial panic of unknowing passed and she stretched, luxuriating in the fact she had a good night's sleep, despite the uncomfortable perch. There had been no intrusions, no noise to rouse her too early — just peace. The branch underneath her swayed slightly in the morning breeze and the sound going through the nettles was like a shushing, calming any anxieties away — like a mother to a child.

But as all good things must do, Claire thought, *it's time to go back and get on with the day, as much as I would like to stay here.* A small idea grew in her mind, and she smiled, thinking that she could maybe bring Matt up here to enjoy it with her sometime. Although that would have to wait for him to make the next move. She had left it with him to decide and was in no hurry herself to push it.

Slowly she let herself down to the ground, making sure no one was about when she reached Mother Earth again. The sounds of the forest surrounded her like a comfy blanket, and she patted the tree she had spent the night in, thanking it for its security, then left for camp.

Claire did not hurry as she walked back. The peacefulness still enveloped her, and she had no intention of letting it slip. She tried to cling to it to the last possible moment. She was about to find that that moment would come sooner rather than later.

"Where have you been, Claire? I was just about to send out a search party." Maggie was blocking her path to her tent.

"I went for a walk in the forest. I had trouble sleeping."

"Well, I presumed that, seeing as you were coming from that direction. I need you to drive me to Killin—I have to pick up a few things." She then came towards Claire and plucked out a bit of tree bark from her hair. "I'm not going to have to explain anything to your uncle, am I?"

"No, I was by myself. And anyway, I'm old enough."

"Mmm, we'll see. Go get ready and I'll meet you by Gerry's car. You should be grateful I'm getting you out of here before they start shooting the first day of that horrid program. To think that Robbie used to be a serious academic." She stalked off towards where the cars were parked and Claire made a beeline for her tent, wondering at the change of heart Maggie had with the program.

The drive to the town at the western end of Loch Tay was a pretty one. The hills running along each side were bare and green with a smattering of trees and craggy rocks poking through the earth. In some ways it again reminded Claire of parts of New Zealand. It was a narrow and winding road, only allowing for one car to use at any time, with plenty of pull-off points to let other vehicles pass. There were hikers making the most of the summer weather, taking the trails up to the top of Ben Lawers or just wandering about by the many rivers and streams that ran in the area. The hikers and other drivers were very friendly, waving to them as they passed, making the trip a pleasant one. Maggie had Claire in stitches trying to get her American accent around the place names as they passed, until she gave up trying and told her she would do no better, to which Claire heartedly agreed.

At the top of the rise they had slowly been making their way up, they found the source of the stream they had been following. It was a small loch nestled where two large hills met with a large dam structure at the other end and the view of the next valley came into sight. Green hills rolled out before them, dotted with the darker green of trees. Homesickness suddenly caught at Claire's heart once more as it reminded her how far away she was from her own little valley that she loved.

The road became even more winding, and they soon caught their first glimpse of Loch Tay. It felt like months since Claire had been on this side of the mountain, and she was enjoying the drive. The road soon dipped, and as they drove over a cattle stop, trees sprung up on either side of the road, sending them into semi-gloom compared to the bright sunshine they had just been in. White billowing clouds marred the beautiful blue sky above.

They came to the junction and chose the right fork to meet the road to Killin. Loch Tay ran to their left, and they caught brief glimpses of it through the large trees that lined the road. Stone bridges and walls sped by as they drove on to their destination. The trees opened up to bare fields speckled with flowers and white puffy sheep, exposing more expansive views of the sparkling waters of the loch.

As they neared Killin, more and more houses were found on the side of the road along with cottage lets, bed and breakfasts, inns, and cabins. Some were charming and picturesque in their setting; others were new builds that tried hard to fit into the landscape. The further into town they went, the more stone houses they saw. Not all were exposed stone. Some had been rendered and painted white.

"Right, I think the first thing we need to do is go to a café and get a decent cup of coffee," Maggie said, folding away the map that had been laid out on her lap for the whole trip.

"If there is a gift shop, I wouldn't mind getting my cousins something and some postcards. I've been a bit neglectful of late."

Maggie gave her directions and they pulled up in a car park. "There's a gift shop just up the road. We'll go there first and then get a coffee across the river. We can walk back to the post office after and send your cards and collect my mail. If Gerry had told me there was a post office closer to site, I would have had it redirected there. Men—they never think of these things."

The walk was a short one, and the shop looked like it used to be a small cottage. Claire selected a few postcards for her aunts, uncles, and grandparents and then went inside to find something for her cousins. Maggie was no help at all in what to get three twelve-year-olds and a sixteen-year-old. She finally settled on some funny T-shirts, flags, and a tartan hat with bright orange hair coming from underneath.

Bag in hand, they crossed the road to the bridge spanning the River Dochart. It curved to the right, and halfway across stood the entrance to the Clan MacDonald burial ground. The river that flowed underneath had the dark peaty look to it as it rushed over the large rocks and boulders in the river. People were lining the sides of the bridge that was both a foot and car bridge, taking photos of the falls, and even more scrambled over the rocks at the edge of the flowing water.

The coffee shop they were looking for was part of The Falls of Dochart Inn, just on the other side of the bridge. A large white building was the inn, restaurant, bar, accommodation, and tea shop in one. Large umbrellas stood open outside, shading the picnic tables that sat on the footpath.

They entered and placed their order, then sat outside under an umbrella that waved slightly in the breeze while they awaited their food and drink. Both were busy writing out postcards, and when Claire was done with her tea and scones, she went to the inn's gift shop while she waited for Maggie to finish with her correspondence.

Inside was more like a gallery than a gift shop, and she found a few more things that her uncle would like. A small, beautiful watercolour painting of the loch caught her eye and she decided to buy it, along with some hand-printed scarves for her grandmothers and a local book on fishing for her grandfather.

Back out in the sunshine, Claire returned to Maggie, who was just finishing her last letter and sealing it in an envelope.

"Are you ready?" Claire asked her.

"Yes, but I could go for another coffee. Can you wait while I get one to go?" Claire nodded and waited outside for her to return.

Claire was miles away watching the falls and listening to their roar when a man caught her attention. He was a big man, tall and thickset, and he was vaguely familiar to her. She watched him for a while, trying not make it obvious. It was only when he took his sunglasses off to wipe his reddened face that she recognized him. It was Richard. She was sure from the scar that David had left on his face when he hit him. That was the only name she had known him by six years earlier. He used to be one of Marcus Ryder's men, and he was the one who had beaten Adam up for his father. He was also the one they suspected of murdering her parents. He kept inching towards her, and she started to feel anxious. The closer he got the more the feeling intensified until it felt like there was a stone in the pit of her stomach. What was he doing here, of all places?

Claire was still miles away as she pondered the sudden appearance of Richard, and she jumped when Maggie placed a hand on her shoulder.

"Come on, sleepy. We had better get back. I promised Gerry that I would back him up against Robbie this afternoon."

As they made their way back over the bridge, Claire kept glancing over her shoulder. A tingle down her spine let her know he was still there and was now following them.

"What are you doing?" Maggie asked when she finally noticed how Claire was acting.

"It's so beautiful, I can't help but look," Claire told her with a smile, hoping that it masked the way she really felt.

The puffy clouds that had been in the sky hours ago were now building and becoming a dark grey, threatening to become a summer storm. There was less blue sky now and the wind was picking up, causing the many trees to bend and sway more. Claire and Maggie hurried back down the main road to the post office, sent their parcels and letters on their way, and made it back to the car just as the first large and heavy drops of rain began to fall.

There was no sign of the man that Claire thought was following them, and she breathed a sigh of relief.

"What was that for?" Maggie asked, buckling herself into the seat.

"Just thankful we didn't get too wet. But I'm not looking forward to being on site with this weather. Let's hope it doesn't make it over the mountain."

"I don't like your chances of that. This is Scotland, remember." Maggie laughed, and Claire tried to smile in return.

The trip back to the turnoff seemed to take no time at all, even though Claire was going slower than on the way to Killin. The rain was now coming down in great sweeping sheets and lightning rent the air, with both bright flashes and loud rolling thunder trailing along behind. The air crackled with the electricity, and Claire was having a hard job seeing the road in front of her.

"Should I pull off until it passes?" Claire asked her companion as she tried to peer through the swishing windscreen wipers and torrential rain.

"No, keep going. Hopefully everyone else is wise enough to be off the road and we can get through," Maggie replied with a note of uncertainty in her voice.

The small running brooks that fed the stream beside the road were now more of a torrent and the stream a raging river. Some of the runoff flowed over the road and Claire slowed down even more, with great sprays shooting up from the tyres. She could feel the wheels lose a little traction with the road and the car start to aquaplane. A bright white flash of lightning lit up the dull day, causing a terrified sheep to dart out in fright in front of them. Claire slammed on her brakes, narrowly missing the creature as they came skidding to a stop. She sat there for a moment breathing heavily, gripping the steering wheel tightly.

"That was close!" she said, and Maggie just nodded.

Claire pulled the car away again and they drove slowly along the narrow road, now scouring both sides for flooding and animals. The windscreen wipers were having a hard job keeping up with the deluge of rainwater hitting the car, even though they were on full blast. The noise of the rubber scraping over the glass was the only sound in the car. But Claire should have been watching behind as well. A large four-wheel drive raced up behind them, flashing its lights. Claire looked for a passing bay and soon spotted one on the left-hand side of the road by the racing waters of the river.

She pulled over and waited for the driver to pass her, but she was shocked when they were shunted from behind. All she could see in the rear-view mirror was the bright headlights. The car was now trying to force her off the edge and into the water, and Claire was pressing her foot harder and harder on the brake pedal. She pulled the park brake on as hard as she could, hoping that it would help keep them safe, but the little hatchback was no match for such a big car. The wheels started to skid on the wet gravel surface, and the car slowly inched its way towards the edge. Maggie tried desperately to get a signal on her cell phone, but there was no service in this valley and she gave a cry of despair.

Claire felt the earth under the front left tire go first, and the car tilted towards the water. Maggie hung on to the dashboard to stop herself from being thrown forward.

"Do something!" she yelled at Claire.

"There's nothing I can do!" Claire was hanging on desperately herself.

The large vehicle backed up a bit and then sped forwards, and with a mighty crash, it hit the small car. The women were thrown violently forwards against their seat belts, and the impact pushed the car farther into the water until the whole shelf gave way. Both women screamed as they began floating along with the brown murky flood water. They bounced off boulders under the surface and were turned around, the sound of their scraping over unseen obstacles was loud in the cabin of the car.

Maggie screamed loudly and gripped Claire's arm as the car was pushed one way and then another. Their bodies were slammed up against the side panels as it collided with rocks, until finally it was stuck fast.

Claire looked over at Maggie, who had lost consciousness with the last large collision and was leaning up against the passenger door. Cold flood water was coming in under the door sills and filling up the footwells of the car. Claire started to panic. She didn't know what to do. She had never thought that something like this could happen to her. Looking this way and that, she tried to find a way out of the car without having to open the door to the torrent of water that was now engulfing them. Her eyes fixated on the headlights of the car that had just pushed them in.

This was enough to make her concentrate and think rationally. Claire knew she could get out of this situation by herself, but that would mean leaving Maggie to the mercy of the river. She knew if she wore a backpack and she made herself smaller, that it would shrink as well, but she was not sure it would work with another person. Claire didn't have time to find out, as the man in the car was now getting out and watching them.

Claire wound down the window a couple of inches, letting in a torrent of rain, and then undid her seat belt and Maggie's. With a great deal of effort, she managed to manoeuvre Maggie into a position where she could grasp her mentor under each arm. Holding her tightly, she quickly shrunk and made them both invisible. To her great relief, it worked, but she didn't have time to congratulate herself. Up and out of the window they flew, to the other side of the river and into the relative safety of some scrubby bushes.

Claire didn't let Maggie go until the man drove away and she felt that they were safe. Slowly she released her energy and brought them both back to normal size, but she couldn't be sure that Maggie wouldn't feel the muscle pains that sometimes came with shrinking.

Rain poured down her face, helping to drench the shirt she was wearing, and she was soon shivering in the gusting wind. Making sure that Maggie was safe and in a comfortable position, Claire shrank herself one more time and flew back to the car. She grabbed their bags and jackets and made her way back to the still-unconscious woman. Claire sat on the wet ground and draped both jackets over Maggie.

The thunder was still booming around them, and Claire tried to keep as low as possible. The rain was still pouring down and the wind started to whistle, chilling the air around them even further. Under the jackets, Maggie started to stir, and Claire placed a hand on her shoulder to stop her from moving.

"It's okay, Mags. We're safe," she told her softly, trying to keep her calm. "Help will come soon." Claire desperately hoped she was right.

"My head…what happened?" Maggie raised her hand, dislodging the jacket from her.

"We had an accident." Claire gently tucked the jacket back in place.

"No, there was a car. He pushed us into the water."

"Shh, Mags, you're upsetting yourself. Just keep calm."

"How did we get out?" her mentor asked, still with a hand on her head where it had connected with the door.

"I managed. Please, Maggie, just keep yourself quiet," Claire instructed through chattering teeth. She did think about putting her to sleep and trying to change her memory but decided against it. The damage to the car may give too many clues away as to what happened.

The storm raged around them for what seemed like hours, but according to Claire's watch, it was only another half hour before it started to dissipate. The sheets of rain eased off, but the wind still howled and whipped the branches of the bushes around them. Her shivering was becoming so bad that her whole body was shaking. The wind was still lashing around them, and the bushes were not giving them much coverage.

She knew she should stay with Maggie, but she needed to go for help. If she left Maggie on the ground for too much longer, she would go into shock or hypothermia or both. The only problem was that the river was still swollen and running fast. If she flew over it, she risked being seen and then she would have to explain how she got there with Maggie on the other side.

Feeling stuck, she just hoped that someone would see the bright blue hatchback sitting in the middle of the river and come to investigate. Realising that if they continued to sit in the scrub bushes they would never be seen, Claire decided that she would need to move Maggie.

It was not easy to try to explain to the muddled Maggie what she wanted her to do. Finally managing to get her to stand up, the older woman wobbled a bit and hung on to Claire's arm as they moved slowly closer to the raging water. Claire quickly laid down one of the jackets and got Maggie to sit on it, trying to reduce the amount of cold water that she was in contact with, then wrapped the other around her shoulders to keep the wind off.

"What about you?" Maggie asked, noticing how badly Claire was shaking.

"I'm fine. I can move around to warm up, and you need it more," Claire reassured her. She looked at her watch and wondered if they had been missed yet. They should have been back by now.

As Claire followed her own advice and started to move around, swinging her arms and walking, she thought of starting a fire with her Light Talent, but dismissed this as a last resort. Finding that the exercise wasn't helping, she started to jog on the spot. It helped a bit, but it soon brought on a headache that grew from a dull ache to a piercing pain at the back of her head. Having experienced a concussion before, she didn't want to even think about the possibility. Her first concern was making sure her mentor was safe.

The afternoon dragged on and on and she started to tire. The pain in her head was worsening, and she found she couldn't concentrate. Sitting down hard beside Maggie, Claire placed her head in her hands. Maggie put an arm around the girl and drew her close, sharing her body heat to warm her. Claire placed her pounding head on her mentor's shoulder and slowly started to fall asleep. Even if she had wanted to create a fire to warm them, the headache was enough to stop her concentration of producing even the smallest of sparks. The cold had invaded her too much.

"Claire! Can you wake up for me?" a voice called through the thick grey mist of her mind. "Claire, come back to us." The voice persisted in trying to wake her.

Claire groaned in response, pain piercing her eye as a light was shone under her eyelid.

"Do you know what year it is, Claire?" a broad Scottish accent asked her.

"It's um… It's… I don't know," she replied.

"It's all right, sweetie, we'll try again later. You've bumped your head," she was told by the kind voice.

"I'm so cold," she managed to say through chattering teeth.

"We're warming you up, Claire."

Opening her eyes slowly, Claire looked around and groaned. She hated hospitals. The smell, the sounds all brought back memories, and for a moment she was confused as to where and when she was.

"Uncle Geoff?" she asked.

"Who, sweetie?"

"Is Uncle Geoff here?" She tried to rise up off the bed.

"No. Keep still and under the blankets. I'll go check for you." The woman in blue scrubs left her side.

Moments later, Maggie was with her. "Claire, honey, it's me. Your uncle is back in New Zealand, remember?" She grabbed her hand and held it close, rubbing warmth into it.

"Where am I?"

"You're in the hospital. Do you remember what happened?"

"No, I don't. Where's Uncle Geoff?"

"Oh, honey, he's not here. You're in Scotland, remember? Just rest. It'll all come back to you."

When she woke again, she was in a bed covered with thick blankets and she was feeling very warm. She tried to throw them off but was stopped.

"Hey, just calm down, Claire. You're going to be fine." Matt was there, so sweet and concerned. "You gave us all a hell of a fright."

"How did… What happened?"

"Well, according to Maggie, someone ran you off the road during the storm. Do you remember? She also said that you're her hero, that you got her out of the car and to safety."

"I remember Killin. There was a man, I think..." she tried to say.

"Not just yet, Claire. The police want to talk to you, but only when you're ready." He pulled his chair up closer and rested his elbows on the bed. "Addy's gone to get a nurse for you."

"Your dad's car!" It came to her that it must be totally trashed and unrepairable.

"Don't worry. It'll be taken care of."

"Nice to see you awake, Claire. Welcome back to the land of the living." A woman in pink scrubs came up to the side of the bed and started to check her blood pressure while Addy stood by her cousin.

"You are doing fine," the nurse said when she had finished. "You missed the docs for the morning, but with that one at your side, I don't think you'll be wanting one of those." She gave Claire a sly wink. "You'll be pleased to know that there's nothing broken, or any major damage and your temp is coming back to normal. The police are coming in this afternoon to talk to you. They've already been this morning. So just rest and you can buzz us if you want anything." She bustled away to another patient.

"When can I get out of here?" Claire asked Matt and Addy.

"When the docs say so, Claire. I'll tell you what, some of those docs are rather dishy. Can I get some numbers for you?" Addy asked, nudging Matt.

"I'm all good, Addy. You can have them," Claire replied, and Matt smiled at her, his eyes sparkling a lovely shade of blue that Claire could lose herself in. "How long have I been here?"

"We found you late yesterday afternoon and you were airlifted here," Matt told her.

"I was in a helicopter? I always wanted to go up in one and I can't remember it. Not fair." She pouted a little.

"We'll have to organize another one for you," Addy told her.

"What about Maggie?"

"She's fine. She was discharged last night. You took good care of her," Matt told her.

"Good." Claire yawned and quickly covered her mouth, but she did not put her hand back under the blankets. Instead, she sought out Matt's.

"Is there anything I can get you? Something to drink?" Addy asked as she smiled broadly at the pair.

"No, but my phone would be good, so I can call home."

"Maggie already did that last night." Addy rummaged in her bag and clothing to look for it. "We tried to stop her until we knew how you were, but she was adamant that your family would want to know straight away." She handed Claire the phone.

"Yeah, I'd better ring. Uncle Geoff will be freaking out." Claire started to flip through her contacts to find *Home*, and she pressed the call button.

"We'll leave you to the call. Back soon." Matt squeezed her hand and they left her alone.

The phone in her hand rang and rang, and Claire felt nervous waiting for it to be picked up, trying to rehearse in her mind what she was going to say. It finally clicked, and a deep, sleepy voice answered. "Hello?"

"Uncle Geoff, it's me, Claire. I didn't wake you, did I?" she asked, her voice sounding a little husky.

"Claire, are you okay? I got a garbled message from Maggie, something about a car accident."

"I'm fine. You know me, can't go a couple of years without giving myself a concussion. I think I had a bit of hypothermia as well. They've got me wrapped up in a ton of blankets."

"What happened?"

"We were pushed off the road. I saw Richard—you remember, he worked for Marcus," she said in a low voice, looking at the door to make sure no one was coming in.

"The one David laid out at the cabin?"

"That's the one. At least I think it was him." She gave another quick look towards the door. "Adam contacted me. He told me that Jack is bent on revenge. I didn't believe him, but I think I do now. He said something about Jack trying to bankrupt Ben?"

"So that's what that was. He couldn't understand why his business was floundering. I'll let him know. Do you want to come home?"

"No, I'll be fine. I've made some great friends and I want to see this through. I do have some other news, something that Aunt Lil would have loved to hear. I think I've found out where The Community comes from—here. The site director's son and his cousin took me to meet their gran and she picked up that I had Talents. She has Foresight." Claire's voice was getting an excited tone to it, and she whispered the last bit into the phone.

"Well, that is news. Do you want me to tell the rest of the Elders?"

"Not yet. I want to find out a bit more first. I told them what I can do, and they seemed very surprised. There's not even a name for what I am here."

"I don't think that was very wise. Be careful, Claire. You trust so easily, and I don't want another phone call like the last one. Is Adam still trying to get through?"

"No, I asked him to leave me alone. I haven't heard from him in the last few nights."

"Good. I hope it stays that way. Now tell me more about your work," Geoff said.

Their conversation lasted for half an hour, and a couple of times Claire had to wake Geoff up. The last time, she told him to go back to bed and she would talk to him later. He bade her goodnight and told her to look after herself. When he had rung off, she laid the phone on her chest and fell asleep herself.

The police did come that afternoon, and Claire decided not to try to hide the truth, as she knew Maggie would have been adamant about what happened. They went through it with her several times, but she stuck to her story. The only thing she left out was her spotting Richard in Killin watching her. That piece of news would have only confused the police, and it was better that they came to the conclusion she wanted them to—that of road rage.

All through the interview, Matt and Addy were at her side. They were only allowed to be there if they didn't interrupt, to which they agreed and adhered to the stipulation. But once the police were gone, they had questions of their own.

"Okay, so now our turn. How did you get Maggie out of the car?" Matt started.

"I used my Talents. I used both Hide and Fly," she answered.

"You shrank Maggie as well?"

"And made her invisible. It was the only way to get out without the man seeing us," she told them.

Addy looked at Claire and then at Matt. "I didn't think that was possible. Did you know that could be done?"

"No. I didn't. How did you know?" Matt asked Claire.

"I didn't, really. I just tried, and it was either that or—I don't know what," Claire told them.

"This guy that you mentioned—who is he?" Addy asked.

"His name is Richard, and you remember I told you what happened when I was seventeen? He worked for Marcus. He was the one who beat Adam up and the one we think killed my parents."

"And you think he was the one who pushed you into the river?" Matt asked, concerned.

"I don't know. I didn't see the driver. All I saw was a figure standing by a car. I couldn't make out anything. Look, when can I get out of here? I'm feeling fine."

"You just about died last night, Claire. The doctor said another hour and we would have lost you." Matt was resting his elbows on the side of the bed. "I think you can stay in bed until the docs say it's okay to leave."

"I hate hospitals," she complained.

That afternoon, after much promising and pleading with the doctor, she was given the all clear to leave and she didn't waste time getting out of there. It felt wonderful to be going back to the site.

Chapter Eight

Sunshine crept down the roof of Claire's tent, and she snuggled down deeper into her sleeping bag. She listened to the world stirring around her and felt safe in her little cocoon. The previous night came flooding back to her. Pulling up to the car park and being greeted like a hero, then being pulled into the site director's tent, and asked the same questions the police had demanded of her. Claire had given Gerry the same answers. One thing she did do differently was to apologize to Gerry for damaging his car.

"Don't worry about it, Claire. It was insured, and I can get another one. I'm just glad that both you and Maggie are safe. Well done, by the way, on getting her out. How did you manage it?" Gerry asked, looking up at her from his seat behind the trestle table that served as a desk.

"I don't know. Maybe it was just adrenaline," Claire replied with a shrug. She wasn't quite sure he had bought it or if Matt and Addy had told him anything, but she stuck to it.

When she left the tent, she saw that Matt and Addy had been waiting for her. They'd already fended off the offers of joining in the merrymaking. Matt ordered her straight to bed and told her not to leave for anything else, otherwise he would make sure that Addy would be sharing her tent. Claire promised faithfully that she would do as she was told.

And so now it was morning, and Claire was listening and waiting for her time to get up. She didn't want the applause or the attention. She just wanted to get on with the work she loved doing—uncovering the past and preserving the memories of those who had gone before, so she could live in the present and hope for the future. This is what she truly wanted. That, and someone to share it with.

Matt. She smiled, remembering him saying goodnight at her tent. How he had taken her into his arms and kissed her tenderly and sweetly, and she had kissed him back. The butterflies had decided to depart, and she was left with only a complete feeling inside. It was only a small kiss, a brief one, but the memory of it lingered still, and she thought she wouldn't need her Talent to fly through the day.

The process of getting up and dressing was slow and easy, Claire wanting this peaceful, happy feeling to linger all day. She pulled on her work shoes and laced them up, tying them off in a double knot. Looking around, she decided the tent needed a tidy. She stuffed her dirty clothes into a plastic bag and moved it to the entrance of the tent. She stacked books and placed them on the small table by her cot, then straightened out her sleeping bag. By the time she had finished, the sun was fully shining down on her tent, and it was time she left if she wanted to eat something before the morning meeting.

Zipping the tent back up after she left it, she heard her name being called and she looked up. Addy was walking across the compound, her hair catching the morning sun and making it look like wildfire.

"How do you always manage to look so good in the morning?" Claire asked as Addy neared.

"No idea. Must be good genes. Should you be working today?" she asked, concerned.

"I want to. I feel fine, really, Addy, I do. I just want to get back to work." Claire was looking around the camp.

"If you're looking for Matt, he is up on site already." Addy grinned at her.

"Don't say anything else, Addy. Please don't ruin the good mood I'm in." Claire turned red and could feel the heat in her cheeks.

"And Maggie said to say you are to stay in camp and not to overdo anything. Like that's going to happen. Come on. I'll walk with you to the meeting. Apparently, there is big news afoot, but Dad wouldn't say what it is." She linked arms with Claire, and they made their way to the cookhouse.

Inside was packed with people waiting to be told what to do for the day. The noise dropped slightly, and heads turned as the pair entered. Claire went red again. Slowly the noise returned to the previous level and they went back to their conversations, but she had a fair idea that some were talking about her escapades of a couple of days before.

Coffee and food were all she was concerned about at that moment, and they headed for the serving area. Unlike some, this dig was fully catered, and the food was surprisingly good. They had the pick from just plain toast to a full English breakfast, but today Claire satisfied herself with a bowl of cereal and an enticing, aromatic cup of coffee, then squeezed onto the end of the first long trestle table.

Not looking at anyone else but her food, she gulped it down and pushed the bowl away from her. The dark liquid had cooled enough by then to start drinking. Gerry was soon on his feet and starting the meeting.

He rattled off names and areas they would work, and when Claire's name was not mentioned, Addy whispered that she could come and work with her. The safety briefing then dragged on, and while Claire was daydreaming about much more pleasant things, she noticed Matt walk in the door and lean against the wall. His eyes sought her out, and he smiled when they found her. The whispered chatter around the room picked up while the safety officer told them the same things he had told them the day before, and the day before that. Gerry got up again and cleared his throat.

"This is it." Addy nudged her in the ribs.

"Thank you, Bernie, for that. Right, if you could all just settle down now, please. Later on today we will be having yet another visitor to our wee community—a VIP, some might say. This visitor is our benefactor, and I would like you all to be on your best behaviour. Let's show him that his money has not been wasted. Just remember, he is responsible for all the good food you lot have been putting away over the weeks we have been here. Also, it is the last day that Archaeology Adventures will be with us, so please be a bit nicer to them. Publicity is good for funding. We may even convince other benefactors to part with their money. They have planned a special night tonight. They will be throwing us a party to show their appreciation. They will also be letting us see some of the footage that they have filmed while being here. That does not mean that you all get so rat-arsed that you can't get out of your tents in the morning. All right; you have your orders, get to it."

"Is that it? Another bloody idiot to bow and scrape to— yippee," Addy said.

"Never mind, Addy, sounds like he is rich. All you can hope for is that he's good-looking, too. Then you might be in," Claire teased her.

"Claire Brown! I will have you know I have standards! Some, anyway." She laughed. "But with my luck, he will probably be old, bent, and hard of hearing. Come on. Let's get you out of here before the olds stop you coming up to site."

"Yeah, I'll be right with you." Claire was watching Matt walk towards them. Unfortunately, she soon lost him behind the overly concerned visage of Maggie Halloran.

"Claire, honey, I've cleared it with Gerry for you to take it easy today. We don't want to overtax you, now, do we?" she said in a very motherly tone.

"I'm fine, really, Maggie. I'm feeling fit as a fiddle. How are you feeling, by the way?" Claire asked. The doubts she had of shrinking her mentor and what aftereffects she may experience still had her curious.

"I'm all right. My muscles are a bit sore still, but I was not as bad as you. Thank you for saving me and looking after me." She bundled Claire up in a big hug. When Maggie released her, tears glistened in her eyes. "Well, I'd better get to work. Get some rest and just relax today."

"What if Claire shadows me today?" Matt asked from behind Maggie. "She can learn a little about being a surveyor, like you suggested."

"What a good idea, Matt. You are such a sweetie. Would that be all right with you, Claire?" Maggie asked her.

"That would be great! Thanks, Matt," Claire said, feeling her smile spread from ear to ear.

"Shall we go?" Matt grinned back at her and they walked out the door.

The day was one of the best that she had spent on site. Not even the squally shower that passed over the hill in the middle of the day could dampen her spirits. They spent the hour it took for the weather to pass under a large elm getting to know each other a little better—and not necessarily with words.

Afternoon rolled around, and they ambled their way back to camp. Gerry had asked Matt to be there when the benefactor arrived, and that time was fast approaching. Some of the crew were already downing tools and getting ready for the festivities of the night, including Addy. She waved as they entered the compound and came to meet them.

"Well, my luck has turned," she told the couple. "That guy has arrived and oh my God, what a looker. Hot and wealthy—what a combination!"

"Where is he?" Claire asked.

"He's in with Uncle Gerry and Dad at the moment. Oh, and brace yourself, Matt—Mum is here. Dad, with his usual brilliance, thought that she would charm some more money out of him. Too bad she's too old for him." Addy giggled.

"Is that him?" Matt asked Addy, pointing to a group of people coming out of the site director's tent.

Claire looked where he indicated and felt her stomach drop. She turned her back on them and started to walk away.

"No, no, no," she kept muttering under breath as she went.

"What's wrong?" the cousins asked in unison.

"I can't believe that he would do this. It's unbelievable!" Claire stopped and turned back just to make sure she wasn't imagining who was there.

"Who?" Addy asked, concerned.

"That's Adam." She started to walk away from them. "I've got to get out of here." Desperately she turned to find an escape route, but she was too late.

"Hey, guys, they want you over there. Including you, Claire," Nick called, running up to them.

"Why me? I haven't got anything to do with running the site," she declared, a little panicked.

"You were asked for by name." Nick shrugged as he walked back to the group.

Claire turned to where Adam stood and could see him staring back at her. She did not want to talk to him right now while her anger was still building, but she followed Matt and Addy, trying to hide behind them.

The flickering thought of disappearing and going off to hide somewhere petered out when she saw so many people milling around. *And that would have done no good either*, she thought to herself. *Adam would just wait around until I reappeared*. Taking a great breath and letting it out slowly, she steeled herself for the meeting.

Matt and Addy were introduced first and then Claire was presented. "We're old friends, aren't we, Claire?" Adam greeted her.

"Friends?" Claire raised an eyebrow with the question.

"I hope, still friends." He smiled down at her. Claire could feel the waves of Charm coming from him and put up her defences to block it. "I was hoping you could show me around."

"Gerry or Maggie or anyone here would be better qualified than me, Adam. I'm still a student, remember?" The tension around them was soon making everyone uncomfortable. "Plus, I have other duties to finish this afternoon."

"Surely they can wait—" he started, until she cut him off.

"No, everyone has to pull their weight around here, and if I don't do it then Addy has to do it by herself, and that wouldn't be fair." To Claire's great relief, Addy came to her side and linked her arm with her own.

"We better get on with it if we want to finish before the party tonight, Claire. It was very nice to meet you, Adam," Addy said with a sweet smile.

Addy steered her friend away towards the other side of the camp with no real destination in mind. When they were out of sight, Claire let out a breath and relaxed, releasing the tension that had built up in her body.

"Thanks, Addy," she mumbled.

"I did it for Matt as much as for you. I don't think you saw how he was reacting. I thought he was going to deck Adam.

You just gave me the excuse to get you away. I wouldn't have had a clue how to extricate either one of them out of that situation," Addy said, giving Claire's arm a little squeeze.

"So, what are we going to do until tonight?" Claire asked her.

"Spend it getting ready, of course. I think a touch of makeup and a nice hairdo should just about do the trick." Addy was looking at Claire speculatively. Then she reached up and pulled Claire's usual ponytail out and started to play with her hair. "I would kill for hair like this," she told her friend.

"Yours is gorgeous! I've often thought about dyeing mine."

"We could slip out of camp and go find some dye if you want. But I don't think Matt would like it." Addy gave her a cheeky smile.

The rest of that afternoon they spent sneaking from place to place as they luxuriated in the freedom of performing a few girly activities instead of digging dirt out of boots and cleaning out their tools. Claire sat patiently on her stretcher while Addy—who was already dressed impeccably—riffled through her clothes, trying to pick out an outfit for her to wear because she had objected to what Claire had dressed herself in. With disgust, she looked at her friend.

"Don't you have any girly things to wear?" she asked, holding up dirt-stained t-shirts and a pair of overalls.

"Well, I wasn't expecting to do any fine dining while I was here. What's wrong with the clothes that I have?" Claire asked, taking the items from Addy, and placing them back into her bag.

"They're all work clothes, that's what. There is only one thing for it—you'll have to wear something of mine. Wait here, I'll be right back." True to her word, she was back in moments with a bundle in her hands that she handed to Claire. "These should fit you—we're about the same size."

Claire lifted each piece in turn and then held up the shoes. "These are the only things that I would wear. I haven't worn a skirt for years."

"Well, it's about time you did. Get dressed and I'll meet you outside. Trust me, Claire. You'll look beautiful."

Pulling on the clothes Addy had given her, Claire's nerves started to get the better of her. She smoothed the top and looked down at herself. It was bizarre to see her legs sticking out of a skirt instead of in shorts or jeans.

"Come on, Claire! How long does it take you to put on a skirt and top?" Addy asked her impatiently.

"Yeah, I'm coming." Somewhere between getting up off her bed and exiting the tent, the nervousness that had been building finally got the better of her. Without her noticing, she had made herself invisible, and as the tent flap opened, Addy gasped.

"Claire, I can't see you," she whispered, looking around to see if there was anyone around.

"Oops." Claire laughed and righted herself.

"Oops? Oops, she says, nearly giving herself away. Let's go before all the good stuff has gone." Addy started to lead Claire over to the crowd gathering in the middle of the common ground where the fire pits were located, but they were stopped by a call from behind.

"Adaira, darling!"

"Oh great—it's Mum." She turned on the spot to face her with a fixed smile on her face. Fiona MacCallum was still a beautiful woman, with long, dark red hair and a slim figure. Claire could see where Addy got her looks from, as the resemblance between mother and daughter was very striking.

"You are supposed to be joining us in the tent for dinner, and your friend, Claire." Fiona gave Claire a brief glance before addressing her daughter once more. "I presume this is Claire?"

"Yes, this is Claire. Claire this is my mother, the great Fiona MacCallum," Addy said and introduced the pair.

"It's lovely to meet you. I've heard a lot about you from Addy." Claire stuck her hand out to shake. Fiona glanced briefly at it and then took her fingers limply in her own for only a second, without a word of return.

They followed Addy's mother over to the director's tent and entered close behind her. A large table had been placed in the middle, and it was lavishly set for the meal. Claire noticed that Adam, Gerry, Robbie, and Matt were already seated, and they all stood when the ladies entered.

Adam pulled out a chair and indicated for Claire to sit beside him. Deliberately she turned and sat next to Matt, with Addy seating herself on her other side. Maggie came running in, apologizing for being late, and took the only other seat available beside Adam.

"Are you all right?" Matt asked as he leaned in to pour Claire and Addy a glass of wine each.

"I'm fine. I would be better if I wasn't here," Claire responded with a tight smile.

"You look gorgeous," he whispered to her as he reached under the table and took her hand in his, giving it a little squeeze. It helped a little to ease her fears, and she took her first gulp of wine of the night.

The dinner started, and they were waited upon by some of the students that Claire recognized. The main point of conversation around the table was between Adam and Gerry, with Maggie interjecting every now and then. It was obvious to Claire that they were lobbying for more funds to extend the dig, and it was just as obvious that Adam was not really listening. Every time Claire looked his way, she could see him watching her. She would shift in her seat, feeling very uncomfortable under his gaze, and look down at her own plate or take another sip of wine.

Addy was more often than not talking to her mother. Claire could not hear what was being said, but she could feel her friend's discomfort as much as her own. Matt was drawn into the main conversation, but occasionally he gave her comfort with a squeeze of her hand under the table.

"Claire, how are you finding the work?" Adam called across to her as the dessert dishes were being cleared.

She blushed under the scrutiny of everyone and cleared her throat. "I'm enjoying it a great deal. The work is enjoyable, and the people are great." She tried not to let the tension show in her voice and quickly finished off another glass of wine.

"I'm pleased that you are enjoying it." His eyes bored into her and she knew he was itching to say more, but she was not willing to give him a chance in front of the people around them.

Building up her courage to face off with him, she was about to let fly when they were interrupted by Nick at the entrance to the tent. "We're ready, Robbie, whenever you are." He looked around at the quiet table and gave a small, almost nervous smile.

Robbie took the opportunity to stand and break the tension that seemed to surround Adam and Claire. "What are you waiting for? Let's go watch," he said, hurrying them along.

Addy and Matt stuck close to Claire and when she stood to leave, she realized she had had too much to drink and was not looking forward to this viewing, hoping that there would be little to no footage of herself.

Her hopes were dashed as some of the first footage to be shown on the large, improvised screen was her digging out the bead with the boar symbol. She stood at the back of the crowd and slowly backed up, leaving Matt and Addy to watch it by themselves. Wandering over to the deserted fire pit, she sat down and stared into the flames, watching them dance and flicker over the coals that glowed deeply underneath. The noise from the crowd ebbed and flowed as they watched themselves, and Claire tried to block it out.

"You never did like yourself on camera, did you?" Adam asked as he came up behind her.

"No. That was your idea," she said shortly to him.

"Claire, I can see I have upset you, and I'm sorry—but I did all this for you." Adam sat down on the seat next to her.

"Oh, I am so touched." Sarcasm dripped thickly from her words.

"I remembered that you had always talked about wanting to come to England and get stuck into a good dig. So, I found one you would love and funded it. I did it before we broke up and I didn't want to cancel it. Think of it as a parting gift from me."

"For a start, this is not England; it's Scotland. And for another, what gives you the right to order my life for me?" Her voice was rising, and she leaned forward in her seat. "You were always organizing everything. I was never allowed to come and see you. You always had to come to me. Were you hiding more girlfriends from me then, or was it just the one?"

"I think you have had too much to drink, Claire. Why don't we discuss this in the morning when you have a clearer head?" He stood up and started to walk away.

"No, we do this now. Did you think you could just turn up here and tell me that you did all this for me, and I would walk right back into your arms? That everything would go back to the way it was?" She walked up to him and pushed against his chest.

"Calm down, Claire." Adam put his hands up and moved back from her.

"Why can't you just get the message and move on? Why do you have to keep hounding me? I asked you not to contact me again and yet here you are." Heads were beginning to turn as her voice began to rise, and soon Matt and Addy were walking their way.

"I did promise, but it was more than just wanting to see you. I came to warn you as well—" he started.

"Just leave me alone, Adam." She spotted Matt coming up behind Adam and she started to go to meet him. As she passed Adam, she left him with a parting shot. "I've moved on. I suggest you do the same."

Claire reached Matt within a few steps and kissed him soundly on the mouth, snaking her arms around his neck and drawing him close. He placed his hands on her hips and slowly pushed her away, breaking the kiss. Quickly Matt put his arm around Claire and guided her away from the increasing crowd. Addy followed behind. Claire did not see Adam's reaction.

In the deserted cookhouse, Matt sat Claire down and went and made her a coffee. When he placed it in front of her, she looked up.

"I'm sorry. I shouldn't have done that," she told him, drawing the cup to her.

"No, you shouldn't have." He sat down beside her and Addy opposite. "It was nice, but are you sure you should've thrown it in his face like that?"

"Probably not." She sighed. "I'm sorry. I've ruined everything for everyone. I let my emotions get away from me."

"Yes, you did, but some guys can have that effect on you." Addy told her while looking significantly at her cousin. "And as for ruining things, there's no way to tell at the moment," Addy said.

"There's no point worrying about it now. You can't change what you've done," Matt said gently as he took her hand and kissed it.

Claire refused to meet his eyes and looked down at her lap. She was feeling stupid and definitely ashamed of herself. They sat in silence for a while, drinking their coffee and listening to the applause outside, which soon turned to loud music and voices yelling over it. Matt suddenly stood up, his arms at his sides with clenched fists. Claire looked up and saw what he was staring at. Adam stood in the doorway with his hands up.

"I didn't come to fight or argue. I just came to see if Claire is okay, but I can see she is being well looked after." He took a step inside and stopped when he saw Matt's darkening glare. "But you and I have to have a conversation soon. It's important. Maggie told me about your accident."

She could tell from the look on his face and the reference to the accident that it was about Jack. Claire nodded to him.

"Not tonight, Adam. We'll talk in the morning."

"That's all I ask, thank you. I'll say good night, then." He turned and left them alone.

Chapter Nine

Birdsong filled the cool morning air and floated on the unsubstantial mist that clung to the side of the hill, wrapping itself around the sloping sides like a blanket. Underneath the tall trees, the world was waking up to the predawn. Small creatures scampered around in the undergrowth, rustling dead leaves as they passed, looking for their morning meal. The thought of food made Claire's stomach constrict. It was not so much the food itself—more the thought of facing everyone else. There had been enough talk about her when she had saved Maggie, but now the gossip would be more salacious. All she wanted was to be left alone, to wallow in her own self-pity.

Pressing on, she ran the full circuit of the trees and came back to camp before the sun had made its presence known. No one was about. The party the previous night had lasted well into the small hours of the morning, but Claire had not slept. Lying in her bed listening to the merrymaking of the others, she had once again felt isolated and alone. As the music stopped and the talking continued, she'd wished she could leave her tent and seek Matt out, but even there she found no comfort. She had embarrassed him as much as herself, and even though he was calm about it, she could tell that he was not happy.

Tossing and turning as the voices outside dwindled away and the light from the fires died down, her mind stayed awake, refusing to let her sleep. Occasionally she had felt Adam trying to get through and did not succumb to the automatic urge to answer him. With the first songbird call, Claire was dressed and out running.

Now back at camp, she was not ready to return to her tent. The exercise had not diminished her restlessness in the slightest. Instead, she went to the cookhouse, where there was always hot water on the go and instant coffee to be had no matter the hour.

"Morning, Claire. I see I'm not the only one to have no sleep last night." Gerry was sitting with his back against the wall and his feet up on another seat, a cup nestled between his hands. He looked tired, with big bags under his eyes and rumpled clothing.

"No, I couldn't sleep either." She went and made a cup of very strong coffee and then returned to join him. "May I sit?"

"Go ahead. I'll not stop you."

"Gerry, I want to apologize for last night. I got a bit tipsy, and that's not a good thing for me. All judgment seems to go out the door," she said as she stumbled through her apology.

"Aye, I would agree with you there. But never mind, lass. Matty explained everything to me. By the way, could you tell Adam not to be so noisy when trying to talk to you in your dreams?" He looked at her over the rim of his cup with raised eyebrows.

"You can hear us?" she asked with some shock at this news.

"Aye, I've been trying to work out who it was, but Matty cleared it up for me last night. As soon as I met him, I could feel the Charm oozing from him. But he's never been taught properly to manage his Dream Messaging, has he?"

"That's because our studies are incomplete. We had no system of learning our Talents from our elders. We were left to study from journals and diaries of those gone before. Also, Adam was a little more isolated in that matter than I was."

"I understand my mother-in-law has had a wee chat with you. As head of the family, she holds all our lore."

"Yes, it was very exciting to meet her. Our Community has hidden itself away for many generations, and where we came from was deliberately made a mystery by our forebears," Claire told him, warming now to the subject.

"It could have something to do with the persecutions of our people around this area and to the south in the borderlands. The Presbyterians and Episcopalians would find any excuse to persecute those they thought were different or to settle old scores. A lot of people from there went to America. I'm sure you have heard of the witch trials over there?" When Claire nodded, he continued. "Some of the accusations were false, but some were true. Our People were hounded there, and they moved on again. We lost the trail as they headed south. It could be your family stems from that group."

They fell silent for a while as each pondered this information. "There is still a large gap of time between the trials and the settlement of New Zealand," Claire added.

"Well, lass, there's your starting point." Gerry gave her a friendly wink.

"Can I ask a question?"

"Fire away," he said, placing down his now empty cup on the table.

"The other day when I dug up the bead, both you and Robbie were getting excited. What is it that you hope to find here?" Claire asked.

"You're not one for missing much, are you?" He laughed as he toyed with the handle of his cup. "That information is for the family. But I will tell you that it is something we have been seeking for a long time and thanks to you, I think we have. But don't tell Robbie I said that."

"I won't."

"You know, when you are finished here, I suggest you go spend a bit of time with Rowena." He saw her confusion at the name. "The old girl would have told you to call her Gran."

"Oh. Yes, she did." Claire smiled over her cup.

"Well, go see her and get some instruction. What she doesn't know is not worth knowing. Now I will make myself another cup and take it back to my tent. You both have some talking to do. No yelling and play nicely." He indicated towards the door as he stood, and Claire turned in time to see Adam walking through it.

"Morning," Adam greeted them quietly.

"I'll be leaving you to yourselves, young man. Mind what I say to you, Claire."

"Thanks, Gerry," she called after him as he headed out the door, then turned to Adam and looked up at him.

"Truce?" he asked her.

"Truce," she agreed, and he sat down opposite. "Well, this is your show. What do you want to talk about?"

"Jack. That's what. I've found some major discrepancies in some of the books. He has been spending money like it was water, and I'm having trouble finding what he's using it for," Adam told her as he sat down heavily, opposite.

"Getting Richard over here could be one." She drained her cup and put it on the table.

"Richard? Dad's old security, Richard?" he asked, his eyebrows knitting together in confusion.

"I saw him the day Maggie and I had our accident. I thought it was too much of a coincidence."

"He was let go. Well, to tell the truth, he was told if he ever darkened our door again, then what he did to me would be only a fifth of what would happen to him."

"It looks like Jack has found him."

"That's not all. Claire, I've just found out that Mum has been hurt." He held up a hand to stop her before she could ask. "She's fine. Charlie and Mum were in the city and a car came out of nowhere. Thank God Charlie was there—she managed to sort out the broken bones before the ambulance arrived. But there was some internal damage that she didn't want to touch. David rang just now. That's why I'm awake, he forgot the time difference. He says 'Hi,' by the way."

"Oh my God." Claire started to fumble for her phone.

"David was calling everyone else after me. Geoff won't know just yet." He watched her check her messages and put the phone back.

"Habit, I suppose. So do you think Jack was behind it?" she asked with a frown.

"That's the problem. I can't say for sure. I have to dig a bit deeper. There may be some old contacts I can access that might give me some clues. Can I keep you up to date?" he asked her hopefully.

"Phone only. I've discovered that our Dream Messaging is not as private as we thought," she said, lowering her voice.

"Come again?"

"Since being here I have discovered that this may be where The Community originates from. And there are those in camp who have been a witness to our talking via Dream Message."

"Who?" he asked, sitting forward and leaning on the table.

"I can't tell you unless they reveal it themselves. But there is a small group here that have Talents as well—though they call them Abilities. So only contact me by phone. I mean it, Adam."

"All right, phone only. I promise. This is big news, you run away from The Community and a branch ends up where you are. That's a bit ironic." He got up from the table. "You want another cup?" Adam picked up her mug.

"No, thanks. I need to get some rest. And I didn't run away, remember." She got up and stretched, then moved to the door. She turned back to Adam, giving him a hard look. "If you are funding this dig, then—"

"Then what?" he asked.

"The students have all paid to be here. I haven't paid, and no one has asked me to." She narrowed her eyes at him.

"Ah…yeah, well, that was one of the stipulations—that Gerry take both you and Maggie on without charge." Claire could see him bracing for her fury.

"Right. Well, I'll be rectifying that, but Maggie doesn't need to know, okay?"

"Okay." He let out a long sigh of relief. "Claire, do you think we will ever be friends again?"

"I don't know, Adam." Claire was just about out the door when something occurred to her. "Hey, if you really can't face not being in a relationship, I may know someone. But she knows our history, so you may have an uphill battle with her."

"Now look who's doing the organizing." He laughed, and she left the room.

Gerry knew how hard the team would party, so he relented and had given all of them the day off, despite what he had told them the day before. Later that morning, with a lightness in her heart that she had not felt in a very long time, Claire dressed. After a couple hours of light sleep, she felt not quite rested, but a bit better than she had earlier that morning. It could also have been a result of clearing the air with Adam. There was no dread from Adam's words, no heavyheartedness from misplaced trust—just a floating feeling of joy and anticipation. For the first time in years, she was about to go on an official first date and she was very much looking forward to it.

At breakfast, Matt had told her that he intended to take her away from camp and away from all the drama, to have a day where they could get to know one another properly. Claire had readily accepted the plan and now tried hard to take care in how she dressed. Sitting back, looking at the pile of her clothing, she agreed with Addy; she had nothing she could really wear. Having no idea of their destination was another obstacle. Shorts or jeans, what was the weather going to be like, should she take a jacket or jumper, flip-flops or sneakers?

After finally giving up and throwing a jumper and light jacket into her bag, she was ready. Matt drove them out of the camp and back over the hills to Loch Tay. Instead of right to Killin, Matt veered left and they were soon passing Lawers Hotel, where she had stayed the first night in Scotland. The mountain stretched up to the sky on her left, and even more stone bridges and moss-covered walls passed them by.

The view opened, and a great expanse of Loch Tay lay out beside them. The shimmering reflection of the sky above created a beautiful watercolour effect on the surface. Claire wished she could look at this view forever; it was spectacular and peaceful. She envied those who lived in the cottages on these shores. Shadows of the clouds dappled the hills across the loch, changing the colours of the vegetation as they passed. The wind danced over the surface of the water, leaving behind little ripples, as if a fairy had dipped its toe in as it flew over. The road now ran right beside the loch, and Claire could see odd glimpses through the trees. As they rounded the bend of the loch, more and more holiday lets and cottages could be found lining the road. And then it just ceased. The trees grew closer together and the bracken on the ground was denser.

They had entered into a forest park. At some points, it was like driving through a tunnel of green and prismatic sunlight.

A building made of rough-cut stone zoomed past on their left, and Claire twisted in her seat to get a better look at it. It was a cross between a church and a castle, and it captivated her imagination. They passed an information sign pointing the way to various sites, including one that read *Drummond Hill Forest Walk*. Claire looked at Matt.

"Our family has been in this area for a very long time," he said with a small smile. "But it doesn't belong to us."

A little further on, they entered Kenmore, a town located at the complete opposite end of Loch Tay from Killin. They passed over the River Tay and its impressive stone bridge, and then turned towards the Crannog Centre.

"This is the first part of our day," Matt informed her.

Claire caught glimpses of the experiment that was the Crannog Centre, built out on the loch on great wooden piles. It wouldn't become an island like the others that dotted the surface of the loch until it had fallen down and been rebuilt multiple times. They parked in the car park and went into the complex for a few hours of listening to stories and watching demonstrations, even participating in a few. Claire loved how Matt threw himself into the activities, and it was nice to be around someone who genuinely enjoyed it.

As she went to cross the long bridge that led to the shore, Claire stopped to look back at the round, thatched building. That overwhelming feeling of déjà vu was back, and she shivered a little. It was as if someone was calling to her to try and remember something. Matt took her hand in his, breaking the spell that seemed to have come over her. The strange feeling was left behind as they made their way back to the car and their next destination, which was only a few minutes up the road. Matt found somewhere to park in the small village, and Claire followed him up a stony track.

"I'm taking you to see one of the most beautiful places around here," Matt said, slinging a bag over his shoulder and grabbing her hand, dragging her on with him.

They walked up the hill with trees to the left and an open field with bleating sheep to the right. Up a bit, he stopped and turned Claire around. The breathtaking view of the loch with the hill dropping away in the foreground and Ben Lawers in the back lay before them. The sky was now clear of the earlier clouds, but there was still a breeze. It was a magnificently warm day. Matt smiled at Claire, taking her hand again gently as the couple carried on up the track. They soon reached a sign pushed into the grass sign that read *Hermit's Cave*.

"This is the first part," he told her and led her down a narrow path, lined on the left with a wooden fence and a sharply rising bank on the right. A right turn revealed the entrance into a rock formation, and inside Claire could see it was pitch black.

"You all right in the dark?" Matt asked with a cheeky smile.

"I have my ways of dealing with it," she told him and then produced a small light in the palm of her hand. His eyes widened a little, but he didn't say anything.

They entered, and the dancing light revealed little niches cut into the walls, just small enough to sit on. Further in and to the left, a grey light penetrated the dark; Matt turned, beckoning her on. The narrow path widened out onto a viewing platform with a metal guard fence and framed-in view with a magnificent waterfall. The ribbons of white seemed to leap out of the trees and cascaded down the rocks to splash their way into a dark pool at the bottom. Trees and ferns made their home on every surface, and the sounds of birds were drowned out by the rushing water.

Matt pulled his camera from his bag and started to take photos. Claire tried to get out of the way so he could have a clear shot of the vista, but he only pulled her back into shot. When he had finished, she held out her hand for the camera, insisting that it was only fair that she take some pictures of him. Deftly she arranged both him and the falls in the shot. For some, she had him looking away, and for others, she zoomed in on his face.

"I want copies of those," she said when she handed the camera back.

When they reentered the tunnel to carry on with their walk, they could hear a large group of people entering the cave. Claire refrained from creating a light spark, instead held on to Matt's hand tightly as they entered the gloom. When they reached the junction, they bumped into the excited group and a torch flickered on. As the beam of yellow light was swung around, Claire for an instant saw a familiar face, and she stiffened.

This mass of strangers was a group of Americans, all talking loudly, their voices echoing off the narrow tunnel. Confusing images flashed in front of her as the torch beam picked up people and rock in stark contrast. She gripped Matt's hand tighter and pulled him out of the scrummage that had blocked their way, desperately making for the other exit and back out into the sunlight.

Some of the warmth of the day had been left behind in Hermit's Cave, and she shivered slightly. Wide-eyed, she looked behind them to see if Richard was following, but she only saw a concerned-looking Matt.

"Not here," she said to him in a voice that was choked with fear. She hurried on to the main track, heading further up the hill.

"What happened, Claire?" Matt asked. Claire could hear his concern.

"Richard. The man I told you about. He was in there. I'm sure I saw his face," she told him hurriedly.

"Could you have been mistaken?" He stopped her and held her hand.

"I could have; I don't know. It was only a flicker, but it was so clear."

"Look, he's back there and we're here. I think we should go have a look at the rest of the falls and forget about him." He put his arm around her and looked back behind them but saw no one following.

Further up the track, they found the turning for the path to the stream and waterfall. It led them through thick green grass and a clump of tall, thin trees. The further in they went, the denser the bush became until they came to a narrow set of dirt stairs, flanked by a wooden handrail leading down to the base of the falls. Standing at the very end, they watched the water falling from one carved out basin to another and then tripping over rocks as it made its way down the narrow canyon. The noise of the water was all-encompassing, and Claire felt herself relax with it, letting it wash away the worries of moments before.

A wooden bridge had been constructed over the flowing waters, and Claire leaned against the railing and looked down into the cleft the water had eroded away. Matt was firing off more shots on his camera, taking in the falls and the trees. He lifted his sights to where they had descended from, and a dark silhouette came into his viewfinder and stood looking down at them.

"Let's get moving. When we get to the bottom, I'll buy you a pint." He tugged at her sleeve to encourage her along.

"Can't we just stay here for a while? It's so lovely," she said lazily.

"I think we're about to have company," he told her quietly and indicated above them.

The silhouette was now making his way to the dirt steps, and Claire studied him for a moment. It was remarkable how much she remembered about the man she had only briefly seen a couple of times in her past. She shook herself back to the present, moving off with Matt. They followed the trail down the hill, watching the river as they went, casting furtive looks back behind where they had just been to see how far back he was.

The path opened up, and the viewing platform attached to Hermit's Cave could be seen clearly across the gorge. Standing watching them with a phone to his ear was a younger man wearing a baseball cap pulled down low over his face, his eyes hidden behind dark sunglasses, staring at them as they passed.

"There seems to be more of them," Claire commented while they descended.

The joy of the day was fast disappearing, and Claire was beginning to get angry. Why couldn't Jack just leave it? He had his father's love, and part of the business was now run by him. What more could he possibly want? She could feel herself becoming more introspective with her thoughts as they went along, and she tried to get her head together.

They turned a corner and were hidden from view from above, and Claire grabbed Matt's arm. "I'm sick of this cat-and-mouse game, so I'm going to do something, but you are going to have to help."

"Anything," he told her.

"Okay, I am going to shrink us and then make us invisible. But I am going to have to have your help to Fly."

"What do I have to do?" She went quickly through the process with him and then took him in her arms. "I'm liking it so far," he said, grinning down at her.

"Later." Claire flashed a quick smile at him before concentrating, pulling her energy in, and encompassing Matt into that process. Slowly they faded from view, and then she began the process to shrink.

"Bloody hell!" Matt exclaimed as it started to take effect. Soon they were as small as mice.

"Right. Lift off now," she told him; she could feel his Talent merge with hers to raise them up in the air.

It was not a moment too soon that they took off into the trees, flying straight down the hill following the stream underneath them, for Richard had caught up with where they were. For a brief moment he searched down the track for them. He raised his phone to his ear and waited, breathing deeply from the chase.

"I think they're running for it. Keep an eye out on their car down there. I've sent Tony down to cover from the other side." He clicked the phone off and carried on down the track.

By this stage, Claire and Matt had managed to get to the bottom and reach the village of Acharn. They sat hovering in the tree line, looking out around them.

"Do we go to the car or try to hide somewhere?" she asked.

"I have no idea; this is your party. I've never been in a situation like this before."

"Let's try the car. We'll do a sweep first and see if there is anyone watching it, then get the hell out of here." They wound their way around the car park, with Claire looking for any signs of Watchers. There were only a few cars, but nothing stood out to her. Landing behind the old Land Rover, she slowly brought them back to size, taking care to tell Matt how to work his muscles so they did not cramp up.

"As long as we are touching, you will still be invisible. What do you say to driving off and maybe freaking out a few locals?" she asked, starting to feel slightly out of breath.

"Can you make the car disappear?" he asked her.

"It's a bit large, but I might be able to make it less noticeable. I really don't know if it will work, Matt. But when we are safe, I am going to need some serious feeding."

"Let's get in first; I'm having a hard-enough time as it is talking to you without seeing you."

Matt managed to open the door to the Land Rover and Claire climbed in first, scooting across the bench seat to let him in. It was an awkward manoeuvre, but they managed it. Matt put the key in the ignition and waited for Claire to do her thing.

The effort she exerted trying to change the molecular structure of the large vehicle put a great strain on Claire. Sweat was pouring from her brow and running down her face.

"Is there a change?" she asked through gritted teeth, straining to get each word out.

"Some. I'm going now. Are you sure this is a good idea? I don't want you to burn yourself out." He started the engine after she gave a quick response, quickly put it into gear, and shot forwards out of their parking space. "Hopefully they will think we have gone back through Kenmore."

Further down the road, Claire released her grip on both Matt and his car and collapsed back against the seat. Her hair was limp and damp with sweat, dark circles were emerging around her closed eyes, and she was breathing heavily from the strain. Matt shot her a worried look and kept driving, going as fast as he could without attracting any unwanted attention. Every time he came to a straight piece of road, he checked behind them in the rearview mirror, making sure they weren't followed.

Matt drove until he came across a lookout spot to view the loch. He entered and parked the Rover behind some trees, hoping it was enough to hide them from the road, then shook Claire awake. He handed her a bottle of water and dragged his bag off his shoulders, where he had left it in their haste.

"Have you got any food in that bag?" she asked while she gulped mouthfuls of water.

Digging around inside, Matt found a couple of muesli bars and handed them to her. They were open and gone within minutes.

"I get hungry when I use more than one Talent at a time," she told him, leaning her head back on the headrest. "I think I have used my Talents more in the last month than I have in the last few years."

"Are you going to be okay?" Matt asked, concerned she had pushed herself too far.

"I'll be fine. But I am starting to wonder if I should leave." She looked him in the eye, trying to judge his reaction.

"So he can follow you there and hurt more of the people you love? No, Claire; don't leave. We can help you...I can call a meeting of the family and we can work something out." He reached out and grasped her hand in his, holding it tightly as if he were afraid she would slip away from him.

"You are a wonderful man, Matt, but I can't take the chance that he would hurt all of you just to get to me. He's not right in the head."

They sat in silence for a while and watched the road through the trees. Cars passed at a leisurely pace, people going about their daily lives unaware of the turmoil that the couple was feeling just meters away. One car did catch their attention as it sped past going towards Killin.

"Well, we are going to have to decide what to do next. Do we go back to site or hide out for the rest of the day?" he asked.

"I can think of a few things we could do." She smiled at him. "But first I really need to get some more food into me."

"Right," he declared, happy to have any sort of plan to follow. "We'll go to Kenmore, seeing as we've seen them racing the other way. We'll get you some food and then we'll go back to camp. I know another way. It's the perks of working in your backyard."

"First, there is something I have wanted to do all day." She leaned forward and pressed her lips to his, moving closer as he drew her into his arms.

While they were otherwise engaged, they did not notice another car drive into the viewing area, make a loop, and then exit again only to pull up further along the road within sight of the entrance. It sat there patiently until the Land Rover pulled out and headed back to Kenmore, following at a discreet distance, always keeping them in sight.

The pair stopped beside a café, and Matt went in to get something for them to eat. The car caught up and drove straight past the old Rover, stopping near the bridge behind another car. The two drivers got out and spoke to each other, watching to see which way they would go. Going back over the bridge, Matt took the road they had travelled on, passing the Forest of Tay and turning just at the edge of it as Claire scoffed down the food he had bought her.

The narrow country road wound its way through the valley with wildflowers lining the sides, bobbing in the wind that was picking up. The hills on either side were planted with pines in neat, straight rows like soldiers on parade, standing dark against the bright green of the fields.

Traffic was light on this road, and in his rearview mirror, Matt saw a car a way back from them, matching their speed. He wasn't entirely comfortable with its presence and sped up a little. Noticing his actions, Claire turned and looked behind, then sat back and watched the world pass by.

"If I had just listened to Adam before I even left, I could have had this all sorted." Her thought tumbled from her lips.

"You weren't to know. How could you? And really, what could you have done?" Matt asked, still glancing at the car behind them.

"I don't know. Marcus was easy to deal with; he was so narcissistic that we used that against him. Jack is a totally different matter—his mind just doesn't work like other people's. It's so messed up with all the lies that were fed to him growing up, that he has no true grip on reality. That is why Aunt Lil refused to help Adam change him. That and she found the whole thing distasteful."

"Could she help now?" he asked, flicking his eyes up to the rearview mirror.

"No, she can't. She died a year ago of a heart attack." Her reply caught in her throat, and he reached over to grab her hand.

"I'm sorry." He looked at her briefly with his blue eyes full of concern.

"Its fine. You weren't to know."

They rounded a bend and crossed over the River Lyon and had to stop in their tracks. The road ahead was blocked by lots of newly shorn sheep going back to their pasture, bleating, and chasing around each other. A black-and-white collie dog was barking loudly as it harried at their heels to move them along.

The car that had been following them soon caught up and Claire tried to see inside it with the wing mirror.

"One guy driving," Matt said quietly, and Claire quickly agreed. "The turnoff is just ahead. We'll see if he will still follow."

Just as he said, within seconds of the road clearing, he turned down another lane and sped up as fast as the old car could go. Pastures and gorse-lined banks passed them by. When Matt looked behind, there was no sign of the other car and his hands relaxed on the steering wheel. But he didn't see the car pulling up shortly after the turnoff and the driver consulting a map, then using his phone to report. As soon as he was off the phone, he turned the car around and took the turning after them.

The views around them were stunning. The River Lyon was to their left down a steep bank with only a low stone wall protecting them from the fall. To the right a hill rose up from where the road had been cut into it, full of rocks poking through a carpet of soft, bright green moss and trees spreading their large branches overhead, creating a green tunnel with those on the other side.

Splashes of rain hit the windscreen intermittently, and Claire prayed that this would only be a passing shower. The gloom that had spread earlier now deepened and the clouds opened up, letting down their heavy load. Sheets of water crossed in front of them, and the windscreen wipers worked double time to shift the rain from the glass.

Matt spied a passing bay ahead through the streaming water and pulled into it, waiting for the weather to pass.

"While we wait, you can tell me how you learned to fly." He loosened his seat belt and leaned up against the driver's door, tucking his left leg under his right.

"There's not much to tell, really, and I have told you this before."

"I want to hear it again. We've got time." He smiled, his eyes twinkled, and the dimples in his cheeks deepened.

Claire suddenly felt shy talking about it with him. He had come from a family where it was openly talked about and celebrated. She—on the other hand—had been kept in the dark until the age of seventeen and then had all the information forced upon her.

"Okay. Uncle Geoff had worked it out and didn't think to tell me anything until I got into that spot of trouble, and then he explained it to me as we escaped from the city. When I got to the village is when I learned that I had all this family that had been kept from me, and I was given books to learn from."

"There were no lessons of any kind?"

"No. What I have learned has come from books and trying to figure out my own techniques."

A car passed by them at some speed and Claire tried to see it through the misting-up windows and heavy rain. All she saw was a dark-coloured streak as it raced by. When she looked back at Matt, he was considering her deeply.

"How do you just learn it from books without anyone there to teach you properly?"

"I had help with Hiding and Light. Jack was actually my teacher for Hide, and for that I am grateful, because my first attempt on my own was not pleasant. Jasper, my cousin, helped me with Light."

"Isn't he younger than you?"

"By seven years. He actually developed it by himself. At the time, his mother was against the Talents, so he was scared to mention it to her. But Uncle David was over the moon when he found out. I had never seen him so happy."

"I'm confused with all the names. Your Uncle David is related by your mother?"

"He's her twin. Okay, I'll go through it, but some may be confusing. My parents were Jess and John. Mum's parents are my grandparents Lynnette and Bob; Bob passed away a few years ago. My mum has a twin brother, David, who is married to Beth and they have two boys, Jasper and Hunter. Beth is

Adam's mother and his father is Marcus. Right. Now for the other side. Dad's parents are Grace and Malcolm, and he has a younger brother called Ben. He is married to Charlie, who is a doctor, and they have two kids—Oliver and Owen—and they are twins. My granddad's twin sister is Lilith, who died last year…and Geoff, who was my guardian, is their younger sibling. Does that make it clear?"

"As mud," Matt said, chuckling. "Let me get this right. Marcus, who was giving you all the trouble back then—his son is Adam, your ex, and he is also the son of your aunt?"

"So, we're going there." She rolled her eyes. "Yes, he is the son of my aunt by marriage and half-brother to my cousins, but as there were no real blood ties, it would have been fine."

"I didn't realize New Zealand could be so incestuous. I thought that honour had always been held by your neighbours in Tasmania." He laughed.

"Not funny—at all," she told him straight-faced with a raised eyebrow.

The weather cleared and they carried on their way, making it back to the camp as the sun broke through the clouds, sending them scudding away to the horizon. On the way back, they did discuss talking to the others about seeing Richard again, and they agreed that forewarned was forearmed.

Claire sought out Addy first and was greatly surprised to find that Adam was with her. They were both in the trench, and Adam was on his hands and knees scraping away at the mud and dirt. She stood for a moment and watched them as Addy tried to teach him the correct way to hold the trowel so he didn't scrape his knuckles.

"Oh, you do prefer redheads," Claire said, laughing. "I don't know how you did it, Addy. I wasted so much time and breath talking to Adam about archaeology, and he never took an interest."

"It's my natural charm, Claire, sweetie," Addy replied with a flick of her hair and a beaming smile. Claire could tell she liked Adam. She just hoped that Adam wouldn't hurt her. "What's up? I thought you and Matt would be gone all day?" Addy asked, grabbing a water bottle.

"We had some company on our date that wasn't really wanted," she said quietly so only Addy and Adam would hear. "Matt and I thought we should get you all together and talk about it. He's just going to go talk to Gerry now."

"So, Uncle Gerry knows about your..." Addy started and looked at Adam.

"It's all right. I know about Claire's Talents and she knows about mine. I take it you also have them?" He looked at her from his kneeling position in the trench.

"Yes, I have Stealth and Music. What about you?"

"Charm and Mind Touch," he told her.

"Another two majors! My God, what crossbreeding went on down in the colonies?" she laughed.

That night Claire and Adam joined Matt and Addy's family after dinner in Gerry's site tent. Matt brought Robbie and Fiona up to speed on the fact that both Claire and Adam had Talents and that there had been problems in the past. He then asked Claire to fully tell them what those problems had been. Claire cleared her throat and told them all, with the help of Adam giving his side.

After the telling, Claire then informed them of the events since the day she visited Killin with Maggie. Of how she saw Richard and had presumed he was the one who drove them off the road. How she had seen Richard again that day at the falls and of being followed.

"There's more than just Richard," Matt finished. "We think there could be as many as three working together."

Gerry, Robbie, and Fiona looked stunned. Several times Gerry went to say something and then just shut his mouth again.

"The reason some guy is coming after you, is because you made his dad a bit nicer to him?" Robbie asked, breaking the silence.

"That and the fact he thinks we are supposed to be together," Claire told him. "His mother and father both fed him that lie to get him to work with them. I don't know what else they told him, but that is what he believes."

"And he is your half-brother, Adam?" Robbie asked.

"Yes. Marcus is our father," the younger man confirmed.

"Why tell us then?" Gerry finally asked Claire.

"Matt and I thought you should know. With him already trying something, we thought to let you know in case he tries anything else," Claire said.

"I really don't know what this has to do with us. Isn't it just a case of you going home and dealing with it there?" Fiona piped up.

"No. They can't do that, sweetheart. Something like this has to be dealt with together. Claire has come to us with a problem, and we have an obligation of The People to help," Robbie told his wife gently. "There's one thing I don't understand: you said that you and your aunt gave this Jack a suggestion to make him think he had lost his Ability. If he has no Ability, then he can't really be a problem."

"He has in his employ some of the same people that Dad had. Some of those were men with Talents, including Mind Touch. If they had managed to find a way to get around Lilith's suggestion, they might have. I know he was trying to get Dad back to the way he was before this all started," Adam told him.

"It's possible," Gerry said, nodding. "If you only gave him a suggestion and didn't actually damage the Ability, then he could regain it."

The discussion went on for a while and Claire began to remember all the talks many years ago between her family of a course of action, and it felt very familiar. In the end, nothing was really decided, except Robbie agreed to go talk to his mother, Rowena.

When they broke for the night, Claire overheard a conversation between Robbie and Gerry that she wished she hadn't.

"Do you want me to pass a message on to Leana?" Robbie asked his brother-in-law quietly.

"I'll only speak with her when she learns to forgive herself. There's nothing I can do or say until she does. I still love her, Robbie. I won't give up hope, but it is in her hands now."

Robbie placed a supportive hand on Gerry's shoulder. "I'll have a word with her. It's been too long."

Addy, meanwhile, was having an argument with her mother, and she finally exploded angrily. "Will you please stop trying to run my life for me? I will decide who and when, Mother." She stormed off, and Claire could see Adam watching Addy leave.

"Go after her," Claire told him quietly with a smile. Adam wasted no time at all in following Addy.

As everyone was leaving the tent, Nick walked in looking very sheepish and went to Robbie.

"I was wondering if I could have a few weeks off and stay on the dig. I would love the chance to really get stuck into some good archaeology," he asked.

"Oh, aye, I bet you would. You can have all the time in world, Nick. If it were up to me, you would be on your bike and pissing off to whatever hole you crawled out of in the first place, ya backstabbing little bastard. Did you really think I didn't know what you were up to? Well, it won't last long. Just be warned. You have only got the job because they're looking at scrapping the show completely, and I decided I wanted to go out on top. Enjoy it while it lasts, laddie." Robbie brushed past him and joined his wife as they left.

Nick stood stunned like a rabbit caught in headlights until he realised where he was and who was staring at him. He mumbled something about good night and left the tent.

"You're not going to take him on, are you?" Matt asked his father.

"Yep, and give him all the shite jobs he's missed out on the journey to become a real field archaeologist." He laughed almost evilly. "Robbie warned me that he might do this. Now go have fun. I've got work to do." He waved them out of the tent and sat at his desk.

Chapter Ten

For the next few weeks, Claire confined herself to the camp, the forest, and the excavation site. But to her, there wasn't a feeling of being trapped. She saw it as an opportunity to get some real work done. This excavation was proving to be a very big deal, with more trenches opening and a great deal of significant finds being made. Soon tourists and locals alike were flocking to the site to have a look at the mounting finds.

Gerry took no time at all in putting Nick's semi-fame to use by having him deal with the crowds that were building. Claire admired the way he took it in stride and his easy manner with them, but she still did not like the man. He always seemed to be on the fringes of their conversations, even though Matt had made it clear to him that there was no going back after the way Nick had behaved towards her.

Another surprise was that of Adam. Having visited the site and been reassured his money had been well spent, he asked if he could hang around a bit and learn some more. Gerry had agreed, solely because it was a request from his financial backer, but he was warming to him. Adam's main reason for staying—Claire had found out by directly interrogating him—was that he was interested in Addy.

Robbie and Fiona stopped by on their way back to London after their visit with Gran and Leana. Fiona surprised her daughter by actually taking an interest in her work in the trench, and a thawing in their relationship seemed to have begun on both sides. Also—Claire noticed—her friend's mother had changed her attitude to Claire herself, and she wondered whether that was a result of something that happened at Gran's, or the fact that Adam was now paying attention to her daughter.

Later, after they had left, Claire was heading to her tent when she spotted a very distraught Gerry being comforted by Matt. The father and son were sitting close together, and she remembered the conversation between Gerry and his brother-in-law. Her heart broke for the family, and she wished there was something she could do to help. Later that day, Matt confided in her that Leana was getting worse.

Matt and Claire's relationship grew in the confines of those weeks. He taught her how to draw at least competent sketches for the dig. Once again, she was a quick study and picked it up easily. Having a teacher who gave his full attention to her helped as well. He finally showed her his other drawings, including the one Addy had teased him about. Claire slipped it out of his pad and rolled it up carefully, telling him she wanted it for herself.

By the end of the two weeks, the trench Claire had opened now showed the uncovered broch fully. It was bigger than the round house that was originally found further down the hill, and the other three smaller ones that now joined it. They had the makings of a small village, and Gerry estimated that it was Iron Age, possibly late Roman. The evidence that a community had been living on the side of the hill for some time was mounting, and it sparked everyone's enthusiasm.

Claire was enjoying a day off, but still, she couldn't keep away from the site. Wandering around handing out water bottles and snacks to those who were still working, Claire joined in with the easy banter that came from working with great people. She stopped under the shade of a tree to watch the newest batch of tourists who had made the climb up the hill. By now she could almost recite the words Nick would tell them. It did not stray much from the normal patter—only if there happened to be a pretty girl or two in the group.

Once the talk was over, they would be led to stand near the trenches where the group was allowed to take photos and ask more questions. Claire was just about to move off when she saw something that caught her eye. Nick didn't follow them like he usually did but was talking animatedly with a man dressed in black, a grey baseball cap pulled down over his face. There was something so familiar about him, but it wouldn't come to mind. The man in black passed something to Nick, who put it into his back pocket as the stranger walked away.

Her curiosity was piqued, but she had no time to find anyone to let them know what she had witnessed. Claire stepped behind the tree and made sure she was not being watched. Slowly she disappeared and then shrank herself. Taking off from the ground, she hastened away to follow the man in black and caught up with him in no time. She studied him closer while still keeping her distance. He was tall with dark hair. She managed to see that his eyes were brown before hiding them behind dark sunglasses, and he had a clean-shaven face. Again, there was a familiarity with him—she was sure she had seen him somewhere before but did not have the time to use her Recall to pinpoint the memory.

Down at the bottom of the hill, cars were parked all alongside the narrow road. This mystery man made his way to a dark blue car and looked around before opening the door. Just before he closed it behind him, Claire snuck in and hid herself in the back seat. He started the car and pulled out his phone.

"It's Tony. I saw him. He's asking for more money," he said into it. His voice had a distinctive New Zealand accent to it.

Claire became mad as she realised this man was working for Richard and that Nick was passing them information. Before she knew it, the car was moving and there was no escape. She maintained her disguise for the whole of the drive and was surprised at how soon he was turning into a gate. She recognised the area, as she and Matt had passed it on their date only a few weeks before.

The car stopped outside a very new-looking cottage, and she flew out immediately once the door was opened. *Now that I'm here, I might as well find out some more*, she thought to herself and followed him to the door. The man she now knew as Tony knocked loudly at the yellow-painted door and waited until it opened. Standing inside the doorway was Richard, still as big as she remembered and his scar an ugly reminder marring his features. Inside, the cottage was a mess, with dirty dishes and food scraps everywhere.

"You could have cleaned up a bit while I was out. This place is a pig sty. No wonder your wife left you," Tony complained as he stepped inside.

"If you don't like it, then you can do one of two things: clean or get out. I'll leave it up to you. Now what did the Irish prick have to say?" Richard sat heavily down onto a chair and watched as Tony started to clean up.

"It was just the usual. Adam is getting on nicely with that redhead, Adaira, and Claire and her new bit are all lovey dovey. But, he still can't find out what all the meetings are about. They keep fobbing him off, saying that it was just a family matter." Claire was pleased that he knew nothing and was just wondering whether Richard had imparted any knowledge of the Talents to this other man when Tony spoke again. "Pity Nick hasn't got a Talent. He could get in and get more info."

"Just be pleased he doesn't. They are all crazy. Look at Jack—used to be a good kid, now more loony toons than Marcus was," Richard told him.

"Don't know about that...never met him before the village incident."

"Well, look at what that other bugger did to my face." He pointed to the scar that ran down the side of his head.

Tony stopped mid-stride and stared hard at Richard. "Are you drunk again? Because you only ever mention that when you are. I thought I got rid of all the bottles?"

"You did. And I am not drunk. I haven't had a drink in over a week, ya bastard."

"Got the shakes still?" he threw at Richard over his shoulder.

"Listen here, Tony. You may be getting orders directly from Jack, but I am still in charge on this one."

"You can't be relied on when you have drink in you, Rick. Look at the bungle the other week. We had her in our sights and then you lost them." He took off his cap and threw it on the table, raking his fingers through his dark, wavy hair.

"That wasn't my fault. I couldn't see in that downpour. The blasted weather in this country is so bloody impossible to read. If I had known it was coming, I would have stayed closer to them."

They had been followed after they left Kenmore that day. It was just as well that Matt had pulled up on the side of the road until the rain passed. She thanked her lucky stars.

"Jack never said what we were to do with her when we do finally get her," Tony said.

"He just wants to know. I think he plans to come over at some point, but Adam still being here is making it difficult for him to leave. Apparently, the old man is a bit unreliable these days. Are those other two still in place?"

"Yes, they are. Stephen should be taking over for George soon."

"Good. They better come up with something more useful than the crap the Irishman is coming up with." Claire could quite plainly see his hands shaking, and he clasped them together trying to get them under control. She wondered how far into detox he had gone and knew it could be quite bad. She stored that piece of information away for later.

Feeling like she had overstayed her welcome, she looked for an escape and found none. It was a great relief when Tony opened the window over the kitchen bench to get fresh air into the fetid room. Just as she was about to leave, she turned and looked at him again closely. With a shock, she remembered where she had seen him as a smiling face on a plane came to her.

Once out into the wonderful fresh air, Claire looked around her. She headed down the road the way they had come and stopped when she got to an intersection. Hiding behind a tree, she came back to full size, pulled out her phone, and made a call to Matt.

"Hi, it's me," Claire said when he answered.

"Where are you? I've been looking everywhere," he replied.

"I had to follow someone…I'll tell you about it later. Can you come pick me up?" Claire quickly relayed to him her location.

"Stay where you are and keep out of sight. I'll be there soon." Matt hung up and Claire was left with a screen that went black.

The minutes seem to drag by as Claire waited by the side of the road. When he turned up, she jumped into the Rover and immediately went invisible. On the way back, she told him what was said in the cottage and what she had seen. Matt remained quiet all the way, and when she finally finished talking, she noticed that he was looking upset.

"Sorry. I didn't have time to tell you what was happening. I had to act." Matt still did not say a word, and Claire carried on. "So, you're not going to talk to me?"

"I don't trust myself to at the moment, Claire," he said tightly, and they drove back in silence.

Matt turned the car off and sat for a moment when they arrived back before opening his door and fumbling with the keys. This gave Claire enough time to slip out of the car. When she did, she gently placed a kiss on his cheek and whispered *Thank you* to him. He turned his head and slammed the door, then stalked off towards his own tent. Claire watched him go, her heart sinking.

Claire went to her tent and stood in the middle of it, her mind tripping over itself with ways of how to make it right with Matt. She was breathing heavily and ignored the hunger pains that were starting to bite in her stomach. Her head came up suddenly when she heard her name called from outside.

"Where have you been?" Addy asked as she came out of her tent.

"I've been asleep," Claire lied.

"Yeah, right. I checked only a little while ago and there was no answer."

"I'm a sound sleeper. What did you want me for?" she asked.

"Adam wanted to take me to the pub, and I said I would if my favourite cousin and his new girlfriend could join us."

"I don't know, Addy. I think I've upset Matt. You guys go and have a good time. We'll catch up later and you can tell me all about it," Claire replied, looking anywhere except at Addy.

"What's happened?" Addy asked quietly.

"Nothing, really. Now go. Don't keep him waiting. He doesn't like it." She smiled encouragingly.

"You sure?" Claire nodded, now not trusting her own voice to not give away how she was feeling. "Okay. I'll come find you when we get back and we can talk then." Addy smiled at Claire and walked to her tent.

Claire searched around her, feeling at a loss. She felt she should just throw herself into work, but the thought of grubbing around in the dirt didn't appeal at that moment. It wouldn't be the same if Addy and Matt weren't there. She so desperately wanted to go talk to Matt, but he had made it clear he was angry with her and didn't want her around. Adam would understand, but he was heading out with Addy, and Claire felt she didn't know Gerry well enough to talk to about what had happened. With a loud growl, her stomach once more told her to get food—now—but her heart and mind were not convinced. She grabbed the sketch pad Matt had given her from her tent and walked out of camp.

Up the hill she went, past the dig sites, until she commanded a magnificent view of the hillside below, with the tents all lined up, the last stragglers leaving the dig sites for the evening, appearing so small as they moved around. She picked out Addy's flaming red hair walking beside the tall, lanky frame of Adam and leaving in his car. She tried to pick out other people and had some success with Maggie and Nick. Matt, she did not see at all.

Taking a deep breath, she sank to the ground and sat cross-legged, pulling her pad onto her lap. The pencil she twirled in her fingers until she found something to sketch. Her hand flew across the page, shading and outlining, building the picture up as she went, pouring her heart and soul into it. When she finished, she looked at her work. It was not a picture of the landscape before her, but those piercing blue eyes that gave her so much pleasure to look at.

They were sad eyes, looking back at her with a tear just about to fall from the lower lashes. In the reflection of the teardrop, she had drawn her own image, looking equally sad. A real drop fell onto the page to join its counterpart, and she dashed at her face in anger at herself. The tears poured from her eyes and ran down her cheeks, and Claire collapsed over the drawing.

"Oh dear. Don't you like what you drew?" a rough voice said cruelly from behind.

Claire quickly twisted around and had a hard job recognizing the body that the voice belonged to, as it was silhouetted against the sky. He came closer, the scar running down his face making her jump as she tried to scramble to her feet. The pad dropped to the grass, now forgotten, the pages blowing in the wind.

"Hello, Claire. Remember me?" Richard asked. Resting against his shoulder was a rather substantial dead branch, which he saw her eyes flicking towards. "Now I never got to thank you or your uncle for giving me such a distinctive look." Lifting it off his shoulder, he cradled it carefully in his hands.

"You know you won't even be able to land a blow on me, don't you, Richard? You know what I can do," she said, trying to warn him.

"But I have had fun making you jump. I could have laid you out just now and you would never have seen it coming." He paused as he stepped closer. "Tell me, why does Jack want you so badly?"

"He hasn't told you?" She took a wary step back down the hill, her foot trying to get some even ground.

A flash flew by her, whipping her hair up at the same time. Claire flinched automatically at the sudden movement and fell backwards, rolling down the hill a little. Righting herself, she turned back to Richard only to see him falling down to the ground and tumbling towards her. Matt, his face red and set with anger, was landing beside Richard, kicking him hard.

"Matt, no!" Claire yelled, and he looked up. The expression he wore frightened her. "No, Matt. Otherwise you will be just like them."

Matt stopped and stood over Richard, looking from one to the other. "He was going to hurt you," he said, panting hard.

"No. He knew he wouldn't have been able to get hold of me." She walked slowly up to Matt, laying a calm, and restraining hand on his arm. "I think he was looking for information."

"We should take him down and—"

Richard's hand shot out and grabbed Claire's leg, and within a millisecond, she had reacted. To Matt's eyes she was there then she was not, gone into the ether, taking Richard with her.

Claire grasped hold of Richard and flew him up into the air, shrinking him as they went, spinning in a spiral to confuse him, then diving back down to the ground just as fast. She could feel him tremble under her touch and hear him scream near her ear. Back up, she took him on a terrifying ride—like a roller coaster out of control, up and down, around, and about, until she let go.

Richard instantly reappeared and regrew nearer the ground than he thought he was, but still screaming. He landed with a thud and lay there, his face echoing the terror he felt and his body shaking all over. Claire came to rest beside him and released her energy to bring herself back to full size once more. Leaning down, she turned his face to her and looked him dead in his wide and wild eyes, breathing hard.

"You go back to Jack and tell him that before he goes after anyone else I love, he had better come and see me first. Do you understand?"

He nodded with short, sharp movements. Still staring at her, his eyes bulged out of their sockets with fright, and he shook like a leaf. Matt helped him to his feet and stood beside Claire.

"Now you have seen what I can do, but that is not the half of it. You and your men better pack up and get out tonight. Because if I see you around here or anyone else who even looks like they may have anything to do with you, I will hunt you down and this will seem like a day out at the fun park." She pushed him to make him start moving.

The first steps were stumbling ones as he kept a wary eye on Claire, his face as pale as a piece of paper and his body beginning to spasm in terror. When he was certain they were not coming after him, he turned and fled back up the hill, running at full tilt until he reached the trees at the crest.

Claire watched him leave, her breathing heavy and laboured as she turned to head back down. Matt was coming towards her with her sketch pad in his hand, and he was smiling. The sight gladdened her heart, and she returned it with one of her own. Suddenly her footsteps faltered and came to a stop. Her vision blurred and then wavered. Claire swayed where she stood and collapsed to the ground in a heap. She heard Matt calling her name before the blackness overtook her and plunged her down into depths of her mind she didn't know were there.

The darkness was all-encompassing. There was no ground or sky above. There was no feeling of floating or standing. Just nothing. Claire could not even tell if she was turning her head to see if there was any change in her surroundings. She just was. Time had no meaning and she had no means to measure it, even if she could remember how. Fear gripped her and she tried to go into herself but found that way was blocked.

Outside in the world that surrounded Claire, Matt gathered her up in his arms and carried her down the hill. Her sketch pad lay on the ground, forgotten and at the mercy of the weather. His stumbling steps under her weight very nearly tripped him up, making him slow down and take more care. Reaching the dig site, he saw that there was no one around, and Claire was still unconscious. He realised that everyone would be at dinner by now in the cookhouse and made his way to his own tent.

He dragged her under the canvas and laid her down on his bed, then knelt back and took a few deep breaths as he watched her. Her breathing was even. She still had colour in her cheeks, but instinctively he knew something was wrong. Claire was not there—he did not know how or even why he felt it, but he was certain that he could not help her.

Getting to his feet and crouching down, he left the tent with a quick backwards glance at Claire, then took off at a run. The site director's tent was his first stop, but it was empty. He looked around, feeling panic rising up inside. His father's tent—empty again, and then he looked at the only other place he could be, the cookhouse.

Calming his breathing and making himself walk at a sedate pace, he hoped that when he arrived, he would have his body under control once more. As he entered, friends called out in greeting, inviting him to join them or wanting to catch up with a beer later. Matt acknowledged them with a wave or a small smile but made a beeline for his father.

"Dad, I was wondering if I could have a word," he urged quietly when he reached his side.

"Later, Son. Come and see me later. I'm currently enjoying the wonderful delights of this perfectly cooked steak." Gerry carved a piece off and placed it in his mouth.

"I'm sorry, Dad, but this can't wait. It really is very important."

"Nothing but a very serious emergency could drag me away from my meal tonight." He took another bite and then looked up at his son. The expression on Gerry's face changed as he took in Matt's. "All right, but it better be an emergency." He placed his knife and fork onto the plate in front of him and then followed Matt out the door.

Back in the tent, Claire had not moved. Anyone glancing in would just suppose she was sleeping. And that is exactly what Gerry thought when he saw her, but then he stopped before he spoke. He knelt at her side and placed a hand on each temple and entered her mind.

Immediately Gerry found himself under attack. First white and then black swirled around him, buffeting him this way and that. He fought to get under control, to find the metaphorical feet under him, and held firm against the onslaught. Pushing back against these images, he tried to calm the environment, believing that this was Claire.

"Claire, calm down. Tell me what's wrong. How can I help you?" He sent out the message through her mind, trying to get through to her.

"Where is she?" a loud, deep rumbling voice answered him back, taking him by surprise. The force of the thought pushed him over, and he broke the link with her mind as he fell.

"Dad!" Matt called out and helped him back up.

"I'm all right. I'm fine." Gerry shooed Matt away as he got back up and then knelt, looking down at her. "That was strange and unexpected."

"What was? What's happened to her?" Matt demanded, his voice rising.

"Shh, let me think." He pondered the situation, but no matter which way he thought about it, the only way he was going to find out was by diving back in. Again, Gerry linked his mind with hers, and again he found himself immediately under attack.

"Where is she? Where is Claire?" the voice demanded of Gerry as the dark smoke flew about him. Gerry found that his feet were bound by a white misty substance, and he could not move against their onslaught.

"I don't know. That's why I'm here. Who are you?" Gerry asked.

"That is not for you to know. We can't find her—she's gone." There was pain in the male voice, an agony and longing that Gerry understood very well.

"I'm here to find her. We are concerned about Claire. Let me help you." He tried to make his words as gentle as possible.

"Who are you?" the black smoke demanded.

"My name is Gerry." He knew giving up his name was giving up part of his power. "I'm Claire's boss, I suppose you could say. I am one of The People."

"People? Who are The People?" There was agitation and confusion mixed together.

"You call it The Community. We are one and the same. We have the same lineage somewhere in history," Gerry told the entity.

"You have Talent?"

"Aye, that is what Claire calls it. We call it Ability."

"Claire knows you have this?" the entity demanded.

"Aye, she does. We have talked about it." He could feel the binding of his feet loosen and then retreat while the black became an undulating column before him.

"How can you help find her?" it demanded of him.

"I don't know, but I will try. First, I have given you my name. I need to know yours." He waited. The air was electric, and there seemed to be some sort of communication between the white and black.

"We are John and Jessica." It gave him their names, and as it did, a figure started to form in the black column.

"It is very nice to meet you, John and Jessica. My son is very concerned for Claire, and he wants to help her. But I have no idea what has happened to her today. Can you help us with that?"

"We have some awareness of the outside. But we are here in the subconscious, and only a few pieces get to us."

"I was going to ask how you came to be, but that can wait for another time. What pieces have you got from today?" Gerry asked, still confused as to what was going on inside Claire's head.

The more the entity named John talked, the clearer he became until he was fully formed. John stood before him: a man in his forties with blue eyes, dressed in dark clothing and anguish across his features.

"Stress, anger, hurt, sadness. That is what has filtered to us." John's hands were balled into fists at his sides, the knuckles white.

"Feelings. All right, it's a start. Was there anything else?"

"Her Talent…she has used a lot of it in a short time." The white mist crept up John, and Gerry surmised that if John was the black, then Jessica was the white.

"We have no name for what Claire is here in Scotland. We have never seen her like before, only myths and legends. I cannot believe the amount of energy she needs to expend to use her Abilities. I need to think about it for a moment. I will be back and try to help her find her way." John nodded to him in acknowledgement. Gerry released his hold on Claire's mind and sat back on his heels, expelling his breath. "What has happened to Claire today?" He looked over to his son, who was sitting beside Claire's inert body holding her hand.

"She saw someone and followed him. She hid, and he led her to Richard. She overheard some things and then got out of there and called me. I wasn't really listening. I was angry with her for not coming to me first, for going off like that where something could have happened to her. Then just now Richard found her on the hill. She wouldn't have been up there, Dad, if it wasn't for me."

"You can play the blame game later, lad. What happened when Richard confronted her?"

"I attacked first, pulling him up off the ground and then dropping him. We thought he was out to it, but he grabbed her leg and it happened so fast. I don't know what she did to him, but they disappeared and then he fell from the air and was as white as a sheet. She yelled at him, warning him off. He ran away and then she was there smiling at me. Until she just dropped," he finished his tale.

"That's something to work with. She may have just exhausted herself today using the Abilities so much. But this is new to me. I could really use your Gran's experience with this one." He fumbled with his phone and punched in the number.

While Gerry waited for her to answer, Matt could hear Addy outside and he went looking for her. She took one look at him and left Adam's side.

"What's happened. Who's hurt?" his cousin demanded.

"It's Claire, we don't—" He fell silent as Addy wrapped him up in her arms.

Adam looked past the cousins and saw Claire lying in Matt's tent. "What happened to her?"

"We're not sure yet, Adam," Gerry said, putting his phone away and exiting the tent. "We think it's exhaustion. She has had a rather busy afternoon."

"She told me that you two had an argument," Addy said to Matt.

"It was all my fault. I got angry with her and she went off on her own." He started to tell her the tale, but Gerry placed a caring hand on his arm.

"We can talk about the why later…what we need now is to figure out how to bring her back. Adam, you're used to Dream Messaging with Claire—have you ever come across anything unusual when you have?"

"You mean the mist and smoke?" Adam answered with a question of his own.

"Yes. It is very unusual. I have never come across it before."

"Claire once tried to explain it to me. She told me that her parents had somehow placed a piece or a sense of themselves in her mind before they died."

"That would explain the reactions I've been getting from them. It's been an experience, that's for sure. They are strong, too," he told them, still musing on the problem.

"I've only been affected by the black smoke."

"John appeared to me in full form. He only appears as smoke for you?"

"I don't mean to interrupt, but can we get back to fixing Claire?" Addy asked.

"Sorry. But I really have no idea what to do." He cast a look towards the cookhouse as people started to emerge. "I think we'd better not talk about it out here in the open. Matt, let's move her to my tent—there's a bit more privacy there."

Between them, Adam and Matt lifted Claire and carefully moved her to Gerry's tent. Gerry then pushed his things aside and off his own stretcher, smoothing out the crumpled bedding. They laid her down gently and Matt placed her arms at her sides.

The small group sat back and watched Claire breathe. Her stillness was unnerving. Addy sat by her head, simply stroking her hair.

"When did she get so thin?" she asked while staring at the hollows that had formed in Claire's cheeks.

Matt lifted the hand he was holding and pushed Claire's sleeve up. The arm that greeted him was so thin, it was almost all bone.

"What's happened to her?" He looked pleadingly at his father.

"When was the last time she ate a decent meal?" Adam asked as he stared at Claire.

"I saw her eat lunch. I was sitting opposite her," Addy told him.

"Has she used her Talents?" Adam now looked to Matt.

"Yeah…a couple of times today—the last one was pretty intense."

"This time I definitely remember what she told me. Her body is taking all its reserves to replace the energy she needs when using more than one Talent. She usually eats like a horse after. You said a couple of times—did she eat after the first one?"

"I don't know—that's when I was angry. I sort of stormed away from her," Matt replied, a little ashamed at his actions.

"We need to get some food into her," Adam declared.

"But she's unconscious…getting her to eat is going to be challenging!" Addy spoke the obvious.

Gerry quietly reflected on the information he'd received from Gran. He shooed Addy out of the way and reconnected with Claire. John and Jess were there waiting for him.

"We think it's a matter of exhaustion and lack of food. Claire is currently wasting away, so we need to act fast to stop her body from consuming itself. But I can't do this on my own. With me at the moment is someone who also has Mind Touch. He has Dream Messaged with Claire before and can add his Ability to mine to reach through to her."

"You mean Adam?" John asked darkly.

"Aye. I do."

"We don't like him. He hurt our daughter."

"They have since made their peace. I'm sure he will lend his energy to help her. But we will also need any energy you may have to spare," Gerry told them.

"I can lend mine, but Jess is already weak, and I won't allow you to access hers," John replied heavily.

"I wouldn't dream of it. Let me go talk to Adam."

Gerry returned and outlined his plan with Adam, making sure he understood all the nuances and pitfalls that came with the plan. And without hesitation, he agreed to do it. Just as they were preparing to join forces, Matt stopped them.

"I have a few concerns…" he stated while looking directly at Adam.

"You're going to have to trust me, Matt," Adam said. "I'm not looking to change anything in her mind, and I don't think her father would allow me to, anyway. We don't have much time." He looked at the man who had replaced him in Claire's affections and realised the jealousy he had felt a few weeks before was gone. And he accepted that Claire wasn't his anymore.

"Okay, go ahead." Matt picked up Claire's skeletal hand once more and watched his father and Adam get to work.

Together, they entered her mind and were greeted by John. It was the first time that Adam had met Claire's father and he could see the pain of loss etched on his face—which caught at Adam's heart.

"I need to go further past the subconscious. The way I understand it, there's a primeval part of our brain we never use. I believe that her life force has retreated into there in order to save herself. The body is consuming itself at a great rate and we need to get her to eat to stop it."

"What is it that you want me to do?" John asked.

"We need to join our energies together. Once we have that connection, I can relay where we need to go."

John nodded and stepped closer to them. They then linked hands and stood in a triangle as the white mist that was Jess curled itself around and up John. He looked down and forcefully told his wife to stay away. Jess retreated beyond their circle and swirled in agitation and frustration.

With their minds linked as well as their hands, the image was sent, and they searched. It felt elusive—rather hard to find as if it was hiding from them, slipping past them while they looked in a different area. They spread their search out wider and wider until John found it and brought the other two together in preparation of entering this dark space.

Each time one of the three men neared the undulating dark sphere, there was a feeling of a growl—a warning to stay away. Gerry could sense Adam's uncertainty and fear and encouraged him to stay strong. Together they pushed against the exterior of the sphere. It moved against them, pushing back and almost overcoming the trio. But with a renewed determination, they pushed on.

On the outside, Addy and Matt watched the two men as their faces contorted and sweat stood out on their foreheads. The effort they were putting into saving Claire was evident and Matt felt helpless and afraid. Addy stood and went to leave.

"Where are you going?" Matt asked her.

"We're going to need food for when she wakes, since not one of you men has even thought of that!"

Inside the sphere, it was dark, and Gerry warned them to not let go of each other. The primal feelings were assaulting them, trying to break them apart and expel the intruders. The hold on each other was strong, and they prevailed against the darkness.

Gerry conveyed to John to send out a searching thought to Claire. Being her father, he thought that John would have the biggest connection to his daughter. Adam added his call to John's, hoping that there was still a bond of some sort with his childhood sweetheart. The calls went out and they waited and waited, but there was nothing.

"Try again," Gerry ordered while adding his own. He wasn't sure whether the others felt the constricting of the blackness—that horrible feeling as if things were closing in on them.

The strength of their call entered the darkness and pierced it as they cried out, hoping that Claire would hear them and latch on to it. Then she was there—floating in a fetal position, drawn in on herself. Her hair splayed out like it was floating in water. They manoeuvred their connection to encompass her body, forming a protective bond with their thoughts to bring her out. Passing through the barrier was going to be the next challenge and with great effort, they thought of light—each thinking of someone who anchored them to the outside world.

To John, it was the thought of Jess waiting for them in the subconscious. To Adam, his mind found Addy with her bright red hair, which surprised him. And for Gerry, his wife of so many years—the broken and damaged Leana—the mother of his children, both living and dead.

The pull of their anchors helped them move through the barrier and back. All three men were grateful to leave the place. It pulsed in front of them, swelling almost to try and draw them back inside and then shrinking back in shuddering fear.

Keeping hold of each other and making sure Claire was still between them, they moved back to the subconscious and back to the enveloping white mist. As soon as they appeared, they gently placed Claire on the metaphorical ground and Jess covered her daughter.

"My turn." The words were faint, but all were heard and understood.

Standing guard and waiting was not something any of them were used to. The time it took for Jess to coerce Claire back to herself seemed to stretch on and on. Gerry hoped that Matt wasn't being too frantic on the outside while he was waiting. He liked Claire and thought she was good for his son. These thoughts brought into mind John, and he studied the man, wondering how they'd managed to imprint themselves onto Claire. It was a question that could wait, he told himself.

Movement under the mist shroud caught their attention. Claire's blond hair moved through it all as she sat up. She looked at her hands first and felt her face while relief flooded through her as she made to stand but stumbled. She felt weak and hungry.

"Claire, my beautiful daughter." The soft, misty voice rose up from the coils that still surrounded her.

John reached down and grasped her hands, carefully lifting her to her feet and holding her gently in his arms. She leaned into his embrace and smiled. "We thought we'd lost you," he said into her hair as he then kissed the top of her head.

"I was lost. I don't understand…how did you find me?" she asked into his shoulder.

"It wasn't just me. I had help." He didn't let her go fully, only relaxed his grip on her.

Claire looked around at the other two men: her ex-boyfriend and the father of her new one. "Thank you."

"You're welcome, Claire, but we have to bring you back properly. You need to replenish your energy and the only way to do that is to eat," Gerry told her.

Nodding slowly, Claire gave her father another hug and kiss on the cheek. The mist enfolded both of them and caressed her cheek.

"I love you two so much," Claire told them and then she let go.

Matt sat still for such a long time—merely concentrating on trying to feel and will Claire's presence to come back. There was no life force there at all, only an empty shell, and he felt frightened. Addy had returned with as much food as she could carry and was laying it out on the little table by the cot.

Like a tsunami, Matt felt the spark of life flow back into her body—wholly filling her up. The relief of knowing she was back hit him in the chest as a tear escaped him.

"Claire? Claire, can you hear me?" he called to her.

"What's happening?" Addy stepped up and knelt between Adam and Gerry.

"I think they succeeded. I can feel her…can't you?" he asked, not taking his eyes off Claire.

"No, I can't. Why haven't they come back to us?" She looked at the men on either side of her.

"I don't know, Addy."

Gerry's eyes flickered and then opened fully. He gently removed his hands from Claire's head and sat back again on his heels. He wiped the dripping sweat from his face on his sleeve and looked at his son.

"We've done it. Adam is guiding her to wakefulness," he told them.

Addy jumped up and then passed a bottle of water to her uncle and watched Adam, waiting for him to finish helping Claire. His eyes opened, taking in the sight of the first person that he saw, and he smiled at Addy.

Claire moved with a groan, and Matt helped her to sit up. Her limbs felt limp still under his touch, and he had to remind Addy to pass him something for her to eat and drink. The water bottle was empty within a few gulps, and she was looking for something more substantial. Her friend then passed her some fruit and brought the rest of the food over.

"I want Claire to stay in here for now, at least until she has regained her strength a little. I'll go find the heads of departments before they come looking for me. We were supposed to have a meeting tonight, but I think I will shout them a few drinks down the pub." Gerry looked at his watch and then at the group before him.

Matt looked up at his father in surprise and was about to say something, but with a look from his father he was quiet once more and turned his attention back to Claire.

"Is anyone going to tell me what happened?" Claire asked after she swallowed a mouthful of food.

"We'll talk later. Just eat," Adam put in before Matt. The two men looked at each other. Matt's face was set with a fixed stare towards Adam. "I'm sorry. It's habit, that's all."

Chapter Eleven

Rain started to pour down during the night, and the inclement weather continued throughout the next day. The safety officer deemed it too wet for work to continue, and the cookhouse was the meeting place for everyone to spend their unexpected spare time. All except for Claire and Matt, since Claire was still looking on the skinny side and explaining how she had lost so much weight in such a short time would be hard to do. So instead, they told everyone she had a cold. Matt and Addy took turns keeping her company in her own tent. After everyone had settled down the previous night, they had helped move her back.

The rain continued into the next day as well, and the next, and Gerry was starting to worry that they were running out of time. It was now the first week of August and they were due to start winding up the dig on the twenty-third.

On the fourth day of constant rain, most of the crew made their way to the pub for the afternoon. Claire was sitting in the cookhouse with her earphones plugged in and the music up loud. She was finally back to her normal, healthy-looking self. Addy and Adam were sitting at the table with her, but she was feeling like a spare wheel. Matt was busy with his father until he came to join them. He walked up behind her and lifted one of the earpieces out to hear what she was listening to.

"That's awful!" Matt laughed and sat down beside her.

"What's she listening to?" Adam piped up.

"I really couldn't tell. I had no idea that her taste in music was so, so…" He looked at Adam. "Tragic!"

"She's been inflicting that lot on me since we were little!" Adam said, laughing with Matt.

"You know, I think I preferred it when you two didn't get along," Claire said huffily before turning her back on Matt and plugging the earpiece back in.

The wet weather continued on and off for the rest of week. Gerry called a meeting after talking with Adam and department heads.

"All right, settle. We have no choice with this weather the way it is, so we're closing the site down. However, we'll be back next summer with the very kind help of Ryder Industries. If you are interested in coming back and being our slaves again, then please let us know how we can contact you. Now, we need to secure the site and pack everything away. When we're done, Adam has kindly told me he'll be getting you all a drink at the pub." A collective cheer went up at that point.

Gerry started to hand off to the department heads—so they could organise the workforce—when Claire's mobile started to ring. Quickly, she headed outside while apologising to Gerry and was soon joined by Adam on his own phone.

"Claire, thank God I got you…I wasn't sure of the time difference," Geoff said with panic clearly evident in his voice.

"What's wrong. Who's hurt?" she demanded.

"No one. Now listen. Jack has disappeared. The Watchers I had put on him lost sight of him yesterday. But I've done a bit of digging and found out that he has left the country." Claire remembered what she'd told Richard and looked at Adam. She could see he was getting the same information even barely hearing what Geoff was telling her. "Both David and I are on our way."

"You don't need to come, Uncle Geoff—it's not necessary." She could hear Adam ask about Beth.

"It's too late, Kid…we are already in Dubai and just about to board our flight to London. I'll call you when we get there. Stay safe."

Both Adam and Claire cursed them and then returned to the meeting, simply waiting for it to finish. After everyone was dismissed, there was a lot of talk and noise and they managed to tell Addy and Matt that they needed to talk now.

Claire sent out feelers to see if there was anyone around the camp who shouldn't be there, but she couldn't find anything out of the ordinary. She refined her search to Jack. Even though she'd only had a small amount of contact with him in recent years, she still had the shared experience while he was teaching her. The feeling she got back in return was—as far as she could ascertain—far away, but a lot closer than New Zealand.

"Claire, there you are!" Maggie called, interrupting the hurried conversation that was going on around her. "I was wondering what you were going to do with your unexpected spare time. We still have a few weeks left until we leave."

"I thought I might do a bit of sightseeing…be a tourist for a while," Claire said.

"Good. I have a bit of family in England, so thought I might take the opportunity to see them. I was hoping you might have plans."

"Actually, Maggie, I'm dragging Claire off to Glasgow to show her the sights there," Matt said, taking Claire's hand.

"If I were twenty years younger, young man…"

"You'd still be too old for me," he said with mock regret and a large grin.

"Cheeky. Have fun. Don't do anything I wouldn't do." She winked at Claire and gave a sideways look at Matt, then left them to it.

For the rest of that day and on into the next, they helped with the packing up of the equipment and tents and said goodbye to friends made on the dig. Exchanges of emails and other social media were made, along with promises to keep in contact. At the end of the day, all was done except for a few remaining tents. With the cooks and food having already packed up and gone, the only option for a hot meal that night was the local pub.

With a full stomach and good company, Claire was enjoying herself. She thought Addy and Adam made a good couple, and her eyes then rested on Matt. He and Adam had become fast friends after her little episode. In some ways, it had concerned her that Adam might be faking the friendship, but she had no doubt in her mind tonight.

With no concerns crossing her mind, the evening was a very enjoyable one and she was more relaxed than she'd been in weeks. That was, until Nick stopped at their table to make his farewells.

"Nicky, Nicky, Nicky...come sit, my boy!" Matt scooted over, pushing Claire into the corner of the booth they were sitting in. He patted the seat next to him. Claire knew that Matt wasn't drunk, but he suddenly appeared to be well on the way—with his accent becoming quite thick. "We've not talked too much lately." He put his arm around Nick's shoulder.

"That's all right, Matt," Nick said, looking slightly uncomfortable. "You've been a little preoccupied." He raised his glass to Claire.

"No, Nick. Ya cannae do that." He placed a hand on Nick's drinking arm and pushed it back to the table. "Ya dannae deserve to even be in the same room with Claire."

"I don't know what you're talking about, Matt!"

"Oh, I think ya do, Nicky. Ya see, we know what you did." He looked him dead in the eye and his voice dropped to a near whisper—while still holding onto Nick's arm and smiling. "Aye, you know what I'm talkin' about."

"I can explain…"

"That would be good, man, 'cause I'm havin' a very hard time working out why ya would do it." Matt moved his grip to Nick's shoulder and squeezed it as he grimaced in pain.

Adam leaned closer across the table. "I'm sure that Gerry and Robbie would be interested in your activities of late."

"What do you want to know?" Nick asked, looking worried.

"So glad we are on the same page. How about you start from the beginning?" Adam picked up his glass and took a long gulp.

"It was in here. These guys came up and asked if they could buy me a drink. We got to talking and after a few more, one asked me if I wanted to earn a bit more money. Well, with my student debt hanging heavy over me, I thought *Why not!* All he wanted me to do was to let them know who Claire was close to—when and who she talked to and where she went."

"So, you could'nae come to an old mate and tell what was asked of ya?" Matt asked him, again squeezing his shoulder and making him wince.

"Matt, what I told them was nothing they couldn't have seen with their own eyes. They had people posted around the camp site taking photos and watching."

"But that's not the point, my *friend*." He placed a heavy emphasis on the word. "You should've come to me, Nicky. I would've put ya straight, and…and you could've kept that money that they gave you. How much was it, by the way?"

"Five hundred."

"Five hundred. Is that all she's worth? Claire, did you hear that? You're worth only five hundy!" Matt turned back to Nick. "Right, this is what yer going to do, pal. *You're* gon' take all the spondoolies in your wallet, and *you* are going to put it in that wee collection tin on the bar there." For further emphasis, Matt poked Nick with his finger.

"But I need that for petrol for tomorrow and for—"

"That ain't my problem, pal." Again, he squeezed Nick's shoulder. "Are ya goin' to be a roaster 'bout this? 'Cause if you are, then I'm gonna have to take ya out the back and skelp ya, till ya cannae remember yer own ma." Then Matt indicated Adam across the table, who was giving Nick a death stare. "And after I'm done, I'm sure my friend over there would like a go, too." He gave Nick a shove off the bench they were sitting on. Nick was still holding on to his drink, and it sloshed all over the front of his shirt and jeans as he landed heavily on the floor.

Nick picked himself up and stood looking down at his once-friend. The murderous stare convinced him that Matt was not joking. He fished around in his pocket and pulled out a battered brown wallet. Opening it up to extract a wad of bills, he then turned to shove it in the collection tin. He turned back to the table and both Adam and Matt were standing up to face him, slow-clapping his action.

"Now, when I see ya next, we're not goin' to say a word about this… 'cause if I see *you*, it'll be me fists talkin'. Got it, pal?"

"Right, well…I'll be off, then," Nick said, backing away.

"Aye, you do that," Matt told him as they watched him leave the pub.

"Okay, two things," Claire said as the two men sat down, still laughing at their antics. "What is a roaster, a skelp, and spondoolies? And secondly, you can be very scary when you want to be."

"Thank you, sweetheart. I practiced hard on that. And as for those others, spondoolies is money, skelp is to hit, and a roaster—well, that's just, um, it means—"

"What it means, Claire, is that Nick was being a C word," Addy told her primly.

"Oh, okay. I understand. But wait…I didn't think you were that drunk! What's happened to all the slurred words?" Claire asked Matt.

"He wouldn't have taken me seriously if I didn't seem a wee tad rat-arsed," he said, lifting his drink in salute and affecting the same slurring he'd used on Nick. And for his efforts, Claire kissed him.

The next morning was the first in a week that it wasn't raining. The sun was shining gloriously down on the site and there were only a few clouds in the sky. The mood in camp was subdued as everyone finished packing up their own tents and made the final preparations to leave the place they had called home for the last two months. Not to mention the hangovers most were nursing from the previous night. When Claire had risen, she was pleased to see that the spot where Nick had pitched his tent was empty and there was no sign of his car.

"Give us a hand!" Matt called out as he crawled from Claire's tent, dragging her bag and bedding behind him. She picked up her sleeping bag and shook it out. "Don't play with it. We'll never get to Glasgow at this rate!" he said firmly.

"Sorry. I just don't want it to end. I've had the best time here and have met the most wonderful people." She smiled down at Matt as he stood and took her in his arms.

"It's only the beginning, Claire." His blue eyes twinkled at her

They were interrupted by Addy, who handed Claire a sketch pad. "Someone found this ages ago and handed it in—I thought it might be yours. Sorry, I forgot to give it to you," she explained.

Matt took the book from Claire's hands and flipped through it, fully stopping when he came to the eyes. She blushed with embarrassment and tried to take it back from him, but he resisted. After pulling the page from the book, he carefully rolled it up and went to put it in his own bag without a word.

Addy just raised her eyebrows to her friend at Matt's actions then called out to her cousin. "You better hurry up…the last one to your place buys dinner!"

Claire missed most of the trip to Glasgow as she was asleep, but Matt woke her as they entered the outskirts of the city. He worked his way through the busy streets until he came to a very narrow lane lined with pubs, bars, and eateries, all painted white. He had to slow for the pedestrians wandering across the road, looking for somewhere to sit and have a drink in the warm afternoon sun.

Rounding a bend, they saw a tall building to their left and the rear fence to a row of terrace houses on their right. Matt stopped at one near the end of the lane and tossed a small key ring to Claire.

"Care to open the gate?" he asked with a grin.

"What'd your last slave die of?"

"Too much attention." He smiled as she went to the double gate in front of the car. A rusty-looking lock hung from a hasp and staple latch and Claire had trouble getting it to open. It soon clicked and released. She pulled the padlock off the staple and pushed open the gates. The hinges protested loudly to all in the area that they desperately needed some attention.

Beyond the gate was a small, paved parking bay. The narrow yard further in was neatly trimmed and cared for, with a winding concrete path down the middle leading up to the white wood and glass door. Matt drove in and Claire closed the gates behind him and latched them again. Matt was waiting by the back of the car for her, their bags in his hands. He smiled at her and led the way up the garden path. At the door, he fumbled with his keys a bit before putting the house key into the lock.

"Welcome home," he greeted as he swung the door inwards and picked up the bags to head inside. She noticed that he didn't say *Welcome to my home*, and she felt pleased about that.

He then put the bags down and gave her a surprisingly short grand tour. The small terrace house had just two bedrooms and a bathroom upstairs, with a quaint living room and kitchen downstairs.

"Shall we go for a walk and get some food in?" Matt asked, peering into the fridge.

"Sounds like an idea," Claire said. She was reminded of a similar time from her past as a shiver went down her spine.

They left via the front door and Claire got her first chance to see the outside. A little path ran down to a wrought iron gate and the hedges that surrounded a small, neatly kept garden. Matt admitted that he gave one of the gardening crew from the university some money on the side once a month— merely to keep it all tidy.

They walked hand in hand to the local shop at a slow pace as Claire took everything in. All the old architecture and Glasgow's sounds and smells were so different to her, but some of it took her back to growing up in the city back home. By the time they returned to Matt's tiny, terraced house, Addy and Adam were sitting on the front doorstep. Addy looked disappointed when she saw the shopping bags, as that meant they'd lost the bet and she had to buy dinner.

She turned to Adam as Matt and Claire opened the gate and started up the path. "Told you we shouldn't have stopped to get wine!"

Once inside, Claire's phone began to ring. "Hello?" she answered, still laughing at Addy.

"Hey, Kid…we made it to Edinburgh. Where are you?" Geoff said while Claire thought he sounded tired.

"We're in Glasgow—at Matt's place. Want us to come get you?" she asked.

"No, David and I are booked in already at a hotel. We're both exhausted. We'll spend the night here and then hire a car to come find you."

"We'll pick them up," Adam told her.

"Did you hear that?" Claire asked Geoff.

"I did. That would be great. Better than us getting lost. I'll speak to you tomorrow. David said to say hi. See you." Geoff hung up before she could reply.

They then spent a pleasant evening in a nearby pub, having a very enjoyable meal on Addy and eventually making their way back to Matt's—where Addy opened a bottle of wine. Curled up on the couch, Claire sat next to Matt and slowly drifted off to sleep.

The noise of traffic woke her the next morning and she stretched out on the couch. Sitting up, she had to remind herself where she was and smiled when she saw Matt watching her from the dining table—holding a cup in his hands.

"Morning, sleepyhead." Matt grinned at her over the rim of his cup.

"Good morning. Are we the first up?" She joined him, leaning down to give him a hug.

"No, you're the last one up." He reached up and kissed her. "Adam and Addy have already left for Edinburgh."

"What time is it?"

"Late. We didn't want to wake you. You looked like you were having a lovely dream." She let him go when he stood up. "I wanted to make sure you were awake before I left." He walked to the kitchen and put his cup down.

"You're leaving? Where are you going?" she asked, following him in.

"Work, unfortunately…but I won't be long. Will you be all right here for a couple of hours?"

"I'll be fine. Go off and leave me—on my first day in a strange city!" she said dramatically while smiling.

"I'm not going far. That big building out the back is where I work. If you need me just call and I'll be back in a flash. There's a spare set of keys on the table if you want to go out and explore a bit." He wrapped his arms around her and gave her a long, lingering kiss.

"Watch it. I might just ring you every five minutes!" she told him when he pulled away.

"Don't tempt me," he said with a pained expression as they parted. With one last longing look at Claire, he grabbed his bag and left.

The narrow room around her was littered with piles of books and papers everywhere. Having been so used to her uncle's neat and tidy habits, the organised mess started to itch on her. But she resisted. This wasn't her house, and these were Matt's items. She knew how she felt when people messed with her things. Instead, she picked up the keys, grabbed her wallet, and headed out the front door. With both her uncles coming, she had decided they needed more food in the house. She retraced their steps from the previous afternoon and found the supermarket Matt had taken her to.

As she was going down the aisles with her basket over her arm, a man brushed past her. Startled, Claire stepped back quickly and started to apologise, but the words got caught in her throat with a gasp. It was the man she'd met on the plane—the one she knew worked for Richard.

"Hello, Claire…nice to see you again. I hope you've been keeping well. How's Maggie?" he asked, smiling pleasantly.

"What are you doing here, Tony?" Claire asked back in a choked whisper.

"So touched that you remember me." He beamed at her. "I just thought we could have a pleasant chat. But I'm a bit smarter than my colleague Richard. He tried when there was no one around to see your special Talents. As you see, I've not made that mistake."

"How is Richard? Has he recovered from our exercise?" Claire looked around for an exit.

"I don't know what you did to him, but I'd like to thank you. Firstly: because he is now no longer in Jack's employ, which makes me in charge. And secondly: he is now so deep down the neck of a bottle, nothing's going to pour him out."

"Well, if that's the case, then I do regret it. Did he not give the rest of you my message?"

"Oh yes, he did—in between bouts of fits. I passed it on to Jack and he took you seriously. I can't honestly see why he would." He looked her up and down, seemingly appraising her.

Claire was keeping an eye on who was in the aisle with them. When the last person left, she stood before him and looked him in the eye.

"Richard seems to have learned to leave me alone and I think it'd be wise if you did the same. You see, I can still use my Talents even if there are people around." She started to draw on her renewed energy and turned it inward to fade herself out slightly.

Taking an involuntary step back, his eyes went wide at the sight. "You wouldn't…you can't…not here."

"Can't I?" She took a step towards him, releasing the pent-up energy and returning to her normal form. "This isn't the only thing I can do, you know." Her hand became hot as a tiny spark formed in her palm and she released it to buzz around his head for a moment. "I suggest you make Jack realise that there's no point keeping this up. He'll only end up getting hurt." She waved her hand dramatically and the spark exploded with a small pop by his ear.

Tony jumped and then kept backing up from Claire. "He won't. Jack is totally obsessed. He will never stop trying to get his revenge on those he thinks have wronged him!"

"Revenge? For what? We did what we had to do. He wasn't hurt, and he got the father he should have had from the start."

"But that is just it. According to him, you changed his father—he didn't want the one who's there now, he wants the original."

"He's mad."

"I'm afraid he is," Tony told her seriously.

"Then why work for him?"

"He pays well to keep my loyalty. Plus, I enjoy the work."

"Don't enjoy it too much, Tony. You may not like the results. Now if we're done here, I think I'd like to get back to my friends."

"Before you do, Claire…be warned. We are watching. I know for a fact that Matthew's place is currently empty." He seemed to regain his previous bravado.

"Don't threaten me or anyone close to me." She pointed a finger at him as her voice dropped to a whisper. "Because I will not hesitate to use every Talent I can to stop all of you, regardless of who is around. Tell that to Jack."

Claire turned on her heels and stalked away, hoping that he wasn't following her. This false hope she knew was only dust in the wind, as he'd already told her they would be watching. She finished her shopping as quickly as she could and walked back to the little terrace house. Every few steps she spent looking around, trying to find who was keeping tabs on her, but she could see no one out of the ordinary. But what did she expect to see? Men in big, dark coats on a late summer's day and hats pulled down over scowling faces?

She pushed the gate open, slamming it shut with a loud clang behind her and taking one more look around before climbing the steps to the front door and inserting the key Matt had given her. After the door opened, she rushed inside to the quiet. No one was there as she let the fear take her over for the first time.

The shopping was dumped on the countertop, and she went to the front window to look out at the street through the net curtains. People were walking past on the busy street. Some to get to their cars, some walking with dogs, and one couple hand in hand. She examined every face as they passed and was becoming very agitated with the thoughts going around in her mind. Forcing herself to turn away from the window, she went back to the kitchen and put the shopping away and then started to tidy up the mess Matt had left before the dig.

Over an hour later, Matt walked in the back door and stopped in his tracks. He put his bag on the bench that separated the kitchen from the dining room and stared at the living area. He wandered in and looked at the piles on the table before him. Each had a note on top and there was not a speck of dust to be found on any surface.

"Claire?" he called out up the stairs. "Claire, you there?" She came down the stairs and flew into his arms. "Hey, I wasn't gone that long!" He gave a chuckle and enjoyed the feeling of her body against his.

"I went to the shop and got some food for dinner, and… "

"And what—what happened?" He smoothed the hair from her face.

"Tony was there. They're still watching." She leaned her head against his chest.

"Tony? Who's Tony?"

"He was the one I followed that day he met with Richard."

"You aren't alone, Claire." He kissed the top of her head. "You are not alone." He held her for a bit longer before asking, "Now, are you going to tell me what you've done to my home?"

She combined a sigh with a giggle and wiped her eyes. "I just tidied. The piles on the table have all been labelled, so you know where they were and what pages the books were open to. Also…" She was warming to the subject and moved over to the dining table. "There is a pile for unopened mail and a pile of opened. Oh, and a pile of other items I didn't know how to class—like photos and other stuff." She stopped. "What?"

"You're a born researcher. I can't believe this only took you an hour. I've been trying to figure out how to tidy it for years."

"Messy on the outside, but organised on the in…is that what you are telling me?" Her smile took his heart in its grip and squeezed it, taking his breath away. "Matt Drummond, you and I are going to make a great team."

Snaking her arm around him, Claire reached up to plant a kiss on his lips. "Do we have time before they get here?" he asked softly, kissing her tenderly over and over.

"Not sure, but we don't have to answer the door." Her arms were now around his neck and he picked her up as if she were a feather, then made his way to the stairs. Halfway up, the doorbell went, and Matt stopped as the pair looked at each other.

"Put me down." Claire said with resignation.

"But you said we didn't have to answer it," he replied quietly.

"We can't leave them standing there—that's my Uncle Geoff and David. You want to make a good impression, don't you?" She turned her blue eyes to his and gave him a doleful look.

He sighed in disgust and turned around, heading back down the stairs with Claire still in his arms. Reluctantly, he released her when they were at the front door.

As soon as the door was opened, Addy pushed past with Adam in tow carrying bags. The tall and lanky frame of Claire's Great-Uncle Geoff—with his twinkling brown eyes, large nose, and a smile from ear to ear—was just behind the friendly grey eyes and strong, comforting presence of David.

Claire ran into Geoff's arms as the old feelings of safety and security rushed back to her. She then turned to David and was enfolded into one of his bear hugs. Matt was still standing at the door waiting for them to finish their greetings, feeling uneasy under the scrutiny of these two large men.

Claire made the introductions to Matt and the pressure from their handshakes left a great impression on him. They then caught up on all the news from home. For the time, Claire had forgotten her encounter with Tony at the supermarket. Matt wasn't sure why she hadn't mentioned it and didn't bring it up himself, thinking that there must be a reason for her not to tell her family.

Watching closely, Matt monitored the relationship between David and Adam and was surprised to not see one bit of awkwardness. Geoff and Adam were another matter entirely and it didn't surprise him that there was an iciness there, considering that Adam had broken Claire's heart. He watched them interact together—both himself and Addy on the outskirts looking in—and recognised the faint traces of jealousy creeping in around the edges, but he shook it off.

"Would anyone like a cuppa? I'm making." He stood and waited for all their requests as Claire came to help.

"Are you okay? You seemed a bit quiet in there." She laid a hand on his.

"Well, it is intimidating meeting them."

"No less than me meeting your family, and this *is* only two of them." She turned and saw Geoff watching them. "Don't worry about Uncle Geoff. He'll soon warm to you." He gave a smile and squeezed her hand.

They brought out the tray and organised the everyone's accommodation. Addy and Adam were to go to a hotel nearby and Geoff and David to share the spare room. They spent the afternoon talking about everything—except for the one reason both David and Geoff had made the very long journey.

After dinner, they relaxed back in the living room and spent a lovely evening together. Addy and Adam left for the night and Claire went upstairs for a moment. When she was about to come back down, she could hear the three men talking. David and Geoff were giving Matt the third degree, and it dawned on her that they had been waiting all afternoon for this moment. Claire sat on the top step to listen to them.

"So, you are Dr. Drummond, then?" David asked Matt.

"Yes, I lecture at Glasgow University…and spend my summers on digs."

"And when Claire comes home, what then? A long-distance relationship? Because the last one didn't work out that well," Geoff asked.

Claire held her breath and waited for Matt to answer. This was a question she hadn't even wanted to consider herself yet. What would happen when she returned to New Zealand? She didn't want this summer to end, as the thought of leaving Matt left a gouge in her insides and it filled with loneliness and emptiness.

"I'm not sure. It's not something we've talked about yet but believe me when I say this: I am not willing to lose Claire and I'll do everything in my power to be with her. If that means she wants me to move over there, then I will."

A small smile crept onto her lips and the gouge slowly closed. Down the stairs she went and sat beside him, taking his hand in hers.

"You heard, didn't you?" David asked her and had the good grace to look ashamed. On the other hand, Geoff gave nothing away.

"Yes. And I would really appreciate it if you didn't give Matt a hard time. All you need to worry about is the fact that I like him, and I know he really likes me. And when the time's right for us," she pointed between herself and Matt, "to discuss what is going to happen to our relationship, that you have faith in the *both* of us to decide what will be right for *us*." She stared Geoff down at that point. She hadn't lived with him all those years without picking up some of his habits and mannerisms.

"Well, we've been put in our places," Geoff said casually to David as he sat back in his seat.

"I mean it, Uncle Geoff," Claire said sternly.

"Have you got anything stronger than coffee, Matt?" David asked the younger man, hoping to break the tension between niece and uncle.

"Yeah, I have…I've got a nice twelve-year-old Scotch somewhere." He got up and went to a shelf, starting to search for the bottle. "Claire, did you happen to see a bottle of whiskey here this morning?"

"It's in the cabinet with the rest of the bottles," she said, getting up and going straight the cupboard.

"I see she's already organising everything for you," Geoff said in jest. "Or did something happen and now Claire's coping mechanism has kicked in?" He sat back and watched Claire carefully while she handed him a glass.

"Claire? Are you going to answer Geoff? Because there is no point in hiding it. It's written all over your face!" David took the glass from her hand.

She sat back down and waited for Matt to join her before starting her tale. Quickly, she slipped into her report—going back to old habits while relating information to her uncles. Her clear and concise words described all that happened in the market with Tony. And in turn, her uncles waited until she had finished to ask their many questions.

Each time they asked to retell a part, she could feel the fear dropping away bit by bit, replaced by an intense anger. Anger that these people threatened her—as well as her family and friends. It was intensifying inside, swelling up and growing impatient to be free. Her hands were clenched into fists and the colour rose in her cheeks.

Matt gently placed an arm around Claire and held on, making her turn and gaze at him. Her words stumbled, and she released the energy she was slowly building to use on something she didn't even know. His presence calmed her and made her come back to herself and she leaned into him, placing her head on his shoulder.

"Where were you six years ago?" David asked as he finished his drink. "You sure you don't have a touch of Charm on you?"

Matt held her close. "No…no Charm on me."

Chapter Twelve

For the next few days, the group played tourists, and Matt enjoyed taking them to all of his favourite places. Claire was also enjoying the guided tour, yet she couldn't shake the feeling of being watched and was constantly looking around. She started to feel suffocated and hemmed in but tried not to show it. She was pleased with how Geoff had taken to Matt, and she loved to watch them interact.

A couple days later, Matt received a phone call from his gran—telling him that it was important for them to come up to the cottage. When Matt relayed the news to the rest of the group, he was surprised by Geoff's eagerness to go and be introduced to his gran.

Claire sat in the back behind Matt, and Geoff was in the front seat of the old Rover, where he kept up a long conversation with Matt. Smiling, Claire was watching him in the rearview mirror. His blue eyes twinkled back with mischief. But Claire wasn't the only thing that Matt was looking at on the drive. He'd noticed a couple of cars that had been with them, matching their speed since Glasgow. He suggested that they stop at Killin so Geoff and David could get a quick look at the area that Claire had been staying all these months. They then asked Claire to call to the other car and tell them that they would be stopping for a break.

As Matt took the road that led to Killin, Claire noticed that he was concentrating more on what was behind them, than the road ahead. Swiveling in her seat she looked back and saw two dark-coloured cars turning the corner behind them. Facing back to Matt the look that they exchanged was significant, but neither gave voice to their concerns. He parked the Rover outside a pub to grab some lunch. Matt deliberately placed himself where he could see the cars from the window.

After eating lunch, Matt mentioned that he had heard a noise and just wanted to check the old girl before going on. He got down and had a good look underneath the Rover. But when he got back up, his face was set with a very unhappy look.

"Everything okay?" Geoff asked.

"Yeah, think we may have picked up a bug or two. You might want to check yours, Adam," Matt suggested.

They all started to feel a little on edge as Claire searched the street and car park. A car that wasn't parked far away looked like one that had turned after them earlier, and there was a man in the front seat. The window rolled down slowly, and Claire gasped as she recognised Tony. He smiled and waved at her mischievously.

Adam was soon back with the group, and he gave Matt a small nod, letting him know that he also had a little hitchhiker attached to his vehicle.

"We might as well leave them on until we get over the other side. I know a few fords we can clean them off in. And our *friends* won't be able to follow in the cars they have, anyway." Matt noticed Claire walking toward the cars he'd just indicated.

Claire reached Tony's car and leaned on it in a more casual manner than she actually felt. "Hello again, Tony…fancy meeting you here."

"Claire, I warned you that we'd be watching. I did enjoy the guided tour of Glasgow. It was very enlightening. Please thank Matt for me, would you?"

"So happy we could be of assistance in furthering your education. You know, we really need to stop meeting this way, since people are going to start talking."

"Only those who matter. Are you having a pleasant drive?" Tony asked, obviously enjoying their conversation.

"Very nice—thank you, but we seem to have picked up a few problems. Any idea how we can get rid of them?"

"No...sorry, I can't help you there. I'm not very technically minded." He smiled up at her. "But I do hope you don't resolve it too soon. You better get back to your party or as you said, people will start talking!"

"Have a nice day, Tony, and I hope to never see you again. No offence." She pushed off the car and walked back.

"None taken, Claire," he called to her as she retreated.

"Shall we go?" Claire asked before resuming her seat in the back of the Land Rover.

It took the others a while to make a move to their respective cars. When Geoff and Matt had entered the Rover, both swiveled in their seats to face Claire.

"What the hell was all that about?" Geoff demanded.

"I was just having a friendly word with our neighborhood Watcher." She smiled back at the pair.

"Your what?" Matt asked.

"That was Tony. Now as we drive along, he's going to be following us. When I release it, he is going to be experiencing a little problem with a bug of his own. This one glows though, and likes to fly." She gave them a satisfied grin. Comprehension slowly dawned on the men, and they smiled back at her.

As they turned back, Geoff said, "Well, you could have told us you were going to do something. You were giving me a heart attack back there!"

Matt pulled out of the car park and followed Adam on the road. "Does she do this a lot?" he asked her uncle.

"Has she not told you? Do I have a few stories in store for you, my boy!" Geoff chuckled and started to regale Matt with stories of her childhood and teenage years. Meanwhile, Claire was having a mini attack of her own.

Walking up to the car and facing Tony had taken every nerve in her body to do—and to talk pleasantly to a man she detested, even more. She'd used the nerves and anger he inspired to ensure her little light "bug" had enough energy stored in it to last a very long time. But those feelings were nothing compared to what she was now experiencing as she faced the thought of travelling over that pass again. Once more, the butterflies in the pit of her stomach were making her feel sick with their constant agitation. And the closer they got to the accident site, the worse they flew.

"Claire, are you listening?" Geoff asked her, looking back from his seat.

"Sorry…I was miles away. What were you saying?"

"I was asking when you would release your bug," he replied.

Claire looked about her and recognised the pass road. Even more, she became aware that they were closing in on the area where she and Maggie had been pushed off the road and into the river.

"Matt, can you slow down and let them catch up a bit? This is a very appropriate spot."

"We're close to the accident site," Matt told Geoff as he reduced his speed.

Claire concentrated and found the connection to her lovely little bug. Pouring her instructions into it, she then released it to do her bidding. Claire looked out the dirty rear windows to the car behind, watching it swerve on the extremely narrow road before it mounted the steep, rising ground on the left. It bounced back onto the road, bringing with it great clods of dirt and grass. The car veered suddenly and sharply to the right, until it tipped over the side of the bank. Plunging down into the small stream, it sent up a spray of water to glisten in the fleeting sunshine. With the car behind them now stopped, a man got out of the following car, and ran to make sure that Tony was okay.

Slowly, they became smaller and smaller as the Rover moved away from them. They disappeared completely from view when they rounded a bend, and Claire turned back to face the front, hoping that Tony wasn't too badly hurt after his ordeal.

The passing bay came upon them fast, and Claire could still see where they'd gone off the edge. Two stakes had been driven into the earth and a danger tape had been strung up between them—marking the spot.

Even though Matt and Geoff had resumed their conversation, Claire remained quiet and didn't bite at any of Geoff's jokes at her expense. The two men exchanged a look, but she didn't notice. Claire was off in her own little world, thinking of how to be rid of Jack. There was only one solution that she could think of, and it was not one she relished. She hoped that something else would present itself as an alternative.

The rest of the journey was uneventful, and as promised, Matt guided them to a deep ford where the water soon destroyed the tracking device that Tony had put on their vehicles. Once relieved of them, they carried on. However,

Claire was still introspective and barely unresponsive to even the simplest of questions.

It wasn't until they were passing the old oak tree that she started to come back to herself. The long gravel track took them to the door of the cottage, and it opened wide as they pulled up to it, with Gran and Leana coming out to greet them all. Introductions were made all the while a biting wind blew down from the hills. Once done, Gran invited them inside.

"It's going to be a tight squeeze, but we should all fit in quite nicely. The girls are back in the Rose Room. Matt, you'll have to give up your room to Geoff and David, and you and Adam will have to sleep in the lounge with the rest," Gran informed as she ushered them in.

"The rest?" Matt asked as his question went unanswered.

"Leana, go put the kettle on…I think our guests would appreciate a cuppa after such a long journey. Addy, can you help? Thank you, dear. Please, sit down. You're making the place look untidy." When Leana and Addy had left the room, Gran turned back to Matt. "We will talk about it later."

Claire had a strange feeling that it had to do with his mother but put that out of her mind as Gran then turned to address them all.

"You must be wondering why I called you all here. To start, there's no time like the present. I have had a vision and I keep having the same one, so it must be important. Claire, the trial that's coming—the one you are going to have to face alone—will ultimately test you to your limits."

"What is this trial?" Geoff said, sitting forward.

"There's someone who hunts her. And he is bent on revenge."

"Jack," David said simply. "His name's Jack Sheridan. He is the son of an ex-Elder. His Talent is Hide. He taught Claire."

"And he's my half-brother," Adam added.

"He feels that he's bonded to Claire. It was one of the lies his mother told him when she was alive to do Marcus's bidding," Geoff said. "We had to deal with his Watchers on the way here."

"I don't understand the term 'Watcher.' Can you explain?" Gran asked.

"A Watcher is a person from The Community who's set to watch someone with Talent if there is a problem—either they're in danger from someone else or they're dangerous to the general public. The Watcher reports back to the Elders if the Talented one has used their Talent unnecessarily."

"There is obviously a great gap in how your community has developed over the years, so I look forward to discussing it more with you."

"Which is why I welcome this opportunity. You have no idea how happy we were when Claire told us about you!" Geoff revealed to her.

"There will be plenty of time for that later. We must find a way to keep Claire safe."

"Is the vision set, Gran?" Matt asked as Addy and Leana returned with refreshments.

"Right, well, I'll leave you to it. I don't think you need my input in this," Leana said after she'd set a tray down.

"Mum, please stay."

"You are sweet, Son…but no. I have nothing useful to contribute and I will only say something silly." She then left the room.

Gran said something in Gaelic to Matt and he sat back down by Claire. The others in the room looked at each other in confusion, not having understood what had just passed between them.

"There is only one thing that must be done, and I am the one who has to do it." Claire sighed. "It feels like I have said this before, but I shouldn't be here with you. I don't want to endanger anyone else ever again. I need to face him by myself, and I already know what it is that has to be done."

There was silence at her words.

"Are you thinking what I think you are?" Adam asked as all eyes turned to him. "It's the original plan you had for my father, isn't it, Claire?"

"Yes, Adam...it is."

"You came up with an alternative then. Why not now? Surely there's another way?" He paused, hoping that she'd agree with him, but she didn't. "I know your aunt didn't think a suggestion would work with Jack, but are you quite sure? After pulling you back from the brink with Gerry, my eyes have been opened as to what we can do with this Talent."

"It is still different. You must consider the mind of the individual. Jack's so suggestable that the smallest change would make things worse—rather than better." She stared at Adam for a moment with narrowed eyes. "But you know this from experience, don't you, Adam? You've already tried to change him. My God, Adam, I made you promise not to try anything. Why did you do it?"

"I had to try something. He'd just broken us up and I was hurting that you had left me. I was so angry. I confronted him about it...it just sort of happened."

"Aunt Lil and I both told you what would happen if we tried. We told you and told you!" Her voice was getting louder, and she felt like she was about to lose control. In short order, she stood up and stormed out of the room, hightailing it out the back door of the cottage. The top of the hill behind the house drew her gaze and she lifted off the ground, flying higher and higher. The wind tore into her clothing—chilling her skin beneath and whipping her hair around her face.

At the top of the hill, she spotted the spring and landed beside it. The water gurgled out of the ground and tumbled down the hill, bouncing off the rocks and finally settling into a running brook before joining the river further down the valley. The green hills of the early summer were now brown as autumn came closer. She looked over the other side and could see the group of standing stones—all tall and thin and covered in lichen. She made her way over to them and felt each as she circled on the outside.

Each stone seemed to vibrate with the wind, and she felt drawn to them. Claire was surprised how smooth they felt under her touch and leaned against the largest of them at the entrance. It hummed as she felt peace and calm wash over her. Her troubles seemed to drain away, and all thoughts were tuned to the rhythm of the stones. There was no other way to describe it. They hummed in concert with each other, with a rhythm that her whole body could feel. But it felt slightly off, as if they were slightly out of time.

Going from stone to stone, it kept shifting. And no matter where she stood, it wouldn't fit together. She stopped between the two entrance stones, and as she was about enter the circle she heard her name called. Across the circle Matt touched down and stood facing her.

"Claire, I was worried…" he told her, his voice carrying on the wind.

"There's nothing to worry about, Matt. It's all going to be fine." Claire placed a caressing hand on the stone to her left and lifted her eyes to it, feeling the trapped energy inside.

In a moment, Matt was at her side and took her hand off the stone, leading her away from the circle. For a brief second, Claire came back to herself and looked at Matt and then the stones.

"Claire, look at me." He stood between her and the circle, trying to get her attention.

"Matt, they're alive." Her voice was low and quiet. "I've never felt anything like it."

"What do you mean they're *alive*?"

"Can't you feel them calling to you…inviting you in to share their energy?" They were still there in her mind—calling out, enticing her.

"Hang on to me. I'll take you back to the house." He lifted her up in his arms and held her tightly, pushing off the ground and following the flow of water down the side of the hill. By the time they reached the bottom, her head was tucked under his chin and her arms were wrapped around his neck.

"What happened up there?" she asked.

"Don't know. I've never seen anyone affected by the stones that way. We need to talk to Gran. Will you be okay to walk?" Matt asked with a great deal of concern for her.

She nodded as he placed her back on her feet. "You seem really good at that." Claire now felt shy, and she didn't know why.

"At carrying you? I seem to have gained some practice in the last few months, but it doesn't necessarily mean that I don't enjoy it." He reached for her hand and pulled her closer as he cupped her chin.

Their lips met in a gentle brush and then more firmly. Claire held him around the waist and pulled his body to hers, sharing his warmth from the cold wind. Claire never wanted it to stop. She wanted this to go on forever and for them to forget the world outside this valley. She felt it within her that this was the man she was meant to be with for the rest of her life.

The intensity of the feeling was more than she could handle, so she broke their embrace. The reality reared its ugly head and inserted itself between them. When she could not even be certain of a future for herself, how could she commit to this wonderful man before her? But those blue eyes melted her heart when she looked at them. And for a moment, she was lost in them until her body betrayed her and she shivered involuntarily.

"Come on…before you end up with hypothermia again." He put his arm around her shoulder as she snuggled into him and put her arm around his hips. He kissed the top of her head as they walked, and Claire had never felt so comfortable and at ease with anyone before. It was like she had known him all her life.

They rounded the corner of the house and saw a car pull up. Matt stopped when he saw who was driving. "What's he doing here? Mum is going to go spare."

Claire saw Gerry climb out and wave to his son. From the passenger seat, Robbie brushed away his long hair off his face. They both walked toward the young couple.

"What are you doing here, Dad?"

"I thought it was time that your mum stopped the pity party she's been throwing herself for the last fifteen years. Robbie has agreed to help me, and I was hoping that I could count on you as well." Gerry held his hand out to his son. Matt clasped it and pulled him into a hug.

"Of course, Dad—anything." They broke the embrace and walked into the house together, with Claire and Robbie following.

The arrival of Gerry and Robbie stopped any further talk in the living room and another round of introductions began as David admitted to Robbie that he was a fan of his work.

"That's very nice of you to say, but what I do is rubbish. Gerry's the real archaeologist," Robbie told him humbly.

With the pleasantries over, Gerry excused himself, Robbie, and Matt, and they left to find Leana.

"Shut the door, Addy dear. I think this might be a bit unpleasant for us to hear," Gran said quietly.

Even with the door closed, they could still hear raised voices—alongside a crash of something heavy and some glass smashing in the back of the house. It went on for a while and they tried to make small talk around the argument. After one particular loud tirade from Leana, Gran suggested that they take a turn outside and go look at their library.

This was an opportunity too good for Claire to pass up, no matter how much she wanted to be there when Matt came out. Books fascinated her and with what Gran had hinted at, there should be older information that she could get her hands on.

They left the warm confines of the house and walked across the windswept yard, stopping outside one of the outbuildings. On the outside, it looked old and decrepit. But inside, it was beautifully fitted, and temperature controlled. The walls were lined with bookshelves and long, thin specimen drawers. Gran encouraged her to look through them whenever she could.

Claire's fingers begin to tingle at the thought of learning more, but there was one thing she really wanted to know. The event up at the standing stones had intrigued and revitalized her. She felt so full of energy and she wanted to know why. The feelers were sent out to the many books and writings that filled the little library, and to her great satisfaction, she got back a few returning signals.

She immediately went to the one that came back the strongest and pulled open one of the shallow drawers. Laid out carefully was an old sheaf of paper. She jumped when a pair of cotton gloves were held out in front of her.

"This is the only condition of looking at our treasures. They must be worn to read them, so the oils on your hands do not damage the old writings," Gran told her while looking down at what she'd opened. "You're going to have a hard job reading that one, as it's Pictish Symbols. Unfortunately, we haven't been able to get to all the documents held here, but we have translated some. There is a full catalogue of the documents held on the computer over there." She shut the drawer Claire had opened and steered her over to the desk in the middle of the room.

Claire couldn't be certain, but it felt that she had been deliberately steered away from the drawers. This piqued her curiosity even more, and she was determined to get Matt into the building to help her as soon as possible.

Gran was explaining the system they were using. Claire had missed it with her own thoughts. The energy was buzzing inside her, wanting release. She found it hard to keep it down. Her fidgeting was getting worse, and a large hand came to rest on her shoulder. She looked up and found Geoff looking down at her.

"You okay, Claire? You look like you're jumping out of your skin."

"I'm not sure. I have all this pent-up energy," she told him. "I honestly want to be here taking all of this in, but the thought of being cooped up in here is really grating on me."

"Why don't you go for a run? It's always worked in the past when you need to think."

Claire realised he sensed she was agitated because of what she'd said earlier in the house. Placing her hand in his, she smiled.

"I might just do that." She saw David watching them. "You up for it, David? Or have you gotten too flabby and sedate?"

"You cheeky little...I can still run rings around you, young lady—any day," he said cockily as he accepted her challenge. "Care to join us, Adam...Addy?"

"I do not run, thank you," Addy informed him.

"Addy, I think being the only family member here, you could guide them around the best places to go. Also, your Ability will get rusty. It needs to be used," Gran admonished her.

"Yes, Gran. Have you got any spare kit, Claire? I seem to have left mine in my other luggage."

"Well, you can count me out. I know for a fact I'll never keep up," Adam said.

A quick stop inside to change and they were soon out again, setting off down the long track. Both Claire and David let Addy set the pace. It was an eerie feeling: the wind whistled past, but not a sound came from the three runners. Their mostly silent footfalls upon the gravel track led back to the road as their breath kept to themselves. Claire lost herself in the sheer beauty that surrounded her.

The wide-open fields rose sharply into the steep hills while the sheep and cattle in the field ignored the trio as they passed them by. Addy pulled up at the sight of the oak tree and sat down on the grass at the edge of the track.

"I'll wait here for you," she told them, staring down the track at the tree.

"Be back soon," Claire told her as she carried on, pulling David with her.

When they were out of earshot, David asked, "What was that about?"

"The oak tree holds a sad memory for Addy, and she doesn't like to be near it," Claire revealed. "Matt had a little sister. She died by the tree."

A shiver ran down her spine as they passed under the large, gnarled branches of the ancient oak tree. The air was cooler in the shade of the leaves that were starting to change their colour. She had passed this tree in the car three times now, and for the first time, she could see a small cross in the bare earth underneath. There were no flowers, no ornaments of any sort to show that the place had been visited. It was if they'd placed the cross and just left—never to return and never to remember the little girl who had died there. It was a lonely feeling place, with the tree being the only feature in the landscape—apart from the small river at the end of the track.

"What was her name?" David asked quietly.

"Breena. Addy told me about her."

"Is that why Leana is—?"

"Yeah. She can't forgive herself that she didn't see it," Claire told him sadly.

They ran on to the ford and turned to run back. Claire was watching the tree as a cloud passed across the sun. She wasn't certain, but she could have sworn she saw a face peering out from the branches. Shivering again, she increased her pace to pass it as soon as possible. The hair on the back of her neck was standing up as they made their way to where Addy was waiting to join them for the run back.

The run didn't really help quieten the energy that had gotten so excited at the standing stones, but Claire managed to get hold of it in her mind and push it down. Matt, Gerry, and Robbie still hadn't made an appearance from the back of the house, but it was much quieter now.

Claire showered quickly after Addy, remembering the limited hot water supply. Leaving the rose room after dressing, she stopped on the landing. From within one of the bedrooms on the upper floor came a sweet-sounding song. It was in a male voice: soft, clear, and soothing. A door opened while the song swelled from within as Matt came out.

He stopped when he saw Claire. His eyes were red from tears and his shoulders were slumped. Matt then closed the door silently behind him and stepped out to meet her. Claire took him in her arms and held him close as he rested his head on hers and burst into tears. She clung to him, simply trying to give comfort as best she could. She stroked his back and let him cry. A sound coming from downstairs prompted Claire to take him by the hand and pull him into the rose room, kicking the door closed behind them.

She led him to her bed and lay down beside him, cuddling him as he let out his grief while his body was wracked with silent sobs. Her hand smoothed his hair and she said not a word. Her heart wrenched for him and for his whole family. She could not imagine what it had been like for Matt growing up. When his sobbing was spent and he lay quiet, she kissed his forehead and held him closer again.

"I'm sorry," Matt apologised quietly into her chest.

"It's all right." She kissed him again.

He pulled himself up on an elbow and gazed at her. His hand reached up and stroked her cheek. His eyes, normally so bright and clear, were now ringed and red from his sorrow. "I suppose Addy's told you about Breena?" He wiped the tears from his eyes and sniffed loudly.

"She has. I didn't want to mention her before you were ready to tell me."

"What on earth did I do to deserve a woman like you?" He gave a small smile.

"I could say the same about you."

"Breena was such a sweet girl. She could be a pain in the butt, but she was so sweet that I would immediately forgive her. She loved that bike." His eyes were looking far away — past the woman beside him. "She'd sped down that track so many times before, squealing the whole time. During summer, she would race into the river and then she'd ride her bike back up the hill and race it down again." He sniffed softly and moved up the bed to lie on his back. Lifting his arm to let Claire lay her head on his shoulder, he pulled her close.

"It was my job to look out for her. Dad was always away working on some dig site and Mum was painting. So, we took our bikes to the hill. I was supposed to keep her safe. I can still see her racing down towards me…her legs were sticking out to keep them from the spinning pedals. A smile spread across her wee face—dark, curly, long hair streaming out behind her. She was so happy that day." He smiled at the memory until he carried on with his tale.

"Breena hit a stone and her bike wobbled. It turned, and the sound—" He stopped, covering his face with his hand.

And Claire did know that sound. It sometimes still haunted her dreams: the sound she'd heard when David had hit Richard in the head with a piece of wood.

"I didn't know what to do. I was only fourteen. I picked her up and flew her home, but I didn't know she was already gone." Another sob escaped him, and Claire reached up with a hand and placed it on the side of his face. He managed to get his voice under control once more. "Mum wouldn't talk to me for such a long time—until she got it into her head that it was her fault for not seeing it. That's when she took to the drink. I was packed back off to boarding school and Dad went back to work. Mum stayed here, since Gran thought she could help her, but it just carried on. She refused to let Dad back—and she told him to stay away, only trying to punish herself."

The door flew open as Addy came rushing in. "Claire, dinner's ready. Oh…sorry. I didn't know—" she said and stumbled back out in embarrassment, closing the door behind her.

"We never seem to get a moment of peace just for us. They all seem bent on interrupting us." He gave her a weak smile and sniffed.

Softly, little white snowflakes fell and collected in Claire's hair. There was a hush and stillness over the hills, and the only sound was the spring—setting forth its icy waters to tumble down into the darkness. Her feet were bare, but she didn't feel the cold, wet grass beneath them as she made her way across the top of the hill to the standing stones, hidden by the large rocks.

The whole night seemed to be like a dream. Claire had woken from a deep sleep with the urge to climb the hill. The pull was so strong, she hadn't stopped to put on any shoes or even a jumper. Her blond hair glowed in the fleeting moonlight and hung down, spreading over her shoulders. The soft clouds gently touched and eddied around the top of the hill, making it seem like a warm and comfortable blanket was surrounding her. But her only focus was on the stones.

They called to her, begged her to listen to their tales with voices that came from far away and long ago—reaching down through the ages for her attention, demanding her notice. Her hand touched each in turn and she stopped at the entrance to the circle. Seven dark and mist-enshrouded figures appeared, clothed in long hooded robes, their hands clasped before them.

Each taking a position in the gaps between the stones, the group turned and faced inwards. Their faces were lost in the dark cloth and their voices were quiet—only mumbling at first. Slowly, Claire entered the circle and stood in front of each one. She was hungry for the knowledge that they could impart to her. At first, their words were a mystery to her—an ancient language hard to pick out. But the more she listened, the more she began to understand until the words were as clear as if they were speaking her native tongue. The knowledge was heavy on her and she stopped in the centre, falling to her knees as it weighed down on her. New knowledge of Talents once hidden—and that of ones she already had—opened up to their fullest for her to use. Claire repeated back what she had heard, increasingly determined to remember their words forever. Each gave up their collective wisdom to her memory, until she felt she could no longer fit any more in. She cried out as she felt it pressing on her mind—extending and making room for this new information.

Once all had been listened to and their knowledge was hungrily taken, the figures turned inwards and walked to the centre of the circle, coming to stand around her. Raising their arms, their hands slipped from the robes, displayed bony and white in the moonlight. Their chanting became urgent and ever so slowly, light emanated from them all. When Claire tried to peer through the bright light, she saw that they had merged. Now, only one stood before her. The hand that was raised over her head now had long fingers, and it seemed to glow as she could feel power in that gesture. The hand came to rest on her blonde head and once it touched, she understood what it was she had to do that night. Standing completely still, Claire watched the figure as it eventually faded from her sight. And somewhere in the far distance, a mournful bell tolled.

White mist crept up the side of the hill, spreading its tendrils out around the circle. It circled as if a great wind had picked it up, and it soon became a wall around the stones. The white was agitated and frustrated as it sought a way in—all the while drawing in the energy from the stones, feeding itself whole again until she saw a beautiful woman standing at the entrance of the circle. Dressed all in white, her features were so familiar, so ingrained in Claire's memory.

"Mum," Claire whispered, her blue eyes wide with stunned surprise.

The same smile and same nose Claire saw every day in the mirror were now worn on this woman who stood before her. Her mother, Jessica Brown, turned to her daughter and smiled.

"Claire." Her voice was vibrant. She ran into the centre and drew her daughter to her, hugging her tightly. "You don't know how jealous I have been of your father—seeing him hug you when I couldn't."

"I've missed you so much." Claire closed her eyes and hoped that when she opened them again, Jess wouldn't be gone. And luckily for her, she wasn't. She was still right in front of her.

"So have I, my sweet, sweet girl." She broke the embrace and held Claire by the hands. "Let me look at you. My, you've grown into such a beautiful woman and I missed it...I missed it all!" A tear ran down Jess's cheek and dripped to the ground unheeded, forming a perfect crystal.

"I don't understand how this is possible."

"Did you not hear them—the Guardians? They gave you the knowledge you needed to do this for me. It was your doing, my wonderful, clever daughter. You summoned me, and I came. I thought you were in trouble, but here I find that you've given me a great gift...the strength to be myself."

"How'd you do it in the first place? Get into my mind, I mean. Aunt Lil didn't know how and couldn't explain it."

"Lilith was a bit of a stickler for protocol and sticking to the rules. I will try to explain, but I'm not sure I am going to make much sense. Before we were killed, I had a very vivid dream. There was a figure—dressed very much like the one in the circle just now. This figure whispered to me and I understood what I was supposed to do. Don't ask me what he said, because I can't remember. However, what I *do* remember is waking up and waking your father. There was an urgency that I had to obey. We went to your room and we connected. John was not happy about it, but I made him do it." She looked sadly at Claire. "I had always hoped I'd done the right thing that night. I put so much time and effort into making sure your father was perfect that I left little energy for myself, so I had to be satisfied with being there…but not."

"But now you are here, in the real world. Will you be whole in my mind after tonight, or will you be gone?"

"I will still be here, as this is just a shade of myself—a ghost, if you'd like to think of me that way. I am still in your mind, and we both will be for as long as you need us." She squeezed her daughter's hands.

"Is Dad around? I want him to see you." Claire looked around, but there was no sign of her father.

"No. I had to be summoned by you to be here and I must go back soon." Jess stopped and looked around her for a moment, frowning. "Strange, these stones look like the ones in your subconscious." The musing soon passed as she turned her attention back to Claire. "There is one more thing I'd like to tell you before I go. I want to tell you how proud we are of you, how much we love you. I am sorry you had to go through your most difficult years without us being there properly, but we've watched over you and tried to help when we could. Oh, and I think Matt is quite nice. I believe you've already decided he is the one. I can see it on your face. I hope you have found a love that is as strong as ours has been." Jess hugged her close again and kissed her on the cheek. "Can you do one thing for me?"

"Sure, What is it?" Claire held on tightly to her mother, not wanting to let her go just yet.

"Tell my brother that I'm the one watching now. He will know what I mean." Jess gave a mischievous wink to her daughter. "I have to go now. They won't let me stay here too much longer, and anyway, there is someone else here to see you," Jess said cryptically.

After one last parting kiss, Jess let go of Claire's hands and walked to the rocks that hid the standing stones. Claire followed, stopping at the entrance of the circle. From behind them came Matt, looking bewildered. Jess walked up to him and took his hand as she was passing.

"Look after her…she thinks she's strong, but she hurts easily." She dropped his hand and walked off into the darkness.

Matt turned back and saw Claire through the falling snow as he made his way over to her. "Who was that?" he asked.

"That was my mother, and she likes you."

"I'm pleased. Where are we?" He looked around him, half dazed and confused.

"By the standing stones—don't you recognise it?"

"It doesn't feel right. I can see snow falling, but I don't feel cold."

"I'm not sure if this is real or a dream," Claire told him while also looking around.

Matt looked at her and then stepped closer. "If this is the inside of your mind, then I like what I see. I was so jealous that Adam got to be in here with you and I couldn't."

"That was a different part—my subconscious. I'm not sure what this is. You were jealous?"

"Of course! I was jealous the moment he came into camp. How could I not be? I mean, I'm a guy and I could see he was good-looking, so how could I compete with that?"

"I like that you were jealous, but don't make a habit of it…it will wear thin pretty quick. Anyway, there was no competition at all. On one hand, an incredibly gorgeous guy who is intelligent, sweet, and sensitive, and who has the most amazing blue eyes I have ever seen." Claire placed a caressing hand to his face.

"And on the other, a guy you've known all your life, been in a relationship with for five years, has access to your mind and knows you like the back of his hand," he finished for her.

"Except that it is you who's here and not him. I don't even know how you are here."

"This is your dream, Claire. Are we likely to be interrupted here in your dream?" His left eyebrow rose up into his forehead.

"It's my dream, so I can make or stop any interruption."

"I like the sound of that." His voice dropped lower as he took her into his arms and kissed her.

"Claire, it's time to get up." Addy's voice woke her. "Come on. Breakfast is ready. Man, you were doing some major dreaming last night. I woke to find you up off the bed! Did you know you did that—the hover thing—at night?"

"Yeah…I do it when I'm stressed, usually," she croaked back to Addy.

"It nearly frightened me to death. Come on, sleepyhead. I've just had a hard time getting Matt to wake up. Don't you make it difficult as well." She threw her pillow at Claire to get her moving.

"Okay, okay—I'm up." Claire sat up and swung her legs out of bed. "Bloody hell, it's cold."

"It snowed last night. The tops of the hills have a light dusting on them. Look!" Addy opened the windows to the morning light and Claire joined her there. And it was as she had said, the brown hills behind the house looked like they'd been sprinkled with icing sugar.

"Wow, that's so pretty! How long will it last? Will it be there all day?" She remembered the night before, being out in it, but she felt sure that it had been just a dream and not reality.

"Depends on a lot of things, but the first snow doesn't really hang around that much. It's just snow."

"In our valley, we are lucky if we see snow once in twenty years, so it is a big thing." Claire hurriedly dressed and pulled on a pair of thick socks from the bottom of her pack, remembering putting them there back in New Zealand.

"See you down there," Addy said as she left the room.

Claire straightened her bed and then tidied Addy's as well. She left the room and bumped straight into Matt. Their eyes met, and the night's dream came flooding back to both of them. Colour rose in her cheeks as she reached up and kissed him.

"I enjoyed last night...now I can't wait till—" he started.

"I know. Neither can I."

"Are you two going to spend all day snogging on the stairs or are you coming for breakfast?" David stood halfway up the stairs watching them.

"We're coming," Claire said, giving Matt one last light kiss. "Oh, and David, before we join the others...I have a message for you." She joined him at the bottom of the stairs and Matt stopped behind her.

"A message from who?"

"From Mum. She said to say that she is the one who's watching now and that you would know what that meant. She also winked at me."

"That is so unfair. She knows I can't win now!" He left them, muttering under his breath as he went back to the kitchen.

Chapter Thirteen

Claire thought it seemed like a perfect day as she climbed the hill to play in the rapidly thawing snow. She laughed and had a great deal of fun with Addy, Adam, Robbie, and her uncles while Matt spent some time with his father and mother. Although the pull was great, Claire made sure not to go near the stones again. The last encounter had her feeling a little scared of them, like she could get lost within them. The sun was shining and there didn't seem to be a care in the world, but she was deceiving herself and she knew it.

"Who wants a trip to the local shops?" Matt called to them as they returned from their morning fun. He was just coming out the door as they approached, with a jacket in hand. The seats were soon filled, and Claire was not one of the party.

"I'm going to do a bit of indulging in that library," she told Matt as she leaned on the driver's door.

"Is there anything you need?" His eyebrow arched suggestively.

"Just bring me back something nice." She kissed him through the window, which provoked good-natured noises of disgust and comments about public displays of affection from his passengers.

Claire then went inside the house to let Gran know that she was heading to the library. She found her in the kitchen baking.

"Hello, Claire. Did you have fun up on the hill?" Gran asked as she was rolling out scone dough.

"I did. We don't get much snow back in New Zealand. It was a real treat," Claire told her as she leaned against the bench.

"You won't think so when it is so thick you're snowed in for a few days! That's why I've sent Matty out to get extra supplies. With all the people in the house at the moment, it doesn't hurt to be prepared." She was cutting up the dough now into squares and placing them on a baking tray. "And it wasn't this morning I was talking about."

Claire blushed and looked down at the floor. "It was an interesting night, to say the least. I'm still not exactly sure what happened."

"Do you wish to talk about it? I get the feeling that you haven't really spoken about it with Matt..."

"No, I have, but only the part that concerned him. I don't know how to explain it. I'm still not clear about what happened myself."

"Can I tell you something? In equal measures, I have seen heartache for both you and Matt. But I've also seen that you were made for each other, and that neither of you would be happy without the other. I will be there for him when you leave him, and I understand why it will happen. I have not spoken to Matt about this, and I give you my promise that I will not speak a bad word about you when you leave him," Gran told her seriously.

"But I'll never leave him, Gran. I could never leave him."

"But you will...I have seen it," Gran quieted her and put the scones in the oven to bake. "I do not blame you, and I know it has to do with dealing with Jack. I don't mean to make you feel agitated about it, my dear, but only to warn you. What's coming is going to change you a great deal and I feel that the change has already begun. It started last night up on the hill with the standing stones."

"Maybe the key will be in the library out there. I was just going out there to have a look," Claire told her as she pushed herself away from the bench. The conversations were starting to worry her, and she didn't like the matter-of-fact way that Gran was telling her what was going to happen.

"I agree. It may be there. Make good use of the peace and quiet while you can." Gran was wiping up the bench and preparing for the next lot of baking.

Claire started to leave, then stopped to face Gran once more. "How is Leana today? I didn't have time to ask Matt before he left."

"It'll take a while for her to be better. Gerry is with her, helping with the worst of the symptoms. But coming off alcohol is a hard thing to do. Now off with you…I'll send your lunch over, since it will be easier that way."

"Thank you, Gran. I'd appreciate that."

Claire left Gran to her baking and crossed the yard to the library. With great anticipation, she pressed the numbers Gran had given her on the keypad. The lights flickered on as soon as she closed the door and she breathed in the purified air. As she walked around the large room, Claire ran a finger along the shelves and over the drawers, feeling the knowledge that each held jumping out at her. This was a new feeling, and it soon began to overwhelm her somewhat.

The draw that first enticed her attention the day before once more called louder than the rest, and Claire stood in front of it. Her fingers tingled as they hovered over the handle and slowly pulled it open to its full extent. The pages lay spread out neatly, waiting for her to pick them up—when she remembered the rule Gran had stipulated. Claire then picked up the cotton gloves that sat on the table in the middle of the room.

The pages were soon laid out on the table's metal surface and Claire found herself studying the beautifully inscribed artwork. She noticed something on the first page she had not previously and marvelled at the workmanship that went into creating it. It was not paper that had been used and it was not vellum, but something else entirely — and she wasn't sure what the ink was made of, either.

Concentrating on the first word, she could make out the individual pen strokes the writer had made. The delicate lines interlaced each other almost like runes. The more she stared at them, the more they resembled those she'd seen before. Almost immediately, she knew the book and the position on the shelf that she wanted. Once it was retrieved, the pages flipped in her hands until she stopped and looked down at the book. She traced the ruin figure with her finger and compared it with the one on the page.

Her mind shifted slightly, and she tried to employ her Recall techniques but found them blocked by something else. Standing up, she shook her hands and walked around for a moment and then went back to the table. Claire cleared her mind again and felt inwards— trying to find what was blocking the one Talent she could always rely on to help her with this. At every turn, she was stymied and failed to find what was wrong. Her frustration levels were building until she gave out a grunt of pure anguish.

Not since she had come into her Talents had she felt this way. They had never let her down and she was at a loss as to what to do. Once again, she calmed herself down and sat staring into space, clearing her mind. Carefully, she sorted her thoughts, tracking their paths until she came to an area of her brain she'd never seen before. It was crystalline and luminescent—the complete opposite to the description Adam had given her of the primeval area they'd rescued her from.

She circled the orb and reached out a hand to touch it.

"What are you?" she mused aloud.

"We are us." The light coming from its insides pulsed as a voice replied to Claire and she stumbled back.

"What are you doing here?" Claire asked it.

"We are here because we are here."

"When did you come to be here?" She was starting to feel her frustration increase.

"Time has no meaning to us here, but we would gauge it to be half a day."

"What is your purpose?"

"We exist as a conduit for our Talents," the crystal orb replied flatly.

"A conduit? What do you mean by that?"

"To be a focus. We believe we are searching for an explanation and these simple questions will take too long. Would you like for us to tell what our function is fully?"

"That would be very helpful. Thank you." Claire was still dubious about this sudden change in her mind.

"We are a gift that was left for us from the Guardians—to help with our task. This gift was left via a tear our mother dropped. It was the seed for us to grow and now we are here."

"Who are the Guardians and why have they given me this gift?"

"The Guardians are the old people who lived in this land. They are the original race and had Talents that far exceed those of today. They are tied to the land and keep its secrets still."

"I'm going to ask a question that everyone seems to ask in situations such as these, and that question is this: why me?" Claire asked, trying not to give a nervous laugh.

"We are a direct descendant of the Guardians. The merging of our parents' lines, and the events that are happening in the world at large, became the perfect time for the creation of us. That is why we—out of all who have gone before us or even after—have all the Talents. We are the One True Child."

"But you're wrong. I don't have Strength or Foresight. You have to be born with those Talents," Claire argued.

"We beg to differ. We were born with those Talents. All of them, including Longevity. That is why we have found it so easy to learn the Talents, because they come so naturally to us."

"What if I don't want them?" Her brows knitted together at this news. Her experience with Marcus and how his longevity caused his apparent madness clouded her thoughts.

"We can pick and choose the Talents we want to utilise. If we do not wish to have Charm, we do not have to use it."

"Well, that is something, I suppose. You mentioned that the Guardians had more Talents than we have now. What are those other Talents?"

"The answers we seek are here in this room. We just need to decipher them to understand," the crystal orb told her.

"That's what I was doing when I felt the blockage on my Talents. Was that you?"

"We may have been in the process of realigning our Talents and that may have been our problem. We have completed that task and we have implemented a new Talent for our use. The Talent is Tongues—this should help with our work."

"Tongues? I presume this means that I can understand different languages?"

"Correct."

"If this was happening in a movie, I would've called this far-fetched. Sometimes I think I'm losing my mind," Claire said, shaking her head slightly.

"We can assure us that we are not losing our mind." The flat tone of instruction was gone, but only slightly. Underlying the words that were spoken by the crystal, Claire detected a slightly mischievous nature.

"That doesn't help," Claire gave a little chuckle. "Is there any way you can stop using the 'we' and 'us' when talking? It makes it very hard to follow what you're saying."

"If that is what we wish. I will try to accommodate you."

"Thank you. We'd be most grateful."

"I believe that was an attempt at humour. Unfortunately, that is located in another part of your brain. Would you like me to integrate it into my specifications?" the orb asked. If this had come from an actual person standing in front of Claire, she could have imagined that they were being sarcastic.

"No, it's all right. What are the other Talents that they've integrated into my mind?"

"There are many. It would take me time to explain all, and that is time we do not have. Someone is trying to communicate with you, and I believe you should answer him before he tries to reach in and find you."

"Thank you. I look forward to talking with you again."

"I will be here," the orb said, and the light dimmed from within.

Claire retreated from her mind and saw with her own eyes again. Standing beside her was Gerry, ready to place his hands on her head to seek her out. She flinched and moved away from his reach before he had time to use his Talent on her.

"Gerry, sorry. I was searching my mind…trying to figure out these ruins," she said, quickly trying to cover up the flinch.

"Thank God you're back. I've been trying to reach you for the last few minutes. I brought your lunch." He seemed embarrassed, indicating a plate of sandwiches on the table.

Gerry moved away and sat down opposite her. "You were so deeply under I was beginning to worry a bit."

"It's a habit that I've formed. Uncle Geoff was always complaining about it." She took the gloves off and picked up a sandwich. "Thank you for this. How's Leana?" She took a bite and was surprised to find how hungry she was.

"Leana will be fine. She's sleeping now, and Robbie's watching over her." Gerry's face was bruised, and one eye was puffy. He saw her looking. "She took some convincing to see things our way. I'm sure you heard the crashes."

"We did. Matt told me about your daughter. I'm sorry for your loss."

"That is very nice of you to say, Claire, and I do appreciate it. I'm not really ready to discuss Breena yet. I would rather do that with my wife, if you don't mind," he said quietly, looking down at his folded hands.

"Of course." They sat in silence while Claire finished her lunch.

"You mentioned ruins? Which ones are you looking at?" Gerry asked, turning his attention to the pages laid out on the table.

Claire nudged the gloves over to him and wiped her hands on her jeans. She watched him carefully put them on and then move the page towards him to study it.

"I'm not sure what the paper is. It doesn't feel like vellum or any plant-based fiber that I know of," she said.

"You're right…it is neither, but that does not matter. The ruins are familiar." Claire passed him the book and he compared the two. "Yes, they are similar—very similar indeed. I can't tell if the page is an earlier version of those in the book or the other way around."

"I think it might be earlier." She sat looking at Gerry and decided to lay all her cards on the table. "Gerry, have you ever heard of the Guardians?"

"Guardians, you say?" He got up and without hesitation, went to a drawer and opened it up. He shifted through a few pages that lay inside and pulled one out. Very carefully, he brought it over for her to see. The page trembled while he placed it on the table. "Have a look at this one. It is the predictions of one of our forebears. I only remember it because it was one of the last ones I catalogued before I left."

Carefully, Claire cast her eyes over the cursive script. And even though it was in Gaelic, she found she could read it. The crystal was right; the musical-sounding language flowed through her mind. *But how to tell Gerry that I can now speak and read it fluently? How can I explain what had happened to me?* she thought, glancing up at him.

"If you're asking about the Guardians, then I believe you have a bit more to tell me." She remained silent for a moment longer than he liked. "Claire, the time to be completely honest is now—if I and the others are going to help you."

"You're going to think that I'm completely mad, because I certainly think I've lost my marbles."

"Try me," he prompted.

"Yesterday when I stormed out, I went up to the standing stones. They had a strong effect on me. I could feel the energy pulsating inside and was drawn to them. Matt took me away from them, but all I could think of was getting back there."

"So, you are a sensitive. Never mind…I will explain later—please continue."

Claire went on to tell him about her heavy dream state and all that happened on the hill. She described the Guardians and the knowledge they imparted to her before calling her mother to her and changing Jess from mist to fully formed.

"That doesn't sound very helpful, but it is what happened. She came together, and I could see her—like I see my father. We talked and then she left. She approves of your son, by the way," she said, blushing slightly as she finished her telling.

"I am pleased to hear it. I approve of you also."

Claire smiled. "Apparently, when my mother was leaving, she shed a tear that turned into a crystal. She told me that it was a gift from the Guardians."

"She? You mean your mother?" Gerry asked with some confusion as he tried to follow her explanation.

"No. This is the part where you're going to think that I'm totally barmy. When I was inside my mind just now…" Claire hesitated for a moment. "The crystal spoke to me. The crystal was a seed planted by the Guardians to help me with my Talents. From what she told me, they are the first people of this land and they had far more Talents than we have today. She said that she was rerouting all my Talents so I can use them more effectively, and that I had more than the normal, including being able to understand languages. According to the crystal, I am a direct descendant of the Guardians due to my lineage. She called me a 'true child.' That is why it has happened to me." She watched his predicted reaction. "See, I told you that you'd think I'm nuts. Do you approve of me now?"

"That's a lot to process." He sighed deeply and shifted a little in his seat.

"You're telling me! I'm still in shock."

"I still approve, Claire. I haven't seen Matt this happy in a very long time. None of his other girlfriends have *ever* had this effect on him." Claire blushed deeply at the praise. "Now, languages. Does that mean both living and dead?"

"Let's give it a go," Claire said, looking back at the original page she pulled out. She put on a new pair of gloves and held it in her hands.

The meaning behind the symbols jumped out at her and it became so clear that she felt that it should've been obvious from the start. She read it and read it again to make sure she understood the writing and looked back at a patiently waiting Gerry.

"Well? What does it say?" he asked eagerly.

"It says…" She placed a cotton-enshrouded finger under the first row of ruins. "'Our people's time is at an end. Others are coming to take our place and we must not resist, but welcome them, learn from them, and be integrated with them. This will not be an easy thing to do, as they are far less advanced than we are. The sacred places shall stand and be used for other purposes, but in the most sacred shall lie our knowledge, skills, and energies. But know that two will come who can once again bring life to our words and wield our Talents in their defence.'" Claire looked up at Gerry.

"I think you and I will be working very closely together for a while, Claire." He looked at his watch. "But I must get back to Leana. I'd be very appreciative if—for now—this new information was kept between us. We must learn more and think on it before we tell the others. Is that okay?"

"More than okay. The longer I have to tell them, the longer until they find out I'm a basket case." She laughed.

"I know it must feel that way right now, but let it sink in. Would it help to tell you that we've been looking for a link to the Guardians? My research into our family led me to that area specifically and it is what we were looking for on that dig."

"You have heard of the Guardians?"

"Yes, we have, and they have many other names, but I'll tell you more tomorrow. Again, just let this new information sink in tonight and get used to it."

Gerry then left her as she sat at the table looking around. She remembered reading that the Picts were thought to not be the original settlers of Scotland, but that they were in fact the descendants of conquerors of a much older race of people. If that was true, then what lay before her was proof that the older race had deliberately bred themselves out of existence. Their bloodlines only surfaced in those who could seemingly handle the Talents.

The other page Gerry had taken out of its resting place still sat on the table where they had left it. She read the cursive script and pondered the meaning of the lyrical language. *Two as close as twins and of the old shall come to be with the new. Abilities so great and untried. Those lives so precious must be protected and hidden. The Ancient Ones will claim their lives as their own.* The last line caused the hair on the back of Claire's neck to stand up and a shiver to creep down her spine.

Claire closed her eyes and leaned back in the hard metal chair. Then she stood, carefully putting the pages back into their respective drawers and returning the book to the shelf she had found it on, before removing the gloves and dropping them down on the table. She stopped just before she got to the door as a sound—or a sense—came over her, like a collective groan at the fact she was leaving. The knowledge called her back, begging her to stay and learn. She tightened her defences in her mind, opening the door to the outside world and stepped through it, back to the present day.

Like a weight being lifted off her, Claire felt light and free in the weak afternoon sunshine, but she did not feel like going back to the house with all its troubles just yet. Instead, Claire wandered down to the field behind the outbuildings and stood by the brook. Looking up, she traced the white of the water as it hurtled and sparkled down the hill toward where she knew the stones were waiting for her to come back.

Now turning her back on the hill, she walked beside the babbling brook, watching it glisten in the sunlight and listening to the burble as it travelled over the rocks down into the next clear pool. It snaked its long way down the valley, splitting the meadow in two with its many twists and turns. The rush of the water was halted only momentarily by placid, deep pools that lay glassy and still, reflecting the billowing clouds in the pale blue sky above. Claire followed it all the way to the end, where it met with the faster-moving, darker, and deeper river that cut the valley off from the rest of the bustling world. She saw the waters mingle and mix as they got carried away downstream. And in her mind, she could see the journey that it took to finally end in the sea. The path it took was clear in her mind and she watched it ebb and flow, feeling the life that it gave to the world.

A blast of icy wind drove through her thin clothing, reminding her that it was probably time to get back. The sun was disappearing behind the gathering clouds, which were turning grey. She didn't want to get caught in the rain again. Slow, hesitant footsteps moved Claire away from her dreaming and carried her to a place she did not expect to go. The leaves were already turning beautiful shades of yellow, red, and orange in patches, making the oak tree seem as if it had been touched by a passing rainbow. The chill she had felt before was not there now. Instead, it was peaceful, calm, and almost warm under the protective branches. But most of all, it was inviting.

Her hand touched the ancient wood and the tree's life force thrummed with hers, welcoming her like an old friend. So many things depended on it for their homes and their lives, and they all called to her in greeting. A low branch afforded Claire a chance to seek her own comfort in the tree and she pulled herself up, climbing higher. It had been years since she'd climbed a tree rather than flying up. Nestled now in its branches, she felt at ease and comfortable as she sat back and listened to the dying day.

"Hello."

Claire's eyes flew open in surprise and searched the branches. She could have sworn she had heard a small voice but could see nothing that would have made the sound.

"You can see me, can't you?" Like a whisper on the wind, it spoke again. "I saw you with a man I don't recognise."

Claire sat up straighter on her perch and peered closer into the gathering gloom. This day was turning out to be a very strange one.

"Who are you?" she breathed softly, her heart beating hard in her chest. Claire had a feeling she already knew the answer to that particular question.

"I'm Breena." A little girl slowly materialised, dancing lightly over the branches towards her. Her hair was caught in a ponytail with a red ribbon, and she was dressed in a blue T-shirt and green shorts. "I live here now," she told Claire. "Do you know my Mum and Da?"

Claire studied the child for a moment and recognised the face from the covered canvas in Leana's studio. "Yes, I do, Breena."

"And do you know Galen, my brother?" the girl asked with her head cocked ever so slightly.

"Yes, but I know him as Matt."

"That's silly! Why would he call himself by his middle name? Are you trying to trick me?" Breena's laugh was like a tiny bell on the wind.

"Why do you live here now, Breena? Why don't you go home?" Claire asked her softly.

"I tried, but there was so much sadness there that I came back here. I like my tree and he likes me. He protects me." The little girl patted the trunk. "There have been a lot of people around lately. I wish Galen would stop on his way past to say hello, but he never sees me when I wave at him."

"Was he a good big brother, then?"

"The best there ever was. He's the coolest. I put a big frog in his pocket one day and he chased me all the way to the ford and threatened to put it down my shirt if I did it again. I laughed and laughed. We had so much fun," Breena told her with a very large, beaming smile.

"It sounds like he loved you very much."

"Doesn't he love me anymore?" Breena tilted her head again, and her eyebrows knitted together. The question was such a simple one, but it held so much pain and heartache.

"I'm sure he does. They all still love you, Breena." Claire tried to reassure the girl.

"Then why don't they come to visit me? I get so lonely with just the tree." She hung her head and played with her fingers.

"I don't know. Sometimes it takes a while for people to understand and come to terms with things."

"I know I'm dead. I watched Galen carry me home. There was a lot of pain at first, but then it went away. Can you make them come and visit me?" she asked with eyes brimming with hope.

"I'm not sure if I can do that, Breena. I don't know if they'll be able to see you."

"They will if you help them." The little girl skipped the last couple of branches and pointed to Claire's head as she stood beside her. "It's in there. All you have to do is look—then you could help them."

"How about if I promise to try to get them to see? Would that be all right?" Claire asked, trying to appease the little girl.

"Yes, please." A glowing smile beamed from her, and Claire couldn't help but smile back.

"It's been very nice talking to you, Breena, but I had better get back before it gets dark. They'll be wondering where I am."

Breena sighed and wandered off to the next branch. "I hope you come again. I like you. What's your name?"

"I'm Claire. Claire Brown."

"No, it's not!" the little girl said, laughing and shaking her head. "You have another name, but it's hidden and secret." She put her finger to her lips and made a shushing sound before slowly disappearing into the deepening shadows.

Claire sat for a while longer, listening quietly to lonely rustling of the leaves and the creak of the old wood in the wind before climbing down and making her way back up the track to the house. *A very strange day, it still feels like I'm dreaming,* Claire thought to herself. Who would believe that she had met a ghost in the tree? But convincing them is what she had to try and do.

Chapter Fourteen

"Addy, are you still awake?" Claire asked into the darkness.

"Mmm," Addy replied sleepily from somewhere under her blankets in the next bed.

"Addy, do you believe in ghosts?" The question hung in the air for a moment before Addy's head appeared. Only the sound of the wind mournfully seeking a way in through the windows punctuated the dark.

"I'm Scottish, so of course I believe. Why, have you seen one?" she replied in her clipped English accent.

"I have," Claire answered.

"I love a good ghost story. Where?" Addy asked eagerly.

"I don't think you're going to like this one."

"Claire, stories don't scare me easily."

"I'm not worried about scaring you. I'm more worried that you won't believe me, or you'll be angry."

"What are you going on about? Just tell me the story and let me decide."

"I warned you." Claire propped herself up on an elbow and looked at the dark shape in the bed opposite. "I went for a walk today and I found myself under the big oak tree." She stopped and waited for a response from Addy.

"Go on," Addy responded flatly.

"Please don't be angry with me, Addy. I talked to Breena."

The wind rattled the window, the house creaked, and the silence between them grew. Claire lay back down with disappointment, cursing herself for bringing it up. She'd thought Addy would be the one to go to with this, but it was just this reaction that she was afraid of.

"What does she look like?" Addy asked quietly.

"She had a ponytail with a red ribbon and a laugh like a bell."

"That was my ribbon. I left it here before she died. What did she say?"

"That she missed everyone. She told me a story about a frog in Matt's pocket."

"I dared her to do that!" She laughed at the memory. "It was after she died that Galen started to call himself Matt." Addy paused for a while as she remembered the incident. "I wish I could talk to her."

"You might be able to. She told me that it was all in my head. Well, that sounded really good." Claire chuckled at the absurdity of it.

"Probably not the best way to put it." Addy laughed with her. "Can we go in the morning?"

"Yeah, if you want. I promised that I'd try, so don't be too upset if I can't do it."

"I'll not sleep now. I'm so excited—nervous—but excited." Claire could hear Addy roll over in her bed.

Claire herself had trouble getting to sleep that night, as her mind was racing with everything that had happened that day. It was all too much. She tossed and turned, but finally gave up in the wee small hours. Climbing out of bed, she pulled on a jumper and socks and crept down the stairs to the kitchen to put the kettle on.

With cup in hand, she sat at the table and used it to warm her in the cold night air. Lost in her thoughts, she stared out the window into the darkness beyond. A whirlwind of emotions colliding with each other, secrets were held close—marring her world with their infectiousness. She hated secrets and hated keeping them and having them kept from her. In a perfect world, she knew that there would be none left, but this was not a perfect world and she herself, was not perfect.

Her eyelids drooped, and her head began to nod as sleep finally came calling. Her head jerked up when she realised she was sleeping, and she blinked a thousand times to clear it. Claire knew she should just go up to bed, but the thought of climbing those stairs was too much for her to bear and she leaned back in her chair.

"Hey…what are you doing here? You should be tucked up in bed—with me, preferably." Matt's smiling face came into focus as Claire's eyes fluttered open. "Good morning, gorgeous. I missed you last night." His eyes were dancing with mischief.

"If this is what waking up beside you is like, then I want to do it forever," Claire mumbled as she stretched and then placed her arms around his neck. "Can we run off and forget about everyone and everything that has happened and just spend our lives alone together?"

"I'd love nothing more." He kissed her gently. "I was hoping that last night you might invite me in again." He rested his forehead on hers.

"I'm sorry. There was just so much on my mind. I *did* have every intention of calling out to you, but I think I prefer you in the flesh."

"Um, good morning, you two." Already dressed and ready to go running, Addy stood in the doorway. "I thought you had left without me, Claire. Remember, you convinced me to go for a run this morning?"

The conversation from the previous night came back to her and she forced a smiled. "Yeah, I remember. Do you mind, Matt?"

"There's nothing that you could do that I'd mind." He kissed her again. "So go for your run...breakfast will be waiting when you get back."

"I love a man who can cook." As Claire stood with him, he looked a bit startled at her words. She felt herself blush with the intense feeling for this man standing so close to her.

"Are you coming, Claire?" Addy asked without looking at the pair.

"Just let me get changed." She broke the hold his eyes had on her and left the room.

Minutes later, the two women were running down the track. The lack of sleep prompted Claire to set an easy pace, but she could tell Addy was in a hurry to reach the great oak. The morning was still—with the wind having blown itself out overnight—and a thin mist lay over the low-lying fields, giving it an otherworldly feel.

The tree came into sight and Addy slowed down, with the enormity of what she'd agreed to just beginning to dawn on her.

"We don't have to if you don't want to, Addy." Claire stood beside her friend, watching her closely.

"No, I want to. I need to see her—to say goodbye." She gave a tight, determined smile and then continued on at a walk as Claire linked her arm with Addy's.

Part of the problem Claire had with the idea was figuring out how to pull this off. How was she going to be able to let Addy see Breena using her own eyes? Breena had said the knowledge was there; she just needed to find it, and Crystal came to mind.

"When we get there, I'm going to have to go inside myself to find what I need…so you will have to bear with me until I do, okay?"

"Yep." Addy's nervousness was spilling over, and she was as now white as a sheet.

As they closed in on the tree, a small figure dropped from the branches and waited for them under its shady limbs. She smiled when she recognised Claire and stared at Addy.

"You came!" the little girl called out. "Addy, it's you!" Breena danced around in circles, happy to see her cousin. Claire smiled at her antics.

"Why are you smiling?" Addy asked.

"Breena is very happy you came. She's dancing around the tree."

Addy looked back at the tree but saw nothing under the spreading limbs. Her face reflected the confusing thoughts that played out in her mind, as she wondered if her friend was crazy. Or was she herself dreaming this?

They stopped at the edge of the tree and Claire turned to her friend. "Can you stay here while I explain things to Breena—if I can even get her to calm down?" Addy gave her a small nod and watched Claire move away from her.

"Hello, Breena. Yes, I did bring her." Claire paused as Addy could see she was listening to something by the large trunk. "You need to calm down and be patient. I still haven't got a handle on what I need to do." There was another pause while Addy felt like she was listening to a one-sided telephone call. "Let me do what I need to do and then we will try, okay?" Claire nodded and then sank to the earth where she stood.

She closed her eyes and found her way back to Crystal. There was music playing somewhere in her mind, and its haunting melody floated around her. Claire felt certain that if she were to pick up a musical instrument, she'd be able to recreate the tune flawlessly. She focused back on Crystal and gained her attention.

"Good morning. We are well this morning."

"Yes...I am well, and so are you. Remember when we talked about this yesterday?"

"I remember everything we do."

"Good. Now, can you help me with letting Addy see Breena?"

"Of course I can, and so can you. It is all here—like that song that we're playing in our head. So happy, yet so sad."

"Never mind that now...can you please tell me what I need to do?"

"I can't tell you, but I can *show* you."

The light from within the crystal casing grew until it was blinding. The moment it encompassed Claire, it was in every fibre of her being. And Crystal was right—she already knew what to do. It was as if a light-switch had come on, illuminating, and bringing to focus the particular Talent she needed.

Her eyes flew open, and she beckoned the cousins to come closer. She stood and brushed the dirt from her knees, then looked at them both.

"Do you trust me, Addy?" Claire asked uncertainly.

"Yes, I trust you." Addy had a feeling a simple nod would not do in this situation.

"Breena, do you trust me?" Claire looked down at the little girl.

"Yes, Claire...I trust you."

"Good. I need the pair of you to take my hands." She held them out and felt one warm, trembling hand and one small, cold one slide into each of her own. "And Breena, can you now take Addy's other hand in yours?"

Addy's eyes widened as an icy cool touch encompassed her hand. She started to shiver even more but held firm onto Breena's hand.

Claire pushed her energy out from her hands and into the two beings beside her. She felt the energy connect at the point where Breena held Addy's hand and then spread to the middle of the circle they'd made.

"Addy, you can open your eyes now," Claire said gently while letting go.

Addy's soft blue eyes had been tightly shut for the whole process and now they flickered open. She looked down to where Breena still held on to her hand and gave a gasp of surprise. Immediately, she was on her knees—hugging the little girl to her with tears streaming down her face.

"Bree, oh, Bree...I've missed you so much," she crooned over and over.

"Addy, you can see me!" Breena hugged her cousin back and was jumping up and down, unable to contain her excitement a moment longer.

"I'm going to leave you two to talk." Claire smiled and wiped a tear from her eye before walking towards the ford at the bottom of the track. Thoughts of her own reunion with her parents were on her mind, so she could understand what Addy must be feeling.

The track ran straight into the river, and Claire could see the wheel marks that had been made over the years underneath the flowing water where it shallowed. She picked up a few stones and started to toss them in, watching the splash sparkle in the early morning sunlight.

A lazy white cloud crossed in front of the slowly rising sun as Claire looked up. Her heart thumped loudly in her chest when she saw who was standing on the other side of the ford from her. Tall and lean and dressed in jeans and a jumper, was

Tony. He smiled and waved at her as he walked closer to the water's edge.

"You're up early this morning, Claire," he called to her.

"You know what they say…the early bird catches the worm." She smiled sweetly at him. "Oh, and that reminds me—how is Jack these days?"

"Missing you, apparently. He sent me to find you yet again. I really must thank you for the lovely gift you gave us in Killin, but unfortunately, it cost us a bit to fix things after it left."

"You are most welcome, Tony. I knew you would like it. Especially in that spot. I take it that it was you—and not Richard—who did the deed on that stormy day?"

"Is my work that recognisable? Richard wouldn't have had the bottle for it."

"As I understand it, he had a lot of bottles…usually filled with amber liquid. Is he any better since the last time I saw you?" Claire asked, remembering the wild-eyed look she had left the man with.

"No change. You truly did a number on him."

"Take it as a warning. Don't mess with me, my family, or my friends. And tell Jack the same thing. It doesn't seem to have sunk in yet."

"I don't think it ever will. You know, I'm beginning to see what he sees in you. You're a feisty one." Tony's gaze took in her whole body.

"Guys like you make my skin crawl. You're old enough to be my father," she threw at him only half-heartedly.

"No, I am not as old as he was." A cruel smile emerged when he saw that piece of news affect her. "Oh yes, I knew your daddy and your mummy. They were such a lovely couple. It really was too bad what happened to them."

"I've had enough of this conversation. You're boring me now. Bye, Tony. And remember what I can do…" The information had shocked her. He had known her parents.

"Don't go yet, Claire. We were having such a lovely chat! I get so lonely out here watching you. You looked lonely yesterday when you were here. It nearly broke my heart."

"I didn't know you were so sentimental or even *had* a heart. Maybe you should get yourself a dog—I think one of those fluffy little white, yappy things would suit you to a tee. Or get yourself a hobby that takes you far, far away from me."

"Why do you have to ruin things with such nasty words? I was starting to love our chats…as I have yet to meet another woman who can match me the way you do." Claire could see him appraising her body again.

"You obviously don't get out much. You should, since there is a beautiful world out there that's just waiting for you to explore. That is my parting advice to you. Goodbye. I would say have a nice life, but then I'd be lying."

"How about we meet tomorrow? Same time, same place! I'll bring a picnic breakfast we can share. Do you prefer bagels or croissants?" he asked with a grin.

Claire turned and waved back to him, not daring herself to say another word. The mere fact he was here was bad enough news, without having to deal with his puerile attempts at humour. Also, the information he'd imparted about knowing her parents had stunned her into remembering that he was in fact a dangerous man.

"Who was that?" Addy asked when Claire returned to the tree. Startled from her tumbling thoughts, she saw both Breena and Addy sitting on one of the lower limbs of the old oak.

"Tony just kindly letting me know that he is around. He's such a creep." Claire shivered and unconsciously looked back to the ford—just in time to see him walking away.

"I don't know why you don't just get rid of him with your…you know." Addy waved her hand in the air like she was performing magic.

"Don't be ridiculous, Addy. Anyway, at least I know where he is. I could get Uncle Geoff to do a sweep of the area and get a lock on him," She yawned, feeling the lack of sleep, and also thinking of how to involve her uncle in some way.

"He's been watching us?" Addy asked, visibly shaken, and shivering at the thought.

"It seems that way. Enough of him. How have you two got on?"

Breena jumped out of the tree and into Claire's arms. "Addy thinks she can get Galen here." Her expression was bright with the thought as Claire placed her down on the ground.

"That is going to have to be up to him." Claire got down to her level and looked the ghost child in the face. "Galen and your parents were very hurt when you died. It damaged their relationships, and it might be still too painful for them. Do you understand what I'm saying?"

"Yes, I do. But I can't go until I have seen them. They are keeping me here with their pain and I feel it every day, even when Da and Galen are away."

"Claire and I will try our best, Bree." Addy joined them on the ground.

"Okay, but they have to come soon, 'cos the man in the long dress said that it needs to be mended before the full moon or I'll never be able to leave. He asked me to tell you." Breena looked into Claire's eyes and she could tell the little girl was telling the truth.

Claire took the child's face in her hands and kissed her cool forehead. "I will do everything in my power for you, Breena. I promise."

"And I promise as well," Addy told her.

"You had better go. They're starting to look for you," Breena said, hugging Addy once more. "Come back soon, Addy."

"I will, sweetheart." Addy reluctantly let her go and followed Claire back to the track. She took one last look behind and saw Breena disappear like mist. A tear escaped her eye and she brushed it away.

"Are you okay?" Claire put an arm around her friend.

"I'm fine." Addy leaned into Claire. "I don't know how I'm going to explain it to Matt. Can you help me?"

Claire groaned inwardly to herself. "I'll try, but I don't—"

"Don't think, just do," Addy fired back. "Come on…or my father will have eaten most of breakfast before we get back."

They ran all the way up the track, not saying a word to each other. Once inside, they found the rest of the household awake and in the kitchen. Claire and Addy each grabbed a plate and helped themselves to the bacon and eggs. The pair helped to clean up and then Claire went in search of Geoff.

"We have a problem," she started as both David and Geoff's heads came up from the map they were looking at.

"What problem?" Geoff asked with an immediate worry clouding his features.

"Tony's watching us again. I met him on our run this morning—at the ford. We actually had a very polite chat."

"Is that your way of saying you went heavy on the sarcasm?" David asked with a short laugh.

"Maybe just a tiny bit. I was wondering if you two could help me…"

"Let me guess. You want us to locate and do a bit of snooping on the snooper?" Geoff asked.

"We could do that, as it beats sitting 'round here all day. I've been getting so bored that I went out and moved the sheep yesterday—just for something to do," David said. "Come on, Geoff…let's get a bit of exercise. I promise I won't go too fast for you."

"All right, but only to shut you up! This might be difficult. I've never spoken to the man myself," Geoff said quickly.

David and Claire watched as he looked out into the distance. Claire noticed he was using more effort these days for such a simple task and it worried her. She was about to offer to do it for him when he came back to them.

"There's someone over the hill—that way. That's all I can get," he told them.

"You said he met you at the ford? How about we take it from there…I can track him back to his camp. It shouldn't take too long." There was a determination to David that reminded Claire of his encounter with Richard.

"I don't want you to confront Tony. I just want to know how far he has been travelling around the valley and where he is camping. Nothing else, David," Claire warned him.

"You have nothing to worry about, Claire. I'll be making sure Geoff's kept out of mischief."

"You will never change. I wonder what my mother would say on that," Claire pondered mischievously.

"Don't you dare bring her into this, Claire Brown. That is so unfair. Even beyond the grave, she's giving me grief," David said with a smile.

The mention of a grave reminded her about the delicate question of how to bring up the subject of Breena with Matt. After Gran's warning about hurting him and leaving for a while, she didn't really want to tackle it at all. But the question was out of her hands. Matt came looking for her and his face was red.

"Is what Addy told me true? You've seen Breena?" he asked Claire quietly and urgently, dragging her into the empty formal dining room.

"Yes. So has Addy." Claire held her breath, waiting for him to explode.

"She told me." He seemed to be at a loss for words, attempting to say something and then stopping before he did.

"Breena wants to see you, Matt. She can't move on until she's seen her family."

"Her family? You mean she—"

"Yes," Claire answered before he could pose the question. "Look, you need to think about it. I'm not going to push this and I—"

"I just wish you had told me yourself!" His anger burst from him in the form of a heavy whisper.

"I was just coming now to do *exactly* that. Addy was supposed to wait for me, so we could talk to you together," she defended herself. "Matt, I'm going to walk away now, so that neither of us can say anything we might regret." Claire left him standing in the dining room, grabbing her jumper from the hall where she'd left it and heading out towards the library. And she did not look back to see whether he was watching or following.

Inside the library, she leaned against the door and calmed herself down. She had known Matt would take the news badly and she'd expected him to react with anger, but it still unsettled her. Her thoughts of Breena and Matt reached out to the collective works in the library, and they shouted back to her. A confusion of information battered her brain and somewhere in her mind, Crystal was soaking it all up and sorting it.

She sat down and laid her head on the table, as her mind was starting to hurt with the forceful onslaught she was just too powerless to control. Claire closed her eyes and let Crystal do her thing, waiting for the slowdown she was hoping would come soon.

A hand touched her shoulder as she lifted her head with a start and forced a smile onto her lips.

"You scared me," she said slowly.

"I'm sorry. I really am. It just surprised me," Matt apologised and leaned down to take her in his arms. When Claire didn't answer back, he looked down at her. "What's going on?"

"Information, so much information. I'm finding it hard to concentrate. Don't worry about it, Matt. I understand…I'd be angry, too." There was a vagueness to her voice that concerned him, especially as there were no books or papers on the table before her.

"How about you give it a break for the moment? It's lunchtime." Matt had to place his hands under her arms to get her to move. "Claire, come on. You're scaring me."

"I'm fine," she insisted, half-heartedly trying to fend him off.

"No. You are not!" Matt picked her up and headed for the door. He tried to juggle her almost limp body while attempting to open it, finally having to put her back on her feet and hold her up.

The door opened, letting in a burst of fresh air with the wind. The smell of autumn that was carried along with it was enough to revive her. Claire pushed Matt away and stumbled outside, bending over, and taking great gulps of air into her lungs and breathing them out just as deeply. She stood and gazed about, noticing that half the day had already passed by. She wondered briefly how long she'd been in there.

"Claire, you're really scaring me now. You all right?" Matt asked her clearly and calmly with a hint of panic as he placed a hand on the small of her back, trying to draw her into an embrace.

"I'm fine. I swear. I'll be fine," she said, breathing hard and stepping out of his arms.

"What the hell happened in there? Was it the air? I'll go make sure it's working properly." He went to step away, but Claire called him back.

"Matt, come back. It wasn't the air. I don't want to keep it secret anymore. I need help."

He was at her side within a second of her asking for it. "What is it?"

"That night…when you were with me in my mind by the stones, something else happened. Mum wasn't the only other person to visit me beside you. I was visited by the Guardians."

She could see him mulling over the word. "Guardians? Claire, I don't understand."

"The Guardians are the original people—before the Picts. They were integrating themselves with the new cultures and kept their Talents hidden. In some way, we are all their descendants, as it is from them we got our Talents. That night, they planted something in my brain to help me focus my existing Talents and the new ones they've given me." She stopped and looked at him. "That is how I can see Breena, and how I can read the ruins on the pages in there…and how I'm now able to just pluck out the information without even taking the book off the shelf. Matt, it feels like I am losing my mind. I don't know how to control any of it."

Her eyes were wide and pleading with him to understand—to accept what she told him completely and not reject her. Matt stood silent and she could see the incredulity on his face. The fight within him to believe was as clear to her as if she were hearing his thoughts.

"I…" she started and stopped. The urge to flee from him overcame her need to stay, so she turned and ran. Her legs worked hard underneath her, taking her as far away as possible, as the track flew beneath feet and her arms pumped at her sides. No sounds carried to her ears—except for the sound of her heart simultaneously beating and breaking.

Passing the big oak with Breena swinging from the branches and through the ford, she realised she had not gone farther since coming to the cottage. When she reached the road, she turned left and ran down the hard, dark bitumen—eating up the miles. Claire ran on and on, pushing herself hard and using up all the energy she could spend through using Stealth, but she still found she had an abundance left.

Finally, she pulled up and sat on the stone wall that ran beside the road. Large, fat tears streamed from her eyes in total anguish, and she sobbed uncontrollably. So much so that she started to retch, and she emptied her stomach over the wall. Wiping her mouth, she stood up and again, anguish filled her very being. The pain was so intense that she felt crippled by it.

The day had started so beautifully with Matt waking her up and her feeling complete with him—to the wonderful reunion between Addy and Breena. But it had started to darken with the appearance of Tony, a harbinger of what was still to come. Then the confession to Matt and his reaction, which had scared Claire. She wondered why she had run, why she hadn't stayed and waited for him to properly talk about it. It confounded and frightened her.

Claire lifted her head with the sound of an approaching car and thought it was Matt coming to find her. To her surprise, it was not. It was a gleaming black sedan. Feeling foolish and wiping away the remains of her tears, she started to walk back to the cottage along the side of the road. The car then rushed by her at a great speed, whipping a wind up as it passed before she heard it come to a screeching stop.

Looking back, she saw the back door open, and a man step out. At first, Claire thought it was going to be Tony—taking the opportunity to taunt her once more. She prepped herself to answer him back. But it wasn't Tony. It was Jack.

"Can we offer you a lift, Claire? You seem to be a very long way from home and all your friends."

"No, thank you, Jack. I can get back on my own." She started to walk backwards slowly, keeping him in sight.

"It's been such a long time, Claire…you know, since we last spoke. I'd love the chance to catch up. I have so much to tell you." He was walking towards her.

She noticed that the life in the city had agreed with him. He was slimmer and better groomed than the last time she saw him in the village—when he'd confronted her outside the hall.

"I don't have time at the moment, Jack. And besides, we aren't meant to meet yet. The time's not right." The words were out of her mouth before she even knew what she was going to say, but instinctively felt they were right. "You are too early."

Jack stopped in his tracks at her statement and stared at her. "I will have you, Claire…you will be mine." The genuine menace in his voice sent a chill down her spine.

"You're going to have to fight me, Jack. Are you ready for what I can do?"

"I can handle whatever you throw at me. I'll be ready."

"Can you give Tony a message for me? Tell him I know." She watched confusion flood his face. "He'll understand." Smiling at Jack, she hoped that this would seed discord between them. She turned and ran down the road and then thought better of it. With ease and grace Claire jumped the stone wall with a single leap and carried on over the hills and fields.

There was no sound of pursuit or of the car turning around. But she carried on until she reached the river and followed it to the ford. Crossing the river was like stepping into another realm, and a peace descended on her. The moment she exited the river, a form rose before her—it was robed, and she recognised it as being one of the Guardians.

"You must stay." The language was definitely not English, but the translation was immediate in her mind. "You have tasks, Carling. And you won't succeed if there is pain here."

"What are the tasks? Please tell me!" she begged the hooded, mysterious figure.

"They will come to you, and you must complete them before the full moon. It is a special moon—a changing moon." The figure disappeared before she could ask another question of him, and Claire walked on. It had definitely been a male voice that had spoken from under the deep hood.

"Claire, Claire! Is Galen coming?" Breena asked, meeting her on the track.

"I'm not sure, Breena. I'm not sure he believes us. If he does, then he's fighting it." Claire left the track and went to sit down with her back leaning against the trunk of the tree. Breena came and sat with her.

"The man said you were sad and I should sit with you. Why are you sad, Claire?" the little girl asked, coming to sit cross-legged beside her.

Claire drew her knees up and rested her chin on them. "I'm sad because I'm in love with your brother, and I think I've just blown it. I'm not sure he understands."

"Galen will come. I know he will, and I will tell him." Breena sat up eagerly and looked so serious.

Claire and the ghost child sat for a long time in a companionable silence, and the day wore on around them. She slept for a time, leaning up against the ancient oak. Her dreams were peaceful. An iridescent green butterfly was fluttering against a window, trying to get in. And as she watched its bright-coloured wings caught the sunlight, a man and a woman watched her—arm in arm—vying for her attention. They were both familiar to her and she couldn't understand why.

A bright star shone down on her, twinkling, and pulsating in the deep blue sky. She knew it was out of place but was fascinated by it and wondered why it was even shining on such a bright day. Claire sat down on the hill's green grass and watched the valley below, seeing a procession of people make their way up beside a sparkling brook and climb the hill to gather near her in the standing stones. They were dressed in bright-coloured clothing, and light seemed to emanate from their skin. Then Breena was there, shaking her shoulder.

"Wake up. You must wake up now, Claire. They are coming."

"They're already here...can't you see them?" Claire replied, her voice curious and mystified by the vision in front of her.

"Not them, Claire—don't watch them. It's not time for you to join them yet. No, look; it's Adaira and Galen. He's come to see me!" Breena said with an excitement rising in her voice.

Claire's eyes fluttered open as she looked over her knees. Addy was jogging down the track with Matt floating behind, keeping pace with his cousin. She groaned and buried her head in her arms, hoping they'd go away and not see her.

But in reality, she knew that they would find her, and that they would be concerned. Claire felt ashamed and guilty for running off like she did—for acting like a prime goose and for once, she didn't feel like facing up to it. She was sick and tired of being responsible for other people's feelings. And even more, she was also tired of being different and having to hide it.

She waited for them to join her and Breena, and as she predicted, they were concerned. Breena was waiting patiently beside Claire for her older brother to notice her, and she took his hand. Claire watched as Matt looked down and shook his hand, but Breena refused to let go.

"She won't let go, Matt." Claire cut across their talk she'd completely ignored, and the cousins then fell silent. "That cold feeling on your hand is your little sister, and Breena's trying to get your attention."

Matt tried to move his hand away, looking at Claire in alarm. "What the—"

Claire didn't wait for him to recover. She grabbed his hand and then joined her other with Breena's. The process was automatic as the energy flowed through their connection. When she opened her eyes, she found Matt staring from her to Breena—with his mouth open. Claire reached up to close his mouth and kissed his cheek.

"I'm sorry…this isn't about you, but Breena." She then left them alone, taking Addy with her.

"What is your problem?" Addy rounded on her when they were far enough away. "What gives you the right to force that on him? If he dumps your arse, then I will have no sympathy for you. And right now, I'm rethinking our friendship."

"Yes, I am a bitch, Addy. I'm a first-class b-i-t-c-h."

"This is not like you." Addy grabbed her hand, stopping Claire from walking away.

"But maybe it is…maybe the namby-pamby, weepy, weak Claire was the fake one. Maybe I am now sick and tired of trying to please everybody. Or maybe—maybe I'm just so tired that I have no idea what I'm saying or doing to the best people I have ever met in my life, especially the man I..." Claire trailed off as she watched Matt talk to Breena from afar.

"The man you what, Claire? Hey, can you hear me?" Addy stepped in front of her and investigated Claire's face. "You love him, don't you?"

Claire sank to the ground and covered her face with her hands. "I love him so very, very much. It hurts." She looked up. "I'm so sorry for talking to you like that, Addy. I shouldn't have. Can you forgive me?"

Addy sank down with her and took her friend's hands in her own. "What's there to forgive? Did you get any sleep last night?"

"No. Well, a bit in the kitchen. Today started so well—so perfectly with Matt waking me up—and it has just gotten a whole lot worse. I got scared. I could see that he thought I was going crazy, so I ran. I ran so far that I bumped into Jack on the road."

"You what?" Addy blinked a couple of times, trying to keep up with the wandering thoughts that were spilling from Claire's mouth.

"I don't want to talk about it just now...I'll just have to do it over and over, and I am so tired, Addy. When we get back, we will get everyone together—including Gerry and Leana. I need to convince them to see Breena, as it has to be done before the next full moon, so she can move on. It's their pain that is keeping her here. They have to let her go."

"How do you—?" Addy fell silent at the look Claire gave her. "All right; later."

Claire watched as Breena took Matt's hand in hers while tears trailed down his cheeks, disappearing into his cropped beard. She wanted to be there for him, but there was still a chance he would brush her aside. And the pain of that would be more than she could bear.

"Addy, why don't you join them. I'm sure they would like to share it with you. I'll be fine right here." She tried not to let her voice betray her feelings as she watched Addy walk over to them and waited for her to sit with her cousins.

Standing up, Claire stretched and dusted herself off, then turned and started the long walk back to the cottage.

When Claire returned, she jumped into the shower and went straight to her room after—thanking her luck that she hadn't bumped into anyone. With her bed waiting, she lay down, enjoying the comfort of it and staring at the roses that surrounded her. They soon started to fade and left her focus, until they became different-coloured blobs smeared across the walls.

Pressure of someone sitting on the bed woke Claire. A hand shook her shoulder gently, but she still did not stir.

"I know you're awake, Claire. I've seen you sleep…remember?" Matt's Scottish brogue startled her, but she remained on her side. "Breena explained everything and so did Addy. I'm sorry you got scared, but I have no idea why you would feel that way. I never want you to feel scared around me." Claire remained silent but did turn over and look up at him. "See, I knew you were awake." He smiled at her and it caught at her heart. "You know something? My life has become decidedly more exciting since you've come into it."

"I tend to do that" She smiled a little at him.

He held her hand and raised it to his lips. "You know, I love a girl who can make life interesting," Matt told her gently.

Claire reached up and pulled him down onto the small single bed with her. "I should be saying sorry for the way I behaved towards you today. It was way out of line and a dumbass move to do. I'm sorry I forced you to see Breena that way. You weren't prepared, and it wasn't your choice."

"I'm glad you did. Seeing her again was just…just…I can't even describe what it was. We talked and talked. She really likes you."

"I like her. She's really sweet and she reminds me of you." Claire snuggled down into his arms and felt his warm body press against hers.

Matt started to play with her hair. "When this is all over, I'd love to take you away from everything and everyone—where we can't be interrupted and we can just be us."

"That sounds like heaven." She sighed and closed her eyes. Feeling comfortable and relaxed in his arms, Claire started to drop off again.

"Are you going to sleep?"

"Mm, I don't want to leave this bed or you ever!"

"We will have to at some stage."

"Yes, I know. I have to get everyone together and tell them everything."

"No, you don't…that's been done."

Claire's eyes flew open and she propped herself up on an elbow. "Who, what—?"

"Hey, don't worry. You were fast asleep, and Addy and I didn't want to disturb you. Dad told us what happened yesterday, and Geoff and David reported back about where Tony is. Addy told us that you'd seen Jack, and that you would say no more until later. So there, all taken care of."

"What about Breena?" Claire settled back down.

"Addy's talking to Uncle Robbie and Gran now. I've already spoken to Dad."

"Your mum isn't going to take it well, is she?" Claire asked slowly.

"I don't expect so, but we'll get her there. I don't like the thought of Bree being stuck here."

A soft knock came at the door, and it opened a small gap. "Um, I don't mean to interrupt again—"

"But you are," Matt talked over Addy.

"Yeah, well, you know..." Addy tripped over her words, embarrassed to have interrupted the couple yet again. "Just thought you should know that I've talked to Dad and Gran, and they're on board. They want to know if there's any chance we can talk to Aunty Leana now."

"You should go," Claire replied quietly. "Get it over with."

"Gran wants you there as well, Claire," Addy informed her while looking between her cousin and her friend.

"Why?" Claire and Matt asked in unison.

"I don't know. I'm just the messenger." She closed the door before they could say anything else.

"I don't want to, Matt. This is a private matter between you and your family."

"I think Gran would have something to say about that." He grinned. "If she wants you to be with us, then there has to be a reason."

"Why do you have to be so wonderful?"

"To make you fall in love with me." He looked up at her with a hint of a smile. "Is it working?"

"Maybe just a little." Claire blushed slightly as she laid her hand on his cheek.

Matt sat up and pulled her close once more. With his strong arms around her, his mouth was on hers in just moments. The passion surged between them, and she was lost in it.

They left the room together and found a crowd on the landing waiting. Gran, Robbie, and Addy faced them as Claire blushed and hid behind Matt. Gerry came out of the bedroom next door.

"Leana is still sleeping peacefully," Gerry informed them and joined the group.

Gran turned to Claire. "Tell us what do we have to do?" They were leaving it up to Claire to get through to Leana, and she felt the responsibility weigh heavily on her shoulders.

"Ma thought these might help." Robbie was holding out a couple of books to her.

Claire stumbled under the onslaught of information coming from the books. Matt caught her.

"Are you sure you're up to this?" he asked with great concern.

"Yes, I'll be fine. Just don't take me to a bookshop anytime soon." She caught sight of his confusion. "Never mind. I'll explain later. Thanks for the books, Robbie, but I already know what's in them." She then turned to Gerry. "Can I ask whether Leana is in a natural sleep or an induced one?"

"A natural one…thank God." He looked even more tired than the day before.

"Good. It'll be easier. I'm going to need a guide, and you know your wife more than anyone else—will you help me?"

"What is it that you are going to do?" he asked nodding.

"Let me just show you. May I?" She held her hand up to Gerry's head.

"I trust you, Claire…you may."

Claire placed a hand on his head as if in benediction. Images flashed between her and Gerry's mind as he nodded his understanding.

"Do you agree that this is the best way?" She looked into his eyes.

"Yes, it is. I just hope it works."

"Is there anything we can do?" Robbie asked.

"No, there's not. Sorry, Robbie. But I'd like to make one suggestion. It might help if Matt was with us." Gerry turned to Claire. "She might listen to him more than us. She is still fighting me."

"If you think it will," Claire agreed.

They moved into Leana's room. The curtains were drawn against the increasing night and the cold that would come with it. The sleeping form of Leana snored softly from under the comforting blankets while Matt and Gerry walked around the bed and stood opposite Claire.

"Matt, take your father's hand and mine," Claire said softly so as to avoid waking Leana. They linked their hands and Claire concentrated on bringing Matt with them, but she found a problem. Nothing she needed was there. She dropped Matt's hand. "I have to…um…hang on, I can't find what I need."

"It's all right, Claire…take your time," Matt told her in a soothing tone.

She turned her thoughts inwards and went looking for the one thing she knew she could find: Crystal. She was there, bright and shining, as she'd been the last time they talked.

"Have you done this?" Claire demanded.

"Done what?" Crystal answered.

"How am I supposed to use my Talents if I can't find where they are? So again, was it you who moved things around?" Claire asked, trying to be patient.

"We have made changes, yes. We have put things to rights and reorganised the information."

"You could've at least let me know what you were doing and let me have access to everything."

"We will do that for you now."

Her shining surfaces reminded Claire about the dream she had earlier—of the butterfly and the two people. She recognised them now as her parents, and she had even more suspicions. "Crystal, are you blocking my dreams as well?"

"We were tired, so we decided that we needed all the rest we could get."

"I'd really prefer that you didn't do that. There are going to be times when that contact will be absolutely vital. Also, never block my parents again, do you understand?"

"Understood. It shall be as we wished."

"And please stop using the collective! Use the individual when talking to me."

"Yes, Claire, I will endeavour to do so." The voice had a hurt tone to it, but Claire didn't have the time to deal with it just now.

The space around Claire changed, and there appeared all the parts she needed to use her Talents. Only now, there were far more than she was used to, and it was daunting.

"Was there anything else I can do to help?" Crystal asked her haughtily.

"Yes. When I come near a book, please help me to not suck all the information out of it before I have even had a chance to open the cover."

"That is something I cannot do. I can only organise that information. I do not collect it. That is your domain, so you need to learn how to block it." Claire could have been wrong, but Crystal sounded a bit smug when she told her this.

"Thank you, Crystal."

Claire moved away and found her subconscious and entered it easily. Standing before her were both of her parents—whole and visible—so she ran right into their arms. The small family group enjoyed renewing their bond until she reluctantly pulled away.

"Could I have some help?" she asked them.

"Of course! We will do whatever we can," John said happily.

"It's really Mum I need…sorry, Dad."

"Sure, your Mum comes back and it's thanks, Dad, but I don't need you now." He laughed as he said it. "Go ahead. I'm not offended or feel left out—really." He walked away, pretending not to stifle a sniff.

"He'll never change." Jess smiled and sighed. "Tell me what is it you want me to do?"

"I know that this isn't really you, but do you still have access to your Talent?"

"To some extent—why?"

"I need you to help me, but it may be a bit difficult. Leana, Matt's mother, is still grieving for her daughter and Breena can't leave the area where she died until her mother accepts it and the pain stops."

Jess placed her hands on either side of Claire's face. "The pain never stops, Claire...we can only keep it at bay." Then she gathered her up in her arms and held her. "I am only glad we were allowed to do this much and be with you."

"As am I. Does that mean you'll help me?"

"Call me and I will come. I promise. Your dad will probably be there, too—he hasn't let me out of his sight since I came back." Jess smiled.

"Thanks, Mum. I'll call you soon." Claire came back to herself and found everyone looking at her. "Let's try again."

She held out her hand for Matt to take and then laid her free hand along with Gerry's on Leana's head, letting him lead both Matt and her into the mind of his wife.

Confusion and pain abounded there within the dark confines of Leana's mind, but there was also beauty in the extreme. Roses like those she'd painted for Breena—in all colours— along with tiny fairies flitting from one to another. Claire had trouble figuring out which way she should turn and was grateful for the steadying force of Gerry to guide her along.

He pulled them through the mess and turmoil to the calmer and more peaceful subconscious, where they found Leana painting another rose. With a final brush stroke, Leana plucked the rose off the canvas and sent it out into her mind to join the others. Gerry made a small sound to let her know they were there, and she turned in surprise; her paintbrush dripping multi-coloured paint from the tip of the soft bristles.

"How dare you, Gerry! You promised never to do this to me! And why have you brought Matty into this, and her?" Leana indicated Claire.

"Leana, we've come to help you," Gerry told her.

"I am doing everything you have asked me. What more do you want, Gerry? What?" Pretty drops of paint flew through the air as she waved her hands around. The droplets hung suspended in space for a moment before transforming into multi-coloured fairies—which flittered away, chasing the roses Leana had painted.

"Mum, please…there is something that you need to do and only you can do it," Matt pleaded with her. "We promise once it is done, you will be happier."

"Happy? I don't want to be happy. Being unhappy makes me happy," she yelled at her son.

"Mum, please just listen to us."

"No, I don't want to listen. This is my space, and you are trespassing on it. I would appreciate it if you could all just go and leave me alone." She turned her back on them.

"Leana, I know we really haven't had the chance to get to know each other, but I honestly do want to help you," Claire said hesitantly.

"Young lady, you just want to please my son so you can get in his pants and take him away from me," Leana threw at her with venom.

"Mum!" Matt was shocked at his mother's words. "She is here because she's the only one who can help you—not because…of what you said!"

"It's all right, Son. She's not herself," Gerry said, moving to his son and placing a caring hand on his shoulder.

"I am myself, Gerry!" Leana said firmly.

"No, you are not!" he shouted back. "This is not the lass I fell in love with and married. Where is she? Because we'd like her back."

"She died the day her daughter did, you bastard! And then died a little more when her husband left!"

"I never left, Leana…you wouldn't let me back. You don't remember, do you?" He raised a hand as a movie screen-like image appeared. Claire could see figures moving on it but couldn't hear anything.

Claire decided that this was the time to bring in her backup but didn't want to add to Leana's anger. "Matt, I thought I'd ask my mother to come to speak with yours—as one mother who has lost her child to another. But I am beginning to think that it might be a bad idea."

"It might help. I'd try anything right now."

Claire looked over to Leana and then Gerry, who was now supporting his wife as she watched his memories. The images reminding her of what actually happened—rather than all her drink-addled ones. Claire watched as Matt joined them and whispered to his father. Gerry looked up and nodded to her as she sent out the call.

"I'm here, Claire. I didn't want to startle her, so for now, only you can hear and see me. Is that Matt's mother?"

"Yes. Her name is Leana. At the moment, Gerry, Matt's dad, is showing her memories."

"Okay. Just say the word and I'll appear."

Gerry dismissed the memories when they'd played out and then prepared Leana to meet Jess. Claire called her mother and she appeared by her side. Slowly, she approached Leana and gently began to talk. Her voice was so low that only Leana could hear it. Gerry and Matt joined Claire and then waited to be allowed back.

After a while, Jess called them over with an arm around Leana's shoulders protectively.

"Claire, Leana has something to ask you," Jess told her daughter.

"I've been told that you can help me see my daughter one more time?" Leana asked in a small voice.

"I can, but only if you truly want to," Claire told her.

"I truly want to, Claire…I really do. Can we go now?" she asked.

"It's night-time, my love. We'll go in the morning, I promise," Gerry told her, coming forward and taking her into his protective arms.

While Matt went to join his parents, Claire took her own mother aside and waited for them. "Thanks, Mum. What did you say to her?"

"My darling, that'll simply remain between Leana and me. A message between mothers." Jess pushed a stray lock of Claire's hair behind her ear.

"Are you ready to leave?" Matt asked from behind her.

"Definitely." Claire smiled at him.

As Gerry left, Jess held on to the connection with Claire and Matt and brought them back to Claire's subconscious.

"Mum, what are you doing?" Claire asked.

"Your father—when he heard what you were up to—asked me to make sure you came back here with Matt, so he could meet him."

Matt looked nervously around and when Claire went to take his hand, John stepped between them.

"Dad!" Claire called out.

"Don't 'Dad' me, Claire…you know the rule."

Matt looked stunned and slightly scared of John.

"Yes, I do. I'm sorry," Claire responded.

"What rule?" Matt asked.

"We can't touch in here in the subconscious part of my mind. Otherwise, we'll form an unbreakable bond—which means that no matter where we are—I can then get hold of you, both in dreams and awake."

"Well, that can't be a bad thing, can it?" His look spoke volumes to Claire as she blushed, remembering their encounter the previous night.

"Seeing as neither my wife nor my daughter has the manners to make them, let me introduce myself. Hi, you must be Matt…I'm John." He held out his hand to Matt, who looked at it and then back up to John. "Don't worry. I don't bite. And there won't be a bond."

Matt shook his hand, pulling him away from Jess and Claire. Claire was slightly worried what her father might be saying to Matt, and Jess didn't help.

"It's okay. He won't be too hard on Matt." Jess smiled, trying to reassure her daughter.

"This is my mind, so why can't I hear what they're saying?"

"Because it is our home as well, Claire. Speaking of which, I am a bit disappointed with the changes that have been made."

"You mean Crystal? I've had a few words with her about that. There should hopefully be no more problems."

"Crystal is her name?"

"That's what I call her, because it's like a crystal."

"Makes sense, then. Look out; here they come."

"So did he say anything I need to be worried about?" Claire asked Matt.

"Nah, of course not, sweetheart," John said as Matt looked shaken.

"We have to go. I love you both so much." She hugged her parents and Matt shook John's hand again. When it came to Jess, she kissed him on the cheek and—to his surprise—hugged him.

"Look after our girl," she said while they left.

Back in the real world, Claire was still holding Matt's hand over his mother's sleeping form as Gerry waited for them.

"Sorry. Claire's father wanted to meet me," he told his father.

"So, it's already at that point in the relationship…meeting the parents?" Gerry teased his son. "It was lovely to meet your mother properly, Claire. She's a very lovely lady. I can see where you get your beauty from."

"Thank you, Gerry." Claire blushed at the compliment. "Where are the others?"

"They've gone back down. I told them that you were still talking."

"I'm starving. I suppose dinner's over," she stated sadly.

"Only by an hour or so, but if you'd like, I can make you something…" Matt said, still holding her hand and moving around the bed to her side.

"I could get used to being waited on." She grinned.

"Don't. He only knows how to cook a couple of things. You'll soon get bored with them." Gerry chuckled as he teased his son.

Chapter Fifteen

Dappled light and autumnal leaves littered the ground under the great oak by the ford the next morning. Sitting on the lowest branch and dangling her feet, Breena listened to the birds singing in her home's upper reaches. She hummed along with their song and played with her dark hair, twirling locks of it in her fingers. Today seemed to her like a happy day—a sunshine and sparkly day. For today, she knew that her family was coming to visit, just as the spirit that lived in the tree had told her they would.

From up the track, she heard their chattering voices. They were familiar voices that gladdened her heart. She jumped down from the branch and waited at the base of her tree, leaning up against it and saying her own goodbye to her companion who'd kept her safe and given her comfort. She waited for her family to come from over the hill as her heart sang in her tiny chest. And then they came.

Walking with Uncle Robbie, Addy was first. Breena thought he looked funny with white hair, since she remembered him with bright red hair like her cousin's. Gran was next, walking beside Galen, and hand in hand with her brother was Claire. She really liked Claire and felt happy that they were going to become sisters. From behind, two more figures appeared...Mum and Da. A smile as bright as the sun lit up her face and her eyes sparkled with delight and excitement. She knew Claire could do it.

Breena waited patiently for them to arrive under the shade of her oak. Her hands clasped in front of her in anticipation for Galen, Addy, and Claire to notice her. She wanted to be on her best behaviour for her parents and for Gran, but the excitement was building up and she couldn't contain it any longer. Dancing on the spot, she just couldn't contain herself any longer as she started to overflow with expectation and delight.

They stopped at the tree's outskirts while Galen, Claire, and Addy came to stand with her. She waited for Claire to begin, knowing what she had to do.

Da was first as she took his large hand—now so worn with age—in her own and clasped Claire's free hand. She felt the energy pass through her and make the connection with Da's. She felt the early recognition and raised her face to his. His eyes widened as she appeared to him and he caught her up in a swinging hug. Tears fell from his eyes and she placed her hands on either side of his face.

"Hello, Da. I missed you," she said brightly.

"I missed you, too, my poppet...so very much!" he whispered, hugging her fiercely and then putting her down. "Mum's turn." He looked up at his wife and called her forward.

Her mother came over hesitantly at first and then stood with her hand out for her daughter to hold. Those wonderful hands she remembered—which always had time to draw her favourite flower or tuck a lock of Breena's hair away from her face. Claire completed the circle and she waited for her mother's reaction. Tears were already streaming down Leana's face in anticipation.

"Mum, you can look now," Breena told her impatiently.

Leanna's eyes opened and turned down to gaze upon the daughter she'd not seen in sixteen years. The daughter she had missed and wanted so terribly. She got down on one knee and bundled her up in her arms, and those lost years just drifted away on the cool but sweet autumn breeze.

"My little Briar Rose," she called her as she cupped her face in her hands and stared, drinking in the little face she had only seen in her dreams. "I'm sorry it took me so long."

"It's all right, Mum…you are here now." Breena kissed her mother's cheek tenderly.

"Gran's next, my sweet Briar Rose," her mother told her as Breena nodded in return.

Gran came forward and held out her hand. There was already a smile on her face as she waited to greet her lost granddaughter. Breena had loved her baking and loved the way she smelled—like lavender and biscuits.

"I miss your biscuits, Gran," Breena said seriously once Gran was able to see her.

"And I miss baking for you. I don't have many people to bake for now," her gran replied with a small sniff, dabbing her eyes with a white handkerchief.

Then came Uncle Robbie, with his long white hair and his round glasses. He'd never failed to make her giggle whenever he managed to come and visit. She held his hand and waited for him to say what he'd always had said when he arrived.

"Where's my goddaughter?" he asked her quietly.

"You're supposed to shout it, Uncle Robbie," Breena told him a little sternly.

"Not this time, lass. This time is special." He lifted her up high and down again into a big hug while she giggled.

Claire had taken each reunion in as they had happened and felt the love in the family group steadily grow with each one.

As they gathered together, she began to feel like an outsider—an intruder in their midst.

"I'll leave you all alone," she said to him as she watched them gather around Breena. Matt nodded absentmindedly before Claire walked to the other side of the track.

Looking up the hill, she started to climb it on an impulse. Claire thought to give them enough space to say goodbye properly. There was no real reason to walk up it, other than it was just there. The higher she went, the farther she could see as the river below sparkled away in the warm morning sunshine, and the long grass echoed the slight waves on the water—swaying in the gentle breeze. Out farther, the large highland cows grazed alongside the puffy white sheep, and she felt a little homesick for her own valley back in New Zealand.

Nearly at the top, she saw a flash of sunshine reflecting on two circles of glass, and within a few more steps, a figure lying prone on the grass could be seen behind them. She walked a bit further until she was level with him before she spoke.

"Getting a good enough look, are you, Tony?" she asked.

"Nah, my eyes aren't as good as they once were. That's why I have to rely on these." He indicated the binoculars in his hand.

"I hear that's what happens when you get old." She turned away from him and looked out at the valley below as the wind pulled at her hair.

"Are you going to tell me what is going on down there?" he asked, his voice soft and low.

"What? And do your job for you? I don't think so. You're just going to have to report that a group was sighted around an old oak tree."

"Come on, Claire. Throw us a bone. I thought we had become friends," he said, resuming his study of Matt and his family.

"Friends? Us?" she asked, turning to him. "The day you turn your back on Jack and leave my family and friends alone, then we *might* become friends."

"I notice you didn't say 'me' amongst that lot to leave alone?" He smiled at her.

"I am not in the mood to take that bait." She sank to the ground and picked at the grass in front of her.

"You seem a bit down. Is there anything I can help with?"

"I don't think so—just working out my own feelings." While staring down the hill at the group under the tree, her mind continued to wander. "Have you ever lost anyone close to you?"

"Wow, we're going deep? I'm touched that you trust me that much!"

"Just answer the damn question," she told him with a little annoyance.

"Yes, I have—many. But the one that meant the most I lost only after I discovered who they were."

"That makes no sense." She turned her head and watched this strange man. Tony continued to watch the scene down the hill as his dark hair was ruffled by the wind and he refused to look at her.

"I didn't know my birth parents. It took me a long time to discover who they were, and by the time I did, it was too late." He was silent for a moment. "I think you should leave now. Your mood seems to be infectious."

"You're no fun today," she declared, tossing the blade of grass that she had been twisting in her fingers.

"You started it." He kept the binoculars trained on the group down the hill.

"I'm sorry."

"I much prefer it when we throw veiled threats at each other, since it brightens my day."

"Next time we meet, I promise I'll be back to myself—if it amuses you that much. But you know what they say, 'Small things amuse small minds.'" A little smile tugged at the corner of her lips.

"That's better!" He chuckled, finally placing the binoculars down. "Did you ever ask yourself why I've never tried to attack you?"

"I was hoping that it had something to do with what I did to Richard."

"That was impressive, but no. It's because I never want to hurt you. I knew your father. He was a good man who treated me kindly and with fairness. You remind me of him."

"Well, that's news. What happened? Why are you working for Jack?" Claire asked, confused by this man who seemed almost at odds with himself.

"I was working for Marcus, and I was told to befriend your parents. Right from the start, your mum didn't like me, but your dad and I became friends. I was shattered when I found out what happened. Yet by then…it was just too late. So, I shut my mouth and got on with work."

"And Jack?"

"He offered me travel and an easy job of watching you, so I thought to myself, 'Why not.' I'd always kept tabs on you, anyway. I promised your father I would, so I thought it was a great opportunity." Tony paused a moment as he seemed to debate something in his mind, before continuing slowly. "Just a warning for you, Claire…Jack's far more dangerous than Marcus. He is truly mad."

"I can handle Jack," she told him, pulling at another piece of long grass in front of her.

"Are you sure? He has a few tricks of his own."

"I'll be all right. Thank you for your concern, Tony."

"I'm pleased you broke it off with Adam." Tony went back to the binoculars and trained them once more down the hill. "I always found him to be a bit of a prat. I approve of your new fella. He seems much more suitable."

"Oh, you do, do you?" Claire couldn't help but give a small smile as she turned to watch him again.

"I do. And you better go down and meet him, because he's coming up the hill now, and Matthew might wonder why you are sitting here and talking with me. I don't want to cause a rift like I did with Adam." He shot a quick look to gauge her reaction.

"You broke us up? So, he was telling the truth?" Claire asked with surprise.

"No, Adam thinks it was Jack. Your breakup was all me, and it wasn't the first time he had cheated on you. I told you...I kept tabs on you." He flicked another glance at her. "He'll see me soon, so you better get going. And close your mouth. There are too many midges around!"

Claire stood and started down the hill to meet Matt. Seeing his smile, it was like the sun had just become brighter and was shining down on only the two of them. She threw her arms around him the very instant she could and kissed him soundly.

"What was that for?" he asked while coming back up for air.

"Just because I wanted to."

"You can do that again whenever you want!" Matt held her tighter, and she buried her head in his shoulder, enjoying the embrace.

"How did it go?" Claire asked him as they headed down the hill.

"It was grand—so grand. I don't know how to thank you for doing this for my family."

"I can think of a few ways…" She chuckled.

At the bottom of the hill, they met the rest of his family. Breena was holding both her parents' hands and smiling at Claire and Matt.

"It's time for me to go now, Claire," the little girl said solemnly as she let go of her parents and ran to Claire, hugging her.

"I am honoured to have met you, Breena," Claire told the girl, enveloping her in a large hug.

"Look after Galen for me. He's going to need you. And don't you worry about parting from him, you'll find each other again. I made sure of it," Breena whispered in Claire's ear and then let go to stand before Robbie.

"Uncle Robbie, you need to slow down work. Aunty Fiona misses you and so does Addy. Can you tell Aunty Fiona goodbye for me?"

"Aye, I will, Breena lass." He caught her up in a bear hug and kissed her head. When he let her go, there was a tear in his eye.

"Addy, I'll miss you." Breena took Addy's hand and pulled her down to whisper in her ear. Addy's eyes widened, and she blushed.

"You can't mean that," she said to a nodding Breena before they kissed and hugged.

"My turn," Gran chimed in while coming towards her two granddaughters. With great difficulty, she went down on one knee and held Breena close. "I'm so happy we have had this time together again, lass. I am just sad it wasn't longer."

"Don't cry, Gran. There's been enough tears." Breena wiped her grandmother's face and then kissed her cheek gently.

When Gran had been helped back to her feet, she, Robbie, and Addy started to walk towards the house. Claire stepped back and let the little family group have one final moment together before they all said goodbye. She wandered slowly towards the track and looked up the hill to where she knew Tony was hiding but could see no sign of him.

"I'm ready, Claire," Breena's small voice originated from behind her.

Turning around, Claire found them standing before her — with Breena in front holding her hand out to Claire. She took the small hand in her own as the world went dark, but she wasn't afraid.

"Do you know what's going to happen to you, Breena?" she asked the young girl.

"Yes. We have to wait for a moment. Galen loves you, Claire," Breena declared brightly.

"I know, and I love him, too."

"Good. I was just making sure. Here he comes," Breena said, pointing towards the tree. Emerging out of the dimness from under the oak was the same hooded figure Claire had seen the day before.

"Are you afraid?" Claire asked Breena as he approached them.

"No. I'm looking forward to it," Breena told her confidently.

The hooded figure stopped before them and held a hand out to Breena. She turned to Claire and gave her one last hug before accepting the bony white hand being offered to her.

"We will look after her, Carling. She was always bound to join us...as are you when your time comes. Our hopes were that you would both work together, but that plan was undone the day Breena left the mortal world. Now the tasks lay heavily on your shoulders alone, we fear. When the time comes, we will do everything in our power to help you, but you will have to face the darkness by yourself," the hooded figure said ominously.

"When?"

"The rising of the blood moon in two days hence."

"What happens if I don't succeed?" Claire felt suddenly less confident than she had ever done in her whole life.

"Then our lands will be lost to us forever." He turned and Breena waved to her as they slowly disappeared with every step away from Claire.

The light then returned to her as she looked up the track to where they'd faded from view. She felt her stomach clench at what the man had told her was her fate but pushed it back and refused to think about it now.

"I want to thank you, Claire. And I'd like to apologise for the way I talked to you last night. I am so grateful to you for giving me this time with Breena." Leana was smiling at her. Quickly, she embraced the younger woman and turned to join her husband for the walk back to the house.

Gerry nodded to her, and Claire could see his eyes were red with tears he had shed. The couple linked arms and started back to the house as Matt followed them.

Claire looked up the hill and raised a hand as if she was waving, but she tucked a stray lock of hair behind her ear and then turned to see Matt waiting for her. She ran to him and snuggled under his arm.

Later that afternoon, she sat on the couch with Matt—with her head on his shoulder—dozing lightly as he stroked her hair. Images of the months she'd been in Scotland played out in her head like a slideshow. Some were good and others she did not want to face again. But play on they did. As images were chased by feelings and snatches of conversations, it all culminated with the moon—which was full and bright in the sky, appearing red and threatening.

"When's the next full moon?" she mumbled into his chest.

At first, Matt thought she must be asleep, but when she moved her head and looked at him, he answered, "I'm not sure, would you like me to look it up?"

"Thank you. I'd appreciate that," she said as she put her head back down, already knowing the answer and thinking that she'd worry about it tomorrow instead. "I really feel like getting out of here. Is there a pub nearby?"

"Aye, there is," Matt replied.

"You guys want to come?" she asked the room. The general consensus was agreeable and all except Leana, Gerry, and Gran agreed.

They piled into the cars and headed out with Matt leading the way. The destination was a tiny little village made up of several cottages and a single pub—the only one for miles. It was a cozy-looking building, and Robbie was greeted like the old friend he was. The barman and he went back as far as their school days, and they were soon reminiscing while he poured their drinks. Robbie leaned on the bar, as comfortable as if he did it every day.

"Not too much, Claire. You don't want to burst into tears!" Addy teased her.

"No, I promise I won't." She laughed with her friend.

Their drinks came and were soon gone. As they ordered more, the barman made them a bargain.

"The next round's on the house if Addy will sing us a song," he called out, pointing at an ancient karaoke machine gathering dust in the corner.

"Ahh, Hamish, yer grand," Addy answered with a strong Scottish accent. "But only if my new friend Claire sings with me."

"No, no, no," Claire protested.

"Come on, Claire, it's only one song," Addy begged.

"Have you heard her sing?" Geoff asked incredulously. "She can't carry a tune to save her life."

"Not anymore," Matt chimed in with a smile while downing the last of his pint. "I'm empty and could use another. Claire?"

"I'm going to kill you, Adaira!" she said, only half threatening.

"Yay! Now what shall we sing?" She pulled the barman's folder of songs open and started to flip through the pages.

"No way, if we're going to sing, it's going to be my choice." Claire pulled it out of Addy's hands. She stopped flicking and held it out to Addy to see what she was pointing to. "This one."

"You have to be kidding me! That one, really? Your taste is all in your mouth, Claire."

Adam leaned across Addy to see what Claire was pointing to, then made a grab for the folder to show it to Matt.

"I have to agree with Addy on that one, Claire. Sorry," Matt said. "That's just too, too—"

"'Tragic' is the word I've used before, and that song is the epitome of it," Adam finished for Matt.

"Fine. You guys choose." Claire gave up and leaned back in her seat.

The discussion became quite heated at the table after that—with Geoff and David both voicing their doubts on Claire's abilities in the singing department. It took a while for them to decide before handing the book back to Addy.

"Really, you want us to sing this one? I hope you know it." She passed it on to Claire, who raised an eyebrow at the choice.

"It's your ears," Claire said as she and Addy made their way to the machine.

"That's what I'm worried about," Geoff called out.

"It hasn't had much use since you stopped coming to visit your gran so much," Hamish told them as the two women picked the microphones up and he bent to adjust the settings.

"Hey, what's this?" Robbie asked, staring at his daughter.

"Well, a girl had to get a drink or two somehow!" Addy told him with a wink.

Robbie started to mutter under his breath as Addy ignored him and spoke to Claire, working out how they were going to sing the song.

The music started with the strains of a guitar and Addy lifted the microphone to her mouth and sang the first strains of "Stand by Your Man" in her clear and beautiful voice.

The nerves were building inside Claire, but when it came to her turn, she joined her voice with Addy's. Both melding into a pitch-perfect harmony. Claire snuck a peek at her uncles and saw their stunned expressions before it was her turn to sing solo.

After the song was finished, they bowed and headed back to the seat to partake in the free drink while both saluted Hamish with a smile.

They enjoyed a good night out with lots of laughs and drinks. Claire was very careful, stopping after one and simply sticking to lemonade afterwards. After they'd eaten some quickly heated pies and chips for dinner, they carried on. Claire was sitting opposite David and Geoff when she noticed David nudge her great-uncle and point at something behind her. She swivelled in her chair and saw Tony leaning on the bar, ordering a drink. She turned back and watched the small argument between her two uncles.

"I'll be back in a tic. I gotta go to the loo," she said to Matt as she got up. The path to the ladies' room took her right past Tony, and she prayed the man wouldn't turn around. After making it past him, she let out a deep breath and leaned up against the door. With her heart thumping in her chest, she hoped that neither of her uncles would cause a confrontation before she had a chance to talk to him first.

Claire opened the door to the bar just a crack to find out if he was still there or if he'd taken a seat. To her relief, she found he had taken a table close to her—out of eyesight of the others. She slipped through the door, keeping an eye on her party, and found no one looking her way. She moved quickly to Tony's table and sat down across from him as he was opening a packet of chips.

"Hello, Tony. Didn't you choose a bad night to follow me?"

"Actually, you guys chose the wrong night to come to the pub! It's my night off. I'm just here to have a pint or two and read the paper."

"Oh, okay. I thought you were coming to make trouble. Sorry to have interrupted you." She pinched a chip from the packet. "Now, if you're not watching us, who is?"

"That's confidential, Claire," he said while folding his arms in front of him and leaning on the table.

"Come on, you can't be scared that I'd like them better than you, can you?" she asked with a grin.

"No, I think you would find them to be a bit more Neanderthal than me. Usually only one- or two-word answers and totally uncouth."

"You're right. I wouldn't like them. Now, I am going to try and control the men at my table, but you need to be aware, they don't like you the same way I do."

"So, you do like me! Don't let your boyfriend hear that." He gave a chuckle as he dove into the packet of chips himself.

"How droll," Claire said, screwing up her face and pinching another chip.

"Which one am I in more danger of?" Tony asked, turning his gaze to the other side of the room.

"I'd say David, since he's a farmer, you know—used to heavy work. Very well built in the muscle department and protective." She quickly followed his gaze and saw David and Geoff still debating.

"I had better finish my drink and be on my way, then. Such a pity. I've been looking forward to tonight."

"You really need a hobby, Tony. This life you lead doesn't seem to be very fulfilling. Enjoy!" She threw the words at him as she stood and started back to her friends. Claire then walked up to her uncles and squatted down between them. "If you're going to do what I think you are about to do, then I would ask that you don't. He's not doing anything except reading a paper. Yes, he is a pain in the arse following us the way he does, but at the moment…what is he going to hear? Think of it as an opportunity to watch the Watcher!" She patted them both on the shoulder and left them to think about it. When she retook her seat, David leaned over the table.

"Is that such a good idea, Claire? Don't we want to discourage them from watching us?" he asked in a low voice.

"What's this?" both Matt and Adam asked.

"The guy who has been following Claire is sitting right over there." David pointed towards Tony.

"He's having a drink and reading a paper," Claire told them. "That's all. And he's not even facing our table."

"Are you defending him?" Adam asked her incredulously.

"No, Adam. I just want to relax and have a nice drink with my friends. I'm tired of looking over my shoulder every day and wondering who's out there. Can't we just leave it?" she asked them.

"If you're sure, Claire, then that's what we'll do," Matt said to the table. "But if he so much as looks your way…" The tone of his voice made Claire feel both slightly scared he'd make trouble and proud he'd defend her. But she didn't encourage it.

"Thank you. Now, whose round is it?" she asked.

"No one's," Hamish said as he placed a tray of drinks down on the table.

"All right…what song do you want to hear now?" Addy asked him.

"No song needed, lass. These are from that man down the way." He indicated with his thumb down the bar.

As one, they turned and saw Tony holding up his glass in salute merrily. Claire turned back in time to see David standing up, about to launch himself across the pub towards Tony. She was over to him in a moment, putting her hand on his chest and stopping him.

"He's not worth it, David. He's not worth it. Nobody do anything. I mean it," Claire warned them all as she then picked up the drink that had been placed down in front of her and stalked over to Tony, deliberately keeping her voice low and her back to her friends. "I'd just convinced them to leave you alone and then you had to go and ruin it by sending us drinks, didn't you?" Not giving him a chance to answer, she carried on. "I'm sorry that I have to do this, but if I don't, then you're in danger of getting a pummelling. And I don't want anyone to get into trouble here." Claire then upended her drink over Tony's head and put the glass down on his table. "Now, we are going to leave, and I hope that you have a nice night and that I haven't ruined your clothes."

"So kind," Tony said as he licked the dripping lemonade and screwing up his face. "Argh, I don't like soft drinks—too full of sugar."

Claire left him and apologised to Hamish for making a mess before heading back to her table. "Mind if we go home now? I'm really not in the mood anymore." They all agreed and gathered their things to leave.

As she walked out the door, she looked at Tony, who was toweling himself off. Why did she think she could trust him? Shouldn't she have known better? She gave a slight shiver as he smiled at her before she passed through the doorway.

They drove back in silence as Claire was once more drawn into a sombre mood. Why was it she had moments of absolute happiness and joy only to be torn down into sadness and despair? When couldn't she ever just be? She would even settle for slightly happy.

Chapter Sixteen

Claire woke very early the next morning, even before the sun had started to rise. She lay in her bed listening to Addy snore softly and felt restless. Rubbing the grittiness from her eyes, she sat up slowly, then dressed as quietly as she could. Carrying her shoes out with her, she waited on the landing for any noise in the house but only heard more snoring coming from the other rooms. Down the stairs she went, using Stealth to avoid the creaky old steps, and at the bottom she stopped only long enough to put her shoes on.

Out the door and down the track she went, as fast as her Talent could carry her. She stopped at the tree for a moment, but it was quiet. It felt like a lonely place now, empty, and bare. No laughter flittering through the leaves, no tiny feet pattering along the limbs. Claire placed a hand on the old oak's large trunk and could feel that he also missed his little resident.

She looked up the hill to where Tony had been the day before and sent out feelers. They snaked up the hill, sweeping for any sign of life—but all she got back was early rising small creatures. Farther she sent them, spreading them out to find him—until a little shiver came back.

Discarding the others, Claire focused her will on that one strand and followed it in her mind. He wasn't in a tent, but a house—a little cottage up the road, not that far out of the village they'd been in the previous night. She strengthened the

Talent and spread a net over the house, searching for anyone else, but she found that he was alone with the exception of one other deeply sleeping male form.

Impulse overtook her and she started to run. But not back to the house and her friends. Instead, she had the urge to run onwards to the road, to follow that strand where it ended. At the cottage. As she jogged, she wondered why she was becoming so obsessed with this man. She didn't find him attractive—well, not that much—and he was definitely not her type. She'd never detected any Charm Talent coming from him and he annoyed her so much. But her feet were betraying her, taking her closer and closer to this man.

The cottage came into view, and Claire slowed her steps until she came to a stop at the gate. Her hand rested on the rusty iron, and she felt the cold seep into her hand, stored from the night air. Indecision played in her mind, bouncing her from one plan to another, but the one idea that she really did not want to acknowledge was winning the race.

Over the gate she jumped and continued quietly up the path. The overgrown garden was creeping over the old concrete, sending out tendrils ready to trip the unsuspecting. The crumbling path led to the door, and she stood there, looking at the tarnished brass knocker and the peeling, faded green paint.

Courage left her at that point, and she started to head back to the old gate when she heard the door open on squeaky hinges. She stumbled over one of the entrapping tendrils and fell. Expecting the hard ground to come up to meet her, she was even more surprised by hands breaking her fall and lifting her back to her feet.

"I thought you had more agility than that, Claire. I've seen your videos." Tony's arm was still around her and his body close to hers when she came back to herself and stepped away from him.

"I…I…um…"

"Good morning, Claire. I presume you've come to apologise again for last night." Tony looked down at her.

"Yeah, I was just coming to say sorry. So, sorry and see ya." She turned and went to leave, but Tony grabbed her wrist and stopped her.

"Why not come in for a cuppa? It's a long way back and I'd hate to think that you might get dehydrated."

Claire knew it was a bad idea but found she could not say no as she followed him into the cottage. Inside, it was dark with the curtains closed and it smelled like man—the room was littered with dirty dishes and clothing. Tony switched the jug on and noticed that she was looking at the mess. Quickly he started to tidy up.

"This guy is just as bad as Richard when it comes to being a pig. That's why I was at the pub last night, I had to break away from his chaos," he told her by way of apology for the clutter that was strewn around the room.

Claire gave a noncommittal sound as a reply and then moved to the kitchen to sit down. Tony cleared a space on the cluttered surface and then made tea for her.

"Is it a nice morning for a run?" he asked.

"It's okay," she replied before taking a sip.

Tony kept trying to make small talk, but Claire would only answer with a word or two. She did not see his frustration rising, since she didn't really see where she was—she was unfocused and distant—unsure of what was happening to her. Halfway through her tea, she realised where she was and wondered what and how she got there.

"Thank you for the tea, Tony. I'm sorry I bothered you so early, but I really have to go. I shouldn't have come here." She stood and made for the door.

Tony was there before her, blocking the path to the exit and freedom. She looked up and noticed something different about him.

"Please, Tony…I should go."

"Not yet, Claire." Tony took her in his arms, and Claire could feel the strength and power in them. He bent his head to kiss her but stopped just a moment's breath away as he whispered in a gravelly voice, "Is this what you wanted, Claire? Why you came here this morning? Are you hungry for a real man to make love to you instead of the boys you've had?"

Claire shook her head and tried to release his grip. Fear rose as his hold tightened around her. Her arms were now pinned to her sides and the pressure of his hold was increasing. Claire tried to concentrate and make her Talents work, but she could not. They were there but wouldn't work. And not because they'd been moved by Crystal. Panic now rose to her throat as she struggled some more.

"Aw…poor Claire, you can't use your Talents? I thought you'd studied them all! Did you not read about Strength—how it can counteract the others and constrict them? Too bad. I thought you would've figured it out when I told you Jack had a few tricks up his sleeve. I could have had you anytime I wanted, and you were making it so easy." His voice had an edge to it, raspy and raw.

"You don't have to do this, Tony, you're better than this!" Claire begged.

"Don't I? I've been doing this all my life. What would you know of it?"

"I can tell there is a decent person inside you. You demonstrate it to me every time we talk."

"I think you mistook me, Claire." She struggled again but he held on. "I tried to kill you, remember?"

"But you didn't want to. I can hear it. Please, Tony, please let me go," she begged again and stopped struggling.

He held her for only a moment more before releasing his arms to free her. She moved away from him, scared of the man who stood before her, as his Strength Talent was a shock and a surprise.

In turn, Tony was breathing heavily and looking at the woman in front of him. Her golden hair had been messed with in their struggle, and her face was pale with fright. She could clearly see he now felt sickened at his actions. She'd been right, he didn't like doing the things he'd been doing for all his adult life, but she could also see he had had no other choice for his skills. He stepped aside from the door.

"Go…just get out, Claire. I don't want you here," Tony told her darkly, struggling to get the words out.

"You don't have to help him, Tony," Claire replied quietly. "You could leave anytime."

"I have to stay. I'm part of this now and there is no stopping it. I have to make sure everything's put right." He pushed a large hand through his dark hair and turned away from her. "Just go. I promise I'll never breathe a word that you were here."

There was a catch in his voice that touched Claire, but she made for the door, leaving it open as she ran down the path and leapt over the gate. Her feet pounded the ground and her fists pumped in rage. She was angry at herself, as it was all her fault. She should never have gone there—should never have talked to him in the first place. *What was I thinking? I'm an idiot!* She abused, berated, and lectured herself, while her heart thumped in her chest at the indignation she'd put him through.

With a great leap, Claire jumped the low wall at the side of the road and then flew across the fast-flowing river, before heading up the hill. The anger she felt continued unabated, and she didn't want to go back to Matt with it still hanging over her. And there was one other problem.

Had she really gone there to possibly cheat on Matt? Was this what would drive them apart? But no one knew where she had been, and nothing had happened from her side. She loved Matt and held on to that thought as she crossed the hills and ended up at the standing stones.

They stood tall and proud as they had for many millennia—like fingers thrust up from the earth. She sat between the two entrance stones and cleared her mind of all except an image of Matt. With her head in her hands, she concentrated and searched out until she found him with a nimbus of blue surrounding his sleeping body. His own dream melted away around him and he stood before her, smiling.

Matt's eyes were like two deep blue pools, his arms strong and comforting. So steady and protecting, he was ready to laugh and have fun, but was so serious at the same time. His smile brightened her day, making her feel special and wanted. She felt connected with him—at one—and she never wanted to hurt this man who was in her mind.

"This is a nice surprise." Matt walked up and took her in his arms and kissed her so gently it shredded her heart into pieces and tears began to fall. "Hey, it can't be all that bad." He stroked her face, ridding it of the tears.

"Matt, I love you."

"I love you, too. What's wrong?"

"I've been so stupid. You'll hate me, Matt," she said, burying her face into his chest.

"No, I won't. There is nothing you can do or say that can hurt me." He tucked a finger under her chin and raised Claire's face to his own.

"But this will. I hate lies and secrets. I never want to keep any from you. I want us to be honest with each other, so there can be no misunderstandings."

"What is it, Claire? You're scaring me."

"I went out this morning. I went for a run. I ran to him. To Tony."

"That was a stupid thing to do," he told her with a frown now framing his eyes.

"I wasn't afraid of him, but I am now."

"What happened?" The frown turned to concern.

"He tried to kiss me. He held me in his arms and tried to kiss me."

"Where is he now?" he said through clenched teeth, anger rising in his whole being quickly as his hold on her tightened.

"Matt, no. He revealed something to me, and it makes him even more dangerous. He has Strength. He has the ability to overpower any Talent he wants." She was restraining him.

"Did he actually kiss you?" Matt asked, staring at her hard.

"No."

"Did you want him to?" he demanded.

"No!"

"Why did you go there, then?"

"I don't know. It was like I had to. Like I was being forced to. I tried to stop myself, but the urge to see him was—I don't know—somehow overpowering. I felt like I was outside of myself. I'm so sorry. I told you I'd hurt you." She looked up into his eyes, pleading for him to forgive her.

"Claire, I'm not hurt." He gathered her up again and held her close. "I told you, you can never hurt me. I'm angry, but not hurt. And if I ever see him again…"

"Don't…please," she said into his chest. "I couldn't stand the thought of you facing him. He could destroy you."

"Are you saying he'd take me in a fight?" He chuckled a little. "You're probably right. Next time you have one of these urges to do something dangerous, come and find me so I can help you." He kissed the top of her head.

The sun broke over the horizon, landing its first warming rays on the standing stones and the couple. A fiery orange glow surrounded them, and the world started to shrug off its nocturnal shroud and wake.

Matt switched the hold he had on Claire and walked with her over to a soft, grassy area, laying her down. They then joined their bodies once more in their dream at this sacred spot— giving to each other their love and ecstasy, unknowingly drawing power from the stones. With thoughts of Tony now forgotten, only their love filled their minds and hearts.

Spent and lying together, Matt leaned on one elbow while playing with a strand of Claire's blond hair. "You are so beautiful," he whispered to her. "Where are you now?"

"Here with you," she said sleepily.

"I meant physically, where are you?"

"Here by the stones." She snuggled up to him.

"Don't move. I'll be with you soon." Matt stood quickly, leaving a cold spot where his body had warmed Claire. He withdrew his thoughts from hers and disappeared.

"Matt?" Claire lifted her head from the crook of her arm, and the real world crowded in on her. The cold morning air hit her with the wind and she gasped at how chilled she was. The sun was up and shining on the stones and they seemed to glow. She looked around and found no sign of Matt, and she felt alone in the world. It had been a wonderfully vivid dream they'd shared and now he was gone. She stood in the entrance to the stones and placed a hand on each at her sides. They hummed in the morning light, and she drew on their energy.

"Can we try that again, only this time in the real world?" Matt asked, coming up behind her and taking her in his arms.

Claire spun around and drew him closer, kissing him forcefully. The need to have him was great, and they lay where they had stood. Just as sweet as the dream but twice as nice, they joined their energies—soaring together. Claire was dizzy with passion, and it was so perfect for their first time together. Somewhere far off, a bell pealed out into the morning air.

They lay panting in each other's arms, enjoying their combined warmth in the cool morning, with the standing stones towering above them. Claire didn't want to move or acknowledge the coming day. She wished to stay just the way they were—in the here and now. She made a sound of contentment and snuggled deeper into Matt's arms. They dozed together, covered in the jumper he had pulled on hastily as he raced out of the house.

"You check over by the stones. I'll go this way," Adam's voice rent through the still morning air startling the pair awake. Quickly they both realised they were about to be found out. They scrambled to move and dress, but they weren't quite quick enough. Addy rounded the rocks that hid the stones.

"Found them!" she called out as she giggled and turned her back to them. "We thought something was wrong. When you were both found to be missing...well, the search party was sent out."

"Oh shit!" Claire exclaimed. "How the hell am I going to explain this to Uncle Geoff?"

"I don't know what you're worried about. Your uncles are going to kill me!" Matt said, pulling his jumper over his head. Claire looked at him and burst out laughing. "It's no laughing matter, Claire. I'm really afraid of those two."

"They're pussycats. You'll be fine." She kissed him again with passion and pushed him against the rocks.

"My God, woman, you're insatiable!" he exclaimed with a cocky grin.

"You started it." She smiled and pulled away from him.

"What a bloody tease you are." He snaked his hand into hers and held it firmly as they walked back to the house—following Adam and Addy, who kept looking back at them and giggling.

"I'm never going to hear the end of this," Matt said.

Matt's predication was a correct one. Every chance Addy got, she sang the kissing song at the pair, usually egged on by Adam. Claire blushed profusely when confronted by the only family she had there in the country and had to explain herself. There were a lot of false starts as she finally made her way through the tale. But what she did not tell them was her meeting with Tony. Matt had already agreed with her that there was no point in anyone else knowing what he'd done or the fact that she'd sought him out.

The rest of the day was spent quietly. Claire tried to enter the library, but the knowledge that she hadn't already sucked up was still clamouring to be heard, and she shut the door on it reluctantly. Her head was already buzzing with the energy she had absorbed from the stones that morning—not to mention the other activity that had taken place up there. There was a warm, tingling feeling inside her when she did think about it.

Whenever she tried to do a task for Gran or even talk to someone, she seemed to trail off. Her mind would wander and think about random things that had no bearing on their discussion.

"Claire, wake up!" Gran told her sharply. Claire jumped at the sound of the old lady's voice.

"Sorry…I just can't keep my mind on things today."

"I'm not surprised with what you two were up to this morning." She sounded disapproving, but Claire caught the twinkle in her eye.

"No one was supposed to find us," she told Gran sullenly.

"No, and it is just when you think you are safe that you're found. Tell me, how close to the stones were you?"

"Close enough," Claire answered in a small voice.

"Were you by the rocks or right beside the stones?" She seemed quite determined to find out exactly where they'd made love.

"Does it really matter?" Claire asked.

"Aye, it does. So…are you going to answer me?"

"We were by the rocks, I think—sheltered from the wind."

"Good. Because I don't know what would happen if you were by the stones."

"Pardon?"

"There's a tale about a lad and a lassie who were in love, and they would sneak up the hill to meet and be together. One summer's night, they made love by the stones and their love brought forth a child that had a touch of the fairies about it. It is not a tale that ends well."

Claire just stood and looked at the old woman as images started to float in front of her eyes. Pictures of people she'd never met—in old-fashioned clothing—but resembling one another. Pictures of her family were then intertwined in them and those of Matt's.

"Claire, will you please watch what you're doing?" Gran suddenly took Claire's face in her hands and turned it this way and that. "Up to bed with you…you're no good to anyone in this state. Sleep and try not to dream too much. And no wandering the hills!" She pointed to the door and Claire obeyed.

With each step she took on the stairs, she could feel her limbs begin to feel heavy and tired. By the time she'd reached the landing, she had to place a hand on the wall to steady herself. It was a great relief when she reached her bed, and she could lie down. It had never felt so comfortable and soft, and she soon drifted off.

The picture gallery continued in her dreams, and she wandered from one to another, desperately trying to piece together who these people were. It occurred to her there may be help at hand and she called them to join her in this stark white hall. From the other end—walking hand in hand—came her parents in white and black.

Running the rest of the distance, Claire flung her arms around them both. She immediately felt the searing need of her parents' comfort and was grateful they had answered her call. For a moment, she felt like that ten-year-old girl again—saying goodbye to her parents and not realising that it would be for the last time. The enormity of her loss crashed into her in one fell swoop as she burst into tears. She missed them every day and cursed those who had taken them from her too soon.

All the things they had missed out on as she grew, now came more into focus. Her first date, first kiss, her first exam, high school graduation, first dance, university. Just everything. All the times she'd needed her parents and they were not there. All the intimate conversations that mothers and daughters shared. All the lectures that fathers would give. The unconditional love and the laughter that had been denied her welled up inside and it hurt to the point Claire felt she'd break from it. The scar on her heart ripped open anew and bled tears of hatred and revenge.

"Oh, my darling daughter," Jess said with tears standing out in her eyes. "We're so sorry we missed all those things." She held her child tighter trying to comfort her.

"What's happened, Claire? Why are you so emotional? Why did you call us?" her father asked concerned, stroking her head as he had done when she was little. Claire thought it was so typical of him to try and find answers for the situations she found herself in.

"Dad, I've missed you both so much. But I don't know what's happening. All afternoon, I've been in and out with people and not been able to concentrate. I know my body is asleep at the moment, but my mind just can't be still. I'm not explaining it very well, am I?" she asked, looking up at him from her mother's embrace.

"No. Take a breath for a moment." John paused as she did so, and Jess released her hold. "Right…now continue."

"These pictures have been going through my mind all day—invading my thoughts along with snatches of memories from when I was a kid. They're all mounting on top of each other. I don't know what it means, and I was hoping you could help me understand."

Her parents looked at the photos on the walls as if they had just appeared before them. Stern looks mixed with happy faces stared out of the pictures. John then walked up to one black-and-white picture and gazed at it for a moment.

"This is Mum and Dad," he said and then looked more closely at the others. Other names came from his lips—some Claire had heard before and recognised, but some were totally foreign to her.

"That's me and David," Jess exclaimed, laughing at a small Polaroid photo of two children playing in water.

It was like they were going down memory lane as they went from one to another, calling to each other to come and have a look. Claire stood back and watched as they did, wondering where she'd seen these pictures before.

"Somewhere in your past, maybe," a woman's voice said beside her.

Claire turned and saw a beautiful woman about the same age as her, with long and flowing curly black hair. She was dressed in a medieval-looking dress of sapphire blue, which matched her eyes, and trimmed in silver. Her smile was radiant, but her eyes seemed to be looking directly into Claire's soul. She took an automatic step back in surprise at this stranger's sudden appearance.

"You don't recognise me, do you?" Her accent was as broad as Robbie's or Gerry's. But Claire had seen those eyes before.

"Breena?" she asked hesitantly.

"Aye. What do you think?" She gave a childish giggle while twirling with her arms held out wide.

"You look so grown-up."

"Aye, that's one of the things the Guardians have done for me. This is how I would have looked if I had grown up normally," Breena replied full of sunshine, giving a glimpse of the child Claire had helped just the day before.

"You are stunning!"

Breena blushed and fidgeted with her dress. By this stage, her parents had noticed the newcomer and came over to be introduced.

"Mum and Dad, this is Breena, Matt's little sister. Breena, my parents...Jessica and John."

"It's nice to meet you." John replied, clearly confused at this turn.

"Didn't you say she was only six?" Jess asked dubiously.

"She was, but it seems things can be changed when the Guardians are involved. What do you know about these pictures?" she asked Breena.

"The Guardians are getting to know you and reminding you where you come from. It's important that they show you what you are fighting for. Oh, and I'm allowed to tell you that I'll be standing with you tomorrow night."

"Tomorrow night? What's happening tomorrow night?" John asked.

"The blood moon rises as a portent to the battle. Claire and I must face those who wish to challenge the Guardians for dominance. If they win, we lose our lands for good, and chaos will run rampant in the world once more. But if we win, then they'll have no claim, and the world will be safe for a while longer."

"This is the part that I don't understand. The Guardians haven't actually lived in this world for a long time, so why is it so important?" Claire asked.

"That's where you're wrong, Claire. They have lived here and continue to live here now. They are all around us and in the very earth at our feet. You are one of them—descended through the millennia and chosen as their champion—as was I. Our coming was foretold. Sisters, but not…joining together to defeat the ancient enemy. My death nearly pulled it apart, as I wasn't supposed to die that day and it wasn't foreseen by anyone. The Guardians have allowed me to come back to a physical form that I should have had, so that we can work as one. Now I can take my place and support the One True Child."

"Is Jack going to be our opponent? He shouldn't be too hard to defeat," Claire said, musing out loud the situation.

"You don't understand. He'll have the power of the old enemy and he won't be alone. He, too, will have a second, and to win, we must defeat both." Her words had a final ring to them, and a chill struck Claire.

"I don't want to kill anyone, Breena. I didn't want to six years ago and I found a way around it. Is there no other option?"

"The man you faced six years ago was supposed to be standing here against us with Jack at his side. Your changing him was our way of evening the balance that my death had put out of kilter. There is no other way, Claire. You must prepare yourself for that. This time, there is no plan B. I must go now and prepare myself. I'll leave you to take comfort from your family and will see you tomorrow. Oh, and I am so glad we're now sisters."

With her parting words, she hugged Claire and then turned to walk down the long, unending hall before disappearing.

"Claire, you don't have to face anything you don't want to. You have a choice and have free will. You could leave tonight, and no one would blame you," John told her.

"But I would," she said simply. "And who's to say that this fight wouldn't just follow me for the rest of my life? You heard Breena. It was supposed to be Marcus. If I leave, it would change again, and we'd just have to start over."

"Are you going to let the others know what is happening?" Jess asked, taking her hand.

"I don't think I will." She left the rest unsaid. Her fear of others being hurt or worse filled her with dread. The lives she'd come to know and love could not be risked for her sake.

"Do you want us to help you prepare?" Jess asked with great concern.

"I don't know how you would. But I think I'd need to delve deeper and figure out how to use these new Talents quickly. Thanks for coming when I called." She looked up at them both.

"You never have to thank us for that. We're your parents and when you need help, we will be there." John kissed her forehead and stepped back.

"Our love is with you always, Claire. If it helps, use it as a shield to protect you. Remember, love is always stronger than hate." She kissed her daughter and then took John's hand.

"Thank you. I'll come and see you tomorrow. Before…" She couldn't finish the thought and just smiled. Before her eyes, her parents faded while their love echoed back to her like a security blanket, which she wrapped around herself.

The images on the walls soon winked out one by one—their job having been done. The white hall remained so quiet and empty, and a moment of peace seeped into her mind. For once, she was completely alone with her thoughts, and she tried to sort them. Each time she brought forth a new type of Talent, it was like a puzzle, and the pieces didn't seem to fit together. Time and again she tried, but frustration—her old friend— kept inserting itself between her and understanding.

Finally, she screamed, and the white walls shattered at the noise. Stepping over the dusty remains, she made her way over to the sparkling orb and stood before it.

"You've finally come to learn." The voice was different this time, as it had a deeper quality coming up from its depths.

"This isn't Crystal, is it?" Claire asked

"No…that entity you have named is still here and will remain once your training is finished. You had to come to seek help with learning your new Abilities on your own. We would never force you to learn but are grateful that you have decided to do so."

"I am ready. Please teach me." She opened her hands and laid them palms-up in supplication.

Claire came awake slowly, her eyelids fluttering open, feeling so much clearer than she had all day. The light of late afternoon was dim, and she could see the clouds building heavily outside in the sky. But inside, she was warm and safe—and it wasn't just her physical being, but also inside. The building blocks that the Guardians had given her days before were now stacked and at the ready for her use. But she was still not prepared for what she ultimately had to do. That still weighed heavily on her, and the thought sickened her.

She rolled over onto her back, but still it persisted within—pestering away at her, churning, and twisting for her notice. A sore that wouldn't heal, festering away on her soul. Feeling annoyed and cranky at the persistence of the dark thought, she got up and went to look out of the window, opening it to let in the fresh, cold air and hoping to wash it away.

"Bloody hell, Claire…you'll catch a cold!" Addy exclaimed as she came into the room. "It's freezing out there." She came up behind Claire and shut the window. "Well, I can already see that you didn't have a good sleep. Gran will be disappointed."

"No, I did. In fact, I had a wonderful sleep. I dreamed of Breena, but she was all grown up and looked so beautiful. She called me her sister…and my parents. And the Guardians helped me to understand."

"For such a great dream, it didn't leave you looking rested. You look so pale."

"I discovered what it is that I must do, and I don't like it, Addy. I don't want to do it, but I must," she told her, shaking her head slightly, trying to dispell the feeling that had surged through her.

"What are you on about?" Addy asked her.

"Never mind. It's nothing, really." Claire told her, still trying to shake off the feeling.

"But it is…you looked scared for a moment." Her soft blue eyes narrowed slightly as she stared at Claire.

"Sorry. I was just still caught up in the dream. Let's go down." Claire made a move towards the door.

"There's something you're not telling me, Claire. And I don't like that. I'll get it out of you, you know," Addy added, grabbing hold of Claire's arm to stop her.

"I know. But that's the fun part, isn't it? Prying out the secrets? You and I are very much alike on that one." Claire laughed and left her friend standing there to try and work out what it was that she'd just said.

Chapter Seventeen

Addy didn't give up her relentless interrogation of Claire. It continued long into the night, and even after they had gone to bed in the room of roses. For her part, Claire was still not telling and rebuffed her friend's persistence at every turn with great amusement and laughter. She found that the evening had passed so quickly and enjoyably trying to fend Addy off, she did not mind the constant prying.

Her reward was a dreamless and restful sleep. Claire woke the next morning feeling refreshed and clearheaded. The day lay out before her like a fresh sheet of paper, hers to do with as she pleased until she was called.

It started so beautifully with a lovely breakfast, as everyone was crammed around the kitchen table. There was laughter and love, which she greedily drank in, savouring each moment and storing them away in her memory. Each person in the room mattered to her and she made sure she spent some time with them during the day. She showed Leana her sketch book and was praised for her efforts. The debate Claire had with her Uncle Geoff, Robbie, and Gerry about the possible path of The Community and how they arrived in New Zealand was long—with many more questions raised than originally spoken, all left to be investigated another day. She was happy when Geoff said he'd help her in the search. It almost felt like a little of her Aunt Lilith was with her.

With David, she went for a jog down the track and out to the road. While they ran, David tried to ask her leading questions. She could sense he had concerns about the way she'd been acting over the day. Claire could see he didn't quite believe her when he asked if she was all right.

The hour she passed with Gran as she tried to teach Claire the secret to her scones was filled with sage advice and a few veiled hints as to what the future possibly held for her. Claire decided she didn't want to know, as she couldn't see past the coming night.

She spent time with Addy discussing things women their age should, as Addy asked her advice about Adam and remained coy when Claire asked what Breena had said to her. This was still fresh in her mind as she went to find Adam. Her chat with him was straight to the point without any possibility of misunderstanding. Their peace was made, and they were friends once more. It was nice to have him back. So much so, that after, she dared to pry into how he was really feeling about Addy. After her talk with Matt's cousin, she wanted to make sure that Adam would not hurt Addy as he had done to her. She left him feeling satisfied with his answers.

Leaving the best till last, Claire managed to spirit Matt away to the barn for a more intimate time together. While their time by the stones had been full of passion with heightened senses, this was even more special. She was tender and caring, taking her time to show how much she loved him. Afterwards, Claire lay in the crook of his arm, running her finger over his chest and up his throat to his chin. Matt took that finger, kissed it, and held her hand close to his heart.

Feeling content and the happiest she had been in a while, she sighed deeply. Matt kissed her head and pulled her closer.

"Addy tells me you now know what you have to do. Care to share?" he whispered.

"I don't want to think about it right now. Please. You make me so happy, and I want to stay that way for as long as I can."

"I'm not going anywhere. Are you?" He pulled a piece of hay from her hair.

"No, I'm not." To Claire, it felt like she'd just lied to him.

"Good…then we can do this again." He rolled on top of her and stroked her face. "I never want to leave here," he told her.

For the rest of the night, Claire continued to watch everyone in the room. She felt withdrawn—like she was watching from the outside. Slowly, they began to drift off, finally leaving only Matt and Claire in the living room. They snuggled up together on the couch, not wanting to let each other go but eventually falling asleep.

"It is time, Carling," a deep voice suddenly called to her. Claire opened her eyes and found Breena standing beside a figure in a long robe. "You must go to the standing stones for the meeting to begin. Breena will be your companion in this trial and your help—for you shall need it. Your opponent will be equally matched to you, but you'll have your wits and logic to guide you."

Breena was no longer wearing the beautiful dress that matched her eyes, but tight trousers tucked into leather boots, with a white shirt and close-fitting vest. Across her back a bow was slung, but there was no quiver in sight.

Careful not to wake Matt, she disengaged from his arms and stood to meet them. Breena moved to her brother's side and kissed his forehead. He then moved in his sleep, unsettled by something in his dream.

"Goodbye, Galen. I'll look after my sister and make sure she comes back to you safely," she whispered to him.

As they left the house, the door opened before them and closed quietly after they passed through. They mounted the steep and narrow path that wound back and forth up the hill.

Shadowy, hooded figures stood silently and peacefully at each switchback, and as Claire and Breena rounded each bend, the figures joined them—forming a procession until they reached the top. Claire waited with Breena as the procession passed them and made their way to the standing stones. The normally calming music of the spring did nothing to soothe her anxiety of what was to come.

They rounded the rocks, and the standing stones came into view. In between each set of stones stood a hooded figure. They were chanting and their hands were in the air, all pointing to the circle's centre. The one who had guided them was waiting at the entrance to the circle for the two women and indicated that both Breena and Claire should enter.

Claire could feel the stones' energy increase around the circle and began to focus on them both as the two women linked hands and bowed their heads. All her actions were automatic, as if she'd known how to do everything all her life. The chanting became louder, and they were surrounded by a nimbus of light as smaller sparks, all colours of the rainbow, were flying around their heads and weaving between their hands. The chanting came to a crescendo and then stopped. All was dark again. Claire looked around. They were alone. The Guardians were nowhere to be seen.

To the east, the moon was rising, and it looked enormous as it clambered up from behind the horizon. The rosy hue that tinged the surface resembled the colour of blood, and it felt ominous to her. Breena and Claire then walked to the edge of the stones and Claire drew on its energy—adding it to her own stores, fortifying herself for the coming battle.

After the chanting of the Guardians, silence hung heavily on the night, as there was no movement of wind or creature to be heard. Claire then watched the moon making its way into the sky, growing in size and colour while tinting the landscape with its bloody glow.

The scuffle of footsteps rang alarms in Claire's brain, and both she and Breena were immediately on alert. Searching around them, they saw nothing until Jack and Tony made their way around the rocks. Tony gave Claire a sheepish look and a small smile in greeting, while Jack's face was split with a grin that held no warmth to it, instead seeming to add an extra chill to the night air.

"Hello, Claire. So nice to see you again. We didn't have much of a chance to talk the other day before you ran off. But I understand that you've been talking a lot to my friend here. So glad you two have become friends." The words dripped with malice from Jack's lips, and Claire could tell he'd already punished Tony for it—judging by the way he winced when Jack tapped him on the chest.

"I can't say the same thing, Jack. It's not nice to see you, ever! I don't understand why you insist on having me followed. Why go to all the lengths to spy on me? Especially when you can just talk to me. I'm sure I can answer any question you may have and put you straight on many more."

"I have to keep an eye on my girl. And I wish you didn't resist me so much. You should really learn how to relax, Claire. Have some fun! Just think of the things we could do together," Jack said with a leer as his eyes wandered over her body and made Claire's skin crawl. Now noticing Breena, he looked her up and down. "Who's your friend?"

Claire couldn't help but notice that Tony was watching Breena as well. "This is a very special friend of mine. One you've never been aware of—my sister, in fact." It pleased her that Breena was a surprise to the two men, as it was one advantage the two women had.

"I'm here to protect Claire. It wasn't deemed appropriate for a lone woman to go up against idiots like you."

"Get a load of her!" Jack laughed. "Love the accent. But I don't think that you two are going to be much of a challenge."

"Have you got nothing to say about this, Tony?" Claire asked. "You're not usually this quiet. Have we stopped being friends?" Claire asked, and he was about to reply when Jack cut across him.

"Tony isn't in charge here, and what he has to say does not matter. He answers to me! Just because you got all matey with him doesn't mean you can talk to him now. Does that boy know what happened yesterday?" He laughed when he saw her reaction. "I guess not."

"What is he talking about, Claire?" Breena whispered to her.

"Nothing. Nothing happened, Breena. He's only trying to divide us…make us vulnerable," Claire replied hastily.

"Claire, you need to be honest with me."

"Tony tried to kiss me. But nothing happened." Then she turned back to Jack. "And yes. Matt does know what happened. There are no secrets on our side. How about on yours?"

"You may enjoy the wordplay, but I'm growing tired of it. Tony, you know what to do." He waved his hand at the tall man behind him.

"Things have changed, Tony. I don't want to hurt you," Claire told him, holding up a hand to stop him moving towards them.

An anguish spread across his face, and she could see he was fighting an inner battle. Somehow, Jack was controlling him, and Tony's eyes spoke volumes to her.

"You may not want to, but I have no hesitation." Breena moved herself in front of Claire and came to meet Tony in the middle of the open grassed space. The pair clashed together with an ear shattering booming sound, while a light, swirling with all the colours of the rainbow, flared up around them. It rose into the air like a great beacon, lighting up the hillside around them. All the while, Claire kept her eyes on Jack.

Claire edged around them to move closer to Jack, already preparing to encase him in light. She was hoping to get this over and done with quickly with little harm to Tony. Slowly, she passed the standing stones—their power humming in her mind and her fingers tingling as they trailed on the smooth surface.

"You must be truly mad to come to this place and threaten us." Claire's voice came like a growl and to her ears, it didn't even sound like her own.

"Not mad, just vengeful, for all that you have subjected me to," came forth an equally menacing voice from Jack. "You took what was rightfully mine and I want it back."

"There's no going back. We're The People—the Sentinels— we are the land. You are nothing and nowhere, a shadow that belongs in the darkness."

"I am everywhere, and I hold everything. This world is rightfully mine, formed from my own creation."

Jack and Claire circled each other, their voices merging with the entities they both represented—locked in a dance of words from these ancient beings.

"That's the difference. We are, and you are alone."

"There is no need for any other. There's only one. Me. I alone must rule and make these people worship me."

Behind them, the light continued to flash and dim in great succession, as Tony and Breena were equally matched. Claire hoped that Tony's Strength Talent would be negated by Breena's wider repertoire of Abilities.

"We will succeed. You cannot win against our united effort. We succeeded once and we will this time also."

"Puny human!" he scoffed with a derisive laugh. "That is all you and your champions are: human. I am the one, the almighty, and I shall squash you like a bug under my foot and wipe your kind from the face of the earth!"

The primeval snarl that erupted from Jack's mouth was deep and menacing as he moved towards Claire, and she knew she must defend herself. Immediately, her walls went up and the defences she'd learned from the Guardians slammed into place in her mind as she rebuffed this initial attack of mental force from Jack. It only took a moment for her to recover from the attack and send out her own—a combination of lightning called down from above and fiery lights sent in rapid succession. They bounced off Jack, leaving behind little burn marks on his all-too-human skin and coming to rest in the grass, scorching the earth with their heat.

Claire could hear Jack breathing heavily with the energy he was expending. Her own breath was more sedate and measured as she controlled each of her movements and actions, drawing on the stones to maintain her attack. A song began to swell in her mind, and then she measured each decision and step with the tempo of it. She was Order. He was Chaos. This was a battle that had been fought many times throughout the eons—good versus evil and one side pitted against another—both believing they were right and the other wrong.

The moon rose higher into the sky, and the deepening red added its light to that on the battlefield below. No blood had been shed so far, but the ground looked like it ran with it.

Using all her mental and physical skills, Claire was becoming adept at anticipating his ever-increasing attacks and evading the rage that was being directed at her by this absolute evil force. She leapt onto the large rocks that were now behind her and started to rain stones and pebbles down on Jack's head—only to have them rebuffed and sent back to her. With each attack, she could feel Jack weaken. He hadn't been taught how to control these new Talents and was expending his stored energy.

Jumping down from her vantage point, she found a long rod of light bursting forth from her hand. The staff she now held was weighty and substantial, straight and true, it seemed to glow golden in the darkness. Gripping it firmly, Claire brought it up, using it to deflect the next assault. Jack drew towards him—at a great expense to his energy—a thunderstorm. He evidently did not know how to create lightning by exciting the particles that were already in the air. He must have felt he had to borrow the electric energy from the weak storm nearby. A large and crackling bolt came bursting from the sky, arcing out and racing towards Claire. The staff held before her in defense drew in the lightning, sparking angrily around the rod of light. Directing the point of the staff, Claire aimed it at Jack and then released the electricity that had been playing on it only moments before.

Leaping from the point, it found its intended victim, and Jack cried out as it shot through his body, leaving him scorched with a faint smell of burned flesh. He turned his maddened eyes towards Claire and his lip curled, giving him an evil cast in the red moonlight. The laugh that came gurgling from his throat was not his. She knew at this point that Jack was no longer there—that the evil entity had fully taken over the man she used to know. Her moment of inattention was to her detriment. She didn't see the flash of shadow that caught at his hand until it was released and hurtled straight towards her. It grazed her cheek as she moved out of its way at the last minute. Feeling like she had just been punched, she spun around, crouching down on the ground, and breathing deeply as she shook her head to rid herself of the effects of the glancing blow.

But Claire did see the next shadow attack, and she countered it with a ball of light. The shadow and light met in the short distance between Claire and Jack with great force. Crackling with their combined energies, they tore at each other until an enormous explosion brought their destruction. The sound of the collapsing energy was sharp and loud in her ears, echoing off the surrounding hills and the rocks nearby like a gun shot. She dove to her right—behind the protective upthrust of rock—as another mass of dark shadow headed towards her.

"Stop hiding, Carling. You cannot run from me," the being inside Jack growled at her.

Above them, light still encased Tony and Breena, flaring as they continued their own battle. Yet Claire couldn't afford to think of them at that moment. She watched cautiously, waiting for Jack to come around the huge rocks as he searched for her, praying that he would walk into the trap she was attempting to lay for him. Harnessing her will, she called the spring that flowed under her feet and fed the brook. She sought its permission to break through the surface under Jack's feet, turning the earth into a sticky, soft mud that would suck him in. With every step he took, the soaked earth pulled him in— rising to above his ankles, anchoring him. Her attack was now coming at him from all sides as the mud held him fast.

Claire could feel him weakening and pushed home her advantage with another barrage of fireballs. Quickly, she pushed her hands together, feeling the heat increasing as she created a large ball of light. Flinging it from her side, it escaped the confines of her hands, wrapping itself around Jack and holding him firmly. The heat began to dry the mud that encased his feet, helping to keep him in place. Calling upon every protection she knew to strengthen it, she felt her own energy begin to wane. With one last mighty effort, she felt it click into place, encasing him in a golden white light. She just hoped it would be enough to contain him so that she could help Breena with Tony.

Lifting off the ground, Claire sped upwards—following the beam of light to where they still fought. Breaking through the blinding brightness and reaching in, Claire forced herself in between Breena and Tony—breaking them apart with difficulty. Tony was singed and bleeding, but not badly. They'd fought equally, and Claire wondered why Breena hadn't used more of the Talents against him but decided this was not the time to ask. Both were breathing heavily as she guided them back to the ground far below. Claire could see the strain on Tony's face from the energy he had expended, as he collapsed to the ground. And to her, it looked like he was almost spent.

"We have to end it soon, Claire, the time is almost here," Breena warned her between gasps. "The moon's almost at its zenith."

Claire looked up at the large moon that presided over them and saw that it was true. The red tinge was now softening and taking on a kinder hue. Her mother's words came back to her: *'Remember, love is always stronger than hate.'* She went over to Tony and looked him dead in the eye.

"If you love me, Tony, and I think you do, then you have the power to stop this. Help me defeat Jack. I can't do it without you. I need you, Tony. Please," she pleaded, offering her hand, and waiting for him to take it while scared that she'd have to condemn him to a fate equal to Jack's.

Tony scrambled up from the ground, stood up straight, and looked first at the outstretched hand offered in friendship, and then down at her. Claire could feel the longing he had for her. She could feel the strength of the love and devotion that he'd been building up towards her all these years. The aspects of a friend, brother, father figure, and lover all vying for her attention. And then pain—so much pain—as it started to squeeze the life out of him. Down onto his knees he was driven, crying out with the scream of the dying.

Without even thinking, she dived straight into his mind to search for the source of the pain—bravely tearing through, hoping she wasn't just doing more damage as she went. And in the darkest reaches, a small white box, carved with delicate filigree work, was being stabbed over and over. Arms of dark metal ending in vicious, razor-sharp claws were tearing the beautiful structure apart in great chunks—on the inside, pictures of Claire broke into fragments.

From deep within, she pulled all her strength and reserves to stop the devastation of Tony's memories. Carefully, one by one, she changed the spikes, replacing them with beautifully crafted gold coils that gathered all the broken pieces together and held them in place around the box. She waited until the last, tiniest fragment was back in place and then went to find Tony's subconscious as she felt his strong call to her.

He was there—tall and handsome—but everything she did not want. She waited for Tony to notice her and when he did, she moved towards him.

"You saved me. Why?" he asked while shaking his head in disbelief.

"Because love is stronger than hate. You tried to warn me that Jack was dangerous. I just didn't realise that it was you who was really in danger. I'm sorry for that."

Tony moved towards her as she backed away. "Please…I only want to thank you."

"Not in here, and not like that. It would create an unbreakable bond that we can never share, Tony. I don't love you in that way. I love Matt."

"We could have a lot of fun together, Claire," he said, trying to invoke his usual cocky air.

"And probably a lot of pain, too. I've restored your memories to you and added some strengthening to them."

"So, you wish to torture me with my own memories of you. To forever hold on to the pain of them? You should've just let them be destroyed, Claire!" he said with anguish.

"No, I couldn't do that. That change would only have changed you, and that's what Jack wanted. He wanted complete control of you, and the only way to do that was to take those precious memories away. He'd have started with those and then moved on to the next lot. You would've been at his complete mercy. I just couldn't let him win that way. The fight was never between Jack and me. It was in here—it was to do with controlling you and I don't know why."

"So now it is you who has control?"

"I have no control over you, Tony. You must take that for yourself and decide what is right and wrong. If you decide Jack should win, then I die here tonight. But know that if I survive by your choice, you still will not have me, and that would be *my* choice."

"I want you to go. I need to think." He turned his back on her.

"Don't take too long." Claire left his mind, more carefully than she entered.

Coming back to herself, Claire found Breena standing over Tony, while Jack still fought the binding light she'd cast over him. She went to the stones and placed both hands on the largest at the entrance, feeling the cool touch of them and communing with the energy stored there. They healed her wounds and sought to drive all exhaustion from her weary muscles, feeding her strength to carry out what she must do — with or without Tony's help.

"Claire!" Breena called out behind her.

Walking back to where Breena stood, Claire saw Tony start to come around. He stood slowly and carefully, stretching out taut muscles and testing injuries. He looked at Claire and nodded.

"Hatred is weak," he growled, looking at Jack.

"What does that even mean?" Breena asked in confusion.

"It means he's going to help us," Claire told her with a small smile.

"Tell me what I have to do so we can finish this, and I never have to see you again," Tony said, not daring to look at her.

"Your Strength is what I need." Claire placed a hand on his shoulder and passed on some of the energy she'd just taken from the stones. She could see him straighten where he stood, but he still didn't glance at her. Instead, he kept staring at Jack.

"You want me to restrain him, and then you'll use the light on his heart?"

"Yes."

"I wish you would use it on me as well. I can't go on—"

"You can and will," she told him strongly, cutting off the rest of what he was about to say. "I'll only use this once, so don't you dare ask me to do it again!" She walked towards Jack, hoping Tony hadn't seen the tears that were welling up in her eyes.

Claire raised a hand while waiting for the other two to get into position. Breena was ready, as the bow that had been strung across her back was in her hands and an arrow of light was drawn. Tony stood at Jack's back, watching Claire over the smaller man's head, his brown eyes full of hurt and pain. He nodded. Claire lowered her hand, releasing the light from

Jack as Tony quickly lifted him up out of the ground with a sharp tug—causing both of his ankles to break with the force. Jack's surprisingly human scream pierced the night, echoing down into the valley below them. The small ball of light that was steadily forming in the palm of Claire's hand felt hot and eager to please.

"You have been found to be the weaker. Go now and be banished from this land forevermore and never darken its sacred earth again with your evil. We have sent our champions against you, and they have defeated you. You must leave!" the Guardians spoke through Claire. Her hand went up and she pushed the ball of light hard into the chest of Jack. She watched his eyes grow wide and his head vigorously shake with the understanding that he was about to die. The little light struck home so quickly that it took Claire's breath away as she staggered back from Jack, who was already sagging in Tony's arms. Jack's eyes were still on Claire, and she watched the light ebb from them as he went limp.

Tony carried Jack over to the spring and he threw him as hard as he could down the hill. The sickening crunch of bones and flesh striking the rocks carried back to them. Tony turned and walked back to Claire, who was still in shock and trying to deal with the enormity of what she had been forced to do. Breena tried to get between him and Claire, but he held his hand up to her.

"I will not hurt her, I promise. Just give me this moment. I have done what she has asked of me."

Breena moved out of his way as Tony gathered Claire in his arms to hold her close. He kissed her forehead and then her cheek.

"It's done. He's gone now. He will never harm you again," he whispered comfortingly.

Claire tilted her head to him, and he brought his mouth down on hers for just a brief moment. Claire's will was so compromised by the horror of her actions that she nearly gave way to this man until Breena's warning broke them apart.

"Claire, you can't! Please don't hurt Galen like this," she cried out in dismay.

Claire looked at Breena and saw the pleading, desperate look in her eyes. It nearly broke Claire's heart in two to think of what she had almost done by giving in to this man. Turning back to Tony, she saw that he seemed so lost. Pushing herself out of his arms, she shook her head.

"You have to go, Tony. You can't be here when the others come. I won't be able to protect you," she told him quietly, fighting for breath.

"Claire, come with me. Please." He held out his hand for her to take.

"My heart belongs too completely to Matt—as does my soul. You and I could never be happy together. You cannot have me."

"I will go only because you wish it—not because of any threat from them." Shouts and cries were coming up the hill, getting closer and closer. He turned his gaze from her and looked to the edge and then back to Claire. "I'll always be watching, Claire. If he looks like he's going to hurt you in even the smallest of ways, then I will be there to protect you." Tony backed away, keeping her in sight until he rounded the rocks and then ran—leaving her far behind him, but always there in his heart.

Claire crumpled to the ground, as her energy was spent, and her mind was simply reeling from everything that had happened. Breena knelt by her side, trying to give her comfort, and letting her know that she was still there. A cry of anger, heartbreak, and terror escaped Claire. It shattered the night air and flung itself wide. Cold hatred of her actions wrestled with the warm love she felt for Matt and her mind reeled—she fought for control, tears streaming down her face.

"I can't be here when they arrive. I can't stay. I must go. Please, Breena. Help me," Claire cried out, taking hold of Breena's arms.

"Can't you wait for Galen? He will know what to do!"

"I can't face him after what I've done. Breena, I killed a man."

"You had to, Carling," the deep voice of the Guardians told her, appearing behind Breena.

"It's still wrong. Taking a life is wrong!" She sobbed and started to rock back and forth.

"That is the first step to healing. We will help you," he told her as he placed an unexpected warm hand on her head. Gentle and reassuring was the touch, and it calmed her frightened mind for a moment.

"Is this what you want, Carling? Really?" Breena asked her in a small voice.

"Yes. I'm sorry, but it is. Can you understand?"

"I feel your pain, so I will help you as you helped me, my sister. I will keep Galen busy while you leave. This is the parting that Gran told you about. It'll get better and you two will be together again, I promise. Go with my love, Carling." She laid a cold kiss on Claire's brow and went off to find Matt.

"You must hurry if you want to do as you wish, Carling," the hooded figure told her while helping her to her feet.

"Why do you keep calling me that?" she asked, confused.

"Because it is your name—the name you have been known by down the eons. Your efforts tonight have once again saved us all. Thank you. We wish you peace and happiness. Go with our blessing and our love until we meet again." He faded into the circle and then she was alone.

The only sign of a struggle was the scorched and muddied ground. The grass, which had once been long, was now trampled and withered. She looked to where Tony had left and sensed him fleeing as fast as he could, happy to know that there was no one following him. But others were close, grouped together and talking. One other, on his own, was coming her way—and she was so pleased it was the steady presence of her Uncle David. She rushed to meet him. As she did the top of the hill became fully restored to its original state. There was now no sign of the battle that had taken place there. Not even a single blade of grass was out of place. She smiled at the thought of the Guardians making things right.

Down the hill Claire headed—as fast as she could go, trying not to stumble on the narrow path. She ran straight into David's broad chest and held on to him, breathing hard.

"Claire, are you all right?" He pushed her out to arm's length and checked her over, looking for any injuries. "We heard screaming and then we found Jack at the bottom of the hill. What happened up there?" he demanded.

"Not now, Uncle David, please. I have to leave. I can't face Matt. Please just get me out of here." She shrugged off his hands and pushed past him to continue down the hill.

"Claire, wait!" he called out, following his niece.

At the house, Gran and Geoff came out to meet them—with Leana not far behind. David took Geoff aside while the two women clucked and fussed around her, wanting to know what was happening as she quickly gathered her things together.

"I'm sorry, Gran, but it was you who warned me that I'd leave him. And now I must go. I can't face him while having these thoughts… "

"It is all right, my dear. I understand." She hugged Claire. "When you are ready, we would love to have you come back to us."

"We will make sure that Matty understands," Leana said with a sad face and hugged Claire properly for the first time. "Hurry back to us. You'll be missed."

David threw their bags into the car before he and Geoff made their goodbyes, giving their thanks. Claire climbed into the back seat and waited for them to join her. Once they were done, they climbed into the front. And as the doors were closing, Claire could hear her name being called, echoing around the end of the valley.

Revving the engine, David pushed the car into drive and took off without a backwards glance. Claire turned in her seat and saw Matt flying towards her at great speed. The set of determination on his face as he chased the car down the track made her heart ache at what she was doing to him, but she was just as determined that what she'd done was unforgivable. David splashed through the ford, and Matt stopped. Claire watched him as he became smaller and smaller until he disappeared completely. She sat in the back and cried silent tears—not for herself, but for the pain she had just inflicted on Matt.

Chapter Eighteen

They drove through the rest of the night and arrived in Glasgow in the early morning. Claire dreamed in fits and starts as she felt not only Adam, but Gerry trying to get through to her. Her parents held her close, protecting her from their attempts as she described what had happened. Bleary-eyed and exhausted, she boarded the plane to London and slept the whole way, waking before landing and feeling more aware, but the raw, raging heartache still tore through her.

The flight from London was full of noisy children all running up and down the aisles, which did nothing to help her relax and get the rest she desperately needed. She was hoping that by pretending to sleep, her uncles would stop pestering her—constantly asking how she was doing and giving each other significant looks over her head.

A baby cried behind her, and Claire just gave up. None of her techniques would work, since she had no patience left to keep trying to relax. She undid her buckle and made David stand so she could get out and go to the small toilet towards the front—narrowly missing two children who were belting towards her. With the toilet occupied, she stood waiting beside the curtain separating them from business class as her frustration grew further. She peered through a gap in the curtain and in the first row of seats, she met the dark brown eyes of Tony. She gasped and quickly turned around, hoping that he hadn't seen enough to recognise her. But she was wrong.

"I see fate has brought us together again. How are you doing?" There was genuine concern in his voice.

"I'm fine. I'm doing just fine," she told him while attempting to keep her voice level.

"Liar."

They were quiet a moment longer. "How are you?" She kicked herself for asking, as she didn't want to encourage him.

"Not bad for having the heart ripped out of my chest. Speaking of heart, where's Matt? I'd like to shake his hand and tell him the best man won."

"He's not here. I left before I could see him. I couldn't face him—not after what I did," she said quietly.

"So, I did the honourable thing for nothing!" He chuckled wryly.

She heard the toilet flush, and a woman opened the door. She smiled and apologised for taking so long. Claire used the facilities and as she left, a hand shot out from the curtain and stopped her.

"I'd like to see you again, Claire. Please tell me that we can meet when we get back to New Zealand," he pleaded with her.

"I don't think that would be wise, Tony. At the moment, I don't want to see anyone." She pulled her arm free and walked back to her seat.

David let her back in and as he sat down, he caught sight of Tony at the curtain and was just about to rise again when Claire held his arm.

"No, I don't need you arrested for causing a disturbance on the plane. How would I explain that to Beth? He's harmless to me, Uncle David. He won't hurt me." The use of his title both shocked and calmed him.

"Haven't heard that in a while." He smiled at Claire. "I'll leave him alone, but believe me, I will deck him one day." For the rest of the journey, David kept a keen eye on the curtain that divided economy and business class.

Claire finally fell into an uneasy sleep. And once more, her mind was under attack. They battered at her poorly constructed defences until she'd had enough and relented. The two men landed quickly into her dream and immediately began to demand answers while their voices competed against each other—overloading Claire until she collapsed on the ground.

"Enough!" John shouted as he stepped between the men and his daughter. "That is enough! She allowed you in, so you're going to talk very nicely to her now, or I will kick you out so hard your heads will be spinning for a week! Do I make myself clear?"

"Yes, we understand," Gerry said, putting his hands up in surrender. "But you must understand something, John, you must know about what is going on back here. Nobody knows what went on. There is a dead body at the bottom of the hill, and the police are all over the place, and Matt..." He turned to Claire. "Matt's inconsolable," he told her gently.

"I'm sorry. I am so sorry to leave you all in a mess. But didn't Gran explain? Didn't Breena?" she asked weakly.

"Breena? What are you talking about? Breena is gone. She has passed over," Gerry stammered.

"Yes and no, Gerry. She has something to do with Guardians. Both Breena and Claire were meant to fight for the Guardians...to save their lands. That is what happened at the standing stones. Jack was the evil that needed to be defeated and that's just what she did."

"Wait. You killed Jack?" Adam asked, looking incredulously at Claire. "I had hoped that he lost his footing and fell."

"Adam, I…yes, I did…and that is why I couldn't face you all—especially Matt. I couldn't handle seeing this look that is in your eyes right now. I'm a killer, a murderer. I took the light and plunged it into his heart. I watched as the light faded from his eyes and I watched as he tumbled down the hill." She turned from them and hid her face. She didn't know why she'd just protected Tony, but she had and now she had to live with it.

"I think you should leave now," John told them.

"At least let me pass a message on to Matt for you, Claire. You have to give him something," Gerry pleaded.

"Tell him I did what I had to do. And that I will miss him." She imagined what would happen when Gerry gave her message to him. She pictured him ranting and raving, demanding what she meant by that. She visualized Adam and Gerry telling him she had killed Jack and congratulating himself on a near miss. It was the only way she could handle it—the only way she wanted to handle it—as any other approach was just too painful.

She awoke to a nudge from her Uncle Geoff, who was holding one leg down while David held the other. She had been floating and she blushed, hoping that no one had seen her in the tight confines of economy class. She internally thanked whoever had invented the airline seat belts.

Geoff then held her hand and gave it a squeeze. "It's going to be okay, Kid…you'll see."

There were no more run-ins with Tony for the rest of the flight and thankfully, he wasn't on board the connecting flight from Dubai. Claire relaxed a bit more and slept, making sure to put up her proper defenses and barriers to those who wanted to contact her. With some more sleep, she was starting to feel like herself. And she thought back on how much she'd changed since she had landed in Scotland three months before with Maggie.

The smiling and welcoming faces of the people she had met along the way made her ponder just how much they'd hate her now if they only knew what she had done. How could she go back to her old life in New Zealand and just pretend it didn't happen?

The plane landed, and Beth was there to meet them with a concerned smile and hug. They drove out of Auckland and with the Bombay Hills now behind them, they took State Highway One south. As they headed out into the beautiful New Zealand countryside, Claire saw that it was waking up from its winter sleep and bursting forth with new life and blossoms everywhere. David and Beth were in the front, chatting about the boys and the farm—already going back to ordinary life. He had a family of his own he should be looking after, not a niece who kept getting herself into trouble.

"Have you given any thought as to what you'll do?" Geoff asked quietly from beside her in the back seat.

"I need to finish my Honours, so I'll throw myself into that. Then I think I might take up the offer the Elders gave when Aunt Lil died. There is so much more that we know now and it's all up here." She tapped her temple.

"Instead you're going to hide yourself away and drown your sorrows in books and research?"

"That sounds about right." She looked out the window at the lush green landscape passing her by. The cattle and sheep grazing happily in their fields were unaware of the turmoil in the world—oh, how she envied them.

"You can't ignore me forever, Kid," he spoke gently. "When you're ready, I'm ready to listen."

They remained in silence for the rest of the drive to their tiny little village that was tucked away in its river valley—mostly surrounded by tall hills. David and Beth dropped them at Geoff's house and drove off with a wave and a promise to come and check up on Claire the very next day.

Claire trudged slowly up the steps to the front porch as Geoff let them in. Her mind wandered to the first time she'd climbed these steps. Jack had been there with his mother waiting for them in the middle of the night. She had seen it then how Jack had watched her, and a shiver went up her spine at the memory.

Inside smelled fresh, with newly cut flowers on the hall table. Claire guessed that Grace and Lynnette had been in that day and aired the house out, so it was ready for their return. She was just grateful that her grandmothers weren't still there waiting for them. Up the stairs she went, dragging her bag behind her and pushing open her door.

Her room was just the same but now seemed smaller than she remembered. The single bed was made with the flowery cover that had been picked out for her and she had never bothered to change. Her desk was covered in books she shied away from—expecting any moment for their contents to throw themselves at her. But they didn't; all was still and quiet. She went and picked one up and flicked through it and felt nothing. She smiled sadly when she saw who the author was: Gerry Drummond. She placed it back down carefully and let her fingers rest on it a moment longer before sitting on her bed and bursting into tears.

"I'm hoping the casserole in the fridge was made by Lynnette and not…" Geoff stopped in the doorway to Claire's room and then was at her side in a flash. He held her close as the tears flowed. They stayed that way for quite some time as Claire let go of her defenses and released her feelings to the world. Sobs wracked her body and tears dripped from her cheeks while she howled at the loss of Matt and Jack's death.

Geoff stroked her hair and held her, simply trying to soothe his goddaughter as his own heart was breaking for her. Her crying took him right back to when Claire's parents had died, and he had tried to comfort her then. He let her cry and waited patiently for her to talk.

When the sobs subsided and the tears finally ceased, Claire wiped her eyes and face and sniffed loudly. Geoff produced a handkerchief from his pocket and passed it to her. She blew her nose loudly and apologised to her uncle.

"What for? Isn't that why I have big shoulders—all for you to cry on?" He managed to get a smile from her. "You hungry?"

"Not really, but I'll try."

They walked down the stairs together and entered the kitchen—the place of many a discussion between them, usually over food or a coffee. Always a safe and comforting room. Geoff loaded up some bowls with a cold and brown gloopy stew, putting them in the microwave while Claire set the table and poured some whisky into a couple of tumblers from the bottle she had fetched from the cupboard.

They sat and ate in silence, with only the ticking of the clock to fill the room. Geoff ate as Claire pushed hers around the bowl, sipping her drink. Yet Geoff never raised an eyebrow at her drinking and kept his mouth shut until Claire was ready— no matter how much he wanted to ask. Giving her the third degree at that point wouldn't be helpful, so he waited patiently.

"I know you're waiting, Uncle Geoff," she said after an indeterminable time had passed between them.

"Am I?" he wiped his mouth on a napkin and waited for her to go on.

"Yes, you are.Do you want me to just start…or do you just want to ask a question first?"

"Whatever you wish. It's your story." He sat back in his chair and crossed his long legs.

"I don't know where to begin."

"The beginning is always good. How about after we all went to bed and left you and Matt on the couch?" he suggested quietly.

"We fell asleep—we were so comfortable, and I didn't want to leave him until I absolutely had to."

"You knew that it was going to happen that night?"

"Yes…I had been told by the Guardians," Claire began, before launching into the description of what happened that night.

She tried to explain how Breena was now fully grown. Claire knew she was delaying the retelling of the battle. It was still hard to think about. And then she started. The feelings were rising again, and her heartbeat increased as she saw it all in her mind. Geoff reached across the table and took her shaking hand in his before she could spill her glass.

Then she reached the part of her convincing Tony to help her. As she told this part, she felt her uncle's hand tighten around hers. It felt comforting and she held onto it, drawing from him the strength she needed to tell the rest. She stopped for a moment to steady her voice and to wipe a tear from her eye.

"Then he kissed me. I pushed him away and told him to leave. Breena came to me then and I told her to delay Matt— that I couldn't face him—and that I was afraid of his reaction to me being a killer. She agreed and left as I ran down the hill and ran straight into David. He followed me down to the house. You know the rest."

"I think I'm missing something here, Claire. Why did Tony kiss you?" Geoff asked.

"Tony's apparently in love with me. He was friends with Dad and when they died, he decided to keep an eye on me. He's watched me grow ever since and he was the one who broke Adam and me up—not Jack. When Jack offered him the job of going to Scotland to watch me, he jumped at it." Claire fell silent and looked off into space.

"Do you have any feelings for this man?" he asked slowly.

"No. I definitely do not. I love Matt. There is no question of that. I'm not so sure what I feel about him. I enjoyed talking to him. It was a challenge in one-upmanship. But there were no romantic feelings on my part."

"Good…because even *I* would have words with you about hurting Matt. I much prefer him to Adam!" There seemed to be a great relief that swept over her uncle, and she was unsure why he would react that way.

"He's honestly the best, and he deserves someone better than me," she said finally.

"You're claiming to know what his feelings are, yet you have no idea if he is actually experiencing them. I suggest you should just leave it for a week or so and then contact him. You may be pleasantly surprised at how he reacts."

"I already know he won't talk to me. Look, just leave it, Uncle Geoff." She rose from the table and gathered the bowls together. "I'll do the dishes and go to bed. I'm so tired of *feeling* at the moment. I just want peace."

"No, you won't. I'll do them. You go have a shower and get straight to bed." Geoff took the bowls out of her hands.

"Are you sure you know where everything is?" she asked skeptically, trying to make a joke of it.

"I'm not senile yet, Kid. Now go, before I change my mind."

"Thank you, Uncle Geoff. Have I told you how much I love you lately?" She reached up and kissed him on the cheek.

"No, and I love you, too."

She left him at the table and headed back upstairs. Her depression was worrying him. She'd never been this low before and he decided that a few things needed to happen to snap her out of it. As he cleaned up, he made mental notes and then went to his study to carry them out.

For the next week, she locked herself away and divided her time between working towards finishing her Honours degree and working in her Great-Aunt Lilith's work room — reorganising and cataloguing the books and papers that had been left untouched since her death. Also, she wrote a few notes to follow up on when she had more time. However, the week still dragged for her, and she would find herself staring off into the distance and thinking of Matt. But then she would get angry with herself and get back to what it was she was supposed to be doing.

The first thing that happened after a week of being home was her grandmothers deciding they were going to redecorate her room and make it more suited for a twentysomething. It kept her occupied, trying to change their minds about what she'd like.

The second was being roped into train Hunter how to start off in the basics of freerunning — something she later learned he had mastered a long time ago and which was helped by his discovering he had the Flight Talent. They spent time after school for three days doing the same stunts repeatedly before she twigged and then challenged him to beat her. She was very impressed with the results and also how her own body had responded after having not much exercise recently.

It was the third event that started to raise her suspicions. Beth arranged to take her to the city and meet with Charlie for a shopping trip. They left early one morning to make it by lunch, and throughout the trip Beth talked about Adam and Addy and how he was bringing her back for a visit. She asked endless questions about Addy: what she liked to eat, what to drink and do, would she fit in with the family, what her family was like, was she really the daughter of Robbie and Fiona MacCallum, etc.

"Beth, how about you just ask me what it is that you want to know," Claire said finally, getting sick of the questioning.

"What on earth do you mean?"

"You're asking me questions that I am sure Adam has answered for you already and you've been talking in circles for the last hour."

"Was I that obvious?" Beth asked unashamedly.

"Yes. Now…what do you want to know?"

"I want to know about Matt and so does Charlie."

"Ah, there you go! That wasn't so hard, was it? If I'm going to be answering about Matt, how about we wait until Charlie is with us? Then I won't be repeating myself," Claire replied, and they fell into semi silence for the rest of the drive.

Again, Charlie was the same at the restaurant until Beth told her the jig was up and that Claire had rumbled her in the car. Charlie looked a bit disappointed with not being able to ask. Claire spent the next couple of hours telling them all about him—how they met and when they first got together. The more she talked about him, the easier it got and the more she smiled.

They spent the rest of the afternoon shopping, and then Beth and Claire went to her apartment to change for dinner. They were having a drink before going out and meeting Charlie and Ben when Beth told her the home phone was blinking.

Claire pressed the *Play Message* button and the first couple of messages were from Maggie, telling her that she'd try her at her uncles. The next dozen were from a tearful and heartbroken-sounding Matt, interspersed with Addy asking where she was and why was she ignoring them.

"I'm sorry. I should've known," Beth told her quickly as she turned the phone off and gathered her up.

"I'm fine…really, I am." Claire extracted herself from her aunt. "Shall we go?"

Beth was unnerved by how calm Claire was being and when they arrived at the restaurant, she pulled Charlie aside as Ben and Claire caught up and told her what happened. They watched her carefully throughout the night as she started to drink. The more she drank, the more withdrawn and sullen she became. Charlie made the call and cut her off, deciding that the night was over and insisting that Claire needed to get home. They poured her into the car and drove her back to the apartment.

While her aunts put her into bed, Ben took the phone and hid it in a cupboard. Beth saw them off for the night and promised to let Geoff know what had happened, and they all hoped that it hadn't set her back.

Sometime in the middle of the night, Beth woke to noise of something crashing out in the living room and came out to find Claire turning the house upside down. The couch was missing cushions, drawers were open, and the contents were strewn all across the floor.

"Where's the phone?" Claire demanded, wobbling on her feet.

"Claire, we'll find it in the morning. You should be in bed."

"No! I want the phone, so where is it? What have you done with it?" Her voice had become whiney.

"If I give it to you, do you promise to calm down?"

Claire nodded and sat down heavily in the chair beside her. She watched while Beth went to the only cupboard she hadn't opened and pulled out the phone.

"No good will come of listening to it again except to cause you more pain. If you miss him so much, you should call him back." She handed it to Claire and went back to bed, leaving Claire alone.

From her bedroom, Beth could hear the messages being played over and over until they stopped, and she went back into the living room to check. She found Claire fast asleep, crammed into the chair with her knees up around her ears and the phone perched on the arm. Picking it up, Beth placed it on the coffee table, gathered up a throw blanket, and draped it over her niece—tucking it around her to keep her warm. She smoothed the hair from Claire's face and then kissed her gently. This young woman had changed her own life so much and she felt genuine concern for her well-being. She vowed to ring Adam in the morning and let him know what was happening. Claire deserved to be happy.

Noises from the kitchen woke Claire the next morning. She stretched out her cramped legs and winced at the throbbing pain in her head. Her eyes slowly focused on the phone on the coffee table and part of the previous night came back to her. The apartment she had trashed during the night was now put back to the way it should be, and Claire felt guilty. She stood and carefully made her way to face her aunt.

"I'm sorry about last night," she croaked to Beth, clearing her throat.

Beth turned away from the sink and gave her a sympathetic look. To Claire, that was worse than having her yell at her.

"You are not yourself, Claire. You must learn to get over this and come back to us. Are you so sure that this Matt would hate you so much? Because judging by the sound of those messages, he loves you a great deal."

"I don't know. Maybe it's me who doesn't deserve such a wonderful man. I love him till it hurts, but I can't face him. I don't want to take the risk."

"Sometimes you have to take the risk to love. You deserve happiness as well—I mean, of everyone in the village, you deserve it the most!"

"Can we not talk about this anymore? No one seems to get how I'm feeling." Claire turned away and went to the bathroom to throw up.

The drive back to the village was an uncomfortable one for Claire, as the silence was deafening between the aunt and niece. Beth wanted to reach out to her but knew Claire wouldn't let her.

Geoff's final plan became apparent to Claire as soon as she walked in the door when they arrived back. Gathered in the living room, the whole family was waiting for her. Geoff stood when she walked in and asked her to sit.

"What is this, some sort of intervention?" Claire laughed and dropped her bag by the door. When nobody else laughed, she looked up. They were staring at her and looking very uncomfortable.

"So, it is an intervention. Wow." She stared at her uncle with disbelief on her face. "No, Uncle Geoff—no. I am fine! I don't need this," she told him determinedly.

"Claire, please, we just want to help you!" Geoff pleaded with her.

"Thank you, but I don't need help. I just need space. Why can't you see that? I don't think this is going to work anymore, Uncle Geoff. Thank you for taking me in and looking out for me all these years, but I think I'll take it from here." She turned and picked up her bag, running to the front door and flinging it open. Out into the fading afternoon she flew and disappeared down the road.

There was only one other place that she felt safe in the village, and that was Lilith's old house. She made straight for the little house covered in budding roses and slipped inside, hoping nobody had seen her. Alone in the quiet, she searched for any hint of her aunt that may be left in the house but was disappointed. She felt sure that if anyone would've understood her, it would be her aunt.

The night was a long and lonely one for Claire, and she started to regret the way she had talked to her uncle, especially in front of everyone else in the family. The mood she'd been plunged into back in Scotland just seemed to get bigger and bigger and she couldn't find a way out of it. It scared her to feel that way and she waited for the tears, but they just wouldn't come. She felt hollow inside—like she was missing a part.

Just like she had asked, the family left Claire alone. She dove into her work and put the last pieces of her paper together. She read it over and over, making changes and tweaking it till she was satisfied. Bundling her things together, she again flew to her uncle's and hid in the tree until he went out. Not knowing how long she had, she quickly packed up her clothes and pushed a few books into her bag and then headed to her uncle's study.

As Claire sat in his chair, she wondered what she was going to write. She owed him a message to at least let him know she was going back to the city. Picking up his pen, she got the shock of knowing exactly where he was and who he was with. *Was this what he felt whenever he wanted to know if I was safe?* Claire thought as a tear rolled down her cheek.

Immediately, it came to her. The words freely flowed from his favourite pen onto the pad in front of her, and she hoped that he'd understand. Laying the pen down, she left and headed to the garage.

Her car had been stored there since Geoff had dropped her off at the airport all those months ago, and she slipped behind the wheel. With one twist of the key, it started up and she could tell that he'd had it serviced. Slowly, she pulled out of the garage and closed the roller door with the remote. With one last look at the beautiful house that had been her home, she drove off down the road and headed to the city. Claire had no idea when she'd be back, or if she would even be back at all.

The door swung open and crashed against the wall. Claire stood in the entrance of the quiet apartment and listened to the emptiness within. Quickly, she pressed the buttons to turn the alarm off and then sighed as she picked up her bags and carried them in, kicking the door shut. The slam echoed against the walls and when she put the bags down, she realised for the first time in her life she was truly alone.

On the coffee table where she had left it, her home phone was blinking out a beacon for her notice—telling her that she had received messages. With great trepidation and a little hesitation, she pressed the button. Geoff's voice was deep— even and apologetic—begging for her to call him and let him know she was okay and safe. There was a beep, and his voice was swapped in an instant by static. For a moment, Claire thought she could hear a whisper, but then it was gone. She played it again and heard the same thing—a soft word like someone was speaking under their breath. She pushed the stop button, afraid of the next messages but too scared to delete them.

Outside, the sun was still shining and there was plenty of afternoon left. Claire looked around her apartment. The thought of being cooped up again grated on her nerves and pushed her into action. Opening the closest bag and pulling out things, she was soon changed and performing a few stretches before heading out the door. She ran to the park and ran alongside the waterfront. The briny air filled her lungs and she felt at home for the first time in quite a while. She remembered the last time she felt that way was when she was in Scotland. The hills around the cottage had welcomed her and put her at her ease. She shook her head to get rid of the image that came with it, running harder and faster. She reached the end of the path before the port began and then ran back the way she'd already come—passing the playground with screaming children, competing with the squawks of the seagulls—past the rowing club and around the bays.

Reaching the end of that path, she ran back again, increasing her speed and making her body work like it hadn't been worked for quite some time. The cares of the last few weeks didn't drop away like she hoped, but it felt good to be out in the air again. Back in the park, she stopped at a public water fountain and pressed the lever down. The water trickled out and she lowered her head to take a sip. A bottle of water came out of nowhere and was pushed into her face. Quickly backing away, she found Tony with the bottle in hand.

"Take it. Those things are covered in germs," he said and offered it to her again. "Don't worry, it's not tampered with."

Claire took it from his hand, opening it and then swallowing half of it in one go. She walked away from him and sat on one of the benches facing the harbour. He joined her— not waiting for her invitation.

"So, still following me, then?" Claire asked while staring out over the choppy water.

"Yep…I can't seem to break the habit."

"I told you that you need a hobby or a pet. There's a really good animal shelter I can recommend."

"Thanks, but I'm a bit nomadic to look after a pet. I've missed you."

"I bet you have. Sorry…can't say the same," she told him.

"But you've been so busy—always here and there—back and forth to the city."

"A girl has to keep busy."

"I'm sorry you heard the messages. I was going to wipe them, but I thought that might tip you off."

"How do you like my apartment? I've been thinking of redecorating."

"Just don't let your grandmothers help. I'm not a fan of their work."

"Of course, you've seen it." She smiled at his audacity.

"Have you rung Matt?" he asked after a small bout of silence between them.

"You've been following me, so you should know."

"Hey, I don't listen in to your phone conversations. I'm not that much of a stalker!" he retorted with a laugh.

"Well done. You admit you're a stalker—it's a good step in the right direction." She patted his shoulder.

"How are you doing…after everything that happened?"

"Not sure. Do you ever get used to it?" Claire asked quietly.

"Used to what?"

"Killing."

"Claire, do you really think I'm some cold-blooded killer?"

"Aren't you?"

"No, and I'm really offended that you think that way about me. Honest to God, I've never killed anyone in my life."

"But you ran Maggie and me off the road."

"Yeah, to scare you, but I wasn't trying to kill. I could never do that to you," his voice softened, and he reached out to touch her, but he dropped his hand again.

"Sorry. It's just me then," Claire apologised and looked down at her fingers, laced around the bottle in her hands.

"Claire, you are no killer. I've met a few and you could never match up to them. Why are you beating yourself up about this?" he asked, turning in his seat to face her.

"I keep seeing Jack's face as he died. How can I go back to a normal life after that?"

"You just have to try. I couldn't understand why you ran away from Matt. When I saw you on the plane, I secretly wished that it was me you were running to."

"Don't, Tony. Don't do that." Claire closed her eyes trying to shut out the almost desperation that was in his voice.

"Why run from him?" Tony asked.

"He deserves better. Every time he looked at me, he would've seen someone who's capable of…that!"

"No. He would have seen a beautiful woman who loves him."

"Can you tell me something? What is it about me that guys seem to obsess about? I mean…there's Jack, you, Adam, and Matt. What is it?"

"I don't know. For me, it's how you don't stand for any crap. You're not a drama queen—"

"Not a drama queen? Have you not been there to see what has happened to me?" She tried to laugh but it came out as a short snort.

"Those dramas are real. I'm talking about the girls who yell at you for supposedly looking at another woman."

"But you do, don't you? Look at other girls?"

"I'm male, aren't I? Anyway, back to what I was saying—you don't spend hours dolling yourself up, and you're kind, funny, thoughtful, helpful, sweet…simply beautiful."

"Stop it. You'll give me a big head!" Claire said, feeling uncomfortable with the praise.

"Humble, too!" He chuckled. "What's not to fall in love with?"

"You know this is creepy, right? You telling me that you're in love with me? Don't you think you're too old for me?"

"Older guys get younger women all the time, so why not?"

"Yeah, but they're only usually after one thing: money. A good-looking guy like you should have women falling all over you."

"Not always. You think I'm good-looking? There may be hope yet." He gave her a short, cheeky wink.

"Sorry. You're not my type. But yes, you are good-looking, and I really enjoy talking to you. I miss having a guy friend to talk to. They're so much easier than girls."

"Whenever you need me, just call."

"Bit hard. I don't have your number."

"Here." He fished in his back pocket for his wallet, pulling a card out and handing it to her. "All the ways you can contact me."

"Thanks…I might just do that. Or I could pass it along to someone I know and fix you up on a date!" She laughed, looking down at the white piece of thin card, with only his name and numbers on it in black ink.

"Please don't. I hate blind dates." He smiled back.

"So, apart from following me around, what have you been up to? What about work?"

"Not much going out there for a guy with my skill set. I thought I might try something different."

Silent again, she looked out at the bay and watched the seagulls diving and swooping on the breeze. People walked past—walking dogs and pushing prams. Couples were hand in hand and enjoying the last of the day's beautiful sunshine.

"I better get going," Claire said while standing up and stretching. "Thanks for the water."

"You're welcome. Anytime." They faced each other awkwardly.

"Please, Tony. Do me a favour and stop stalking me. It's not helping you."

"I'll try, but you're a hard habit to break, Claire Brown."

Claire reached up and kissed his cheek, moving away again before he could get any ideas that it was more than just a friendly peck.

"Call me if you need anything. A friendly ear or…well, *anything*," he told her.

"I will. Bye, Tony." Claire walked away from him and made for the busy street. She called out to him without looking back. "Walk away, Tony…stop watching me. My arse isn't that great!"

Tony chuckled at how she'd known exactly what he was thinking. He did as he was told and walked to the edge of the harbour. Pulling out his cell phone, Tony punched in a number and watched the clouds change colour with the setting sun—turning a fiery red.

"Yeah, it's me, what's happening?" He waited for the other end to report. "Nothing? He's just sitting in his house in Glasgow…not going out, and only going to work?"

Again, a pause. He then turned just in time to see Claire cross the road and head down a side street.

"Have you been able to get anyone close to him?" He waited again. "Shit, what am I paying you for? I told you to get some bimbo on him as soon as possible. What do you mean he's *always* with someone?" Tony lowered his voice as a woman looked at him sharply for yelling.

"The redhead's his cousin, you dumbass! Get some blonde. He likes blondes. The next time I hear from you, you had better have proof." He switched off his phone and jammed it back in his pocket. The good mood Claire had put him in had evaporated with the call, and the news wasn't what he'd wanted to hear.

Claire ran home and felt her mood had lightened some, as the fading day seemed much brighter and the city less gloomy. She dodged people leaving work for the day and ran past fast-filling bars with their loud music and even louder chatter. Shops were shutting for the day, pulling heavy metal security screens down over their windows and doors while streetlights were starting to flicker on.

She reached the door to her apartment and let herself in. Kicking off her shoes, Claire checked for messages again, but there were none. So, she decided to head for the shower before going to get dinner. Just as she was about to turn on the water in the bathroom, the phone rang. Thinking it would be Geoff, she picked it up straight away.

"Oh my God, she lives!" a clipped English accent shouted on the other end.

"Addy?"

"Who else would it be but me?"

"Addy, this isn't a good time!" Claire froze at the sound of her friend's voice and tried to get off the phone.

"Oh no you don't, Claire Brown. I have been trying to get hold of you for so long. Your uncle wouldn't let me talk to you, and your damn answering service was the only other way. Now you are going to stay on this line and we're going to talk. Do I make myself clear?"

"Yes, Addy, perfectly clear."

"Good. Now, how are you?" she asked in a kinder tone.

"I'm as to be expected."

"What the hell does that mean?"

"Addy, please. Don't."

"No! You were the one who ran away from us, so you don't get any sympathy."

"I'm going to hang up," Claire warned her.

"And I'll just keep ringing until you talk to me. Claire, we're worried about you."

"We?"

"Yes, *we* in all that it applies. *We* are all concerned about you, since you just disappeared, and *we* miss you."

There was a click on the line, and it made Claire stop for a moment. "What was that noise?"

"What noise? I didn't hear anything. Stop trying to change the subject."

"I'm not. Did you just put me on speaker?"

"Why would I do that? I'm the only one here. I've just seen Adam off to the airport and Matt's at work."

"I miss you as well," Claire said quietly.

"Thank God for small mercies. Now, are you going to tell me what happened or are you just going to keep fobbing me off?"

"Didn't Adam tell you?" Claire lay back on the couch and tucked her legs up underneath her.

"Yes, but I want to hear it from you. Can you please tell me?" Addy asked determinedly.

"All right. I'll talk!" She gave a great sigh and started to relate the story. She got to the part where she was leaving the cottage and watching Matt chase after the car and then burst into tears.

Addy waited for her to finish before asking her more questions.

"So why did you leave...*we* still don't understand that part!" Addy told her.

"I killed a man, Addy—that's why. I stood and watched his life drain away. How could I face Matt again with that hanging over me? Knowing that he couldn't trust me."

"Have you had any homicidal tendencies since you got back home?"

"No, but—"

"Then you're not a murderer! Claire, you did what you had to do to protect yourself, and you didn't even give Matt a chance to react."

The crackle on the phone was all that played between them for a little while, until Claire sighed deeply.

"Was it bad after I left?" she asked slowly.

"No, it was a bundle of laughs! We had a great time with the cops crawling all over the place. We managed to convince them that he was a tourist who was there to see the stones and must've tripped and fallen down the spring. They found his car and all the maps and bits in it, so they didn't need much to convince them. Matt was inconsolable. He was angry at you for leaving and at your uncles for taking you away. Gran tried to talk to him—with something about you two being together again soon—but he wouldn't listen."

"I'm sorry. I wasn't thinking straight. God, I've made a mess of things."

"Yes, you have. You've ballsed it up right royally." Addy stopped, and Claire could hear her breathing. "So do you still love him?"

"Who? Matt?"

"No…I mean the bloody Tooth Fairy!"

"Oh, I love the Tooth Fairy—who doesn't?" Claire said, trying to lighten the mood a little.

"Claire, please give me a straight answer. Just a *yes* or *no* would do."

"Yes."

"Good. So, there's still hope?"

"I don't know…maybe it'd be better that he moved on and found someone else." Claire had her suspicions at that point and wondered whether Matt was there listening.

"You don't mean that, Claire. I know you. You're still in love with him and he still loves you, so why make it difficult to be together? Why not just take a risk and give it a go? What are you so afraid of?" Addy asked her.

"I don't know what I'm afraid of. I'm afraid of him running in the opposite direction when he sees me—of him being so angry at me. I'm afraid I've hurt him too much, to the point that he'll never want to see me again. I just afraid."

"You don't know my cousin very well, do you?"

"Maybe that's the other problem. We sort of got together when all this drama was going on, and now it's all over and things have changed."

"I don't think things have changed for him," Addy said quietly.

"Addy, I've tried to be as honest as I can with you, so can you be honest with me?" Claire asked her, now believing her suspicion was real.

"Of course—always."

"Good. Then tell me…is Matt there with you now?" There was another click and silence.

"He is," Addy admitted flatly

Claire closed her eyes and tears welled up and fell from them. It took her a moment before she could speak again.

"Why? Why did you do that?"

"Because he needed to hear from your own lips that you still love him. You should have seen his face when he heard your voice say those words," Addy shot back.

"I don't think you should call for a while, Addy."

"Can I at least see you when I come over next month?"

"I'll think about it. Goodbye, Addy."

"What about Matt? Don't you have a message for him?"

"I…tell him that I…I miss him." She hit the *End* button before Addy could say anything. She sat for quite some time and stared into space. Why did everyone have to rake over the pain, making her feel worse than she already did? She got up off the couch and headed for the shower.

A week later, Claire was at the university visiting Maggie and going over the paper she had just written. Maggie's office was a collection of bookshelves all stuffed to bursting with books and photos. Her walls were covered in posters and pictures and her desk was a pile of papers, magazines, unopened mail, and coffee cups. As she entered, she was surprised that the information the books contained wasn't struggling to gain her notice yet again. Maggie was as eclectically dressed as usual with clashing hues and bright-coloured glasses perched on her head. She was searching her desk for something when Claire knocked on the door.

"Ah, there you are. How have you been?" she asked distractedly.

"I'm good, and you?"

"Oh…just the same, you know. Now come in here and help me find my glasses. I know I put them on my desk, but I just can't see them."

"You're as bad as my Uncle Geoff," Claire told her, plucking the missing glasses off Maggie's head, and handing them to her.

"Yes, well, it happens. Now, your paper's superb, Claire!" She handed a folder over to Claire and sat in her big chair. Claire moved some books off the only other seat in the office and sat down.

"You liked it?"

"*Loved* it. But I have made notes—and they're all in there—so once you've done that, then we can pass it on for evaluation and your presentation. But I wouldn't worry about that right now. I have a very big favour to ask."

"Oh yes, and what is that?" she asked warily.

"Nothing really major. Look, we're thinking about hiring a new lecturer for next semester and we thought we'd try him out for a bit. He'll be here next week, and I wondered if you could give me your opinion on how he does. You know, if he engages the mind well enough and all that sort of crap," Maggie said expressively while waving her hand in the air.

"If you want me to, it's not a problem."

"Good! Now, I've forgotten all the details, of course...so I'll text you where and when later—when I find them in this mess. I really should sort it out. Things sort of piled up while we were away. Never mind. I'll get to it eventually." Maggie ran a critical eye over Claire. "Are you looking after yourself? You're looking very thin and tired."

"I'm fine, Maggie! Stop fussing."

"All right. I'll stop. Well, that's all, I've got to get to a head of department thing, so get that work finished and you can drop it off next week when you come back for that lecture."

"What's his name—this lecturer?"

"I forget, but I'll let you know soon. I really must go now." She pointed to the door and Claire left with her. As Maggie almost ran down the corridor, Claire marveled at how she managed to get anything done.

Claire concentrated on finishing her paper and was pleased when it was all over. With it clutched in her hand, she crossed the campus to the administration building and dropped it into Maggie's box. The heavy *thump* of it landing on the other papers in there was a satisfying sound to her, and she walked away happy. The only other task she had that day was the favour that her professor and mentor had asked of her, and she walked to the lecture theatres. There was no one around and as she slipped into the back stalls of the empty theatre, she looked at her watch. She was early.

Out came her phone and her earbuds were pushed in. The music was loud in her ears, and she waited. Up in the back, she had a good view of the whole room, and she knew from previous experience that if she could hear him up here, then he was already doing well in her books. The door opened again, and students began to arrive, all once fresh-faced first years, who were now looking forward to the summer break.

Watching them file in, she remembered what it had been like when she first started. Not really knowing anyone and being shy. But by the end of the year, having made friends and a bit of a social life had changed her. University had been fun for her and now she was finishing. Or was she? Maybe she could do her doctorate. She made a mental note to talk to Maggie about it when she saw her in an hour for coffee.

The noise level in the theatre was rising as they all vied to be heard. People were on their phones, laptops were opened, pads and pens were pulled out, and bags were stuffed down at their feet. The room was getting warmer with all the bodies in it, and Claire shrugged off the jacket she was wearing just as the door near the podium opened. She quickly grabbed her phone and was in the process of turning it off and putting it away when she heard a familiar voice coming from the front.

"Good morning, ladies and gentlemen. I am Dr Matt Drummond, and we are here today to talk about archaeology—in particular, landscape archaeology. Now before I begin, can everyone understand my Scottish accent?" A general agreement was given back to him from the scattered group, and he went on. "Wonderful. But what about up in the back…can you hear me?" Again, a collective *yes* was given.

Claire sat stunned and watched as he sorted his papers and began his lecture. He looked nervous and fidgety, but she just chalked that up to being in front of a different crowd. His talk was very informative, and she blushed when he began a slideshow of pictures—all to do with the dig they'd been on. There seemed to be quite a lot with her in them, and she was horrified.

Laughter brought her back to listen to what he had to say as she looked around at the students. They seemed to be enthralled, and he had them eating out of the palm of his hand. He was funny when he needed to be and serious when getting his point across. She could also see that he had won some fans in the female sect of the group. And she couldn't blame them. He came across as charismatic and she smiled, leaning forward to watch him for the rest of the hour while he talked.

Questions at the end were fired off, and he answered easily without hesitation. When he finally wrapped it all up, he waited at the front as a few of the students came down to talk to him. Claire picked up her bag and jacket and started to descend the stairs to the exit. She was keeping an eye on him when he looked up and caught her eye and stopped for a moment. Indecision grasped her firmly until she forced herself to move. She was out the door and down the steps with such a rush that she almost fell. People were watching her as she pushed past them and out into the fresh air. Claire took a deep breath and made herself walk calmly over to the coffee shop across the road, finding Maggie sitting under a red umbrella comfortably reading a book.

"There you are! How was it?" she asked as Claire sat down opposite her.

"You know how it went. God, you are such a meddling cow—why didn't you tell me?" Claire demanded.

"He didn't think that you'd come. And don't blame me. He rang offering his services for free…with an option for a job next year. So don't you waste this opportunity, now, Claire. He told me that you two had a bit of a tiff and that he wanted to surprise you. Matt's a lovely man and if you don't take him, someone else will."

"I have my reasons, Maggie."

"That isn't good enough. Claire, you can't go through life pushing people away! At some stage, you're going to end up like me—old and alone. And take it from me, it's no fun. Now you stay there, and I'll go order you a coffee. We can talk about how he did, all right?" Maggie got up and picked up her wallet. "Stay!" She pointed a finger at Claire.

Claire leaned on the table and put her head in her hands. Life was just too complicated, she thought to herself. Why couldn't it ever be simple? And more importantly, why couldn't everyone just butt out of her life?

"Is this seat taken?" That beautiful lilting Scottish accent caught her attention and she looked up to see two bright blue eyes smiling down on her. He sat down before she could even answer.

"I…um…" Claire stammered while her face made the same shade as the umbrella above.

Matt took her hand in his and held it, never once breaking the stare he had fixed on her face.

"I am here, and I'm not running away, because I love what I see. I've missed you, Claire! And I have dreamed of this moment since you left. You broke my heart so much it felt like you tore it out as you left. There's no one else but you. There will never be anyone else but you. You are my soul—there can be no me without us. I can't look at someone else without comparing them to you, my perfect, perfect, Claire." He raised her hand to his mouth and kissed it.

"But I—"

"I know, and I don't care. All that matters is our love and our being together. I never want to be parted from you ever again."

"I don't know how you can forgive me," she said, shaking her head.

"There is nothing to forgive. I understand." He gathered her up in his arms and held her tight. Tears escaped her eyes, but they were good tears—all tears of joy. His mouth sought hers and he kissed her gently at first and as she responded, he touched her much more fervently.

"Thank the Lord! Common sense has prevailed at last! Now you two go and be happy. Leave this old woman to her book in peace," Maggie said with a smile.

Claire jumped up and hugged her mentor. "I will call you later. I need to talk to you about something. Oh, and I think you'd better hire that lecturer before someone else does. He was amazing." She smiled and then placed Matt's hand in hers.

On another table farther away in the café, a man with a baseball cap pulled down over his face watched the reunion of Matt and Claire. His fists were clenched, and spasms rippled through the muscles in his jaw as he ground his teeth together. His brown eyes were like pinholes—deep and dark as they bore into the happy couple's retreating backs. The reports from Glasgow had all been the same. Matt had rebuffed every blonde they could find to throw at him, and he had remained true to Claire. And now Matt was there, walking away with the girl Tony loved while jealousy trampled through his heart. He couldn't help himself, so he got up and followed them— knowing full well that Claire would not approve.

To be continued...

*Pokarekare Ana is a traditional Maori love song. The translation in this novel is one English version only; there are others.

The One True Child saga continues…

Claire's young daughter has been kidnapped by Marcus Ryder. To save her, Claire agrees to join Marcus, but a darkness looms over all of them.

Can her husband, Matt, and her Watcher, Tony, work together to save them both.

REDEMPTION
Book 5 of the One True Child Series

The house was deathly quiet, and it suited the moment as Claire Drummond hung up the phone with a frown. She had always known that this time would come, but it still made her heart feel heavy. He was the last of his generation, and now her Uncle Geoff was seriously ill and in decline. The last four years had felt like one long funeral, as her grandparents had passed away one by one. But Lynnette, Grace, and Malcolm had all been there for the two most important moments in her life since meeting them when she was seventeen: her wedding to her wonderful husband, Matt, and the birth of their daughter, Breena, a year later.

No matter how much she had come to love her grandparents, Geoff held a special place in her heart. It was her uncle who had taken her in and cared for her since she was ten years old after her parents had been murdered. He had been her strength and support when at seventeen she had learnt about her past, her Talents, and the truth of where she had come from. Then again with her ordeal both in Scotland and back home, until Matt had found her again—even though she had not appreciated it at the time.

Quickly she glanced at her watch; it was almost time to collect Breena from school. Claire grabbed her jacket and scarf and headed out into the bitter cold southerly wind. Clouds, dark and threatening, raced overhead; she shivered as the cold winter air blasted around her, creeping under the layers she was wearing. The walk was only a short one, but today her feet felt heavy, dragging as she made her way down the street. She stopped for a moment as the news finally sunk in; a tear escaped her eye and she let it fall.

Steadying her breathing and calming not only her mind but also her heart, she carried on. Claire brought forth the image of her daughter—her long, dark curly hair that refused to stay in a ponytail for longer than a few minutes, the bright blue eyes so much like her father's, and the image of her namesake—Matt's long-passed sister. Sometimes when they were alone together, Breena would look up at her and smile. It had a depth to it that suggested something to Claire, but she always put it out of her mind as soon as she thought it, refusing to face what might be true.

The gates of the school were already open, and children of all sizes streamed out of them into the waiting arms of parents or walked together for the trip home. The noise of their chatter and squeals of delight turned to shouts and calls of farewell. Claire smiled and waved at friends, promising to get together for a coffee or a playdate with the kids while she waited for Breena to skip out of the narrow entrance. Normally her daughter was very punctual and the wait at the gate was a short one, but today there was no sign of her.

Glancing around frantically, Claire could feel panic starting to rise inside her chest. Today of all days, Breena had decided to tarry. She searched for her daughter in the still-moving crowd of little people, but she was not there. Claire headed in through the gates and made her way to Breena's classroom; her teacher was at the door, talking to another mother. She smiled as Claire approached, then pointed inside. Looking through the door, Claire found her daughter still sitting at the table, drawing.

"Bree, what are you doing, sweetheart? School has finished," Claire said as she entered.

"Hello, Mum. I just wanted to finish this." Bree indicated the paper she was drawing on. The little girl turned back to her task and the long, wavy black hair fell over her face, free from the hair ties Claire had put in that morning.

"We have to go; you can't stay here after school. How about you bring it home and finish it there?" Claire knelt down and pushed the hair off her daughter's face. "What are you drawing?"

"It's a picture for my friend," she told her mother.

Claire looked at the picture; it constantly surprised her how well Bree could draw, knowing full well she had inherited it from her father and her grandmother. The picture Bree was so determined to finish before going home was clearly of her and a very tall person.

"Who's that with you?" Claire asked her.

"That's my friend—I told you about him. He's funny. He asked me to draw a picture of us." Bree smiled and stood up. "Can I really take it home to do?"

"Yes, of course you can. Come on." She held out her hand for her daughter to take and they collected Bree's bag from the hook outside. As they walked up the street, Claire pondered the person in the picture with a little concern. "So does this friend have a name?" she asked Bree curiously.

"No; he won't tell me what it is, so I call him Mr Man. He laughs when I call him that." Bree smiled.

Claire took her daughter's hand, and she started to skip beside her mother. Her backpack bounced on her back, and Claire could hear something rolling around inside.

"Did you eat your lunch today, Bree?" She looked down at her.

"No; I told you I don't like cottage cheese and cucumber. It's yucky."

"But you liked it last week."

"Now I don't. What I do like is peanut butter and…" Bree stopped skipping while she thought, making Claire come to a halt as well.

"What do you like with peanut butter?"

"Shh; I'm thinking." Her little finger was pressed against her mouth as she contemplated.

Claire waited, starting to feel frustrated. It seemed her daughter's taste in food changed from one minute to the next and trying to keep up was becoming difficult. Fat raindrops started to fall, landing heavily on the path around them, leaving dark splatter spots on the pale concrete.

"Come on, Bree, otherwise we are going to get drenched!" She tugged her daughter into action and they raced down the street together, laughing and squealing whenever they got hit by a raindrop.

After they reached their front door, Bree raced inside and dumped her bag in the living room, then headed straight for the kitchen. Claire picked up the bag and pulled out the lunchbox. Everything she had put in it that morning was gone, except for the offending sandwich. The picture Bree had been so busy drawing caught her attention.

Taking it with her, she walked into the kitchen. Already strewn across the countertop were bread, butter, peanut butter, and three different types of jams. Bree was attempting to spread the peanut butter on the bread, but she seemed to be smearing it on everything else as well.

"You make the mess, missy, you clean it up."

"Yes, Mum."

Claire pinned the picture up on the notice board and looked at it clearly for the first time. It was beautifully done, and Breena had captured her own face very well, but the drawing of her daughter's mysterious imaginary friend gave her an uneasy feeling once more. He was not quite finished, but already she could see some of his features and they seemed almost familiar.

"Mum?" Bree called her.

"Mmm?" Claire broke her gaze at the page and turned to face her.

"Can we go see Granddad soon?" she asked, taking a bite from her jam-dripping sandwich. As soon as Bree could talk, she'd refused to call Geoff by any other name than Granddad; it had made him so pleased that Claire never corrected her.

Her question stunned Claire, especially after the phone call she had received. "Why's that, Bree?"

"I just get this feeling we should go see him." Jam was now smeared on her face, not just the countertop.

"As a matter of fact, my little oracle, we are leaving in an hour and will be there tonight." Claire grabbed a cloth and handed it to Bree. "So when you have finished eating that sandwich and cleaned up your mess, then go and find some things to take with you. And I don't mean half of your toys."

Claire finished packing their bags and dropped them at the front door on the way to the kitchen as she listened to Bree chatting about her day. The evidence of her daughter's cleaning was still on the bench, with smeared lines of peanut butter and jam heading towards the sink. Claire shook her head and picked up the cloth, rinsed it off and finished the job, then went looking for her daughter.

In her bedroom, Bree was sitting in the middle of the floor and staring at a couple of her dolls. She picked one up very carefully and then whispered to it. "I'll take you; I think you will be good on this trip." She placed the doll carefully into the bag at her side and then put the other away on her bed. "You can come on our next trip, to Scotland."

"Come on, Bree; we have to go pick up Dad."

"I'm ready." Bree picked up her bag and put it on her shoulder, then took one last look around her room.

Claire hated the rush-hour traffic that was already starting to build and knew that getting out of the city would be a nightmare—even more so now that the rain had set in. She threaded the small car in and out of the lanes and waited impatiently for the many traffic lights that were determined to delay her. Finally, she made it to the university, pulled into the car park, and took out her phone.

"Here he comes, Mum!" Bree squealed from the back seat.

Matt Drummond was running down the steps from the administration building and splashing across the rain-soaked car park with his bag over his head. He jumped into the car and slammed the door quickly behind him.

"How's my girls?" he asked and then leaned over to give Claire a kiss.

"We're going to see Granddad," Bree answered him from the back.

"Aye; I know, my wee angel." Matt looked hard at Claire. "Have you had any word?"

Claire nodded instead of answering in case she started to cry. "Charlie rang," she said softly, pulling back onto the road and into the madness of congestion.

"Do you want me to drive?" Matt placed a reassuring hand on her shoulder.

"No, you can take over after we stop for dinner." She smiled weakly back at him.

After the stop-start congestion of the city and suburbs that surrounded it, the journey to the village was an uneventful one. The small family only stopped once when Bree started to complain about being hungry and then got back on the road as soon as possible. Once Matt was in the driver's seat, Claire could relax and take a breath. She remembered the first time Geoff had taken her on this journey; it seemed then that her life had been turned completely upside down.

But that had been nothing compared to her first trip to Scotland, where she thought she was going to be on an ordinary excavation. The discovery of the heritage of The Community was still ongoing, thanks to what she had learned in Scotland, but also of her own heritage and learning the purpose for which she had been born. The Talents that the Guardians of the land had given her still had not found their limits, and sometimes that scared her—just as much as the death of Jack at her hands had. And always in the background—supporting and caring for her—was Uncle Geoff.

She had always hoped that one day he would find love again. He had told her once that he hadn't enough time left to train a new wife. Claire knew this was only an excuse; he had found his love and lost her, and he didn't want a replacement.

Claire looked over at her husband and thought the same thing. How on earth could she replace him? He was so perfect for her, always knowing when she needed extra love, when she needed calm. He made her laugh—a lot—and kept her on an even keel. The day she met him was still so vivid in her mind. The first thing she had noticed about him was his eyes, those beautiful, bright blue eyes.

It was a little bit after nine in the evening when they pulled up outside Geoff Brown's house in the village. The porch light blazed a warm welcome with its golden glow, and a curtain twitched briefly, showing a patch of light from the living room. The door was opened before they even reached the steps, and her Uncle Ben and Aunt Charlie came out to greet them.

Ben pulled Claire into a big hug and welcomed her home, then turned to Matt and shook his hand. Charlie was next, with a warm smile and an even warmer hug, and then she guided her into the hallway, telling one of her tall sons to go get the bags from the car.

"Do you want to go straight up, or do you want a cuppa first?" Charlie asked her softly.

"I'll go up. Matt, can you make sure Bree gets ready for bed?"

"Go on up; don't worry about a thing, my love." He gave her a kiss and watched as she climbed the stairs to Geoff's room.

Claire hesitated at the door; taking a deep breath, she opened it quietly. The inside was lit softly by a single lamp at his bedside, and what she saw made her heart break. Geoff, who had been so full of life and vigour, now lay quiet and thin. His breathing was even and shallow, his skin a pallid colour. The full head of hair, which had stubbornly remained mostly dark with a couple of distinguishing bits of grey at the sides, was now almost fully white. His illness had ravaged his body, and he was now so wasted away she nearly didn't recognise him.

A chair had been pulled up to the side of the bed, and Claire sat in it. She held his hand and kissed it, his skin dry and thin like paper under her touch. She brought it up to her forehead and did something she had never done with him before—she sought out his subconscious.

As she had expected, Claire found an orderly and tidy mind. Everything was compartmentalised and in its place. She found him with ease; it was almost as if he had signposted it for her.

"I wondered if you would," Geoff said to her as she entered. He stood before her just as he had been when she was a teenager. Tall, with dark hair and eyes, and a grin from one large ear to another, stretched out under his equally large nose.

"Uncle Geoff!" She ran to him and before he could say no, she hugged him close.

"Claire!" Geoff tried to push her off at first, horrified, but she resisted until he hugged her back, wrapping those ever-reassuring arms around her once more. They stayed that way for some time, and by the time she did release him, her face was awash with tears.

"That was a foolish thing to do, Kid," Geoff told her as he held her at arm's length. "But I thank you."

"How are you? Are you in pain?"

"No, I'm fine. I find that I am quite comfortable and happy. It's my time, Kid, and nothing you do is going to stop it."

"I know." She nodded.

"Now, have you brought that little firecracker with you? I would like to see her one last time."

"Bree is with us. She even asked this afternoon if we could come and see you."

"Good. She reminds me so much of you. So full of energy and enthusiasm. And Matt—has he been well, not missing Scotland too much?"

"No, he is going back in a couple of months. His mother isn't too good."

"Oh, that's not good. I liked Leana; I'll keep an eye out on the other side for her."

"But you don't believe in God and the afterlife."

"Ahh, a human failing it is to change one's mind when the end is nigh." He laughed, then his mood changed. "There is one thing I would very much like you to do for me before I go."

"Anything, Uncle Geoff. Just name it," Claire promised.

"I would dearly love to see John and Jess one last time. Can you call them here?"

She nodded with another trickle of tears chasing each other down her cheeks. Claire closed her eyes and sent the call into the dark reaches of her own mind, and she heard the answer at once.

On either side of her, a man and a woman materialised. John, her father, was in black, and Jess, her mother, in white. They greeted her with a kiss each and then went to meet Geoff. Claire had to swallow a lump in her throat as she watched them greet each other and stood back to give them some time together.

Sitting on a large green leather chair, Claire waited while they talked until she felt a tug at her mind. She grasped onto it and brought it in, and she found she was holding on to Matt's hand.

"I didn't want to disturb you," he said quietly, taking in the scene before him.

"That's all right, Matt. I was feeling a bit alone." He wrapped his arms around her, both mentally and physically, and she cried into his shoulder.

"Hey, I don't want tears in here, thank you; you'll make everything wet," said Geoff's deep voice, and he grasped Matt's hand and pulled him into a hug. They became close while they stayed at his family's home in Scotland and had remained just as close when Matt came to New Zealand.

"Thank you for looking after her; make sure you keep it up. And that gorgeous girl of yours," Geoff told him.

"I will always. I promise," Matt vowed.

"Now, I thank you all for visiting me, but I would very much like to wake up for a second and tell Bree goodnight. John and Jess, I have missed you, and it was a very great privilege and honour to look after your daughter. She is the daughter of my heart."

"It is us who should be thanking you, Uncle Geoff. You have raised her to be such a fine woman." John shook his hand and hugged him one last time.

"Thank you, Geoff," Jess said and kissed him on the cheek.

"Right—the lot of you, out," he said gruffly, trying to hold back his own tears.

Slowly John and Jess faded out, and Matt gave Geoff another handshake. They spoke no words to each other, just nodded.

Finally it was just Claire once more, and Geoff gathered her up again in his arms. "I meant what I said. You are the daughter I never had, and if you were truly mine I couldn't have been prouder, Claire."

"I love you, Uncle Geoff, and I am proud to be called your daughter. I am so lucky to have had two fathers who have cared so much for me." She kissed his cheek and then pulled away.

"Go get Bree; I want to see her one last time." Claire felt him push her away and she left, very carefully, and finally detached her mind from his.

Geoff's eyes fluttered open, and Bree was by his side in her pyjamas and ready for bed.

"There she is! How are you, my firecracker?" he asked softly and smiled at her.

"I'm good, Granddad. Are you just about ready to go?" Her voice was very low, almost a whisper.

"I do believe that I am, but I waited till I could see you again." Bree climbed up on the bed and gave him a hug.

"Matt, can you go get Ben and the others? It's nearly time," Claire whispered to her husband. He nodded in reply, gave her shoulder a squeeze, and left to go downstairs.

When Claire turned her attention back to the man who had raised her and the child she loved, she noticed that Bree was whispering something to him. Geoff's eyes widened, and he looked at his granddaughter with surprise and love.

Ben, Charlie, and their two boys, Oliver and Owen, filed into the room, followed by Matt. Ben sat on the other side of the bed and held his uncle's other hand. Geoff smiled and took one last look around the room at all who were left of his family. Bree, still at his side, rested her head on his shoulder, and he closed his eyes.

His breathing, which had been so shallow when Claire first stepped into the room, now began to falter and become ragged. They watched over him into the small hours of the morning, until his last breath escaped his lips and he became still.

"Owen, can you and Oliver take Bree out of the room, please?" Charlie asked her son.

Bree reached up and stroked Geoff's face. "Goodbye, Granddad. I love you." She stood up and went around to Owen and held his hand. Before Bree left the room, she took one last look at Geoff and sighed.

Claire was still holding Geoff's hand in hers, and she didn't want to release it. One of the most important men in her life had just left her for the last time, and she felt that a piece of her heart went with him. Tears coursed down her face and dripped onto her lap. A tissue was produced in front of her, and she took it. Finally she let go of Geoff's hand and laid it gently back on the bed by his side.

Matt was there immediately to gather her up into one of his comforting embraces, holding her gently and letting her cry. He stroked her hair and kissed her head. When she was ready, he led her out of the room and down the stairs, followed by Ben and Charlie.

The bottle of whiskey was produced from its high cupboard in the kitchen, along with some glasses. With a measure each, they raised them in salute to the man who had meant so much to all of them. Bree climbed onto her mother's lap and cuddled in, as she had when she was a baby, and fell asleep.

The next few days were a whirlwind of emotions, endless tasks, and cups of tea. And skipping through it all and giving bright smiles and cuddles was Bree; she made sure that everyone benefitted from her sunny nature. Claire had often observed when she was with her friends that this child could make anyone smile.

The day of the funeral, Bree stuck close to her mother all day. Whenever Claire turned around, there she was, slipping her small hand into her mother's larger one. Claire would instantly feel calmer as she looked into her daughter's beautiful eyes.

It was a simple service; Geoff had insisted on that. He hadn't wanted anything too over-the-top or sad. The elders each got up to speak; Claire thought this would have horrified Geoff, as he had often complained about how long their meetings were each month. Claire couldn't face standing up in front of the large crowd that had gathered in the hall, and she had asked Ben to do the eulogy on behalf of the family.

Ben stood up behind the podium on the stage with a few notes in front of him and cleared his throat. Claire noticed how much he had grown to look like his brother, her father, and reminded herself to tell him. He looked out at the crowd and began. Tales of Geoff from a nephew's perspective garnered laughter from the gathered mourners. Ben spoke eloquently and long, something he seemed to have inherited from his uncle. He touched a little on Geoff's relationship with Claire and their history without going into too many details, which had Claire both grateful and a little teary.

The wake was held in the village hall, and it was full of people; he had touched many lives, and they had come from far and wide to farewell him. But the core was the family, and Claire watched them carefully. The boys were now young men; Owen, Oliver, and Hunter, now nineteen, were all at university. The twins were studying architecture, and Ben had great hopes of them joining his construction company. Hunter was following in his father's footsteps and was studying agriculture. He had declared at the age of twelve that he wanted to take over the farm from his father, much to the horror of his mother. The oldest of Claire's cousins was Jasper, and he had just graduated with honours in teaching.

As she talked to them, she realised how much they were like their parents. Owen had his mother's gentle nature and also her Healing Talent, but he confessed to having a phobia of blood. Oliver was more like his father, ready for a good laugh and a joke; he had the Seek Talent. Hunter had Flight and regaled Claire with his exploits in freerunning, something he had long loved, having been taught by her. Jasper, now twenty-three and with Light Talent, told her he'd had enough of study for a while and was about to embark on his own adventures overseas before taking up his first teaching job.

Adam and Addy and their two children had come from the city the day before, and Claire was glad they had. Their twin boys, Cameron and Dominic, were great friends with Bree, and they took her mind off the serious and sad nature of the gathering. She decided she still had a great and supportive family.

At one point, Claire found herself sitting in the corner alone, watching everyone as they mingled. Beth was there, but now the laughter and smiles were no longer forced. She talked to everyone with ease, so unlike the Beth Claire had first met that night all those years before. And she had a flashback to the welcome party and Jack approaching her.

"Claire? You okay?"

She looked up and found David standing before her. He was her mother's twin brother and a great support to Claire; she had taken to him at once with his easy nature.

"Just going down memory lane," she said and smiled.

He sat down beside her. "A lot has happened."

"It has indeed. How's the farm going?"

"Oh, you know, still the same. I can't wait for Hunter to be finished with his studies so I can take a bit more of a back seat. I thought I might take Beth on a trip to Scotland." He winked and smiled at her.

"Do you think she will be able to handle all the midges?"

"She'll be all right. Do you think Gerry, Leana, and Gran would welcome a couple of visitors?"

"I'm sure they would love to see you. They always ask after you and your family. You made quite an impression on them."

"We get a card from them every Christmas. Even though it was such a strange trip, I really enjoyed myself."

Claire spotted Addy and Beth talking. "So are they getting on any better?" she asked him with a small grin.

"No, they still have arguments on how to raise the grandkids. I still can't believe that I am a grandfather!" He laughed at the thought.

"Just remind Beth that her mother-in-law also had small issues with her. That might change things a bit."

"Are you kidding me? That would be like a red rag to a bull. Just keep that nose of yours out of it, Kid." He watched his wife a bit more, then stood. "I'd better get over there and split them up before it gets too heated. Come for lunch tomorrow; I know Beth would love to fuss over you for a bit."

"We will. Thank you, Uncle David." David smiled at Claire; she hadn't called him that in years, and he left her with a warm heart.

The afternoon dragged on, and Claire kept herself occupied by cleaning up cups and plates in between talking to the elders about the work she was carrying out for them. With everyone gone, she shooed out those who had volunteered to help clean up, declaring that she needed a bit of time to herself and would finish cleaning the hall on her own. She asked Matt to take Bree back to the house; he kissed her after making sure she was all right and left her to it.

The kitchenette was scrubbed and the rubbish bags tied and waiting by the door to go out. Out in the main hall, she held a broom in her hands and started to sweep; it was a great time to be lost in her thoughts in the quiet. Memories of Geoff made her smile and cry in turn. The peace and silence of the large room was just what she needed, having had people constantly around her for the last three days. Her defences were down as she reminisced, and she didn't hear the silent footsteps enter the foyer.

She turned in front of the stage to make the final run down the length of the hall when she saw movement. Standing in the doorway was a tall figure with wavy dark hair, now with the touches of time showing, and dark brown eyes that stared at her with such intensity.

"Hello, Claire."

"What are you doing here?" Claire asked.

"I came to give you my condolences." He started to walk towards her slowly.

"I don't think you should come any further, Tony." She leaned on the broom as she watched him get closer.

"I really am sorry for your loss, Claire, for all your losses." Tony stopped and never took his eyes off her.

"Have you been following me all this time?"

"No, I took your advice. I got a job overseas and got back about a month ago. I've only checked up on you once since I returned."

Claire gave him a small smile. "I'm pleased to hear that. And have you gotten over your obsession?"

"I did hope so, but then I read that Geoff died and I found myself halfway out the door to come see you. You seem to be a hard habit to break."

"Maybe you need to go see someone, get some therapy for it."

"Oh, I did that too; I ended up in a relationship with her, and she accused me of transference and then broke up with me. So even that didn't work." He chuckled.

"You're a hopeless case, then."

"Probably. Or maybe I'm just crap with women."

"So you couldn't just stay away, stop yourself from coming all this way. A card would have done."

He stepped closer to her involuntarily. "I needed to see for myself that you were okay. No matter how hard I try, I still care very deeply for you."

"Ah! You said care, not love," she told him. "There is a difference."

"Yes, there is, but I try not to say it, because if I do…" He trailed off. He was closer now, and Claire did nothing to stop him.

"Your daughter is beautiful."

"Stay away from her, Tony."

"Don't worry, I'm not interested in her." He smiled down at her; he was close enough to touch her now. "I still remember that night—it haunts my dreams. That kiss."

"This is not helping." She took a step back from him, unsure whether he would hurt her. Slowly she gathered her energy around her and held it in place, ready for anything.

"No, it's not." He ran a hand through his thick, wavy hair. "Look, my offer is still there. If you ever need me for anything, call me."

"I threw the card away. I found it when we were moving," Claire told him.

He pulled his phone from his pocket, dialled a number, and waited. Over by the wall, Claire could hear her phone ringing.

She turned automatically to answer it before realising that he had her number already. She turned back to him.

"Hi, Claire; just a gentle reminder that I am still around." He hit the *End* button on his phone and put it back in his pocket. "There you are; you have my number now. I told you I will always keep tabs on you."

"Are you ever going to stop this?"

"Probably not. If I haven't by now, what's the point?"

"I'd like you to leave, Tony." She carried on sweeping down the hall and when she reached the end, she turned to find he had followed her.

"You are still the most beautiful woman in the world, Claire. Matt is a very lucky man; I hope he realises how lucky he is."

She stood up straight; to her, it sounded like he was threatening her husband. "He does. Every day he tells me how much he loves me and how lucky he is, and I tell him the same right back."

"Good. Because I have tried everything in my power to break you two up, and not once has he taken the bait." He had a grin on his face that made Claire very uneasy.

"Please leave—before I do something I might regret."

"Remember, Claire, I was on that hilltop as well that night. The Talents given to me by the Guardians are still with me. I think we would be very evenly matched."

"Why stand there and throw veiled threats at me, then? Why scare me?"

"I'm sorry if I have; it was never my intention."

"Well, you did. You have said what you wanted to say; there is nothing more to talk about." She leaned the broom up against the wall. When she turned back, it was to find him standing only inches from her.

Stepping back hurriedly, Claire tripped over the broom and started to fall. He grabbed her, wrapping his arms around her body, standing her up on her feet once more. She looked up into his eyes and had a hard job pulling away—from both his gaze and his touch—but finally she did both and moved away.

"Please, just go," she begged him quietly.

"I think I should," Tony replied. He turned, and Claire watched him leave the hall. He stopped at the door and looked back at her. "I know you were looking at my arse." He smiled and left, his chuckle of laughter floating back to her.

Claire stood staring at the doorway and shook her head, a wry smile tugging at her lips. Her own parting words the last time she had talked to him came floating back to her. *Walk away, Tony…stop watching me. My arse isn't that great!*

She finished cleaning, turned the lights off, and headed out of the hall, shutting the door behind her. Out in the cool wintry air, she shivered and pulled her jacket around her more tightly. She hoped the walk would help get rid of any thoughts of Tony that still remained. Just the thought of him made her look around nervously; she could feel him still near and reached out with her mind.

Having already been inside his mind once before made it easy for her to gain access again. She walked through the various compartments, looking for one particular part. When she found it, Claire noticed that it had changed slightly. The white filigree box with golden coils was now very glossy and slightly larger. Slowly she felt the surface; it was warm and slick, and she trailed her hand around it.

"Now who is intruding on whose life?" his rich voice spoke from beside her. "And how did you get in here?"

"I just wanted to see it again, and it is amazing what I can do now. I can access any part of you that I wish, not just your brain. If I wanted, I could stop your heart. If you wanted, I could make you stop loving me."

"But I don't want that, Claire. I would rather you stopped my heart. But I know you. I know that you could not hurt me in any way. You proved it on the hill that night. In your own way, you love me."

"Please leave the village; don't stay." Claire withdrew her thoughts from his and walked down the street. The wind was starting to pick up and the moon was rising over the hill. From behind her, she heard a car starting and then driving down the road in the opposite direction. She listened to it leave with a tear in her eye.

Redemption available July 2022

PREORDER NOW FROM ALL MAJOR BOOKSELLERS

Loraine Conn grew up on the outskirts of Upper Hutt, New Zealand. Her backyard encompassed the surrounding farmland, river, hills, and mountains which she wandered with her brothers and fed her imagination. After discovering a love for writing in English class at the age of eight, she continued to write in secret. It was not until much later in life that Loraine turned what she thought was a hobby, and something fun to do, into her first completed novel. Now married, Loraine moved from New Zealand to Perth, Western Australia in 2008, and became a stay-at-home mum. While caring for her family and after battling breast cancer, a series was born from a kernel of a dream. Loraine has now published the seven book fantasy series, The One True Child Series, and Realm of Dragons, Fight for the Crown. Both the series and book have been released with the American based indie publishing company Between the Lines Publishing, under their Liminal Books branch, using the pen name L.C. Conn. She continues her career with many more stories waiting in the wings to be released, and even more ideas to be written.

CONNECT WITH L.C. CONN

Email: raindropc1970@gmail.com
Facebook: http://www.facebook.com/LCConn
Twitter: https://twitter.com/ConnLoraine
Instagram: https//www.instagram.com/l.c.conn
Web Page: https//lcconnwriter.wordpress.com/

www.ingramcontent.com/pod-product-compliance
Lightning Source LLC
Chambersburg PA
CBHW011156190726
48286CB00009B/2808